X
WAYS TO
DIE

THE FABIAN RISK THRILLERS

STEFAN AHNHEM

X

WAYS TO DIE

TRANSLATED FROM THE SWEDISH
BY AGNES BROOMÉ

HEAD
of ZEUS

Originally published in Swedish as *X sätt att dö* in 2019 by Forum
First published in English in the UK in 2020 by Head of Zeus Ltd

9 7 5 3 1 2 4 6 8

A catalogue record for this book is available from
the British Library.

ISBN (HB): 9781786694645
ISBN (XTPB): 9781786694652
ISBN (E): 9781786694638

Typeset by Divaddict Publishing Solutions Ltd

Printed and bound in Great Britain by
CPI Group (UK) Ltd, Croydon CRO 4YY

Head of Zeus Ltd
First Floor East
5–8 Hardwick Street
London EC1R 4RG

WWW.HEADOFZEUS.COM

'God does not play dice.'

A. EINSTEIN

Previously, in *Motive X...*

IN THE WAKE of the presumed suicide of his colleague Hugo Elvin, Fabian Risk discovers a set of notes in his desk at the Helsingborg Police Headquarters. The notes suggest that their colleague, forensic scientist Ingvar Molander, not only murdered Elvin, but is also behind several other recent murders. Fabian secretly starts to investigate whether there is any truth to Elvin's suspicions, and just as he unearths definitive proof of Molander's guilt, he also realizes Molander is on to him.

At the same time, a string of seemingly unconnected murders of the most brutal kind are committed in Helsingborg and neighbouring towns. Several complex investigations eventually lead to the arrest of two perpetrators. But something's not right and Fabian can't shake the feeling they've missed something pivotal.

Fabian's daughter, Matilda, has recovered from the gunshot wound she received a month and a half earlier, when the killer whom Fabian was trying to catch had forced an entry to the family home. But the trauma has had a profound effect on her and Fabian struggles to recognize his own daughter in the girl who comes home from the hospital. His relationship with his wife, Sonja, is better than it has been in a long time, but she is still holding back about what happened when her lover turned out not to be who she thought he was.

Fabian's son, Theodor, has felt tormented since he witnessed a brutal murder in Helsingør, committed by a group of his girlfriend's friends. They have been remanded in custody and are awaiting trial in Denmark. The guilt drives Theodor to attempt to take his own life, but Fabian intervenes at the last moment. The end result is that Theodor decides to do the right thing and agrees to testify in court.

Meanwhile, a ruthless killer with no discernible motive is rolling dice to decide who his next victim is going to be, and how that victim is going to die.

PART III

24–27 June 2012

THEY SAY THERE'S a motive behind every murder. Revenge for past injuries, a nightmarish childhood that compels us to repeat what was once done to us, anything to explain the unfathomable horror. Cause and effect that together make the world easier to understand and help us feel slightly safer.

Unfortunately, in some cases, it's wishful thinking. Pure evil never has and never will need a motive.

1

THE LOCK MECHANISM in the door to the three-storey block of flats across the street from the train station in Klippan likely hadn't been oiled in twenty years. As a consequence, the door hadn't shut completely and was easily opened without a code, a key or violence.

Leo Hansi had been on the verge of giving up. But when he slunk into the lobby without turning on the lights, he felt optimistic, for the first time in several hours, that the night, the very last one before he was finally going to get real about turning his life around, might on balance come out positive after all. He couldn't remember when he'd last had an okay night, and this particular June night, which was rapidly moving towards dawn, had up until this point been exceptionally terrible.

And that was despite him being out in the field, working hard for six hours straight. He had checked off one house after the other along Bjersgårdsvägen, Fredsgatan and Vallgatan, and all he'd managed to get his hands on was a relatively new buggy and a pink kid's bike, which said a lot about how low he'd sunk. Stealing from children and new parents. Could it get any tawdrier?

Together, they would net him at most five hundred kronor – in other words, less than a hundred an hour. If you counted the petrol, a coffee break and lack of overtime pay, he was operating at a loss, and suddenly, going back to finish college, taking out a student loan and getting a master's degree seemed the only sensible way forward.

It had been the Weber grill that had convinced him, after all these years, that enough was enough. That he had to make something of his life, something real that made a difference and wasn't just about sneaking around suburban gardens, breaking windows and hot-wiring mediocre cars.

The grill had been the size of a small outdoor kitchen and gas fuelled, of course, which from an environmental perspective was unquestionably the worst alternative. But judging from the four-wheel-drive Jeep in the driveway, the planet's looming climate crisis was not something its owners cared about. He wouldn't be surprised if they never barbecued anything but red meat. Big fat steaks with an enormous carbon footprint that would take their stomachs weeks to digest. Those bastards probably took a plane whenever they were going anywhere, too.

Given all this, he hadn't felt the slightest twinge of guilt when he spotted the shiny grill sitting unlocked on the wooden deck in the garden. New, it would have cost at least thirty big ones, so he should have been able to get a few thousand, maybe even five.

His problems had started the moment he set foot on the deck, in the form of two powerful spotlights. Suddenly, it was like he was being interrogated at Guantanamo. But that hadn't been the worst part. The real headache had been the fucking dog that had woken up and started barking like it was rabid, eventually waking its owners, who, naturally, let the manky thing out.

The only thing worse than climate offenders was dogs.

Not only did they shit everywhere, they reeked like furry bins and insisted on barking like their life depended on it as soon as they laid eyes on him. It didn't matter how small they were, or if it was the middle of the day or they were tied up on the other side of the street. As soon as they saw him, they went nuts.

At least he'd made it back to the van and it had started on the second attempt, which it normally never did.

He was amazed he'd been able to keep going for so many years. Particularly considering suburban developments. Just a few years ago, all it had taken was a rock through a window, and you were in. Today, every last goddam house came equipped with either a tinnitus-inducing alarm or a slobbering dog.

More people had safes these days, too, in which they kept everything that used to be so easy to steal. Not even TVs were worth taking any more. These days, it took so long to get them off the wall they were obsolete by the time you heaved them into the back of your van.

Flats were different, though. People who lived in flats still felt safe, for whatever reason, and didn't think they needed alarms. Some were even naive enough to leave their front doors unlocked. With a bit of luck, you could just stick your arm in and rummage through jacket and coat pockets for keys and wallets at your leisure.

Even so, you couldn't count on more than one out of a few hundred doors being unlocked, and, as expected, all three doors on both the first and second floors were locked. His simple lock pick didn't stand a chance against the new secure locks they'd all had installed. There were only two flats on the top floor, lowering his odds further.

The first one was locked, of course. He walked over to the other and stared at it.

This was the last night he was going to spend humiliating himself like this. The decision was made. Come what may, this is the last building and the last door, he thought to himself as he placed his hand on Evert Jonsson's door handle and barely had to push at all for the door to swing open.

After recovering from the surprise of actually coming across an unlocked door, he stepped into the darkness and paused for a few seconds before gently shutting the door behind him and listening for any sounds from Evert Jonsson or, worse yet, a dog. But everything was quiet. As though the air had stood still for weeks and grown so thick it clung to his face. It smelled sweet and fusty, too.

He turned on his torch and pointed the beam at the coatrack, where two jackets and a blazer were neatly lined up on hangers. But apart from an unopened bag of Fisherman's Friend, a loose shirt button and a handful of old supermarket receipts, he found nothing of interest in any of their pockets. The key cabinet on the wall was just as uninspiring. No keys to a car or a safe as far as the eye could see.

He moved further into the hallway and tried to shake his growing sense of unease. But, like the air, it clung to him. Something was wrong. Something that made him consider turning around and going home to start his new life right then. But he wasn't going to give up that easily. An unlocked flat. Talk about low-hanging fruit.

The first door on his left was closed and would remain so for now, since it probably led to the bedroom. He didn't want to risk waking the old man. Instead, he walked through the door on his right, which stood ajar and led to the kitchen.

It didn't smell particularly nice in there, either. But at least it was a smell he recognized. Old food, rubbish and sewer. The stove was still on and, without thinking, he walked over and turned it off. He couldn't bear seeing precious electricity wasted.

There was an empty plate and a knife and a fork and an equally empty glass on the small round table behind him. Also, a half-empty ketchup bottle, a jar of Piffi seasoning and a carton of milk.

The milk had expired on 27 May, almost a month earlier. That explained a lot. Evert Jonsson was dead and likely still to be found in the flat. He'd seen a dead body once before, but only for a split second as he passed a traffic accident ten years earlier. Quick as it had been, he still had nightmares sometimes about the many details seared into his memory.

Hopefully, that kind of scene wouldn't be repeated here; the old man had probably had a stroke or something along those lines. On the other hand, he had no idea what a body looked like after a full month in this kind of heat.

He went back into the hallway, walked up to the closed door and braced himself before opening it. As expected, the room was dark. The blinds were down but not fully shut, allowing the first light of the early dawn outside to trickle in and settle like a striped blanket across a nightstand piled high with books and a desk on which sat a desktop computer.

And across the bed.

The empty bed.

Leo Hansi didn't understand. Was there another bedroom? Or had Evert Jonsson managed to phone an ambulance and was now in the hospital? Was that what had happened? Had he just not been able to lock the door behind him?

The computer on the desk was a Dell, nothing special. But it did look relatively new, and depending on the RAM and processor, it could conceivably fetch him a few thousand.

When he moved the mouse aside to disconnect the keyboard, the screen flickered to life, revealing a desktop littered with files and documents. So it wasn't password protected, which was pretty much the computer equivalent of an unlocked flat. He sat down in the office chair and studied the various files, all of which had names that were just incomprehensible combinations of letters.

Except one. *Bitcoin Core*.

He'd heard of bitcoin, that it was a kind of virtual currency that some unidentified Japanese guy had invented and that each transaction consumed an obscene amount of energy. Apparently, the bitcoin network used as much electricity as Switzerland. But how the currency worked and how it was used, he didn't know.

He opened the programme and clicked around aimlessly until he found what looked like a main window with two separate columns. One was labelled *Wallet*, the other *Recent transactions*, and as far as he could make out, Evert Jonsson had accumulated 2,400 bitcoins over the past six months.

That didn't mean much to him. It could be a couple of hundred or a couple of thousand. But maybe he'd finally be compensated for the hard work he'd put in tonight.

He found the browser, went online and typed 'bitcoin currency' in the search field. The page it directed him to was a blur of rapidly changing numbers in different columns. It felt like an impenetrable wall of mathematics. But when his pulse suddenly started to race, he knew his heart had realized something it would take his brain a few more seconds to see.

A bitcoin was worth seven dollars. Seven dollars, he repeated to himself while he quickly calculated that the old man's bitcoins were worth over a hundred and fifty thousand Swedish kronor. That was a fortune and it could go straight into his pocket. No middlemen and, more importantly, no guilt at stealing from new parents and some little girl who had just learned to ride a bike.

He disconnected the screen, carried it out into the hallway and was just about to go back to pick up the rest when it struck him that he hadn't so much as glanced at the living room, which should be located at the far end of the hallway, behind the glass door.

What he wanted to do was take the computer and leave, but there might be an old vase in there, or, with the kind of luck he was having, a piece of art.

But the moment he opened the door, his thoughts were no longer on valuables, but on the pungently sweet smell he'd managed to ignore so far, but that now made him pull his shirt up over his mouth.

Two steps into the room, that was all he needed to know exactly where the smell was coming from. But less clear was what the thing was. He moved in closer and aimed his flashlight at the cylindrical contraption in the middle of the floor. It was just about two feet across and six feet long, dark greenish-brown and made of some kind of taut plastic. Like a tent. Or a greenhouse. The kind people might have to use the day Earth is no longer habitable and it's time to colonize Mars.

He aimed the torch beam at the near end of the cylinder. On closer inspection, the plastic looked like the bottom of a transparent bin bag, and when he gingerly touched the rounded edge, he realized the frame underneath was actually a bicycle wheel. There was probably a wheel at the other end, too, and the plastic bags were held together by several layers of heavy-duty duct tape in the middle.

The thing was clearly home-made. But for what purpose?

He bent down closer to the cylindrical plastic tent and shone his light into it, but all he could see was various hues of dark green and brown. As though it were full of algae or something like that, growing on the inside.

But it was the thing hidden behind the outer layer, behind all that green stuff, that drew his attention, and only at that point did he realize it was moving.

2

Everything you know is wrong...

An impenetrable wall of legs blocked the view in every direction. About twenty people of various ages with shopping trolleys, all staring at him. He pushed himself up into sitting position on the polished stone floor and turned towards the girl's voice behind him. It was Matilda, his daughter. She was sitting with her legs crossed, regarding him with that new look in her eyes he would never get used to. The one that wasn't her own and so clearly proved she was no longer herself.

'What did you say?' he asked.

Everything you know is wrong...

The brittle voice was coming from her. He could see her lips moving as the words were spoken. But it wasn't Matilda's voice – at least, not his Matilda.

'Fabian, can you hear me?' Fabian looked up and saw Sonja bending over him. 'You passed out.'

'No, Sonja.' He shook his head. 'I didn't pass out.'

She gave him an insistent nod and a smile. 'Come on, I'll help you up.' She managed to pull him to his feet and then turned to the people ogling them. 'You can stop staring now and go back to doing your shopping. Show's over.' The spectators scattered, but out of the corner of his eye he noticed a man in dark clothes sweeping past them on his way to the meat counter, which abruptly made him aware he was at Ica Maxi in Hyllinge.

Sonja took his face in her hands and made him look at her. 'You and Theodor. You had an argument and were yelling so loudly everyone stopped and stared. I tried to calm you down, but...' She shook her head. There was no trace left of her earlier serenity. 'I had no idea he was so strong. You fell and hit your head on the floor and now he's... Matilda and I, we tried to make him stay, but it was impossible. Do you understand me? And now we have to find him before it's too late.' She was on the verge of tears.

'Sonja, don't worry.' He patted her cheek. 'I'm sure we'll find him.'

Everything you know is wrong...

He whipped around to glare at Matilda. 'Is it you saying that over and over again?'

'Why ask when you already know the answer?'

Greta. The ghost. Was she the one trying to tell him something? Was that what this was all about? He didn't even believe in ghosts. Or spirits, as Matilda insisted on calling them. And that dark-skinned man over by the meat counter, waiting to be served. Why couldn't he take his eyes off him? What was the matter with his face?

Suddenly, the man was sprinting towards the counter. Then, in one smooth motion, he put his left hand on the rounded glass case and practically flew over it to the other side, where he snatched up a knife from a cutting board and buried it in the neck of the customer assistant, who Fabian suddenly recognized as Assar Skanås, the man with the beige Sweden Democrats jacket and his jeans pulled up too high.

Skanås screamed with pain, while doing his best to stem

the blood flow with one hand and fend off his attacker with the other. But the blood was pumping out of his carotid artery with such force that everything within a ten-foot radius was splattered. And the attacker kept stabbing and stabbing as though he was never going to stop.

Fabian had never seen anything so savage. And yet it felt oddly familiar. Like an echo of something much worse.

Everything you know is wrong…

And that brittle girl's voice. Why couldn't she just leave him alone? Matilda was the one who had asked for and received that cryptic answer during her séance. Or… Had it been meant for him? Was that why it was playing on a loop?

'No, please, don't go.' Sonja tried to hold him back. 'We have to look for Theodor. You, me and Matilda, together. Otherwise we'll never find him.'

But he'd already pulled free of her grasp and was on his way towards the blood-soaked meat counter, where Skanås was now collapsing onto the floor.

'Goddammit, you have to listen to me,' Sonja was screaming behind him. 'Our son's missing and we have to find him before it's too late!'

It was up to him to apprehend the perpetrator, he could feel it. There was no one else. No superior. No team. Just him.

Scrambling over the glass display case, he slipped in the widening pool of blood around Skanås, who was lying lifeless on the floor with a meat fork stuck in his face.

There was blood absolutely everywhere. On his hands, clothes, face. He could taste the sweet, sticky iron on his tongue. But other than the door to the staff area, still swinging slowly back and forth, there was no sign of the attacker.

Everything you know is wrong...

He hurried after him and abruptly found himself in a laundry room. The killer was standing at the far end, next to a big yellow washing machine, bending down to push one of the buttons.

'Hey!' he shouted, reaching inside his jacket to pull his gun out of its holster. 'Get down on the floor! Face down, arms out!'

But there was no gun. Or even a holster. And the man was on his way out through a heavy metal door. He ran after him, but the door slammed shut just as he reached it and no amount of banging or pulling could get it to open again.

Panting, bloody and dripping sweat, he turned to the row of washing machines and walked over to the yellow one, which had just started a programme and was filling with water.

Everything you know is wrong...

He bent down and looked through the glass door, straight into the spinning, almost mesmerizing dark.

It was only when a hand smacked against the glass in front of him that he realized there was someone in the washing machine. Someone desperately struggling to get out as the drum kept spinning. First one way, then the other.

In an attempt to stop the programme, he pushed all the buttons, and when that didn't work, he started punching them. But the drum kept spinning while it filled with water and the hand was banging ever more desperately on the inside of the glass door.

He followed the thick power cable from the back of the machine to an outlet with a switch. But even after he turned the outlet off, he could hear the drum continuing to fill with water and spin.

Overcome with despair, he sank to the floor next to the glass door and peered into the dark, rotating hell on the other side, unable to help.

Everything you know is wrong...

Even when he realized it was Theodor's face pressed against the glass, he remained unable to save him. His own son. There he was, fighting for his life while the spinning drum kept pushing his head under the water, again and again.

Theodor screamed. Fabian screamed, too, at the top of his lungs. And yet the only sound was the sloshing water and the drum rotating faster and faster until Theodor's screaming face became a blurred smudge.

Fabian opened his eyes and found himself staring at the ceiling light that the house's previous owner, Otto Paladynski, had left behind and which was still hanging in their bedroom even though neither he nor Sonja liked it.

It had been a dream, he told himself. A nightmare. In real life, things were better than they had been in years. With Sonja lying naked next to him in bed, Swing Party Killer Eric Jacobsén under arrest and the boarding cards that knocked the bottom out of Ingvar Molander's Berlin alibi safely hidden away, it would be greedy to wish for more.

Even Theodor had come to his senses and decided to head across the sound that very afternoon to report to the Danish police, tell the truth and offer to testify in the ongoing trial of the Smiley Gang.

Nonetheless, he could feel his heart pounding like a galloping horse in his chest. Like the onset of a panic attack that at any moment might trick his brain into thinking he was unable to breathe and about to die.

Was it because of the dream? Because it had been a dream, hadn't it? It had certainly been strange and twisted enough that he'd suspected as much long before he even woke up. But no, it wasn't the dream itself that had scared him, he realized now. It was what it was trying to tell him that had set his adrenaline pumping.

He got out of bed, quietly so as not to wake Sonja, hurried out into the hallway and threw open the door to Theodor's bedroom. To his immense relief, Theodor was in his bed. His beloved son, who was breathing heavily and didn't even stir when he gently kissed his forehead and tucked him in. Proof positive that Matilda, that Greta person and his entire dream had been wrong. No one in their family was going to die.

Or maybe the dream hadn't been about Theodor at all?

He tried to recall what had happened in it and eventually concluded the dream had got almost everything wrong. In reality, the victim behind the meat counter had been Lennart Andersson and not the paedophile Assar Skanås. He was under arrest for the murder of Moonif Ganem. Moonif, not Theodor.

Nothing had been right. Absolutely nothing.

Which was exactly what that brittle girl's voice coming out of Matilda's mouth had kept repeating.

Everything you know is wrong...

And now, he finally understood why.

3

IT WAS ONLY quarter to six in the morning when Fabian entered the conference room on the top floor of the Helsingborg Police Headquarters. In a few hours, the whole team would be there to hear what Klippan had to report about the CCTV footage from Ica Maxi from the week leading up to the murder of Lennart Andersson. He'd spent the past few days going through it, and they were all hoping he'd found something that could lead to a breakthrough in the investigation, which had so far come up short in terms of both suspects and strong leads.

But that wasn't why Fabian was there. In fact, he was trying to avoid the others. Whatever his general opinion was on the subconscious and dreams, there was no denying his most recent one had put a finger on a feeling he'd been doing his best to dismiss for some time, and the jam-packed whiteboard walls were the only company he needed right now.

He studied them closely until he felt assured everything was still there. Even though two of the investigations were more or less closed, the walls remained filled with pictures of victims, crime scenes and perpetrators. Lists of potential motives jostled for space with notes and ideas, some crossed out and others circled, and everywhere arrows of various colours, tying everything together.

From close up, it was possible to make out various reasonably logical trains of thought. But from a distance, it resembled nothing so much as utter chaos, which in hindsight seemed the perfect illustration of how their work had progressed over the past few weeks.

But then, they'd been dealing with three major investigations simultaneously. Three parallel murder investigations that seemed to have nothing at all in common. Three fundamentally different worlds, each with victims and suspects, clues to be followed up on, crime scenes to be analysed, theories to be examined from every angle, dismissed and reintroduced.

He had no idea how many interviews they'd conducted in the past week or how many CCTV tapes they'd scrutinized. But it was a very large number, and even though there were things they'd missed, they had, by and large, conducted each investigation by the book, and in the end they'd arrested two perpetrators who were going to be convicted and sentenced.

But in all honesty, as far as motives went, they'd been groping in the dark, and much as it hurt to admit it, they still were.

As the brittle girl's voice in his dream had kept telling him, everything they knew was wrong.

There could be no doubt broadband entrepreneur Eric Jacobsén was guilty of installing hidden cameras in various women's homes, or that Molly Wessman's had been one of them. It was also abundantly clear that, disguised as his alter ego Columbus, he'd had sex with Wessman and tattooed his symbol between her legs. He had admitted as much. But when it came to him poisoning her with ricin, they had neither proof nor explanation. Much less a viable motive.

The same was true of Assar Skanås. No one was questioning the fact he was a paedophile who would have given all the fingers on his left hand to complete his rape of six-year-old Ester Landgren in peace. But paedophilia alone didn't come close to explaining why he would have forced Syrian boy Moonif Ganem into a large washing machine and centrifuged him to death.

It was the same with Lennart Andersson. Maybe the meeting Klippan had called would change things, but so far they'd been unable to come up with a plausible explanation for why anyone would stab him to death in front of a crowd of witnesses in Ica Maxi.

Since the three murders had taken place within a few days of each other, they'd searched far and wide for a motive that could connect the investigations, a common denominator.

When that had failed, they'd moved on to looking for three separate motives. They'd considered everything from xenophobia to sex addiction, turning each theory over and over to try to make it fit with known facts.

Motive, motive, motive. It was what their discussions had revolved around. It was as though the motive was the key that would unlock all the other mysteries. If they could just find it, the perpetrator would be within their grasp.

Fabian pulled out a chair, sat down in front of the whiteboard walls and began to formulate a thought he would have preferred to dismiss. A thought that ran counter to everything he and his colleagues believed in. Counter to their hard-earned experience as detectives. But the longer he stared at the chaos of pictures and notes, the more obvious it became.

A while later, the chaos in front of him was gone, as

though it had never existed. Suddenly, it was all so clear. The geography and time frame, for one thing. Everything had taken place in the north-west corner of Skåne during a relatively short time period. What he saw in front of him now was something else entirely.

The similarities hidden in the dissimilarity.

Each murder had been so spectacular and different from the other two that maybe the common denominator should be sought in the extreme differences. The thought was mind-boggling, but after another minute or two, Fabian felt he was beginning to make out the pattern they'd been looking for.

'Well, what do you know. Hard at work already, eh?' That was Klippan, entering the room with a coffee urn in one hand and a laptop in the other. 'You're early.' He put the urn down. 'It's only just gone twenty past six.'

Fabian shrugged. 'You know what summer mornings are like.' He couldn't tell him yet. Not yet. 'The light woke me up and I couldn't get back to sleep.'

Klippan nodded, but his eyes, darting from the whiteboard wall to Fabian and back again, revealed he was less than convinced. 'So you decided to come in and have a sit-down in here of all places. Interesting.'

'I had nothing better to do.' He needed more time to think and, above all, to come up with a better story than that his daughter had held a séance in his basement and summoned a spirit, which had then wormed its way into his dreams and made him see things clearly. 'And you? I didn't know you were such an early bird.'

'Then you don't know me at all. Unlike Berit, I wake up earlier and earlier. Once she gets up on the weekends,

I'm ready to go back to bed. I guess that's why we're still married.' Klippan laughed and opened his laptop. 'But today, I just wanted to make sure I was here on time and that the technology's up and running before our morning meeting.'

'Right, you've been going through the CCTV footage.'

Klippan nodded. 'And I've found some interesting things, if I do say so myself. But more on that when everyone's here. Why don't you tell me what you're doing instead?'

'Pardon?'

'Fabian. You're sitting there staring at the investigations, two of which are practically wrapped up.'

'But not the third one. We don't even have a suspect for that.'

Klippan sighed and shook his head. 'Fine, you don't have to tell me if you don't—' Before he could finish, his mobile started to vibrate. He looked at it and frowned. 'Yes, this is Klippan… Sverker Holm, that's right.'

It wasn't the terse exchange that followed that made it clear to Fabian something serious had happened.

'Okay… Right… We're on our way.'

It was how quickly the colour drained from Klippan's face.

4

It wasn't the first time Fabian had smelled the sweet, sickly odour of decay, far from it. During his first few years as a police officer in Stockholm, he'd regularly responded to calls from people who had reacted to corpse stench in their stairwells, particularly in the summer. In this case, it was remarkable how faint the smell was. Particularly considering that most signs pointed to Evert Jonsson having lain undiscovered for over a month.

That it was the hottest time of the year only compounded the mystery. The stench should have been overwhelming enough to make the neighbours notice and call the police two weeks ago at the latest. Instead, it had taken until today, and the reason hadn't been the smell but a letter from the local power company addressed to Evert Jonsson that one of his neighbours had found on her doormat when she went to fetch the morning paper.

If I were you, I'd check on Mr Jonsson next door, someone had scrawled across the envelope. *And after that, I might possibly pick up the phone and call the police.*

The reason the smell was so faint became obvious the moment he and Klippan stepped into the living room and saw the six-and-a-half-foot-long, cylindrical plastic cocoon in the middle of the room.

Klippan stopped halfway into the room and seemed

incapable of doing anything other than shake his head. Fabian walked the last few steps over to the dark green plastic tent alone and squatted down to try to see what was in it. But although the sun had climbed high enough by then to shine straight in through the window, he couldn't see through the plastic.

He turned to Klippan, who had clearly read his mind and was already holding out his Swiss army knife, with which Fabian cut a three-inch hole in the plastic.

Even though the hole was relatively small, the putrid stench hit him with such force he instinctively backed away, trying to avoid the worst of it. But it was too late. In seconds, the air in the room was so thick with the foetid smell, it was a good thing he'd skipped breakfast.

Klippan had managed to pull on a face mask and tossed him one, too, and although his nostrils still prickled and itched, it did take the edge off.

At least a couple of dozen white maggots had already crawled out of the hole and dropped onto the floor, where they were now fanning out in search of more food. How they had got into the seemingly hermetically sealed plastic cocoon in the first place was anyone's guess. Granted, bacteria existed everywhere, but maggots could only appear where flies had laid eggs, and so far they hadn't seen or heard a single fly, though it was surely only a matter of minutes now before the stench attracted swarms of them.

He leaned in and peered through the opening in the plastic but couldn't see much beyond a pair of shins and feet mottled every shade of green, red and purple. In places, the decomposition was so far advanced the skin had turned black. Something greenish brown was growing on the inside of the plastic walls, and a viscous brown mixture of moisture and corpse juice had pooled at the bottom.

'Talk to me,' Klippan said. 'What can you see?'

'Pretty much what you might imagine. It's too soon to tell if this is Evert Jonsson, but it's certainly someone.' Fabian stuck the knife into the hole and cut a three-foot horizontal slit, which made a large section of the plastic sheet curl outward, creating a large window into the cocoon.

Klippan took a step closer, squatted down and studied the body, which was on its back with its arms and neck tied to a thick metal pipe that ran through the cocoon like an axle, connected at each end to what appeared to be bicycle wheels.

'No, this is too much.' Klippan shook his head. 'Not another case. Not when we've finally managed to wrap up two investigations and were about to focus all our resources on the Ica murder.'

The parts of the body not covered in maggots were dark and swollen to varying degrees – the eyeballs, for instance, and the tongue, which was too engorged to fit inside the mouth cavity. But the stomach was the worst, so distended it looked like it might burst and release its contents at any moment.

'If you have to kill someone,' Klippan went on, seemingly unable to stop shaking his head, 'why not just get it done, like in the old days? Why do they have to make it so sick and bloody elaborate? Like that.' He pointed to one of the victim's wrists, where the strap had ripped off most of the skin, revealing parts of the skeleton. 'Do you get how hard he must have struggled to free himself?' He sighed. 'Honestly, I don't know how we're going to do this. Another case on our desks will be the end of us. And if you ask me, this looks at least as complicated as the rest of them.'

Fabian nodded, though he was convinced Klippan couldn't be more wrong. This wasn't another case. In all likeliness, it was connected in the same way as all the other cases.

5

IRENE LILJA PULLED her juicer out of a removal box and put it on the kitchen counter, next to the dish rack. It was hardly ideal, but it was the only kitchen gadget she used every day, and there was no other free surface close enough to an outlet.

In a way, it epitomized her retreat from Hampus and their house out in Perstorp. She had no idea how she was supposed to fit all her things into a small one-bed flat in south Helsingborg. Even though she had already unpacked about fifteen boxes, she had at least as many to go.

But she would make it work, and whatever she couldn't cram in, she would either get rid of or put in storage until she could afford something bigger. The important thing was to make sure Hampus didn't get to keep so much as a hair that belonged to her, which is why even the hideous flamingo oven mitts her mother had given her for Christmas were buried somewhere in one of the many piles.

She was lucky to have had Klippan to help her. If not for him, she wouldn't have made it. He hadn't complained once, not even when everything took considerably longer than she'd anticipated. He had just calmly and methodically made sure everything got done and fitted it all in the van and he had even brought his trailer without being asked.

When the last box had finally been brought up to the

flat, she'd offered to take him to Sam's Bar across the street, and they had ordered steaks with extra Béarnaise sauce and a pint each. Then she'd gone back to her flat to try to get organized, but within half an hour she'd fallen asleep among piles of clothes on the bed.

She'd slept through the night, not waking up until eight the next morning, surprised Hampus hadn't once tried to call her since he'd got home from the car racing in Knutstorp. She'd assumed he would reach for his phone the moment he discovered both she and all her things were gone.

Later on, she realized that was exactly what he'd done, but her phone had run out of battery. The moment it started back up, she could see that he'd called repeatedly throughout the night. Twenty-two times, to be exact. Twenty-two voicemails where he unloaded about how awful she was.

She had blocked his number now and was going to change to an unlisted one herself as soon as possible. Hampus was out of her life, and she was out of his. She was finally done with worrying about him drinking too much. About the fights and harsh words. She was finally done with grinning and bearing it. She didn't have to give a toss any more.

The only real problem with the move was that it had taken her so long to pull the trigger. Even though she'd only been back in town for about twenty-four hours, her years with Hampus were already starting to feel like ancient history. As were her recent experiences with the diehard neo-Nazis who had broken into their home and sprayed swastikas all over the walls.

It all seemed like a different life, one she would soon remember only dimly. As though it hadn't been her who burned down their clubhouse and threatened to frame them for all kinds of things if they so much as looked her way ever again.

For another day or two, she was determined to believe the local police's feeble explanation that everything pointed to it being the result of internal rivalries in the criminal underworld.

She carried her toothbrush mug to the bathroom and put it on one of the shelves in the cabinet. It smelled different. Not bad, just different. Moving was always like that. New smells and new sounds to get used to.

She had signed a two-year contract. That was a long time, considering the flat was on the small side and located in the wrong part of town. The south side had never been her thing. But right now, anything was better than Perstorp, and maybe she would even learn to like her new neighbourhood.

She didn't know much about her neighbours, but they were bound to be no different from neighbours anywhere else. An old lady lived next door to her; she had stopped by while she and Klippan were moving things in. She'd seemed nice but was apparently stone deaf when her hearing aid wasn't on, as Klippan found out when he tried to talk to her.

On the other side of her lived *P. Milwokh*. She didn't know who that was. And yet there was something familiar about the name, which she had reacted to on her very first visit to the building when Molander's triangulation had located Assar Skanås's phone somewhere in the vicinity.

But yesterday, when it turned out Klippan had bumped on the name too, and was equally unable to put his finger on why, she decided to clear up the mystery once and for all. To that end, she had gone over after she woke up that morning and rung the doorbell.

No one had answered, and since the doorway was blocked on the inside by a thick, dark curtain, peeking through the letter box had proved futile. She'd stood there with her finger on the small button for five whole minutes before finally giving up and going back to her boxes. They were the reason she'd taken a day off work, after all.

But now a noise made her change her mind again. The distant sound of a toilet flushing. She could hear it very clearly but had a hard time pinpointing where it was coming from. She couldn't hear any water rushing through the pipes in the corner, which meant it wasn't the flat above hers. Also, she seemed to recall Molander telling her sound waves spread downwards more easily than upwards, so she should be able to rule out the flat below hers as well.

That left only the flat next door.

The one with *P. Milwokh* on the door.

She walked over to the bath and pressed her ear against the white-tiled wall she shared with her unknown neighbour. But the only thing she could hear was the sound of her own pulse.

It was only when she pulled on the thin chain that opened the white iron ventilation hatch up near the ceiling that all doubt evaporated. Not only could she hear water streaming into a basin next door and a few seconds later the squeak of a tap being turned off, she could even hear the last few drops hit the porcelain, before everything went quiet once more.

6

EVEN THOUGH THE Hallberg-Rassy was a relatively large yacht, it nimbly zigzagged out of the Råå Marina, and after leaving the harbour turned into the wind and hoisted its mainsail.

Shielding his eyes against the sun high above him, Fabian stood on the north pier, about a hundred feet away, watching the boat with intense interest as the crew trimmed the mainsail until it stopped luffing and took over from the engine, almost like magic.

He'd spotted the beautiful yacht the moment he'd climbed out of the car, and now couldn't take his eyes off it. He'd met the owners late last night during his search for Hugo Elvin's boat, and they'd told him they were heading over to Humlebæk on the Danish side as soon as the weather improved and after that they were planning a night sail up to Gothenburg.

It felt like a sign, and somewhere deep inside he decided he was going to give in to his children and invest in a yacht once things had calmed down.

He picked up the box that contained the contents of Elvin's desk drawer and started walking towards his late colleague's abandoned old wooden boat, which sat alone in its cradle. So far, there was no sign of Hillevi Stubbs, which was remarkable. She was almost never late. On the contrary, she had a habit of arriving long before everyone else. He'd lost count of how often, back when they'd worked together in Stockholm, she'd expressively rolled her eyes at him because the second hand had ticked past their agreed meeting time.

On the other hand, it was a thirty-minute drive from the police station in Malmö, and she'd made it abundantly clear she had neither the time nor the inclination to come out, and had only agreed to meet because it was him asking.

Stubbs was far from easy to deal with, but he had no other options. She was efficient and indisputably one of Sweden's best forensic scientists, and he'd reached a point in his investigation of his colleague, Ingvar Molander, where he could no longer carry on alone.

He needed someone to run things by, someone from outside the Helsingborg team, if only to make sure he'd met the burden of proof before he laid his cards on the table. Besides, it was beginning to feel increasingly important to ensure the work he'd done wasn't lost in case something happened to him.

Not that he was looking over his shoulder every second. But at the same time, there was no getting past the fact that Molander had killed Elvin when he realized his co-worker had been on the verge of blowing the whistle on him.

With the box under his arm, he climbed the ladder propped against the transom of the boat, only to find the dumpy Stubbs stretched out in the cockpit, lapping up the sun.

'There you are,' he said, and stepped onto the boat.

'Where else would I be? Late?' she countered without opening her eyes.

'No, why would you be?'

'That's almost as incisive a question as "Why am I here?".'
She opened her eyes and sat up. 'Yes, I puzzled out that this
is Elvin's old boat,' she went on before he could get a word
in. 'And I'm fully aware you want me to go over it, just like
I did his flat. But why?'

'I think maybe you should just see for yourself.' Fabian
pulled out one of the two blue keys he'd found in Elvin's
desk drawer and walked over to the door leading down into
the cabin.

'Now, I don't want to disappoint you, but I'm not here to
see things. That's not why I took time off and drove all the
way out here. I did it so I could make you understand that
you have to let this go. Believe me, nothing in Elvin's flat
suggested his death was anything other than suicide. Aside,
of course, from what might generously be termed your far-
fetched science-fiction theories.'

'Actually, you're wrong about that.' Fabian carefully
inserted the key into the lock and turned it. 'But we'll get
back to that.'

'I feel like you're not hearing me. There's nothing to get back
to. I have countless shootings to deal with down in Malmö,
and unless I'm misinformed, you just found yourselves a new
case out in Klippan. And yet, here you are, grieving an old
colleague, asking me to examine his boat.' She threw up her
hands. 'I mean, you do hear how that sounds, right?'

'I certainly do.' Fabian pushed the double doors apart and
disappeared below decks. 'That's why we should get started
right away. I have a team briefing in an hour and a half.'

Stubbs heaved a sigh that was no less loud than it was
long, before finally climbing down after him. 'I already

knew you were a pain from when we worked together in Stockholm, but my God, you're like a stubborn two-year...' She trailed off as she looked around the cramped cabin, where every available surface was littered with stacks of folders, pictures and notebooks, labelled plastic containers and evidence bags, electronics bristling with cables of every colour known to man, a computer flanked by a whole collection of external hard drives, a microscope and various other things. The room was so cluttered it was impossible to move without knocking things over.

Fabian flicked a switch to turn on a number of small lights that illuminated the whiteboard, which was covered in photographs and notes, and the piles of documents around the computer. It was exactly the reaction he'd been hoping for and he waited silently while Stubbs took it all in. After a few minutes, she finally turned to him.

'All right. Let's hear it.' She moved a pile of books from one of the berths and sat down.

Fabian made room on the table in front of her and took out a series of black-and-white pictures of a woman in a summer dress walking towards and climbing into the passenger seat of a Saab.

'Until the summer of 2007, Molander was having an affair with this woman. Her name was Inga Dahlberg and she was his next-door neighbour. But over a year before the relationship ended, Molander's father-in-law, Einar Stenson, had become suspicious and gone so far as to follow them and take pictures, which you are looking at.'

Stubbs studied the pictures while Fabian got out a crime scene report.

'Stenson died on 21 April 2007, in the kitchen of his rural

home out by Ringsjöstrand. According to the investigation, the local police concluded that it was a tragic accident. Stenson supposedly slipped on the freshly waxed floor and fell headlong onto the pulled-out dishwasher rack, where a knife had been placed point up in the cutlery basket. But if Elvin and his notes are to be believed, it was no accident, and after looking into it myself, I'm inclined to agree. Four months later, Inga Dahlberg was killed in what became known as the Ven Murder.'

'She was the one screwed to a wooden pallet that floated all the way from the Rå river to Ven?'

Fabian nodded.

'I seem to remember that someone was convicted for that.'

'You're thinking of Danish rapist Bennie Willumsen, who was terrorizing the Swedish side of the sound at the time. Apparently, the brutality of the crime was so similar to his MO that once he was finally apprehended, he was charged with the Ven Murder too. The only problem was that Willumsen had an alibi for that day and was therefore cleared of all charges.'

'Fine, so he offs his father-in-law to keep his affair secret, I'm with you on that. But why kill her?'

Fabian shrugged. 'Maybe she was sick of sneaking around and threatened to talk unless he left Gertrud.'

'Gertrud. Is that his wife?'

'It is indeed, and at this point you'd think he'd calm down. The problem had been done away with, so to speak. But three years later, in the summer of 2010, he strikes again. I had just moved down here and was in the middle of investigating a case with victims from my old primary-school class.'

'Yes, I heard about that. It must have been horrible.'

Fabian nodded and paused for a second before pushing on. 'The thing was that the attempted murder of Ingela Ploghed, who was also one of my old classmates, was different from the rest.'

'In what way?'

'Nothing big, just enough for me to notice. She had been kidnapped and put through a forced hysterectomy to have her uterus removed. In this case, too, the MO matched the other murders fairly well. The only difference was that she was raped before her surgery, which didn't happen to any of the other victims.'

'And what did the rest of the team think?'

'No one ever agreed with me, and Molander was particularly vocal in his opposition, for obvious reasons. And once the perpetrator had been identified and locked up, the whole thing was forgotten. At least, I thought it had been. As it turns out, though, Hugo Elvin was watching Molander and had started his own investigation, the results of which ultimately got him killed and are now spread around in this cabin.'

'And you think you can back this up with evidence?'

'I assume everything I need can be found here.' Fabian spread his hands. 'And I'm hoping you'll agree to help me go through it.'

Stubbs looked around. 'There's certainly a lot of stuff in here. But that's not to say any of it is binding. If it had been, wouldn't Elvin have acted on it and gone public?'

'Maybe he was about to.'

'And what's to say Molander doesn't have an alibi? Just like this Willumsen. I mean, that would instantly make the whole case against him fall apart.'

'As a matter of fact, he does have an alibi for the day Inga Dahlberg was murdered. He was celebrating his anniversary with Gertrud in Berlin that weekend. But take a look at this.' Fabian pulled out the binder with *Berlin* written on the spine and flicked through it until he found a printout of two boarding passes. 'These prove that he flew from Berlin to Copenhagen and back again with just enough time to commit the murder.'

'That's good, but is it good enough? If I were to play devil's advocate, I'd say it might not have been Molander who bought those tickets. It might have been someone else who was out to set him up. But let's assume it was him. That he even went so far as to check in. That doesn't prove he got on the plane. And even if he did, it might have been for a different reason than to kill Inga Dahlberg.'

'Absolutely, you're right. It's not watertight. But I'm completely convinced that with your help, I can find more than enough to have him locked away for life. Take this, for example.' Fabian held up a translucent figurine no more than two inches tall in the shape of an owl. 'It looks just like the crystal owls Gertrud collects. But it's made of plastic and Elvin has drilled a tiny hole in the base just big enough to fit a microphone with a transmitter and a battery.'

'I had no idea he was into DIY.'

'Nor me. I actually think he stole the idea from Molander himself because he used the same audio software.' Fabian walked over to the computer, turned it on and clicked his way to the last of a long series of recorded audio files. 'This was recorded at 11.49 last night, when I happened to be here.' He clicked the triangle symbol and the time marker started to move across the screen.

'*Hold on a minute. What did you talk about?*' Molander could be heard saying. '*Gertrud, I said wait!*'

'*Ingvar, you're scaring me.*'

'*I want to know what you talked about!*'

'*I'm going to have to ask you to calm down.*'

'*I am calm! I just need to—*'

'*No, you're not! And besides, it's late. We'll have to discuss this some other time, because I'm going to bed in the guest room. And I would appreciate it if you would respect my privacy.*'

'*I'll give you all the privacy you want, as soon as you tell me what in God's name Fabian Risk was doing here!*'

They heard Gertrud sigh.

'*If you really want to know, he was here because I asked him to come over. And I did that because he and I were going to try to come up with an idea for surprising you at work this winter for your birthday. There's no need to look so incredulous. You're turning sixty, after all. And as you know, I don't like doing things at the last minute, so I'm actually well under way with plans for a big party for all your friends and colleagues. But I guess it's not going to be a surprise. Not any more. And now if you excuse me, I'm going to bed.*'

They heard Molander clap his hands together. Once, twice, three times, in slow motion.

'*Wow! A stunning performance. You're quite the actress. I almost believed you.*'

'*Whatever do you mean? Invar, what—*'

'*You're lying! Don't you think I can tell when you're lying? I want the whole truth, and until you give it to me, you're not going anywhere!*'

'*What truth are you talking about? The one about what our anniversary trip to Berlin was really about? Is that the truth you're referring to?*'

'*I don't see what our trip to Berlin has to do with—*'

'*Oh no? Are you sure about that?*'

'*I have no earthly idea what you're talking about, and if you think you can get out of this by changing the subject—*'

'*Ingvar, I don't know what you're up to.*' Gertrud's voice was breaking. '*But I know one thing. If anyone's being dishonest here, it's you.*' They heard her burst into tears. '*Oh my God, and you're supposed to be my husband...*'

'*Gertrud, hold on.*' Molander's voice was sounding more distant. '*Gertrud, don't walk away from me. Don't you walk away when I'm talking to you!*'

They heard a door slam shut. Then silence.

Fabian looked up from the computer and waited for a reaction from Stubbs.

'Have you made sure she's okay?'

'I called a few times this morning, and she finally replied with a short text asking me to leave her alone and saying I should contact Ingvar if I have any further questions.'

'She's afraid, and no wonder. The easiest thing for her to do right now is to stick her head in the sand and pretend like none of this happened.'

Fabian nodded.

'On a different note,' Stubbs continued, turning to Fabian. 'I'll admit I was nodding off up there in the cockpit and might have misheard, but I thought I heard a car parking nearby just a few minutes before you came. That wasn't you, by any chance?'

'Probably.'

'So you drove right up to the boat?'

'Yes. Why?'

Stubbs closed her eyes and shook her head. Then she was on her way out, and before Fabian could get up to the cockpit, she'd already climbed down the ladder and was jogging towards his car, which was parked a stone's throw away.

He was about to call out after her and ask what she was doing, but then the penny dropped and he hurried towards the stern instead. Suddenly, his fateful mistake was so glaring it hurt.

How long?

The question echoed through his mind as he ran towards the car. When he got there, Stubbs was already on her back, pushing her head in under the rear of the car. A vague worry had been building inside him for a while, and over the past few days it had grown in strength like an approaching storm. And even so, the thought hadn't occurred to him.

He couldn't say how long he stood there waiting before Stubbs was finally done and got back on her feet.

'Just as I thought,' she said tersely.

He felt every word like a slap in the face. Four blows in quick succession.

She held out the small black plastic hockey puck. 'I honestly don't know what you were thinking.'

He stared at the battery-powered tracker in her hand, and the question that had echoed in his head since she climbed off the boat reached a crescendo.

How long?

How long had it been there?

How long had Molander known?

7

HE STUDIED THE picture of the meticulously groomed white poodle sitting on its hind legs, staring into the camera with black eyes and tilted head. As per the instructions on the website, its owner, a woman – it was almost always a woman – had placed it in front of a solid-colour backdrop.

Not that he had anything against dogs as such, but poodles were probably his least favourite breed. Their only purpose in life was to prance around looking cute, and they didn't even manage to do that. And yet, in the pictures he received, they outnumbered every other breed by a wide margin. And he uncomplainingly cut them out and inserted them into one of the many backgrounds available on his website.

Four thousand kronor he charged for his services. Clients who wanted their picture printed out and put in a gold frame as well had to fork out at least another fifteen hundred, depending on the size. So no, he didn't complain. Indeed, on the whole, he had very little to complain about.

Since he had first rolled the dice five weeks and one day ago, life had been one long thrill ride, which was exactly what he'd wanted. Every task the dice had set him he'd undertaken to the best of his ability, and even though some had seemed virtually impossible, he'd completed them.

On occasion, he'd felt the dice had been wrong, had

wanted too much at once, had made things unnecessarily complicated or had been too mean and unfair.

Now, though, he could clearly see it had been right every time. If not for all the Xs that had added so many extra requirements, the police would probably be further along in their investigation. He might already have been under arrest.

His only failure so far was the six-year-old girl, Ester Landgren. She should have been drowned, but she was still alive. The problem was that the dice had ordered him to let someone else complete the task. If he had been trusted to do it himself, that little girl's parents would have been planning her funeral now.

And yet, he'd found the perfect candidate in Assar Skanås, who had been wanted by the police at the time. Aided by the most improbable lucky break, with chance firmly on his side, he'd managed to find him before the police did. Up until that point, everything had been going his way.

But then, things had started to go pear-shaped. Among other things, that lady detective, Irene Lilja, the one who had called him in for an interview, had suddenly been outside his door, ringing his doorbell while Skanås was tied up on his bed, listening to the voices in his head.

He couldn't understand how they'd found him, and after going over everything he'd done and said and not said during that interview, he'd concluded that the only reasonable explanation was Skanås's mobile phone.

He'd overlooked it until the moment he helped Skanås out of the car in front of the building. The battery had been on its last legs, but apparently it'd had enough juice for the police to track its last known location.

He had decided to make sure the phone was fully charged

and turned on when he sent Skanås off to complete his task. The idea had been for the police to locate it again and this time to find and arrest him. But only after he was done with the girl. Not mid-act. How was he supposed to know the paedo freak needed more than two hours to get things done?

Regardless, it had been an error in judgement on his part, a failure that irked him like a pebble in his shoe, which was why he'd been unable to shake the thought that it had to be put right. But there was no rule to say he could just go back in and tidy up after the fact. Besides, on a fundamental level, it hadn't been his assignment; that was the whole point of the addition from the X notebook.

On the other hand, it could hardly hurt to ask the dice and see what it had to say, could it? After all, it was in charge, and it might agree with him that something had to be done before they could move on.

He tried to think of something else and resumed his work on the poodle, whose owner had decided to place it in front of the Palace of Versailles. But the moment the picture was done and sent off, his thoughts stubbornly returned to the incomplete assignment, and he finally accepted that only one thing would shut them up, so he took out his collection of six-sided, anodized aluminium precision dice.

One of them would tell him if he should proceed at all. A one, two or three meant yes, a four, five or six meant no. After shaking the dice for a long time, he dropped it onto the green felt.

A *two.*

In other words, the dice wanted to be consulted. He picked it up again, closed his eyes and shook it for a long time before making his throw. All he had to do now was open his eyes and see if it said yes or no. Not that it was trivial, he mused, his eyes still closed. For Ester Landgren, a childhood and most of a lifetime was at stake.

He was just about to open his eyes when the grating sound of the doorbell reverberated through the flat, penetrating all the way into his secret room. No one ever rang his doorbell, and even though he could easily just ignore it and carry on with what he was doing, the moment was ruined.

He needed peace and quiet to enjoy the outcome of his throws. If it was something he just rushed through, there was no point to it. He got up and walked through the bedroom to the hallway, where the doorbell was ringing aggressively.

He cautiously peeked behind the curtain blocking the door, and after making sure the person on the other side wasn't looking through the letter box, he slipped between the curtain and the door and pressed his eye to the peephole.

As soon as the doorbell had started ringing, he'd had his suspicions. That was probably why he hadn't been able to continue his game of dice. Now, those suspicions were confirmed, but that didn't make him feel better in the slightest.

It was that fucking detective Irene Lilja again. For the second time today, she was standing out there ringing his doorbell, as though she were determined to carry on until he opened up. He couldn't understand how she'd found him. Fine, she'd been by once, looking for Skanås. But he'd been arrested days ago.

The whole thing was very odd. If the police suspected him, wouldn't they have sent several uniformed officers instead of a lone detective?

He'd considered disconnecting his doorbell after her

most recent visit, but that could be taken as proof he was in the flat and risked piquing her interest further. Instead, he retreated from the hallway and lay down on the sofa to pass the time until she gave up again. If she continued to terrorize him, he would have to do something about it.

Seven minutes later, the flat was silent once more, and as soon as he had calmed down, he got up from the sofa and returned to his dice.

And there it was, its answer. Its verdict.

A one.

He chuckled softly and wiped the sweat off his forehead. The dice had given him a resounding yes. It was finally on his side again. The mistake was finally going to be rectified and order restored.

Finally.

8

FABIAN WAS SITTING alone in the conference room, attempting to adopt an air of calm before the others arrived, which was easier said than done. The battery-powered tracker Stubbs had found under his car had very effectively brought home the imminent threat against him.

There was no longer any doubt Molander was aware of his investigation and was coming for him. The question had instead become what his colleague's next move was going to be, when and how he was planning to strike and whether there would be enough time for them to secure binding evidence against him.

His immediate inclination upon seeing the small black tracker had been to throw it on the ground and stomp it to pieces. But Stubbs had stopped him, insisting that was the worst thing he could do. Not only would Molander know his cover had been blown, he would also be able to see exactly where the signal had been interrupted, which might motivate him to investigate that location.

Listing one argument after another, she'd eventually succeeded in persuading him that the best thing he could do would be to replace the tracker and keep using the car like nothing had happened. Their only advantage right now was that Molander thought they didn't know he was on to them.

In case he was also triangulating the location of Fabian's mobile, they'd agreed to purchase new, pay-as-you-go phones as soon as possible. They also had to move Elvin's boat, and since Stubbs drove a big Jeep equipped with a tow bar, she'd offered to drive it over to her friend Mona-Jill in Harlösa, east of Lund.

'Blimey, you're early!' Astrid Tuvesson exclaimed as she entered the room with sunglasses in her hair and a coffee in her hand. She looked bright-eyed and bushy-tailed, particularly considering she'd fallen off the wagon and been well and truly inebriated when he called her late the night before to inform her about Molander.

'Yes, I wanted to make sure I was on time. Since I have to leave around three.'

'Right, what was that about, again?'

'Theodor and I are going over to see the Danish prosecutor, remember?'

'Quite right. I hope it goes well. If there's anything I can do, just say the word. Okay?'

Fabian nodded.

'Lilja's off today, too, so we'll see how this goes.' She took a sip of her coffee and put the cup down. 'From what I'm told, this murder in Klippan is unlike anything we've seen.' She shook her head. 'And here I was, thinking we were finally going to have some peace and quiet. Had I known this was coming, I wouldn't have given you or Lilja time off. By the way, on a completely different note, since we're the only ones here.' She closed the door and turned to him. 'Did we speak on the phone last night? Because I have a vague memory of you calling and waking me up.'

Fabian considered how to respond before realizing he was already shaking his head. 'Not that I recall,' he said with a shrug. 'Why would I have called you?'

'That's what I was wondering.'

'Maybe it was a dream.'

'Dream?'

'You said I woke you up. Maybe it was just a dream.'

'Sure, maybe.' Tuvesson gave him a very sceptical look. 'Or maybe there's a different explanation. One in which you actually—'

She was cut short by the door opening to admit Klippan and Ingvar Molander.

'Crikey, you're both early.' Klippan set his laptop down on the table. 'We might even have time for my run-through of the CCTV footage from Ica.'

'Let's start with the murder in Klippan, and then we'll see where we are when that's done. Fabian has to leave around three, so we may have to push Ica to tomorrow.'

Klippan sighed and shook his head.

'Sigh all you want,' Tuvesson said. 'But tomorrow's actually better, because Lilja will be back, too.'

'What's the rush?' Molander's question was almost inaudible, and to Tuvesson and Klippan, who knew nothing, apparently completely innocent.

In truth, it was a poison barb, fired across the room.

'I'm going to a meeting with my son,' Fabian replied, and was unable to stop himself adding: 'Why do you ask?'

'Oh dear, aren't we in a good mood today.' Molander put on a big smile.

'Ingvar, maybe it's none of your business,' Tuvesson interjected.

'No, maybe not,' Molander said, without taking his eyes off Fabian.

'So let's get going instead.' Tuvesson waited for Klippan and Molander to take a seat before continuing. 'As you all know, we have another murder on our hands. One that doesn't look like any of the others. I've just been in touch with Flätan, who tells me Evert Jonsson died approximately four weeks ago from asphyxiation caused by the hermetically sealed environment inside the cocoon, or whatever you want to call it.'

'Was that all he had?' Klippan asked. 'That just confirms what we already knew.'

'You've seen the body. According to Flätan, the decomposition is so advanced he was unable to perform a number of standard tests. But a severely fractured skull indicates the victim was knocked unconscious before being tied to that contraption and woke up only after it was sealed. There are also clear signs that he tried to get out and fought hard for his life. One of his shoulders had been pulled out of its socket, for example, and some of the straps around his wrists had cut all the way through to the bone. If Flätan is to be believed, it should have been close to three hours before he passed out permanently.'

'A fairly unpleasant way to go, in other words,' Molander put in.

'That's putting it mildly. But let's start with the victim. What do we know about him?'

'At the moment, not much beyond the fact that his name was Evert Jonsson and he worked as a taxi driver in Ängelholm until about a year ago, when he retired,' Klippan replied. 'His wife, Rita Jonsson, passed away from breast cancer in 2008.'

'No other relatives?'

'No, he had neither children nor siblings and his parents have been dead for over twenty years.'

'That explains how he went undiscovered for so long.' Tuvesson walked over to the whiteboard wall, put up a picture of Evert Jonsson and wrote *no relatives*. 'And speaking of which. That handwritten message his neighbour received.'

'You mean this?' Klippan held up an evidence bag containing the envelope from Sydkraft.

'Exactly. What do we have on that?'

'Ingvar has managed to secure some prints that I ran through the database and, would you believe it, we found a match. This is our guy.'

Klippan passed around a police photograph of the man who had broken into Jonsson's flat, holding up a sign with his name on it. 'His name is Leo Hansi and he's been arrested for burglary more times than he can count, I'd wager.'

'You're not seriously saying it's him, though, are you?' Tuvesson took the evidence bag and studied the handwritten message on the envelope. 'Why would a simple burglar put someone through something like that and then return several weeks later to put a handwritten message through the neighbour's letter box?'

Klippan shrugged. 'According to him, it was sheer happenstance. The door was unlocked, and he went in.'

'What, you've already interviewed him?'

'I figured it was a better use of my time than sitting on my hands. As you know, I've finished going through the CCTV footage from Ica.' Klippan smiled to take the edge off his remark. 'Regardless, I find it hard to believe it's him, unless he's the world's most talented undiscovered actor. He was still deeply shaken and assured me again and again that he was never breaking in anywhere ever again. He's starting a new life.'

'Yeah, right,' Molander said, shaking his head.

'Did he take anything? From the flat, I mean,' Tuvesson said.

'According to him, there was nothing of value in it, and from what little I've seen, I'm inclined to believe him. But maybe Ingvar will spot something missing.' Klippan shrugged.

Tuvesson nodded. 'All right. So the question we now have to ask ourselves is what makes someone want to do this to another human being.' Next to the picture of Evert Jonsson she put up a picture of his decomposing body in the cocoon. 'Because hard as it may be to wrap our heads around, there has to have been a motive. If we can just find it, we'll also find—'

'But what if there isn't one?'

Tuvesson and the others turned to Fabian. 'If there isn't a what?'

'A motive,' he said, despite it still being little more than a theory based on a confused dream he'd had. 'Why does there have to be a motive?'

'Because there always is,' Klippan said. 'Behind every action there's a motive.'

'And if we can find it, we'll find the perpetrator,' Tuvesson added.

'Yes, I've heard that old truism a number of times,' Fabian said. 'But what if that's not the case here? Then what do we do?'

Silence fell.

'Look, I'm not sure I follow,' Tuvesson said finally. 'Are you seriously saying there's no motive?'

'I don't know. There might be, but I'm not convinced it's one that's going to help us move this investigation forward. So I suggest we drop the motive talk for a while.' Fabian got up and walked over to the whiteboard wall. 'It seems to me we've been so focused on a thousand different motives we can't see the wood for the trees any more. Take the laundry room murder, for instance, or the poisoning of—'

'Hold on a minute,' Klippan broke in. 'As you are very well aware, we have motives for the murders of both Moonif Ganem and Molly Wessman.'

'We do? How can you be so sure?'

'Fabian, come on, we've arrested the perpetrators,' Tuvesson said. 'Högsell is preparing charges as we speak.'

'I know, but I'm no longer convinced we have the right people. Take Assar Skanås. He's a paedophile and clearly into little girls. How does that explain why he'd shove a Syrian boy into a washing machine?'

'He was there, Fabian,' Molander said. 'His fingerprints were on the washing machine door.'

'Sure, but fingerprints and motive are two different things. Fingerprints are forensic evidence that could have ended up there some other way. From what I understand, he knew someone in the building. The bloke with all the dolls, right? Maybe he was just there to visit and noticed that the basement door was open and popped down to have a look.' Fabian shrugged. 'Same story with Eric Jacobsén. He has confessed to installing hidden cameras in a number of women's homes. He has also engaged in quite a lot of rough sex. But that's neither illegal nor a plausible motive for killing Wessman. Especially in view of the fact she was poisoned with ricin. I'm sorry, but it just doesn't hold up.'

'So according to you, we're back to square one,' Tuvesson said. 'With both Moonif Ganem and Molly Wessman.'

'Not entirely.' Fabian swallowed and chose his words carefully. 'Because I think everything's actually connected.'

'What do you mean, everything?'

'All the murders, all our cases from the past few weeks. Everything we've been working on.' Fabian nodded at the cluttered whiteboard wall.

The others looked, but no one spoke until Tuvesson turned to Klippan and Molander. 'What do you think?'

'I'm not sure how to put this.' Klippan sighed. 'Fabian, sometimes I feel like you just blurt out theories without any substantiation. Don't get me wrong. I hear what you're saying, but—'

'I would go so far as to say there's nothing to suggest a connection as things stand,' Molander broke in. 'First of all, the cases are completely different. Take the method, for instance. We have everything from knives and poisoning to a washing machine. And now a hermetically sealed cocoon, to boot. And the same goes for the victims.'

'That's my thinking, too,' Tuvesson said. 'And besides, this is hardly a new notion. We've already considered whether everything might be connected, but we haven't been able to find a common denominator.'

'That's true, and that's the point. I think the reason they're all so different is, in fact, the common denominator.'

9

KIM SLEIZNER TOOK a sip of the juice that Laura's Bakery, a hipster café on Nørrebro in Copenhagen, had dubbed 'The Health Booster', which was ironic since it was sweeter than Jolly Cola. He could almost see the damn spare tyre around his waist growing with each sip.

It had been weeks since he'd weighed in. Lately, the scale, and the hallway mirror, had been no-go zones. But there was no escaping the fact that he had put on weight. Lack of exercise was starting to leave its mark; if he didn't do something soon, he risked the wobble becoming permanent.

But it was going to have to wait. He had other things to see to. Other things that were so much more important he had, for the first time in his life, put himself second. The reason was spelled Dunja. Or Dunja Bitch Cunt Hougaard, to use her full name.

She'd gone to ground, and she'd done it with such brazen defiance he hadn't slept for days.

If she'd just stayed in her hole, burnt by everything he'd put her through. Then he would have felt calm. Then he could have gone for his usual run past the opera house and all the way out to the Refshale peninsula and back. He would even have been able to resume his strength training, his yoga practice and so on.

But that wasn't how this was going to go.

She was after his scalp. He'd sensed it, like the first vague symptoms of flu, of an Ebola virus about to break out. And when he found the message from her in her flat, warning him that she would take him down at any cost, he'd realized she was taking things to the next level. A level where his only option was to utterly annihilate her. Harassing her and rattling her cage wasn't going to be enough any more. The time for that was long past.

This time, it was about squeezing her goddam throat until her tongue turned blue and her eyes bulged like ping-pong balls. It was about severing her limbs and cutting her head off. About smashing her maimed body parts with a sledgehammer and throwing whatever was left to some hungry fucking sow.

But not even after doing that would he be done. He wouldn't relax until the pig was slaughtered, roasted and on his plate. Only after he had chewed, swallowed and shat her out would he truly be done.

He just had to find her. And that, despite his extensive network of contacts and the investigative routes open to him as the head of the Copenhagen Homicide Unit, had proved considerably harder than he'd initially thought. The little bitch had apparently planned things out rather carefully.

He'd already found her once. Granted, only for a few seconds in CCTV footage from a bank in Malmö. But that was enough to stay on her scent.

That was why he was now installed in the outdoor seating area of a restaurant in central Copenhagen, feet away from her flat on Blågårdsgade 4, trying to blend into this blasted hipster land by sipping his pathetically colourful Health

Booster, having swapped his suit and shirt for a pair of jeans, a hoodie and an equally pathetic baseball cap.

He'd even gone so far as to acquire a bicycle. Even though he despised anything to do with bikes and loathed the people who rode them even more. To him, they were scum, barely worth being lined up and shot at dawn.

And he wasn't even waiting for Dunja, but for that cocky elephant Chinaman living in her flat. He claimed his name was Qiang Who, but there hadn't been a single person by that name in any of the databases, despite searching both 'Qiang' and 'Who' separately.

Who the fuck did he think he was? Doctor Who? It was like some fucking joke. Him and his goddam elephant fetish.

There was nothing to suggest he had any connection with Dunja, but at the moment the Chink was his only lead. For that reason, he'd spent the entire day, save for a few brief minutes, watching the door of his building from various cafés.

He pulled out his phone and scrolled through his inbox. He'd had another email from Mikael Rønning in the IT department regarding some security update for his phone.

But he didn't have time for technological bullshit right now. A few months back, the same department had done work on their email server, which had resulted in it being down for almost two days. The newspapers had written about it and—

Sleizner stopped himself mid-thought when he realized none other than the pudgy Chinaman himself was stepping out onto the street. With elephant prints on both his baseball cap and his T-shirt, there could be no doubt it was him. He was carrying a backpack and some kind of round, black case.

Sleizner downed his juice and walked over to his bike, stifling the urge to jump on and give chase. He would be too conspicuous. Besides, the Chinaman hadn't even made it to his own bike yet; he was just standing there in the middle of the pedestrian street, bent over the small round case as though he was looking for something. Probably a stuffed elephant he couldn't leave home without.

But then he suddenly started gliding forward, seemingly hovering a few inches off the ground. What the fuck? He was moving fast, too. Sleizner didn't understand until the Chinaman whizzed past him with his feet on either side of the black case, which apparently wasn't a case at all but rather some godforsaken electrical unicycle.

He'd never seen anything like it, and before he could react, the elephant gook was zooming away from him at a speed that was bound to be illegal in the pedestrian zone. Much too late, he threw himself on his bike and started to pedal after him.

But the bike turned out to be significantly less effective than a unicycle on the crowded street, and when he finally made it out onto Nørrebrogade, he'd lost sight of the man, only to catch a glimpse of his ugly mug a few seconds later at the back of bus 3A, thundering past on its way into the city.

Seven intersections later, it had reached Nørreport Station, where it stopped long enough for Sleizner to catch up and pause for a minute. He was panting like a dog trapped in a parked car and desperately needed something to drink. But before long, the bus was indicating to pull out and the Chink had made no move to get off.

When they reached the Central Station, Sleizner was so exhausted and thirsty he would have given anything for some water. Even another Health Booster would have been gratefully received. But before he could get to the bus, he saw the fat prick get off and get back on his unicycle, which immediately shot off up the wheelchair ramp and disappeared into the station.

Sleizner hurried after him through the open doors, dragging his bike, and saw the Chinaman hover through the crowd without so much as a drop of sweat on his balls. Sleizner used his bike as a scooter, ignoring the shouting guard and ringing his bell incessantly to give people a chance to jump out of his way.

Getting down the escalator to the S train was trickier. Where the elephant man could simply pick up his unicycle in one hand and hurry past the queue to the platform, he had no chance of squeezing by with his bike. People refused to step aside, even though he worked the bell and rammed their bloody bags with his front wheel. In the end, he saw no other way than to simply abandon the bike and push through the doors of the southbound S train before it pulled out.

The Chinaman got off at Sydhavn Station and after walking down the stairs to the pavement, he got back on his bloody unicycle and zoomed off. Sleizner had to run to keep up.

What if the gook was just toying with him? What if he'd spotted him on Blågårdsgade and was now just making him run in circles like a picador tiring out the bull before the matador went in for the killing blow?

Sleizner stopped on the central reservation in the middle

of Teglholmsgade and looked around. But there was no sign of Dunja. The Chinaman, on the other hand, was gliding on towards the large building straight ahead, and just like that, hope sprung anew.

The building belonged to the TDC Group, whose president, Stig Paulsen, wasn't just one of Sleizner's closest friends, but was also one of the most active members of The Club. If it turned out Qiang Who, or whatever his name was, worked for TDC, he could zip around on his little toy as fast as he pleased. He would still never be able to escape him.

10

FABIAN TURNED INTO Kungstorget Square outside Knutpunkten Station in Helsingborg and parked in a bay where a sign warned him the maximum stay was ten minutes. He picked one of the seven anonymous pay-as-you-go SIM cards he'd just purchased and pushed it into his old Nokia, whose functions were restricted to calling, texting and showing the time.

Then he found Gertrud Molander's number in his iPhone and dialled it on the Nokia. True, she'd asked him to leave her alone, but he wanted to talk to her and hear her voice to make sure she was okay.

'*You've reached Gertrud Molander. Unfortunately, I'm not available at the moment, but leave a message after the beep and I'll get back to you.*'

Why wasn't she picking up? It would have been understandable if she were in the same room as her husband. But she wasn't. Far from it. Molander was in the police lab, busy cross-matching all prints, hairs and trace DNA samples from the different crime scenes, and it would likely be late before he was done.

Her phone could obviously be out of battery or turned down so low she couldn't hear it. Or maybe she just had better things to do than to stare at her phone all day long.

He unlocked his iPhone and opened Facebook, where

he had a profile, though he'd never posted a status update. He'd created the account mainly so he could have a poke around to see how it worked, and unless he misremembered, Gertrud had sent him a friend request sometime last spring.

He hadn't accepted it. He almost never did. Instead, her request had sat unanswered in a growing line of requests from people who, for some unfathomable reason, wanted to stay in touch with him. Some were former colleagues and friends from Stockholm, others childhood friends from Helsingborg and yet others complete strangers.

He couldn't explain why, but even though he never shared anything about his life, it felt like he was selling himself and giving out keys to his home whenever he accepted a friend request.

Gertrud didn't seem particularly active on social media either, though she did post things from time to time, mostly pictures of food, flowers and cats. But on this particular day, there seemed to have been quite a lot of activity on her wall. Congratulatory messages with pictures of flowers, hearts and champagne bottles had been and were still streaming in from one Facebook friend after another.

Of all the days, this one had to be her birthday.

Was that why she wasn't picking up? Maybe she was out celebrating, treating herself to a spa session or whatever. As he skimmed the list of congratulations, an idea slowly took shape in his mind. When he spotted Hjalmar Bergfors' *Haaaaapy Birthdaaaaay from Hörby*, he decided to give it a go.

Gertrud was originally from Hörby too, so it didn't seem too far-fetched to assume Hjalmar Bergfors was a childhood friend. He pulled the Nokia back out and started to compose a text message.

> Hi Gertrud, since you're not very active on Facebook, I thought I'd send you a big Haaaapy Birthdaaaaay this way, too. Hope you have a great day. I haven't seen you in a long time, but I happen to be on my way to Helsingborg for a meeting right now. Which leads me to ask: can I buy the birthday girl coffee later today? Love, Hjalmar Bergfors. P.S. If you don't recognize the number, it's because I lost my phone a few days ago.

With only ten keys and a maximum limit of 160 characters, it took four texts and a considerable amount of time and focus to type up and send the whole message. Consequently, he was completely caught off guard by a hard tap on his window and only just had time to look up before his door was thrown open.

'Hello!' Sonja smiled and waved. 'We're here.'

'Hi there.' He made sure the last text had sent, climbed out of the car and turned to Theodor, who'd had his hair cut and was dressed in a freshly ironed white shirt, a blue blazer and a pair of khaki chinos. 'Don't you look fancy!' He moved to hug him, but Theodor evaded him and started walking around the car to the other side.

'Maybe you should get going, you don't want to be late.'

Fabian nodded and gave Sonja a hug. 'See you soon.'

'Good luck.' She kissed him on the mouth and walked over to the other side of the car, where Theodor was buckling his seat belt. 'Hey, you. Don't I get a hug?'

Theodor said nothing, just stared straight ahead.

'All right, fine. I'll try again when you get back tonight.

Just so you know, I'm making lasagne. That'll be nice, won't it?' She waited for a reaction but got none. 'Oh, right, and if you want something special for dessert, just say the word.'

'Sonja.' Fabian caught her eye across the roof of the car. 'I think we should just get this over with.'

Sonja nodded and stepped aside so Theodor could close his door.

'Hey, it's going to be fine, you'll see.' Fabian buckled his seat belt and turned the key in the ignition. 'And don't worry, I'm going to be with you the whole time.'

Theodor responded with silence while Fabian put the car in gear, indicated and watched Sonja dry her tears in the rear-view mirror as he left Kungstorget behind and continued down Järnvägsgatan.

11

FABIAN KILLED THE engine and studied the building in front of them, which looked like a secret research laboratory with its series of low, connected, orange sandstone buildings, shiny metal roofs and seemingly random scattering of tiny windows.

Theodor was sitting next to him, his eyes vacant. The journey had felt like a silent film. He'd been on the verge of speaking several times, but had stopped himself, convinced his son had enough on his plate dealing with his own thoughts.

'How are you feeling?' he asked at length.

'I'm not sure,' Theodor replied, without looking up. 'How am I supposed to feel?'

What could he say to that, when his own feelings were all over the place? He was proud and relieved his son had finally made the difficult but correct decision to tell the truth. But he had been the one pushing for it. He was the one who had laid down the law and with simple, irrefutable arguments persuaded both Sonja and Theodor. And now that they were here, his conviction was suddenly undermined by a nagging worry.

Had he pushed too hard?

'I think the important thing is that this is what you want to do. That you feel it's the right thing for you.'

'I do. My mind's made up.'

That was exactly what he'd said back home. That he wanted to start over by going to Denmark and telling them exactly what had happened. And Fabian wanted nothing more than to believe him. That the decision had really been his, that it wasn't just the only way he could see to make the nagging stop.

'But if you've changed your mind, this is the time to—'

'Let's go already.' Theodor cut him off and was already out of the car and on his way to the entrance fifty yards or so away before Fabian had even unbuckled.

The Danish prosecutor was waiting for them at the reception desk.

'Hi, Peter Lange.' He held out his hand. 'And you must be Fabian and Theodor Risk.'

They nodded and shook the prosecutor's hand.

'My mother was Swedish, so I speak and understand Swedish almost fluently. And I love crispbread and Lucia saffron buns. There's nothing better,' he went on with a chuckle. 'Theodor, if you wouldn't mind filling out your name, address and personal identification number on this form. Right, and do you have a passport or some other kind of photo ID?'

Fabian handed over his passport while Theodor completed the form and signed it.

'Great. Then please follow me.' Peter Lange swiped his ID, held the door open and showed them into a long hallway with windows along one side and closed doors along the other.

A hundred feet further on, the hallway made a ninety-degree turn and continued as far again before Lange finally stopped and opened the door to an office, where a desk faced two armchairs on either side of a small table set with bottles of sparkling water and two glasses.

'Please, have a seat.' Lange closed the door and sat down behind the desk. 'I want to begin by saying how happy I am you've chosen to come forward to tell us what you know. It's unusual for witnesses to turn up out of nowhere in the middle of court proceedings.'

'From what I hear, you haven't had many witnesses of any description,' Fabian said.

'That's correct, and that's one of the reasons we've been having such a difficult time. None of the plaintiffs are alive to give testimony. And the defendants are blaming each other while also swearing they have no idea who did what.'

'We've encountered the same strategy in Sweden in a number of gang rape cases, and in those, all the defendants got off because their guilt couldn't be proven beyond reasonable doubt.'

'Exactly. If I want to have even a small chance of getting all of them convicted, I need to be able to show that there was shared intent. And how can I do that when no one's confessing and there are no witnesses?' Peter Lange threw up his hands. 'That's why I'm so happy you're here, Theodor. With the help of your testimony, I'm hoping we'll be able to break down their pact and figure out who did what. But let's start at the beginning. Why don't you tell me what happened, in your own words?'

Theodor swallowed and nodded, and then he tremblingly picked up one of the two bottles, filled his glass and downed it in one.

'This isn't a police interview, just a regular conversation, so there's no pressure, just take your time.'

Theodor nodded again, poured himself another glass and drank it. 'She went to my school. Alexandra, I mean. I'd been in love with her for a while but hadn't dared to talk to her.'

'Sure, that can be scary. I was very shy myself at your age.'

'Anyway, some people were being mean to her and took her baseball cap, so... so I got angry and helped her get it back and, well...' Theodor shrugged. 'After a while, we started dating.'

'Nice work.'

'That was when I first met her friends. They all belonged to the same martial arts club as her. Henrik was one of them. I don't remember the names of the other two.'

'Why not?'

Theodor shrugged.

'I didn't like them and didn't want to hang out with them. But Alexandra did, and one morning after we'd been over to Denmark, I found a video on her phone.' He reached for the bottle to pour himself more water, but it was empty.

'Here, take mine.' Fabian topped up his glass from his bottle and handed it to Theodor, who again downed it before continuing.

'It was the one from the motorway when they pushed that man in the trolley into traffic. We were at her house and I just wanted to get out of there, leave both her and her sick fucking mates. It turned out Alexandra didn't want to keep doing it either. She'd never wanted to be part of it. At first, she hadn't realized what they'd asked her to film, and afterwards it was too late. That Henrik bloke had just kept forcing her.'

'So you're telling me Henrik is the brains of the operation.'

Theodor nodded. 'He calls the shots. Anyway, Alexandra and I destroyed the phone with the video on it and called him up and told him she was out. That she didn't want to be part of it any more. But he refused and said she was in until he said otherwise. Then he said something about there being a witness, the sister of one of the victims.'

'Sannie Lemke?'

'Yeah, that's it, so he forced us to do it one last time. I didn't want to, but—'

'Hold on.' Lange straightened up in his chair. 'Are you telling me you were present when Sannie Lemke was murdered?'

Theodor swallowed hard and nodded. 'But I didn't do anything. The only thing I did was to—'

'But you were there as one of them, wearing a smiley mask?'

'Yes, but all I did was stand watch.'

Peter Lange had already got out his phone and pressed speed dial. 'Thanks. Yes, as quickly as you can.'

'Dad, what's going on?'

'Just stay calm.' Fabian took Theodor's hand. 'What my son is trying to say is that he was at the scene but that he played no active part in what took place.'

'That's exactly what the other four are claiming, too. If they are all to be believed, Sannie Lemke forced the firecracker down her own throat and lit the fuse.'

The door was opened by two security officers, who entered and moved in on Theodor.

'Dad, what the fuck?'

'Hey now, hold on.' Fabian got to his feet. 'What are you doing?'

'Do something! You have to do something!'

'This has to be a misunderstanding. You're not arresting him, are you?'

'I'm sorry, but I wasn't aware your son had participated as one of them. That makes him guilty of—'

'Guilty? He was bloody forced to come along as a lookout.'

'That's called being an accessory and it makes him just as much of a suspect as the other four. We're going to have to conduct a full investigation with thorough interviews, during which he obviously has the right to legal representation. Until that can be arranged, we have no choice but to remand him in custody.'

'Dad, you have to stop them!' screamed Theodor, who was now being ushered out of the room by the two officers.

'For God's sake, he's sixteen years old!' Fabian looked from the prosecutor to the two police officers and back again. 'This is completely unacceptable! My son came here voluntarily to give testimony. To help you. And you arrest him like he's some kind of monster.'

'I'm terribly sorry, but—'

'Sorry?'

'Dad!'

'Hey, look, can you just hold on a minute?' Fabian hurried over and grabbed Theodor, forcing the officers to stop halfway out of the door. 'You can't bloody drag him off just like that!'

'Normally, he would have been fine to reside at home,

under surveillance, and only come in for interviews, but given the seriousness of the crime we can't let him leave the country,' Lange said. 'You're a police officer, you know how this works.'

'I do, and I demand that we straighten this out before you do anything at all.'

'Straightening it out is exactly what we'll be doing, and as soon as we've made sure there's no risk of him reoffending, impeding the investigation or absconding, he will be allowed to return home to await the resumption of the trial. Which will hopefully happen as soon as tomorrow.' Lange nodded to the security officers, who forced Fabian to back away from Theodor and continued out into the hallway.

Fabian was about to object again but realized all he could do was watch as the two guards dragged his son away. He wanted to call out after him, to show his support or say anything that might give him a measure of strength, but before he could open his mouth, they'd turned a corner and were gone.

12

On the second floor of Kärngränden 4 in central Helsingborg, a light switch was glowing red, trying to attract attention. But he'd left the lights off. His eyes needed to adapt. Ten minutes later, he stepped into the flat and quietly shut the door behind him.

It was the same flat and yet completely different. Then, when he'd been here to find out who lived on the other side of the window on the far left, it had been tidy, everything in its place. Now, it was showing clear signs of neglect.

That their perfect middle-class existence had been seriously rocked by Assar Skanås's treatment of their daughter was in one way understandable. But that they'd taken it so hard they couldn't even be bothered to do dishes and pick up after themselves any more seemed fairly over the top. It was as though they were so busy feeling bad and sorry for themselves, they had no time for anything else.

He stopped outside the door to the parents' bedroom. Last time, it had stood ajar. Now, it was closed. To make sure there'd be no squeaking or sticking, he pulled out the can of lock dry lube and attached it to the red three-inch nozzle, which he inserted into the keyhole. He gave the lock and the hinges a few squirts each.

The door opened without a sound and he entered and looked around. After seeing the hallway and parts of the kitchen, he wasn't surprised to find the floor littered with clothes and both nightstands covered with Kleenex, water glasses and open boxes of Zolpidem and Imovane, which reassured him they were fast asleep.

Maybe the fact that they lay facing away from each other at the very edges of the mattress wasn't entirely surprising either. It wouldn't be the first time a relationship had foundered after a child was hurt. What was more remarkable was that the little girl in question wasn't lying between them in bed. That, if anything, would have been expected.

Goddammit. The thought hadn't even crossed his mind, and now he was standing there with no clue as to what to do next. What if she wasn't there? Then what would he do? What if they'd shipped her off to her grandparents because they didn't feel capable of caring for her? What the fuck would he do then?

He went back into the hallway and past the door where wooden letters formed the name *Ruben* and stopped outside the door on the far left, where the wooden letters spelled out *Ester* between a number of taped-up drawings of flowers, hearts and, if he had to guess, princesses.

He gave the lock and hinges a once-over with the lock dry lube before opening the door and stepping into the room. To his great relief, she was in her bed, and just like the last time he was here, she was curled up in foetal position with her thumb in her mouth, surrounded by an army of teddy bears.

After closing the door behind him, he moved over to the edge of the bed, where he squatted down and started to empty his backpack. He set the two plastic bottles of water and the bowl to one side. He pulled a rag soaked in paint thinner from a plastic bag and held it close enough to her face to make her breathe in the fumes.

He waited like that for a few minutes before judging that she was sufficiently passed out, then gently pulled her thumb out and covered her mouth and nose with the rag. There was no reaction, not the slightest twitch or attempt at resistance as she drifted further and further into the haze of unconsciousness.

He was probably doing her a favour. Not that he cared. Not in the slightest, actually. The only thing that mattered was that the task set by the dice was carried out to the letter. That little Ester didn't have to wake up and realize her hours with Assar the Paedo hadn't been a nightmare was something more akin to a happy side effect. Judging from her parents' bedroom, she would probably have grown up in a broken home with no clear boundaries and ended up a junkie ready to do anything for another hit.

He unscrewed the bottle caps and emptied the water into the bowl until it was about two inches from the top. He flipped the unconscious girl over on her stomach and turned her until her head was dangling off the side of the bed. Then he picked up the bowl, slowly raised it up to her face and held it there.

There was no reaction to that, either.

Not a sound. No resistance. Nothing but a few bubbles.

13

FABIAN HAD LONG since lost count of how many attempts it had taken him to squeeze his car into the free parking spot across the street from his house on Pålsjögatan. Granted, it was still crooked and one of the back tyres was on the pavement, but it would have to do.

He crossed the street and realized his sense of balance had abandoned him. But at least he didn't fall over, and he found the right key almost immediately.

He'd never driven drunk before. On occasion he might have got behind the wheel after a glass or two, enough to register on a breathalyser if he'd been pulled over. But he'd never driven as drunk as he was now.

But then, the trip to Denmark had been a disaster. Instead of going home with Theodor to support and prep him for taking the witness stand, he had, after several hours of trying to persuade the Danish prosecutor to change his mind, been forced to go back across the sound alone. He'd been unbelievably naive. He'd tricked himself and his family into thinking everything would be okay. If they just did the right thing, everything would turn out right in the end. As though that were a natural law, universal justice.

Nothing could have been more wrong.

He had called Sonja to tell her on the ferry back. She'd taken the news surprisingly calmly, her thoughts seemingly elsewhere. He'd asked what was on her mind, but she'd simply told him to take all the time he needed.

The alcohol had definitely helped. After just a few glasses, all thoughts of Theodor had grown diffuse and fuzzy. After a few more, his anxiety had more or less evaporated and he'd managed to persuade himself everything was going to be all right. But when he entered the house and was greeted by the aroma of lasagne, anxiety about what the future might hold crashed over him again.

To avoid waking Sonja, he undressed downstairs and brushed his teeth and washed in the guest bathroom before going up to their bedroom and crawling in under the blankets. But when he rolled over towards the middle of the bed to give Sonja a hug and whisper in her ear that he was home, he discovered her side was empty.

He sat up and looked around in the dark, struggling to sober up. Had she given up and left? Packed her bags as soon as Matilda went to bed and just abandoned them? After everything that had happened, it wouldn't surprise him.

He'd been telling himself they were finally doing okay. That all the trials and hardships were eventually going to bring them closer together, back to something that would, in time, be really good. They hadn't quarrelled at all recently. They'd agreed on virtually everything. In the middle of the chaos, they had stood united and for the first time in ages were pulling in the same direction.

Maybe it had been too good to be true. A charade. A false face put on things to lull him into a false sense of security so she could disappear at the first opportunity, leaving everything behind. *Take all the time you need.*

If it hadn't been for the distant music, he would have

fallen asleep in the middle of that thought. But as it was, he got out of bed instead and went back out onto the landing. The music was still too faint for him to hear what it was. But a flickering light filtering down the stairs pointed him to the studio.

The studio belonged to Sonja and was one of the reasons he'd bought the house. She'd always wanted a home studio. A room that was just hers, where she could go to make art whenever the spirit moved her without first getting on the metro, like back in Stockholm. While making dinner, before the rest of the family woke up or well into the small hours.

But she hadn't been up there in over a month now. Since her lover, who had posed as an art dealer, had instead turned out to be the killer he was hunting, she'd refused to set foot on the second floor. She'd been so badly burned that art was now a closed chapter to her.

He'd been hoping it was a temporary crisis, that it was only a matter of time before she pulled on her dungarees, stiff with dried paint spatter, and got back to her art. But she hadn't.

Not until now.

Because there she was. On her back, eyes closed, in the middle of the room, motionless in her white bathrobe. Thirty or so tealights flickered around her and out of the speakers poured Bruce Springsteen's *Nebraska*, one of her favourite albums, which she only ever put on when she was really sad. That was the only time it was ever played. When nothing else helped.

'Sonja...' he said, and he stepped into the room. But she didn't respond. Instead, she just lay there, supine, her arms by her sides. 'What are you doing?' he continued, trying to push down the thought that maybe Greta had been referring to her. 'It's half one in the morning.' But he was unsuccessful and eventually frantic anxiety broke through the haze of alcohol. Had she done it? 'Sonja...'

When she got up, he was unsure whether it was really happening or if he was just having a booze-fuelled dream sprung out of his deepest fantasies. He wanted to ask but stayed silent as she walked towards him with her finger pressed against her lips and let her bathrobe fall.

She smelled wonderful and when she leaned in to kiss him, he could feel the droplets from her hair, still wet from the shower, trickle down his leg as though it were real. The kiss was slow and tentative at first but quickly grew increasingly intense and hungry.

But why now? He didn't understand. Had she been lying up here waiting for him, even though it was the middle of the night and their son had been remanded in custody? Or wasn't it up to her at all? Had desire suddenly just bloomed out of feelings that had been suppressed but never truly gone? Because enough time had passed.

She wanted him. For the first time in a long time and like never before, she wanted him.

He kissed her back and tried to parry her ravenous lips with his own while moving his hand up to cup her breast and caress her nipple. That was his usual move. Meanwhile, he slowly inched his other hand down her stomach.

But not this time. Without breaking the kiss, she slapped away both his hands, grabbed him by the hair and pushed him down. Down along her neck, towards her breasts, which she let him caress with the tip of his tongue.

'Lick,' she said. 'Lick them.'

And he licked. Again and again, he circled her nipples, painting them with his saliva.

'Blow,' she said. 'I want you to blow on them.'

He obeyed and felt a shiver run through her as she pushed him down between her legs.

He'd been there many times. But not like this. Never this intensely. With her vice-like grip on his hair, she forced him ever deeper into places he'd never been before. He liked it and she liked it. Her moans were growing louder and louder. Her muscles tensed, making her body tremble for more. Seemingly insatiable.

She'd always been so quiet. Had always wanted to turn the lights off and keep things tidy. Had always hurried to the bathroom to rinse off the moment they were done. She was like a different person.

'Horny... I was so horny,' she said, forcing him down onto the hard but warm wooden floor. 'So fucking horny...' She grabbed his throbbing erection and squeezed it as she started to move her hand up and down.

'Me too,' he replied, wishing she would never stop.

'But not for you,' she went on, and started flicking her tongue against the head of his penis. 'I didn't want you at all.' Then she took him in her mouth, and he tried to understand what was happening. What she meant. But his questions remained unanswered and soon all his thoughts revolved around her caresses again. The way she took him deeper than ever, only to then kiss and play with it as though she wanted to taste every part.

If she kept this up, he wouldn't be able to hold back much longer. It had been a long time, too long. The tip of her tongue teasingly playing along the edge of the head, coupled with her hand squeezing the shaft so tightly… it was about to explode, he was so hard. He could feel it now. It was building and he wouldn't be able to fight it for much longer.

'Right then, you were the last person I wanted to let in,' she said, and pressed her thumb into the spot right underneath the head, trapping his load. 'Anyone, so long as it wasn't you.'

He was thrown back into confusion. Disappointed and yet not. The load was still in him, throbbing with each heartbeat. When she straddled him, he prayed dawn would never arrive.

'When he pushed into me…' she continued as she slowly began to ride him. 'I had never experienced anything more satisfying.' She leaned down and let him taste her breasts. First one, then the other. 'It was as though he freed me… from all the things I thought I was.' She straightened back up and started thrusting harder, up and down as though she couldn't get deep enough. 'There was a hardness to him I didn't know I'd missed during all my years with you. A primal force stronger than anything else…'

She upped the tempo and he helped with his hands under her taut bottom, pushing it up so far he slipped out of her and slamming it down again so deep and hard it must have hurt. But she moaned with pleasure and begged for more, so he thrust harder and let his hand feel its way closer to her opening, until he could feel himself sliding in and out.

'I even liked it when he hit me… The throbbing pain and the rush of blood. Even then… It was as though I'd been asleep for years and was finally waking up… When I realized who he really was, it was too late…'

Without warning, she climbed off him and got down on

all fours, a position she'd never liked and thought was too pornographic. Now she was asking for it, with her bottom in the air and her fingers spreading her labia, and the moment he pushed inside, she moaned so loudly he was sure the neighbours must be able to hear.

But he didn't care, just kept thrusting into her harder and harder and faster and faster as rage boiled inside him. So many times, he'd wanted her to tell him so they could expel all the secrets that had built a wall between them. And now when she finally did, he wanted nothing more than for her to stop.

'I tried to run...' she went on, and he slapped her buttock so hard it turned red. 'To get out of there...' He slapped her again and heard her burst into tears. But the thought of stopping seemed as remote to her as to him. 'But I couldn't...'

It was as though their bodies had taken over. 'I was nothing to him...' As though it were no longer up to them. 'I was just a way of getting to you... It was all about you...' They sped up, racing towards the climax. 'Once I was used up, he was going to discard me...' Every time he thrust into her, she pushed back harder. 'So he forced me into my own piece of art... Like it was a coffin... I could hear the screwdriver tighten each screw in the lid...'

The beginning of the end began as a quiver in her voice. 'The hole had already been dug... He'd prepared the whole thing...' Then it spread like a shudder through her body. 'He was going to bury me...' And over to him. 'Alive...' Until it finally took over with such force, they both screamed.

14

FABIAN TOOK A sip of the scalding hot coffee and rubbed his knees, which, despite a double dose of paracetamol, ached like he'd run a marathon. Waking up that morning, he'd been unable to figure out why they hurt. But as soon as he discovered the bleeding abrasions, the memories came flooding back.

Neither the wounds nor the persistent tenderness bothered him. Quite the opposite; they were among the few things he had going for him right now. A reminder that last night's exertions with Sonja on the floor of her studio hadn't been a dream.

She'd finally told him everything, filling in the gaps in the narrative of what had taken place during those fateful days when she'd left him for her new man. It had been a hard telling, for both him and her. That there had been some kind of trauma had been clear to him. But that she'd been buried alive, trapped in her own work of art *The Hanging Box*, was hard to take in, though it did explain why his colleagues had insisted on confiscating the wooden box for forensic examination.

It also explained her sudden aversion to her own art. Even why she'd waited for him in the studio, of all places, and until tonight, of all nights, had been explained; she'd been informed by the police earlier in the day that they were done with the box and that she had five business days to come and collect it before it was sent off to be destroyed.

And yet, the thought alone made him feel unclean. As though the whole night was tainted because they'd lain there, wrapped up in themselves and their own anxieties, allowing themselves to feel pleasure while their son spent his first night in police custody. It wasn't like him, and it definitely wasn't like Sonja.

'Well, well, what do you know. Mr Risk is first to arrive again.' Molander looked around as he entered the conference room. 'Who'd have thought it?'

'Happy to be keeping you on your toes,' Fabian replied, playing along with a smile.

'Though you do look a bit pooped. Late night?'

'A bit. There's a lot of work to be done.'

'Yes, there certainly is.' Molander put a stack of documents down on the table and took a seat. 'So no "private excursions" today, then, I take it?'

'Actually, yes, but not until this afternoon.'

'Theodor again?'

Fabian nodded. 'And what about you?' Theodor was the last thing he wanted to talk to Molander about.

'Are you crazy? How can I fit in personal escapades with all of this going on?' Molander gestured around the room.

'I was actually thinking about last night, whether you had a late one. It was Gertrud's birthday, wasn't it?'

'Eh... Right...' Molander seemed to shudder briefly. 'I'm sorry, what was that? My mind was elsewhere—'

'Gertrud, your wife. I noticed on Facebook that it was her birthday yesterday. I hope you took the time to celebrate and didn't spend the whole night working.'

'Oh, right... Well.' Molander forced out a smile and laughed mirthlessly. 'Hope springs eternal, I suppose. I'm afraid I have to disappoint you. Luckily, Gertrud knows what to expect – she knows what I'm like when we're in the middle of an investigation.'

'Voilà! I told you so,' exclaimed Tuvesson, who arrived together with Klippan and Lilja. 'They're here. Perfect. Let's get cracking. Unless you were in the middle of something.'

'Not at all,' Molander replied. 'We were just discussing our workload. And while we're on the subject, I can tell you I spent the whole night in the lab, cross-matching all the samples we've collected from the crime scenes. And I did that even though, as Fabian rightly pointed out just now, yesterday was Gertrud's birthday.'

'So you'll be sleeping on the sofa, in other words,' Klippan said, and he started to plug in his laptop.

'I happen to have a very understanding wife, so I think I'll be all right.'

'And what did you discover?' Tuvesson asked.

'That Fabian was right about the investigations being connected and not the work of several perpetrators with different motives, but rather of one single person.' He held up one finger. 'Fabian, you don't have to look so surprised. Even you have to get it right sometimes.' He flashed Fabian a smile and a quick wink before turning back to the others. 'It turns out that we have unwittingly been collecting DNA traces in the form of skin fragments, hairs and saliva from a single person present at all three crime scenes.'

'Does this mean we can technically link this person to the murders of Moonif Ganem, Lennart Andersson and Molly Wessman?' Tuvesson asked.

Molander nodded. 'And most likely Evert Jonsson, too, though in that case I've only managed to match one fingerprint from the cocoon with one from the laundry room.'

'This is amazing news. But why are we only discovering this now, when the evidence has been in your lab the whole time?'

'There are several reasons for that. The DNA results have only just started to come in, and no one seriously considered the idea that it might be a single perpetrator until yesterday, when Fabian—'

'Yes, we did,' Lilja broke in. 'We just couldn't figure out a motive that fitted.'

'Exactly. And given that, I didn't prioritize cross-matching all the prints and samples we've collected. But sure, blame me, if it makes you feel better. Go ahead. As though I have twenty-five – or why not twenty-six? – hours a day to work.'

'I actually do think a large part of the blame for this belongs to you.' Tuvesson closed the door. 'That's not to say you, and the rest of us, haven't gone above and beyond in the past few weeks. But in all honesty. Wouldn't you agree that it's a bit peculiar that it's only now, after four murders, that we realize this isn't one-offs but rather the work of a serial killer? A serial killer who is probably busy planning a fifth murder.'

'I don't know about peculiar.' Molander shrugged. 'I'd say everything about these cases has been and still is extraordinarily peculiar. Everything from the different methods to the choice of victims. Take the timings, for instance. Evert Jonsson suffocates in his cocoon sometime around 25 May—'

'Ingvar, I'm—'

'Would you let me finish, please. Then almost twenty days go by before Moonif Ganem is centrifuged to death. Three days later, Molly Wessman dies of poisoning, the same day Lennart Andersson is stabbed to death in front of a crowd of witnesses at Ica Maxi.' Molander threw his hands up. 'So no, given the circumstances, I would actually be inclined to say we've been pretty quick and efficient.'

'I'm fully aware this investigation is unlike anything we've seen and that the NFC, despite us being a priority, didn't give us the results of the DNA analyses until now. But the fingerprints, for example – you've had access to those the whole time.'

'Yes, but as I just said, we haven't—'

'It's not about what our theories have been. Or about how busy you happen to be or how many hours there are in a day. I have laboured under the assumption that you continuously cross-match everything you get, without me having to ask you to. Especially under these circumstances. Who knows where we might have been today if you'd realized a week ago that one of the fingerprints from the laundry room in Bjuv was also found in Molly Wessman's flat?'

'What do you want me to say?'

'You don't have to say anything. We all make mistakes and we all miss things. It just normally doesn't happen to you. It leads me to wonder why *now*. Are you having problems at home? Has something happened that makes it difficult for you to focus on your work? Should I request additional resources?'

'No, no, I'm fine. Perfectly well.'

'Are you sure? Because I understand if you've been

running on fumes for too long and need a break. I just need to know what I'm working with here.'

Fabian watched Molander nod like a dog with its tail between its legs. Had his own sins finally caught up with him?

'Listen, I suggest we move on,' Lilja said, turning to the others. 'One thing I'm wondering is if there's just one perpetrator, he must be considered well organized and prepared, to say the least, right? So isn't it strange that he's leaving so many prints behind? Losing a hair here and there, fine. But saliva, fingerprints and whatnot. It doesn't make sense.'

'Are you saying it's part of a bigger plan?' Tuvesson said.

'No idea.' Lilja shrugged. 'But if it isn't, he's incredibly careless.'

'Or maybe he's overconfident,' Fabian put in. 'Since the murders are so different from each other in every respect, there's no incentive to connect the cases. On that, I agree with Ingvar – it's not surprising we haven't until now.'

'Besides, he hasn't exactly been running around leaving prints everywhere,' Molander said. 'Only in the laundry room and at Evert Jonsson's. If you don't want to leave any DNA behind, you basically have to walk around in a diving suit.'

'And another thing,' Lilja continued. 'If there's no underlying motive, then why do it at all? And why the disparate methods and victims?'

'If I had to guess, I'd say it's part of a game.'

'A game?' Tuvesson turned to Molander.

'Sure, why not?' Molander shrugged.

'But I don't understand. What do you mean, a game?'

'It wouldn't surprise me if he's just in it for the kicks, and the more varied the murders, the more thrilling. Right? For him, I mean.' Molander was met by querying looks. 'Whatever, I don't know.' He shrugged. 'It was just a thought. I have nothing to back it up.' He waved his hand dismissively. 'So, let's move on.'

'Yes, we have quite a few things left on the agenda,' Klippan said. 'And who knows. Maybe we'll find some answers in here.' He opened his laptop.

Fabian was surprised to find himself nodding. Not at Klippan, but at Molander, of all people. He'd managed to hit the nail on the head, but had almost immediately tried to back-pedal. As though he'd just realized he was the only member of the team who truly understood the perpetrator. Maybe he could even relate to him.

'Klippan, what are you showing us?' Tuvesson checked her watch.

'Don't tell me you've forgotten?' Klippan said, without attempting to hide his annoyance.

'I'm sorry, forgotten what?' Tuvesson said.

Klippan sighed. 'That I've been going through every single CCTV tape from Ica Maxi from the week before the murder of Lennart Andersson and that I'm supposed to share my findings. You know this. I was supposed to do it yesterday, but Evert Jonsson got in the way, so I think we should get it over with right now.'

'I understand, but I would still prefer if we could hold off until tomorrow, or at least later this afternoon. Because we have a few other things to discuss. Then I have to go see Högsell and let her know the charges against Eric Jacobsén and Assar Skanås need to be completely reconsidered.'

'No, I've waited long enough. I think we should just get this done.'

'Klippan, all due respect to you and your hard work, but I've decided that—' Tuvesson was cut off by her phone. 'This is Astrid, in the middle of a meeting. What's this about?'

Fabian and the others watched Tuvesson grow increasingly pale as seconds turned to minutes. She said almost nothing at all until it was time to hang up.

'He has struck again.' She swallowed hard in an effort to maintain her calm. 'The bastard has done it again.'

'Oh my God.' Lilja heaved a sigh. 'Who's the victim?'

'Ester Landgren, the little girl you saved from Assar Skanås just a few days ago.' Tuvesson was unable to hold back her tears.

'What? What are you talking about?' Lilja shook her head as though to convince herself she'd misheard. 'Are you serious?'

'Yes. I don't know what to say.'

'But why would he... What had she done to... I don't understand.'

'When did she die?' Molander asked. 'And how?'

'From what I'm told, she's been dead for hours.' Tuvesson wiped away her tears and took a deep breath to compose herself. 'Her parents only realized about an hour ago that she wasn't asleep, she had drowned.'

'Drowned?' Lilja exclaimed. 'What the fuck? She can't have drowned in her own bed, can she?'

'I know, but we have to wait and see what Flätan has to say. According to her parents, water came out of her mouth when they tried to wake her. And like you were saying,

Fabian, this is too spectacular and different from the other murders for there not to be a connection.'

'But? I don't understand,' Lilja said, fighting down her feelings. 'Can someone tell me what Ester Landgren, an innocent little girl, has to do with our killer?'

'Irene, I don't know. That's what we have to find out,' Tuvesson replied. 'All I know is that we have to catch this sick bastard before he kills anyone else. Ingvar, I want you to go over there and process the scene, and this time I assume I don't have to remind you to cross-match whatever you find with what we already have.'

'Of course.' Molander immediately started to gather up his folders.

'Irene, you talk to the parents, and Fabian, you keep on Flätan, even if he's not done yet. Klippan, you're in charge of knocking on doors and taking statements from the—'

'No.' Klippan shook his head.

'What do you mean, no?'

'I'm not going door to door. At least, not right this minute.'

'Why not? What's the matter with you?'

'And the same goes for the rest of you. You're all staying here until I'm—'

'Bloody hell, Klippan!' Tuvesson walked up to him and fixed him with a level gaze. 'I'm in charge of this investigation!'

'That may well be,' retorted Klippan, his face bright red and his voice strained. 'But right now, I don't give a shit and I'm telling you and everyone else that you are going to stay seated for another fifteen minutes and you're going to listen to what I have to say.'

15

HILLEVI STUBBS LAY on her back on the cabin sole in Elvin's boat. She was only just five foot tall, and yet there was barely room for her, what with all the things her old friend Hugo Elvin had managed to cram into the small cabin.

Transporting the boat had been unexpectedly easy. The cradle had had enough air in its tyres, and she hadn't found anything remotely close to a tracker on it or her Jeep. Even Mona-Jill, who was usually extremely curious, had accepted her explanation that an old friend's boat was going to sit in the garden for a few weeks without too many nosy questions.

And now she was lying in the cabin, imbibing the clues, thoughts, evidence and ideas Elvin had collected. That was what she always did first when she arrived at a new crime scene. On the floor, in the middle of the room, flat on her back with her eyes closed or staring up at the ceiling. That way she could breathe the air and let the atmosphere and mood, which resided in the walls as much as in the furniture and knick-knacks, suffuse her senses.

Elvin's boat was like a crime-scene concentrate, even though no crime had been committed on board. She had never seen so many clues, samples and notes in such a small space. There was probably more than enough evidence in here. The question was how they were going to find it among the white noise of irrelevant details before time ran out.

Molander was probably already plotting his next move against Fabian and they had to find enough to arrest him before he could act. Only Molander knew exactly how much time they had. A week, a few days or maybe just a few hours.

She got up and waited until she no longer felt dizzy, then slowly started to turn, round and round, letting her eyes rove up and down, scanning as much of the crowded cabin as possible.

Fabian had hypothesized that the Berlin boarding passes had been what pushed Molander into killing Elvin. She, for her part, wasn't sure that would have been enough. Granted, it blew up Molander's alibi. But it was hardly proof that he was guilty of murdering Inga Dahlberg. In the harsh light of a courtroom, it was very far from it indeed.

So Elvin must have found something else. Something absolutely watertight. It should be one of the last things he discovered before his death, since he hadn't had time to show it to anyone else on the team or make sure Molander was arrested. It should follow that whatever it was would be sitting on top of one of the countless piles.

After turning around one last time, her eyes fell on a rolled-up sheet of paper next to a half-empty bottle of Explorer vodka. She pulled off the rubber band holding it together and unrolled it.

It was a printout of a map, clearly downloaded from the Land Registry's website. There were no names on it, only a handful of symbols showing the positions of various buildings, property lines and a few indecipherable scribbles à la Elvin.

She decided to hold off on taking a closer look and

instead turned her attention to the open shoebox next to her. In it lay a number of transparent plastic owls that Elvin, according to Fabian, had used to bug Molander's home.

She picked up one of the owls and studied the hollow base Elvin had enlarged to fit a microphone, transmitter and battery. She recognized the Chinese surveillance equipment. It was the smallest on the market and had a range of a hundred feet, which meant there was a receiver with a SIM card somewhere near the house.

She put the owl back and pulled out some of the photographs piled next to the shoebox.

They all looked like they were from the same crime scene. A living room with watercolours on the wall, painted by someone who had taken one or at most two teach-yourself-to-paint courses, long rows of souvenirs on the mantelpiece and an old CRT TV in front of a leaded light window. Along one wall there was an oversized beige leather sofa, and on the floor next to the smoked-glass coffee table lay the victim, a woman.

Again, a woman.

Stubbs sighed and shook her head. As a younger woman, she hadn't reflected much on that particular aspect; a victim was a victim. She was there to interpret the crime scene so her colleagues could identify and arrest the perpetrator. Who was almost always a man.

That the victims were almost always women whenever there was a close relationship between killer and victim was something she'd only woken up to in the past few years. The fact of the matter was that, in Sweden, every three weeks a woman was murdered by a close relative.

This particular woman looked about sixty years old. She

was slightly overweight, and except for socks that covered
her thick calves, she was naked. Next to her lay a ripped
floral-print blouse, a denim skirt that had been cut open and
a pair of torn knickers.

The insides of her thighs were dark from the blood that
had gushed out onto the carpet beneath her, and protruding
from her vagina was something that had to be a fire poker.

In a plastic folder marked *The Vodka Murder* sitting
underneath the stack of photographs, she found the case file
from back in April. The lead investigators had been Sverker
'Klippan' Holm and Irene Lilja and it didn't seem related to
any of the cases Fabian had mentioned.

The victim was Kerstin Öhman, who lived on Östra
Storgatan in Munka-Ljungby, just outside Ängelholm,
together with her husband, Conny Öhman.

According to the investigation, she had reported her
husband to the police for assault several times and each time
she had later changed her mind and retracted the accusation.
But on the night of 5 April, things had clearly gone so far she
hadn't had time to report or retract.

Instead, Conny Öhman himself had called the police
after he'd slept off his intoxication on the sofa. The forensic
investigation found her blood on his hands and secretions
from her vagina on his penis. On the whole, a fairly open-
and-shut case that in today's media world didn't attract
much attention.

Even so, Elvin had taken an interest for some reason,
and unless she was mistaken about him, he'd based that on
something more substantial than mere intuition.

Granted, Molander had been the one to conduct the
crime scene investigation, but that was not to say he had

committed the murder. Maybe his behaviour had made Elvin react.

That gave her an idea and she walked over to the box containing the contents of Elvin's desk at work, found his diary for the present year and flipped to the first week of April.

The fifth had been a Thursday, and Elvin had tersely noted two times, 8.12 a.m. and 4.18 p.m., which, according to Fabian, corresponded to when Molander arrived at the station and when he left again.

The next day contained more information. He hadn't arrived until 9.17 a.m., over an hour later than the day before. No second time had been logged, probably because Molander had been at the crime scene, working late. Instead, there was a single line of Elvin's characteristic abbreviations.

Kerstin Ö, assau, rape, vodka murder, husb. Conny (?), Klipp, Lilj & M on it.

Nothing about the note stood out to her. But the smiley next to it did. There were other smileys here and there in the diary; they were one of the things Fabian had been unable to figure out. But the moment she lay eyes on it, she knew what it symbolized.

The smiley the day after the murder was so happy its mouth literally extended beyond its head.

Molander had, in other words, been in a good mood.

A remarkably good mood.

16

ESTER LANDGREN'S MURDER had changed everything. Having felt numb to and almost blasé about the evil they were dealing with, they were now once again in the same boat. The other murders notwithstanding, the killer had now crossed a line that had left even Molander shaken.

The atmosphere was tense and subdued at the same time, and everyone except Klippan looked like they wanted to leave so they could start the investigation. But no one said anything. They just sat there with their heads bowed, anaesthetizing themselves with their phones while Klippan worked on making his laptop communicate with the overhead projector.

No one counted the minutes, but everyone knew it took far too long for the device to finally flicker to life and project Klippan's wallpaper – a picture of his dog, Einstein, chasing a tennis ball – on the wall.

'Finally,' Klippan said, wiping sweat from his brow. 'Let's go.'

'A quick question before you get started.' Molander checked his watch. 'How long is this going to take? Don't get worked up. I'm not leaving. But we've been here a while already, and I just want to let the lads know since they're waiting in the van.'

'It'll take as long as it takes. So I would suggest we stop

wasting everyone's time.' Klippan flashed Molander a smile
and turned to the others. 'As you all know, Lennart Andersson
was stabbed to death in broad daylight on Saturday 16 June
while he was working behind the meat counter at Ica Maxi
out in Hyllinge.'

'Please, there's no need to cover things we all know,'
Lilja said.

'I need to do what I need to do. No more, no less. So
for everyone's sake, why don't you just let me finish. And I
promise I'll tell you when I'm done. Okay?' Klippan looked
at each one of them in turn and was met by stony silence.
'Great, then maybe we can move on.' He downed the last of
his now-cold coffee. 'Where was I?'

'Andersson was stabbed to death at the meat counter,'
Lilja said, rolling her eyes.

'Right, and we've all seen the CCTV footage showing that
event once or twice. So what I've done is, I've gone through
all the tapes from a week before, up until the murder itself.
I've edited together a number of sequences showing people I
feel are behaving suspiciously. But since we're short on time,
I'm happy to go straight to my main suspect.'

It took Fabian a second to realize where the vibration in
his pocket was coming from, since his iPhone was sitting on
the table in front of him. It was his old Nokia.

Klippan scrolled down to the file labelled *Friday 15 June
2012* and started a video clip that showed a short man
sauntering in through the entrance to Ica Maxi, from the
simultaneous perspective of several CCTV cameras. He was
wearing ragged jeans, dirty white trainers, a maroon zip-up
hoodie with an Adidas logo and a baseball cap from Biltema
pulled down over his eyes.

While Molander and the others watched as the man picked up a basket and moved further into the supermarket, Fabian pulled out the Nokia under the table and opened the text, which turned out to be from Gertrud Molander.

'And what's so suspicious about him?' Tuvesson said, and instantly found herself on the receiving end of a glare from Klippan. 'Seriously, what's the matter with you? We have to be able to ask questions and discuss things. Otherwise this is completely pointless.'

'I was under the impression we were in a hurry. But all right, far be it from me to be difficult. Let me explain.'

Hej Hjalmar! Thank you for remembering my birthday and I'm sorry for not getting back to you sooner. It would have been nice to meet for a cup of coffee and a catch-up. Do let me know the next time you're braving the big city ;)

Gertrud

'What first stood out to me was the way he moves through the shop,' Klippan said.

'What about it?' Lilja studied the man, who was walking through the kitchen utensil aisle. 'It looks normal to me.'

Was it an invitation or a no, thank you? Fabian didn't know how to interpret Gertrud's message, but still typed out a short reply under the table.

I'm actually going back to Helsingborg today, too, and I would be happy to renew the invitation for this afternoon instead. How does that sound?

'I would say virtually every aspect of it,' Klippan told Lilja. 'Just look at the way he moves through the aisles. Then compare it to what other people do, and you'll see that it's completely unnatural.'

Thanks, but I'm afraid I've come down with a proper summer cold and I'm in bed with a fever, so I'll have to take a rain check. But let's talk again soon.

Gertrud was at the house. So he could pop over and try to persuade her to testify and offer her a hotel room until all of this was over.

'Note the way he keeps his face hidden by continually looking down and turning his back,' Klippan went on, as the video showed the man standing by the Tex-Mex aisle with his back to the camera. 'See? It doesn't matter where the camera is.'

'Klippan, I think we get your point,' Molander said. 'Or what do you say, Fabian?'

'Absolutely. I have no questions.' He allowed himself a smile as he pushed the Nokia back into his pocket.

'You don't? That's odd,' Tuvesson said, 'because I certainly do. Like, for instance, what makes you so sure this is our guy?'

'I said I suspect it. Not that I'm sure,' Klippan retorted. 'But the fact is that everything about him is suspicious. Just look at this.'

The man on the screen walked over to the pickled herring fridge.

'He's just been down the Tex-Mex aisle to pick up taco

shells and guacamole. I don't know what you like in your tacos, but I doubt it's pickled herring.'

'What's to say those things are for the same meal?' Lilja objected. 'The tacos might be for that night and the herring for—'

'The thing is, he doesn't actually buy anything,' Klippan cut in. 'There's no direction to his movements and no plan for what he puts in his basket. In a while, he's going to take vegetarian patties out of a freezer, only to then pick up a pound of mince.'

'Maybe his girlfriend's a vegetarian.'

'Maybe. But how do you explain that he's already been to the fruit and veg section, where he picked up super-expensive organic tomatoes, but later on, he's going to go back there and grab a regular, pesticide-infused cucumber even though the organic cucumbers were only two kronor more?'

'Fine.' Tuvesson nodded. 'So he's not there to shop.'

'If he is our perpetrator, he might be scoping the place out,' Fabian put in to try to make it look like he was participating.

'That's what I assumed,' Klippan said. 'But if that were the case, he should be looking for the cameras, and during the twenty-two minutes he spends in the shop, he doesn't look up once. He also never pulls out his phone to take pictures or pays any attention to the escape route behind the meat counter that he ended up using.'

'So what *is* he doing?' said Lilja, who was starting to look impatient.

'Thanks for asking. That's exactly what I've been pondering. And after studying this sequence I don't know how many times, I've concluded that he's searching.'

'What do you mean, searching? For what?' said Tuvesson.

'We'll get to that.' Klippan held up his hand to stop any further interruptions. 'But first I want to ask if any of you noticed that a while back, he stood over by the new potatoes staring at another customer? An older lady dressed all in blue, who was manhandling every last mango in the shop.'

'Yes, I saw her,' Lilja said. 'Even her glasses were blue. But I didn't notice what the guy was doing.'

'But I did, and right now, he's doing the same thing again.' Klippan pointed at the wall where their suspect was standing by the herring fridge, watching a man who was hurrying away from a mountain of strawberries towards the meat counter.

'And what is that?' Tuvesson said. 'Other than staring at people.'

'Like I said, I think he's searching.'

'Right, you did say. The question is what he—'

'His victim,' Klippan said, cutting her off. 'He's searching for his next victim.'

The mood changed instantly. None of them spoke and the silence was almost palpable as Fabian and the others recalled what they'd seen and tried to digest the realization that Klippan's theory might have merit.

'But hold on,' Tuvesson said at length. 'Why would he be searching for a victim?'

'Fine, maybe selecting is a better word.'

'Searching or selecting.' Tuvesson shrugged. 'Lennart Andersson is over by the meat counter. All you have to do to find him is go over there.'

'My point is that he doesn't seem aware of that at this time. I think he simply hadn't decided yet who it was going to be.' Klippan extracted the last few drops of coffee from the urn. 'Besides, Lennart's shift doesn't start for another three and a half minutes. But watch this.' He nodded at the video, where the man was still hovering next to the herring. 'At first, I thought he was choosing among the different flavours. But he's not. He's not even looking at the fish, he's watching the man in the white shorts and boat shoes standing over there with his son.'

'Hold on, isn't that Eric Jacobsén?' Tuvesson turned to Fabian, who nodded.

It certainly was Eric Jacobsén and his son, Rutger, apparently oblivious to the fact that they were in danger of becoming the killer's next victims. Their paths had, in other words, crossed both here and in relation to Molly Wessman.

'If it's true what you say, that he's there to select a victim,' Tuvesson said, 'then what makes him finally settle on Lennart Andersson at the meat counter and not someone else?'

'That's a good question. And I honestly haven't the faintest idea. For all I know, he just goes for whoever happens to bother him.'

'I'd wager he has a plan for how the murder itself is supposed to go,' Molander said as the suspect pulled something out of his right pocket. Something that flashed before he closed his hand around it. 'And what he's doing here is walking around, looking for the most suitable victim.'

'Then shouldn't he be looking by the meat counter instead of all over the shop?' Tuvesson said.

'Or maybe he's just looking for a person who's as different as possible from the other victims,' Klippan suggested.

Tuvesson nodded. 'Fabian, what do you reckon?'

Fabian stopped pondering what it was the suspect had
pulled out of his pocket and was turning to Tuvesson when
Lilja cut in.

'I'm sorry, but are you seeing what I'm seeing?' She
pointed to the suspect, whose right arm was moving slightly
back and forth. 'It almost looks like he's... playing pocket
ping-pong.'

'Sadly for him, that's not it,' Klippan said. 'My best guess
is that it's some kind of tic to keep calm. He actually does
the same thing several times, and at other times his hand is
clearly not inside his trousers.'

'So, Klippan, I just want to make sure I'm getting this
right,' said Tuvesson. 'You're telling us he's walking around
selecting his victim completely at random.'

'Yes, unfortunately, it looks that way.' Klippan turned to
Fabian. 'And isn't that exactly what you were talking about?
That there might not be a motive?'

Fabian nodded, even though it sounded strange to his
ears, too. But he couldn't see any other explanation.

'I just don't understand why a person would run around
killing strangers for no reason,' Tuvesson said.

'Maybe because he thinks it's fun and gets a kick out of it.
At least, that's what you said.' Fabian turned to Molander.

'Me? No, when would I have said that?' Molander shook
his head.

'Okay, but the selection has to be based on something,'
said Tuvesson. 'Whether or not there's a motive. I mean, it
can't be pure chance.'

'Except. Why can't it be?' Molander said.

'Because something apparently makes him pick one victim
over another, and if we can figure out why, we might even be

able to predict who's next. Or what do you think, Fabian? You're unusually quiet today.'

'I am?' Fabian said, his thoughts once again firmly on what the suspect was holding in his hand in the video. Could that be the key?

'And you, too.' Tuvesson turned to Lilja, who was sitting with her mouth open, staring into space. 'You haven't said anything in a while, either.' She leaned forward and waved a hand in front of Lilja's face. 'Hello, I'm talking to you.'

Lilja reacted, but when she spoke it was to Klippan, not Tuvesson. 'Could you play the video again?'

'Sure. All the way from the start, or—?'

'No, from when he's standing over by the herring and turns to that man with the beard.'

'Absolutely. No problem.' Klippan dragged the time marker back and the video played from just before the suspect looked over his shoulder at the man behind him.

'Pause it and zoom in on his face.'

'Irene, I know what you're getting at. But it's pointless. I already tried.' He leaned closer to his open laptop and zoomed in on the suspect's face, which was half-hidden under the visor of his baseball cap. 'Granted, we get a glimpse of part of his face, which, if I had to guess, I'd say is Asian, but other than that—'

'It's him.' Lilja stood up. 'It's him. I recognize him.'

'Who?' Tuvesson said. 'What are you talking about?'

'I interviewed that guy in my office a week and a half ago.'

17

SLEIZNER HAD JUST pulled out his lock pick and was about to slide it into the lock of the flat in Valby, just outside Copenhagen, when his phone let him know he had mail.

From: michael.ronning@politi.dk

To: kim.sleizner@politi.dk

Subject: Security update of mobile phone

As you will be aware from previous emails, we are in the process of installing a series of security updates on the mobile phones of certain key members of the Copenhagen Police. Since you are one of the people affected, I have set aside time this Wednesday at 1 p.m. Unless I hear from you, I will count on seeing you in my office at that time. The update will take approximately 120 minutes to complete.

Sincerely,

Mikael Rønning, IT Manager

As you will be aware. He was getting too big for his boots, that IT bloke. *I have set aside time.* True, he had received a number of emails about that damned security update, and true, he had ignored them like the spam they were. But that didn't give this loser licence to be insubordinate. *Count on seeing you in my office.* Who the fuck did he think he was?

He was going to let them install that update, all right. But it was going to happen when it suited him, not some bloody IT minion. Not that he could see that there would ever be time when he could be without his phone for two hours. Besides, he had to back up the contents to his computer, so he could delete all the things that were for his eyes only.

Sleizner shoved the phone back into his pocket and started working the lock pick. It had been at least forty years since he'd last used it. And yet, it felt like only yesterday that he'd emptied his piggy banks and converted every penny he owned into German marks before their road trip.

The plan had been to secretly buy a stiletto. Not because he was planning to use it. He was just going to carry it around in his pocket and pull it out from time to time to make sure it worked. In Karlsruhe, he had finally managed to slip away from his parents and had found a shop that carried the largest selection of knives he'd ever seen. Not just stilettos, but throwing knives and machetes. They'd even had karambits, his favourite knife of all time.

But instead, a lock pick had caught his eye, and once they were back from their holiday, it had felt like walking around with a magic wand in his pocket. Most of his childhood, he'd been able to get through any door he pleased. He'd break into his neighbours' house, where there were always sweets and sometimes even cash. His girlfriend's, when he'd had one, to go through her things. Or the teacher's lounge at night, to copy down the questions that were going to be on the next day's test.

Then suddenly one day, his neighbour had lain in wait and caught him red-handed, literally rummaging through the box at the back of the closet where they kept their savings.

After a number of hard slaps, he'd been given a choice. They could either go over and tell his father everything the moment he got home from work, or he could unzip his trousers and pull them down right then. It had been an easy decision, though he'd felt dirty for months afterwards.

He hadn't used a lock pick since. Not until now. But it was like riding a bike. Once you knew how to use it, you apparently never forgot.

The lock clicked and he was able to quietly pull open the door, step into the little flat and shut it again behind him.

The door said *Thor Rindflygt*, but he could tell from the smell the moment he stepped into the narrow, dark hallway that he was in the right place. This was elephant Chink Qiang Who's real address. Or Qiang-Wei Hitomu Oisin, as the Population Registry had it, which explained why he'd been so hard to find.

But everything had turned out all right. In fact, most things had gone his way, and even though he still experienced faint rumblings of worry about what Dunja was up to, they were relatively easy to dismiss. He had seized control and was once again a player to be reckoned with after spending too much time on the bench.

As he had suspected, the Chinaman was an overweight little IT slave in the basement of the TDC bunker. His good friend Stig Paulsen had been happy to give him a list of his employees. An hour and a half later, he'd found the unmistakeably ugly mug, whose real address wasn't Blågårdsgade but rather a flat out in Valby, on Sylviavej 22, fourth floor.

He continued into the small but pleasant kitchen and noted that there must be no bathroom in the flat since there was a shower enclosure next to the sink. Dorm-like and charming if you were twenty and believed in peace on Earth. Pathetic if you were an overweight gook riding around on an electric unicycle.

He'd hoped this might be where Dunja was hiding. That they'd swapped flats temporarily, she and the Chinaman. Then this protracted story would finally get the end it deserved. But there was no trace of her. No piles of clothes on the floor, no dirty dishes or smelly bins. Instead, everything was neat and tidy. Like the many types of tea that were not only perfectly stacked against the wall on one of the kitchen counters, but alphabetized as well.

He couldn't explain why, but for some reason swapping the Ginger Guru Chai and the Ginger Lemongrass made him feel a bit better. Then he continued further into the flat, which even though the Chinaman no longer lived in it was still crammed full of elephant crap. Like the rug in the hallway or the ceiling light in the living room, which consisted of five elephant trunks that ended in light bulbs.

Plates with burnt incense sticks were scattered about the room, which had to count as another sign Dunja wasn't the one living here. Granted, he couldn't be sure, but he would have been surprised to find out incense was her bag.

He'd hit a dead end. No point denying it. He'd decided to give up and leave the flat when, on his way out of the living room, he spotted a neon backpack in an armchair in the furthest corner.

It was one of the most hideous backpacks he'd ever seen, which was why he clearly remembered seeing it once before, in the CCTV footage from the Danske Bank branch in Malmö where Dunja had withdrawn all her money. It had been carried at the time by the skinny Indian man helping her. So he was the one who lived here.

The pieces were finally starting to fall into place and he could feel his good mood returning. The Chinaman was in contact with the Indian, who was in contact with Dunja, which meant he was one step closer to her.

One step closer to ending this.

He went through the contents of the backpack but was forced to conclude that there was no money in it, only a long, narrow box of incense and a folder, which he pulled out and opened. In it were a stack of grainy and in some cases completely blurred pictures, all showing the same flat.

His flat.

18

LILJA WAS FRANTICALLY searching her folders and binders and the loose documents stacked on the floor when Klippan entered her office together with Tuvesson and Molander, all three with cups of freshly brewed coffee in their hands.

'Where did Fabian go?' Klippan turned around and popped his head through the door.

'He had to leave and won't be back until tomorrow,' Tuvesson said, and closed the door.

'Leave? He can't just take off when we're in the middle of a—'

'He has his reasons.' Tuvesson cut him off and turned to Lilja. 'How are you getting on?'

'It's in here somewhere.' Lilja pulled a folder from a pile with one hand, using the other to make sure the rest of the pile didn't topple over. 'I know it's in here.'

'I'm assuming he's gone to visit his son, who's behind bars in Helsingør,' Molander said.

'Theodor? Arrested? Are you serious?' Klippan turned to Molander. 'What for?'

'You haven't heard? He was arrested in connection with the Smiley Gang trial—'

'He was there to give testimony, that's all we know,' Tuvesson broke in. 'Irene, would you mind telling the rest of us what you're looking for?'

Without replying, Lilja quickly scanned the first few documents in the folder before letting it fall to the floor and starting to smack her forehead repeatedly.

'Irene, we're all very busy.'

'Right.' Lilja hurried over to the equally messy desk. 'Here. This is him.' She handed over a folder marked *(un) interesting interviews*.

Tuvesson opened the folder and studied the printout of a scanned driving licence. 'Pontus Holmwik. And who's he?'

'I brought him in for questioning. His car was caught on CCTV in Bjuv, parked just a stone's throw from the laundry room where Moonif Ganem was murdered. I even think you can see the car drive away about half an hour after the murder.'

'Is he Asian?'

Lilja nodded and turned to Klippan. 'You don't remember him?'

Klippan shook his head.

'Really? Well, you're the one who insisted I bring him in.'

'I did?'

'Yes, when Astrid was in rehab and you were in charge. You even barged in here in the middle of the interview. I don't understand how you can have forgotten that. You'd just managed to identify Assar Skanås.'

'Right, that does ring a bell.' Klippan brightened. 'I wanted to bring in anyone who had behaved even slightly suspiciously. And you were grumpy and against the whole idea, to put it mildly.'

'You were right. I was wrong. Can we drop it and move on?'

Molander came up to join them. 'Not that it's that important at all, but I was actually the one who happened to notice that car, and unless I misremember, I checked the plates and noticed it was a rental, which made it extra interesting.'

'Right. From Hertz on Gustav Adolfsgatan.'

'Gustav Adolfsgatan.' Tuvesson turned to Molander. 'Isn't that close to Carl Krooksgatan, where you located Skanås's mobile phone?'

'It's certainly not far from it.'

'Are you telling me Pontus Holmwik and Assar Skanås were in contact?' Lilja said.

'It could be a coincidence.' Tuvesson shrugged. 'But let's do a search and see if we can get a home address.'

Lilja sat down in front of her computer.

'His personal identity number is 790825-3324,' Tuvesson continued.

Lilja typed in the numbers, but quickly looked up again. 'There's no one with that number.'

'Odd.' Klippan went over to see for himself. 'Shouldn't Hertz have discovered that when they put it into their system?'

'You would have thought,' Molander said. 'But then again, we didn't.'

'That's my fault,' Lilja said.

'They probably did the paperwork by hand, simple as that.' Molander took the folder and flipped through it. 'Besides, not a lot of people can tell a fake driving licence from a real one.'

'What, it's fake?' Lilja exclaimed.

'It has to be, doesn't it, with that personal identity number? The best way to find out is to drop it from a few inches and listen to the sound it makes when it lands.'

'What do you mean, listen to the sound? What sound?'

'The plastic, it's different. A real one sounds harder, more like metal.'

'Fake or not, you have to have reached him somehow,' Tuvesson said.

'Yes, I contacted Hertz, who gave me his name and mobile phone number.' Lilja pointed at her notes. 'That's it there.'

Tuvesson, Klippan and Molander exchanged looks.

'Are you telling me I should call him?'

'No, it's better to ping his location and surround him. Or what do you reckon?' Tuvesson turned to Molander.

'Sure, we can do that. But don't expect too much. Given what he's managed to pull off so far, he seems smart enough to get rid of that SIM card as soon as Irene was done with him. And also, I have a crime scene waiting to be processed, which is going to take hours.'

'All right, but as soon as you have time, I want you to try it.' Tuvesson turned to Lilja. 'When you interviewed him. What reason did he give for being in Bjuv at the time?'

'He was going to photograph various backgrounds, or some such.' Lilja took the folder back and flipped through her notes. 'Right, here it is. PetFrame. From what he told me, people send in pictures of their pets and he photoshops them onto another backdrop.'

'And he has the audacity to charge four thousand kronor for it,' Molander said, his eyes on his phone.

'You found the website?'

Molander nodded. 'Unsurprisingly, there's no organization number, address or phone number. The only thing I can see is an anonymous info@ email address.'

'Maybe we can track his payments,' Klippan suggested.

'According to the website, he uses cash on delivery, which makes the payments difficult to track since we don't know what name he uses to send the packages. The best thing would be if we could get access to the email account and start from the other end, his customers.'

'That's going to take at least a week,' Klippan said. 'The question is how many more victims and investigations we'll have on our hands by then. I suggest we put out an APW.'

'That would be tipping our hand, plus we run the risk of having him pick up and leave the country,' Tuvesson countered. 'I don't know about the rest of you, but I have a feeling we're getting really close.'

'I don't know about that,' Molander said. 'We have a face and a fake personal identity number. And not much else.'

'I'll bring it up with Högsell and we'll see what she thinks. But I'd be surprised if she didn't agree with me that the best thing we can do right now is to keep things quiet.' Tuvesson made as if to leave.

'Just one more thing before we break this up.' Klippan turned to Lilja. 'That neighbour of yours, what was his name again?'

'What neighbour?'

'You know, the one next door to you whose name we both recognized but couldn't place.'

'Oh, right. P. Milwokh with a W and a silent H at the end. What made you think of that?'

'It's the same letters, just in a different order.'

'What?' Lilja looked from Klippan to the others and back.

'It is. P. Milwokh and P. Holmwik.'

'What, the rental car bloke? He spells his name with a W, too?'

'Yes.' Klippan went over to the whiteboard, wrote one name above the other and drew lines between each letter until they were all paired up.

Lilja stared at the two names in disbelief as though it couldn't possibly be true. But it was. Klippan was right. They had all the same letters. An H in each. A K. A W.

No amount of wishful thinking could make that a coincidence.

19

GERTRUD MOLANDER HAD made herself perfectly clear. Under no circumstances did she want to meet or have any form of contact with him. Fabian had no trouble understanding why. He sought her out to ask questions that had shaken her entire existence to the core. She had gone from believing everything was right as rain to being forced to realize just who she was married to.

Now she was home in bed, sick, and he was once again going to jam his foot in the door and barge in against her will. This was his chance – and maybe the last one he was going to get – to make her understand that she was no longer safe in her own home. That she had to get out of there as quickly as possible. So he had ducked out of work an hour earlier than planned.

Ingvar Molander was bound to be using his phone to keep track of where Fabian's car was, and it had to be assumed he was tracking his mobile as well. Consequently, he'd left the car at home with the phone safe in the glove compartment and arranged for Sonja to drive it down to the ferry for their first trip to see Theodor in Helsingør.

Fabian himself had walked down to Kopparmölle Square, where he'd caught bus number 2, which he'd then disembarked twenty-five minutes later at Ramlösa Brunn. He'd continued across the tracks and past Ramlösa

Wok-Express, where just over a week ago he'd run into Gertrud when he was interviewing her neighbour about the murder of his wife, Inga Dahlberg.

It had been the worst possible timing. Gertrud had instantly reacted to the investigation having been reopened and questioned why neither she nor her husband had been told about it. Since then, it had only been a matter of time before Molander caught on to what was happening.

Lindhultsgatan was only a few hundred yards away, and when he rounded the corner he realized he only had twenty minutes before he had to start heading back into town to meet Sonja.

He continued up towards the house and noted that Gertrud's car and bike were both missing from the driveway. Once he reached the front door, he rang the bell and waited. Maybe she was asleep. He leaned over the porch railing to peer in through the kitchen window. The lights were off inside and everything looked neat and tidy. No food sitting out, no plates or glasses. Nothing. The countertops were so spotlessly clean they'd pass for mirrors.

Gertrud was the epitome of the dedicated housewife, always cleaning. Probably one of the last of her generation. And yet, something about the advertisement-clean kitchen made him feel uneasy. He pulled on his leather gloves and took out the keyring he'd found in Hugo Elvin's desk drawer.

He'd already found the doors that three of them unlocked, which meant the other four were possible candidates. Two of them were marked with green cloth tape inscribed with handwritten question marks. The other two were marked with white tape; there was a fish on one and a six-digit code – 759583 – on the other, and since a rectangular code lock with two columns of numbers was mounted on the wall next to the door, he started with the latter.

It went in smoothly. At least at first. After a while, it seemed to get stuck, but with some wiggling, it went all the way in. But he couldn't turn it. He tried both directions, applying as much force as he dared, not wanting to risk having the key break in the lock. The other white key didn't fit at all, and nor did either of the green ones.

He gave up and instead went around to the back of the house and up onto the wooden deck, past the grill, which, in true Molander style, was meticulously covered up and sitting next to garden chairs that were propped against the table in case of rain.

Nothing had been left to chance. Not even the electric whirring that abruptly started up underneath his feet. He instinctively reached for his gun before realizing it was a robot lawn mower emerging from its bespoke charging alcove under the bottom step of the deck.

He went over to the terrace door and used his hands to block out the light so he could peek inside. The living room looked like it always did. The rug, the furniture and the curtains, all different shades of beige, and on the walls nondescript landscape paintings jostling for space with pictures of birds and dried flowers.

The white key with the six-digit code fitted into this lock, too, but this time he could turn it. After slipping inside, he quietly closed the door behind him and listened for noises. There was only silence.

Gertrud's collection of owls was set out on a shelf in the display cabinet, just like last time he was there. And in the middle of the crystal parliament, he spotted Elvin's surveillance owl. In many ways, the location was far too obvious given that the objective was to bug a canny forensic scientist in his own home. But the owl collection was probably so entirely Gertrud's domain that Molander hadn't even thought to check it.

He continued towards the bedroom and tapped the closed door gently while pondering what to say. When the only response was more silence, he eventually pushed down the handle and opened the door.

He couldn't say what he'd expected to find, except possibly Gertrud, asleep. The bed was made and the pillows fluffed like in a hotel room. No clothes on the chair in the corner, no tissues, no glass of water, nor anything else for that matter. And no Gertrud.

In her message, she'd explicitly said she was home in bed. Was she resting somewhere else in the house or was it all just a— Had it actually been Molander texting him back? Had he taken her phone and sat there across the table from him, typing out replies to make sure no one noticed her missing?

The place did look extremely clean.

He went over to what looked like Gertrud's side of the bed and pulled out the drawers in the nightstand. First the top, then the bottom one. Both were empty. Same thing with the chest of drawers and the two wardrobes on her side of the room. No clothes anywhere. The room smelled of cleaning products and when he dragged a finger across the bottom of the wardrobe he couldn't see so much as a speck of dust.

Had he cleaned her away? Was that what he was looking at? As though she never existed. But when would he have had the time? Less than two days had passed since their row

STEFAN AHNHEM

in the living room, and if Molander was to be believed, he'd spent the entire night in the police lab.

Judging from what he'd heard of their fight, Molander had been caught off guard by the extent of Gertrud's knowledge, which made it less likely he'd had a plan in place for what to do with her and more likely he'd been forced to improvise.

Fabian went over to the other nightstand. On it lay an old physics textbook he recognized from his school years. A piece of paper stuck out from among the pages. He flipped to the marked page, halfway through the chapter on electrical theory, with page upon page full of flowcharts, equations and all kinds of computations. There were also a few hastily jotted notes in the margin.

Self-ionizing. Conductive. Hydronium: HO- (hydroxide), H_3O+ (trihydroxide)

It was definitely Molander's handwriting.

$200l/24h=8.33l/h/60=0.14l/min$

But what it meant exactly was less easy to decipher.

Impedance of human body = skin resistance + internal resistance = approx. 1000Ω

Could it have something to do with his plan for Gertrud?

$>50mA. X sek \rightarrow \dagger$

Fabian hurried out of the bedroom and threw open every door he could find. One led to a small storage room crammed full of winter clothes, shoes and cleaning implements, another to a small guest bathroom with an old magnetic soap holder by the basin, a third to a small study cum guest room, complete with bed, desk and desktop computer.

In the basement, he found a boiler room and a utility room with a door leading straight out into the garden. In addition to a washer and dryer, it also contained a sink that was as spotlessly clean as the rest of the house. A pair of thick waders for fly fishing hung on a hook on one of the walls and along another were shelves that housed an impressively large wine collection.

The last door in the basement was made of metal and had neither handle nor keyhole.

'Hello! Gertrud, are you in there?' he shouted and banged the door as hard as he could. 'It's Fabian!' He pressed his ear against the cold metal but heard nothing.

Turning around, he discovered a small hole in the wall on his right; when he gingerly inserted a finger, he realized it was a flap that could be opened. Behind it was a keypad with numbers from 0 to 9.

He pulled out the key with the six-digit code and after he punched it in there was a faint rush of air as the metal door slid open, disappearing into the wall. The room behind it was reminiscent of a small museum, full of shelves, display cases and glass counters.

He had seen inside it two years ago. Molander and Gertrud had invited the whole team and their partners to a barbecue, even though they were in the middle of a very demanding investigation. Lilja had taken him down to the basement and the metal door had been open. Inside was everything from handguns to knives and small glass phials full of toxic substances. She'd even shown him a collection of mangled bullets that had killed their victims.

He opened a built-in freezer and found that it was full of plastic containers, small, transparent plastic bags and various other sundries, all labelled with combinations of letters and numbers.

Lilja had told him it was all stuff from closed investigations, and she'd claimed it was the urge to collect, coupled with unadulterated geekiness, that made Molander such a capable forensic scientist. There was probably truth in that, but it also explained why he'd become a serial killer.

It would take him hours to go through it all, and right now his priority was Gertrud. Unfortunately, she wasn't in the room and, as far as he could tell, there was no trace of her anywhere.

He was too late. He could feel it. The only question was when Molander had found the time to move her from the house. If that was what he'd done.

The garage. Why hadn't he thought of that?

The thought triggered a flood of images, each more gruesome than the next. Whatever Molander had done to his wife, he'd obviously done it in the garage. That was where his workshop was. That was where he kept his tools, and that was where he could work late into the night without drawing suspicion.

He hurried back out of the room and up the stairs, through the living room towards the terrace door, all the while picturing Molander backing his car just far enough into the garage to load up the black bin bags full of body parts without being seen.

After locking the door behind him, he hurried across the deck and down onto the lawn, where the robot was still attacking the grass. The side door to the garage turned out to be unlocked, and just as he'd suspected, there was a worn workbench with a vice inside. There were also saws, hammers and pliers, all hanging on their designated hooks, and on a shelf he saw a drill next to a circular saw and a few rolls of black bin bags.

But there was no visible blood. Not on the workbench, not on the floor and not on any of the saw blades. Not so much as dry spatter anywhere. What he did see was a crumpled sheet of paper on the workbench, next to a roll of white electrical cord. He went over, smoothed it out and started to read.

Ingvar,

I didn't know where to put this letter to make sure you'd find it as quickly as possible. You've been so busy lately we barely see each other, and the few hours you've been home you've spent either in the basement or out here in your workshop.

Right now, you're probably thinking what a coward I am for not being brave enough to say what I have to say to your face. But the truth is that I'm afraid. Yes, I'm afraid what you might do to me.

You always had this darkness inside you, a temper whose short fuse has at times had you on the verge of violence. That's something I've been well aware of ever since we first met. My father warned me about it and wanted me to leave you. But I dismissed his concerns, and I want you to know that I've never felt threatened. Not until last Sunday.

You didn't do anything, but you thought about it. I could see it in your eyes, and I've never been more afraid. You probably think I'm exaggerating and being hysterical. Be that as it may, but I've come to realize it was probably exactly what I needed to finally take this step.

STEFAN AHNHEM

It might come as a surprise to you, but it's actually something I've been thinking about quite a lot over the past few years. But as with the concern my father expressed, I just dismissed it and kept pretending everything was fine. That the constant, nagging worry about who the man I'm married to really is was exactly that, exaggerated and hysterical.

But I can't turn a blind eye any more. Despite all the good years we've had together, you and me. Even though you've been the most important man in my life and a part of me still loves you, I've decided to leave you.

So I'm going away for a while. It doesn't matter exactly where to. The important thing is that I need time and space to find my way back to who I am. So please, Ingvar, I beg you. Don't try to find me so you can 'set me straight'.

Believe me. I know what I'm doing.

Gertrud

124

20

I**T WAS ONLY** when he got down on all fours and started scrubbing that he realized just how dirty they really were. That they weren't white any more, but rather speckled with filth. He liked things clean and tidy.

He'd read somewhere that, contrary to popular belief, floors and sometimes even toilets were among the cleanest things in people's homes. The dirtiest and most germ-laden were apparently mobile phones, remotes and computer keyboards, closely followed by, that's right, skirting boards.

Last night's task had been a type of clean-up, too. Everything had gone according to plan, and he felt several pounds lighter. The task had been completed and the earlier debacle, or whatever you wanted to call it, was no longer an open, inflamed wound. It had been disinfected and cleaned and would in time become a beautiful scar.

He was going again tomorrow, but he didn't feel stressed about it. It was under control for the most part. He'd done his laps in the pool that morning and for the first time come in under two hours. He'd also reserved a rubber dinghy with an outboard engine, purchased provisions and packed most of the equipment.

Just then, as though it was a law of nature that there had to be a fly in every ointment, the doorbell started ringing. This time, he didn't even flinch. That detective had been by so many times now it would almost be more surprising if she didn't keep disturbing him.

But she was becoming a problem. The harmony and focus he needed in order to proceed was being shredded by that grating noise. If he'd been able to ignore it, he could have just let her keep at it indefinitely. But he wasn't. He couldn't finish his thoughts. He couldn't even finish scrubbing the goddam skirting board.

Maybe it would be as well to get it over with. Let her in, hear what she had to say and then do away with her using whatever method the dice chose.

There wasn't much time, so he started with a simple yes or no question to determine if he should take care of it now or leave it be. He pulled off his rubber gloves, took out one of the six-sided dice he always carried with him, shook it and let it roll onto the floor.

A three.

Along with the one and two, three represented yes, which meant the dice was with him again. Now it just had to decide how he was supposed to do it and then he'd be ready to open the door. He rolled the dice again to find out which category he was dealing with. As usual, uneven numbers meant *murder weapons* and even ones *ways to die.*

A five.

He knew the list of weapons numbered one to twelve by heart, so he could go straight to the pre-roll to decide whether the choice of weapon should be determined by one or two dice.

A three.

That meant proceeding with one dice. Accompanied by the shrill sound of the doorbell, he picked up and shook the dice before releasing it back down onto the floor and watching it until it stopped.

A two.

The dice had spoken, and its decision was undoubtedly prudent. He was supposed to use a rope, which, since he was at home, had to be considered the perfect weapon. She wouldn't be able to scream or make much of a racket. And there would be no blood or mess to ruin his cleaning. And what's more, he'd already bought rope and packed it with the rest of the equipment he was taking tonight.

He knew exactly in which pocket he'd put it and so it took him only seconds to find it before going out into the hallway.

She looked more muscular through the peephole than he remembered from the interview. In other words, there was no point waiting for her to act first; he should just pull her into the flat as quickly as possible and kick her legs out from under her before she realized what was happening.

He put the rope down on the floor so he could reach it easily when the time came. Then he turned the many locks and opened the door. But before he could take more than half a step into the stairwell or do more than start to raise his hand to grab hold of her jacket, his brain managed to process the visual stimuli relayed by his eyes enough to tell him something wasn't right.

'Wow. So you are home,' exclaimed the woman standing in front of him. 'I was just about to give up.' She was the same height and had the same haircut as the lady detective. But this woman was from the post office, not the police. She smiled and held out a large package.

'Good thing you didn't, I've been looking forward

to getting this.' He took the long package, relieved and disappointed at the same time.

'And a signature here, please.'

'Of course. No problem. No problem at all.' He shot her a smile and signed.

'Have a good day.'

'I'm sure I will. Especially now that this has been delivered.' He held up the package, shot her one more smile and retreated into his flat.

After securing all the locks, he opened the package and the box it contained. Then he wrapped his fingers around the hilt, slowly pulled out the sword and studied the polished blade.

21

THEIR WALLETS, MOBILES, keys. They'd even been forced to hand over the bag Sonja had filled with Theodor's favourite sweets to get through security at the Danish prison. What were they worried about? That they'd stuffed the sweets full of drugs and skeleton keys?

The moment they rolled off the ferry in Helsingør harbour, they'd been overcome with a sinking feeling. A feeling that everyone and everything was against them. The contemptuous looks the guards – who refused to understand Swedish – gave them when Fabian asked whether it was really necessary for them to be strip-searched. The increasingly loud bangs of gates closing behind them as they moved further into the building. The cold blue glare from the light overhead coupled with the echo of their shoes against the floor as they were led down one corridor after another.

That their son had spent a full twenty-four hours in here was almost impossible to take in. The fear he must have felt lying on the hard cot in his cell, which was probably no more than a third of the size of his room at home.

What was worse was the prosecutor's unexpected decision to remand him in custody until the trial was over. A decision that had been delivered without any explanation beyond that they had reasons to keep him detained.

He'd been so certain. So sure he was right. That the truth was the only way forward and that nothing else mattered. Now, he didn't know. Whether all of this was wrong. His fault. Whether he should have listened to Sonja's initial protests, before she gave in and sided with him. Or to Theodor, who had been prepared to go so far as to take his own life just to get out of this. He had no idea. All he could do was hope for the best. Hope that everything would somehow come out right.

The visiting room they were taken to was sparsely furnished with a sofa and armchair in a speckled shade of light blue, a round table with four chairs and a bed with a plastic-covered mattress. The fluorescent lights did nothing to help the cheerless impression. No pictures on the wall. No mirror. Not even a rug on the ugly linoleum floor.

Six minutes past the agreed time, the door opened and Theodor entered, flanked on either side by a guard. His eyes were on the floor and his grey prison overalls were too small. Yet another thing to make them feel bad. But the handcuffs were the worst. Fabian knew the rules and using handcuffs on Theodor was a clear breach of them.

'Why have you handcuffed him?'

One of the guards turned to the other and said in Danish. 'Do you understand what he's saying?'

The other guard shook his head.

Fabian switched to English. 'The handcuffs. What are they for? He's not a murderer.'

'That's yet to be determined.'

'Honey, there's no point.' Sonja put her hand on his knee to keep him seated. 'You're only making it worse.'

'Smart lady,' the first guard said and undid the handcuffs.

'And nice-looking, too,' the other muttered under his breath.

Fabian both heard and understood every word, but since Sonja seemed not to, he took her advice and let the grinning guards leave the room.

Theodor sat down across from them and stared at the table. Fabian wanted to get up, to go over and hug him. Show him how much he loved him and give him all the warmth, energy and affection he could muster. But instead he just sat there, contributing to the silence.

'Hi, Theodor,' Sonja said at length. She leaned forward. 'How are you doing?' She waited for a response that didn't come. 'Theodor, it's not that I don't understand that you're feeling awful and like this whole situation is incredibly unfair. I feel the same way. It hurts me that you're locked up here with guards that handcuff you when you're coming to see us. And it's obviously so, so much worse for you. But please, talk to us. What was last night like? Did you get any sleep?' She waited, but there was no reaction.

'The way they're treating you, us, this whole situation is just terrible,' Fabian said. 'But we're going to get through it. I promise. I'm going to make sure you have the best lawyer there is and we're going to do everything we can to get you home as soon as possible. Do you hear me? Whatever happens, we're always here for you.'

'And another thing,' Sonja said. 'When you get back and all of this is behind us, Dad and I have decided we're going to buy a yacht like you and Matilda wanted.' She turned to Fabian and smiled. 'It'll be fun, right?'

Fabian nodded and felt his energy returning. 'What we're trying to say is that you're not alone.' He got up and went over to Theodor. 'Understand? We're in this together.' He bent down and hugged him. 'You, me and Mum.' But it felt wrong, all wrong. 'And in just a few weeks, this will be behind us and we'll be setting sail together.' Theodor's cold rigidity made him break off the hug out of sheer self-preservation.

Then there was finally a reaction. Theodor straightened up. 'I think we're done here,' he said. 'You're just going to keep saying the same things over and over.'

'What do you mean, done?' Sonja said. 'We only just got here, there's more than forty minutes left. What? You want us to leave?'

Theodor nodded. 'And I would appreciate it if you left me alone and didn't come back.' He stood up, turned away from them, walked over to the closed steel door and pressed a button.

'But, Theodor, what are you saying?' Fabian followed him. 'We've come to see you, you can't just leave?'

'Leaving is one of the few things I can do, actually.'

The door opened and one of the guards entered.

'We're done,' Theodor said.

The guard nodded and put the handcuffs back on. The only thing Fabian could do was put his arms around Sonja as Theodor was led out of the visiting room.

22

CALLING IT A phobia would be overstating it, but Lilja had never liked lifts. Especially not the old, cramped kind that might give up when you least expected it. But the decision had been made. She was taking the lift and the others were climbing the stairs, so the only thing she could do now was pray the rickety thing held together all the way up to the third floor.

Her new flat with the temporary strip of tape with her name on it lay straight ahead when she stepped out of the lift. But she wasn't going home. Not any time soon. In fact, it would probably be hours before she was ready to go home.

Instead, she walked over to the door marked *P. Milwokh*, took a few deep breaths to compose herself and pushed the grey button next to the door, triggering an angry ringing on the other side.

It was absurd, really, that he was the one they were after, her own neighbour. But thanks to the unusual name, identifying him had been a cinch and even though he'd had a beard in his passport photo, they'd all agreed he'd been the one scoping out Ica Maxi in Hyllinge.

According to the Swedish Migration Agency, he was a Chinese citizen who had been granted asylum on 9 August 2010. Unusual enough in itself. But as a member of the political, qigong-inspired movement Falun Gong, he'd been able to claim political refugee status.

The harrowing story he'd told about being apprehended by the Chinese authorities on Sunday 15 September 2002 and placed in the Masanjia labour camp in the Yuhong district outside Shenyang in north-east China had apparently been enough to convince the Migration Agency.

The camp was one of several live organ factories in China, and he and thousands of other Falun Gong members had been imprisoned and forced to perform what could only be described as slave labour under horrifying conditions.

High-paying customers on the illegal organ market could, via Chinese websites, order organs that were then harvested from the inmates. During the seven years Milwokh had spent in the camp, he had lost his left kidney. When the decision to sell his heart and the rest of his organs was announced, he'd managed to stage a violent jailbreak and flee the country, all the way to Sweden, where he'd finally been granted citizenship under the assumed and slightly peculiar name Pontus Milwokh.

Lilja took her finger off the doorbell and studied the circular indentation on her fingertip while the ringing inside the flat subsided. 'As expected,' she said and turned around. 'He's not going to open the door.'

'All right, then we're going in,' Klippan replied, emerging from the dark stairwell together with a locksmith and a three-officer arrest team.

Lilja nodded to the locksmith, who immediately started to drill through the top lock. While they waited, Lilja and Klippan donned bulletproof vests, checked their weapons and prepared to follow the uniformed officers into the flat.

Before long, the first lock was unlocked, then the second, at which point the locksmith stepped aside to make way for the head of the arrest team, who grabbed the door handle and pushed it down to let the other two in. But the door didn't budge. It still appeared to be locked.

'What's going on?' Lilja turned to the locksmith, who shrugged and went back to the door. This wasn't good. Not good at all. This was the time to apprehend him. Now, before he could barricade himself in there with all his weapons, blow himself up or whatever else he might have in mind.

'Odd. Really odd,' the locksmith mumbled as he opened his toolkit and pulled out an extendable stick with a small rectangular mirror, which he inserted into the letter box. 'Well, well, what do you know. Interesting. Very interesting.'

'Could you get to it? We don't have all day.'

The locksmith retracted his mirror and turned to Lilja. 'There are espagnolettes.'

'And what does that mean? That the door is barred from the inside?'

'That's another way of putting it.' The locksmith nodded.

'Okay.' Klippan turned to the arrest team. 'At least we know he's in there then.'

'Does this mean we have to destroy the door?' Lilja asked.

'Not entirely, but it's going to need replacing, and I don't know who's paying for—'

'Never mind that,' Lilja cut him off. 'We'll take care of it. Just do what you have to do. And quickly, if you don't mind.'

'At least it's not a security door,' the locksmith said as he changed the bit on his drill with a practised motion and started drilling into the middle of the door. 'Be grateful for

STEFAN AHNHEM

that.' Then he took out a reciprocating saw, inserted the blade into the drilled hole and enlarged it until it was big enough for him to push his hand through so he could open the espagnolettes from the inside.

The whole thing took just over a minute and then he stepped aside and let the uniformed officers throw open the door and storm the flat, closely followed by Lilja and Klippan.

Lilja didn't know what she had expected. An ambush. A jumble of barricaded furniture. A hostage situation that gave them no choice but to let him get away. But the only thing that greeted them was silence. A silence that, together with the lack of furniture, the black ceiling and completely bare walls in the hallway, made it clear nothing was going to be as expected.

The uniformed officers seemed overcome with the same unsettled feeling and so continued into the flat at a considerably slower pace, making sure to cover one another. All communication was conducted in sign language as they secured each room in turn.

The ceiling, walls and floor had been painted black in the bathroom, too, as well as the bath, basin and toilet. Everything was bare and clean; the only thing sitting out was a toothbrush and a tube of toothpaste. Same thing in the kitchen. Everything was black, nothing was sitting out and the countertop, cupboard doors and handles were all spotless.

Lilja walked over to the balcony door, which was locked from inside, opened it and stepped out onto the black concrete floor of the balcony. Other than a stool and a small table, it was empty. She went back inside and joined

136

Klippan in the living room, which, despite its size and extremely sparse furniture, felt completely claustrophobic with its black ceiling, black walls and black floor. Even the sofa, the curtains and the dining table and chairs were black.

'There's no one here,' said the head of the arrest team, coming out of the bedroom. 'The place is empty.'

'But? I don't understand.' Lilja looked around. 'The door was locked from the inside. As was the balcony door. He has to be in here.'

The officer shrugged. 'I don't know. But he's not here. We've secured the whole flat. So unless there was something else you needed, we'll be on our way.'

'Hold on a minute.' Lilja held up her hand. 'Did you really check everywhere?' She went back into the kitchen and opened one cupboard after another. 'Like here, or here. Or why not here?' She opened the fridge, which was black even on the inside.

'Irene, seriously,' Klippan sighed. 'Do you actually think he'd hide in the fridge?'

'If you ask me, this guy's capable of anything. Like going to the trouble of painting the inside of his fridge black. Who the fuck does that?'

'Irene, I don't know.'

'Me neither. What I do know is he has to be in here.'

'But apparently he's not.' Klippan turned to the head of the arrest team. 'It's okay. You can go.'

He nodded and left the flat with his two team members.

'Would it be okay if I left, too?' said the locksmith, popping his head in diffidently. 'I put in new locks, so you can lock the door while you wait for it to be replaced.'

'Okay.' Klippan took the keys the locksmith held out to him and waited until he'd left before turning to Lilja, who was going through the contents of the fridge.

'I know what you're thinking,' Lilja said as she pulled out the vegetable drawer. 'But we're right. I know we're right. He's our guy. I mean, look. Guacamole, pickled herring, a pound of mince, a few organic tomatoes and a pesticide-infused cucumber.' She turned to Klippan. 'That's pretty much exactly what he purchased in the surveillance video you showed us.'

'Irene—'

'The only thing missing is the taco shells, and I bet they're here somewhere, freshly painted black.'

'Irene, I'm not saying we got it wrong. But the thing is, he's not here. So I suggest we look around and see if we come across anything of interest. If not, all we can do is wait until Molander has time to come out here.'

'But if he's not here...' – Lilja pulled out her phone and dialled a number – '...then how do you explain the door being locked from the inside?'

'I don't know.' Klippan spread his hands. 'Hopefully Molander can think of an explanation. Who are you calling?'

Lilja put her phone on speaker and held it up.

'*You've reached Ingvar Molander of the Helsingborg Police Forensic Department. Please leave a message after the beep.*'

She ended the call with a sigh. 'He never picks up any more.'

'I guess he has his hands full, like the rest of us.'

'Doing what exactly? He started on Ester Landgren's

room more than three hours ago, and unless he's found anything particularly riveting, he should at least be able to answer his phone.'

'I'm sure there's a good reason.' Klippan turned around and walked over to the sofa. 'Let's have a look around instead and take it from there. Okay?'

Lilja didn't move. She wasn't ready to let her guard down. Not yet. Things had unfolded too quickly. It hadn't even taken them ten minutes to conclude Milwokh wasn't in his flat, even though there was no obvious explanation for how he could have got out.

After a while, she walked over to the bedroom, where the walls were, surprisingly, not all black, but rather covered with a greyish-blue 1960s' wallpaper. Clearly this was the only room he hadn't had time to redecorate to look like the ninth circle of hell.

Apart from a small nightstand, a wardrobe and a men's valet over by the window, the neatly made bed took up most of the room. Bedrooms didn't have to be spacious, of course, but this one was unusually tiny. She would panic if she barely had room to walk around her bed.

Suddenly, her uneasiness returned. She could feel it all over. Spreading from the pit of her stomach. As though she'd come too close for her own good. As though she'd be able to hear him breathing, if she could just be still enough. If her heart could just beat slower.

She looked down at her Dr. Martens, almost invisible against the black floor. It was a silly notion, of course. The arrest team had searched the room.

Even so, she was unable to shake the idea that maybe they'd been rushed and overlooked something. That he was hiding under the bed. That any moment, hands might grab her ankles and pull her feet out from under her.

He'd be on top of her before she could so much as cry out. Her pulse, her damn pulse was drowning out all other sounds when she finally got down on her knees and slowly bent down to check under the bed.

It was dark and she couldn't see all the way to the wall, but once she got her phone out and turned on the flashlight, she could plainly see there was no one there. But she didn't feel relieved. Where was Milwokh? He couldn't have just disappeared like some Houdini.

She stuck her arm as far under the bed as she could reach and dragged a finger across the floor. Not so much as a speck of dust. He hadn't just cleaned. He had scrubbed and scoured the entire flat clean of every last hair. There probably wasn't a fingerprint to be found in here, and the toothbrush in the bathroom was probably completely devoid of DNA.

She stood up and heaved a sigh. The only place left to check was the wardrobe on the left side of the room. But it was the same as the bed. Why couldn't she just trust that the arrest team had done their job?

Clutching her gun in one hand, she closed the other around the small door knob and opened the wardrobe. What had she expected? That he would be sitting in there behind the clothes as though they were playing hide and seek?

There were hangers with clothes in the wardrobe. But only a handful. As a matter of fact, it looked remarkably empty. And there were no baskets of socks and underwear, only a single rail at the top.

Without a clear idea of what she was looking for, she pushed the hangers to one side and turned the flashlight on her phone back on.

'Irene! Where are you?' Klippan called out.

'In here! In the bedroom!'

'I think I've figured out how he got out! Come and have a look!'

Lilja turned the light off and went back out to Klippan, who was standing in the doorway to the kitchen, waving for her to join him.

'There's a balcony out here.'

'I know, and I already checked it. The door was locked from the inside.'

'The balcony door, yes. But not the window.' Klippan pointed to the window next to the door. 'See? It's closed, sure, but not latched.' He pushed the frame with his index finger and it opened. 'Once he was on the balcony, he probably just pushed it closed as best he could and climbed down the drainpipe, one balcony at a time. Even I could pull that off, if I were a few pounds lighter.'

The window latches, that was what she'd missed. That meant he was still on the loose. Even so, she felt a measure of relief.

'Maybe he saw us through the window when we drove up,' Klippan said, and she nodded.

At least the puzzle pieces fitted together again. This wasn't some supernatural being they were hunting, it was a flesh-and-blood human who was subject to the same natural laws as them.

★

Lilja's and Klippan's voices grew increasingly muffled further away from the kitchen. From the bedroom, they sounded like a distant murmur, the words impossible to distinguish.

The wardrobe door stood open, like Lilja had left it, and the handful of hangers were still pushed to one side, exposing the back and the small round hole just big enough for a person to stick their finger in, reach the narrow metal plate above the hole and push it aside to open what was in reality a secret door.

There, on the other side of the hole, behind double layers of soundproofing materials and a closed blackout blind keeping the harsh glare of the fluorescent lights from seeping out, was a windowless space of a few square feet.

On the floor lay a packed backpack. Next to it stood a desk with a computer, a notebook with a big X on the cover and a round board with an inch-high rim covered in green felt. A map of Skåne was pinned to the wall, divided into a twelve-by-twelve grid of squares, a few of which had been marked with tiny symbols.

The wall opposite was almost entirely hidden behind a built-in bookcase. Some of its shelves were empty, others were littered with everything from a large collection of dice and syringes to a severed ponytail and a dark-skinned, photorealistic mask.

Underneath the bookcase, on a narrow cot, lay Pontus Milwokh, waiting, completely still with his eyes open and his sword resting on his chest.

23

THE BYPASS TOOL slid into the letter box unhindered and he managed to catch the thumb turn on the inside on the second attempt. Then he just had to turn it, open the door and enter.

There was no way of knowing for sure, but something told him this might be his very last hurrah. That what had started as a rash overreaction, and then slowly but surely evolved into a severe addiction, was irrevocably coming to an end.

The flat looked as expected. Two rooms, bathroom and kitchen. Most of the rooms could have done with a renovation. Ikea furniture, a bookcase with no books in it and a few Tarantino posters on the walls. A TV with a video game console, a pair of hand weights and a rolled-up yoga mat.

That was exactly why it was so important to get everything right. Not just superficially and generally, but down to the smallest detail. His plan was complex and full of steps that could go wrong. But if he pulled it off, it would not only provide release for all the pent-up energy raging inside him – it had been over two months, after all – he would also free himself of all suspicion. Not even Risk would think to look his way.

The fuse box was located in the hallway, and though the

fuses were unmarked, finding the one for the bathroom didn't take long.

The reason was that he didn't really have time to do this. Even though night had fallen, he had so many things to get to it was virtually impossible to plan and execute something of this magnitude, and in a way, this made him immune to suspicion.

After unscrewing the fuse and replacing it with his own modified one, he went over to the kitchen and searched the cupboards and pantry until he found what he was looking for.

As far as choosing his victim was concerned, he'd imposed only one criterion, that they were sufficiently different from Moonif, Molly and all the rest of them to fit the pattern; and after searching various databases, he'd identified the perfect candidate.

The bucket was one-third full. He poured half of the powder into the sink, rinsed it out and mixed in his own. Then he snapped the lid back on and put the bucket back on the bottom shelf of the pantry.

Mattias Larsson of Tryckerigatan 27B. The address was in Planteringen – a forgotten neighbourhood in south Helsingborg surrounded by motorways and adjacent to the South Harbour, an industrial port. The flat was on the second floor of a square brick house with recessed balconies.

There was no outlet by the basin in the bathroom, so he had to run a cable from the light socket in the ceiling all the way down behind the bath.

Mattias Larsson was a twenty-seven-year-old plumber. He hadn't been able to find an active Facebook profile, and hadn't had the time to try to worm his way in through friend requests anyway. It had to happen today, or, rather, tonight.

He stripped the last six feet of cable and removed the insulation at the end of the brown and blue wires. Then he secured one with sturdy tape a few inches from the foot of the bath and the other at the same height at the head.

Luckily, he'd been able to find Mattias Larsson on Instagram. Even better, he had a public profile where he was in the habit of posting an endless series of pathetic workout selfies. If Instagram was to be believed, he put his poor body through the wringer practically every day, and on Tuesday nights it was all about legs.

Grounding the bath was slightly more complicated because the floor was covered in dark green vinyl and the pipe leading down into the floor drain was plastic. He had no other choice than to connect the yellow and green wire to the ground of the light socket and tape the other end to the bottom of the bath.

After sealing the bath's overflow drain with silicone, he just had to mix the two-component glue, fasten the metal loop to the bottom of the bath and test how far he had to turn the tap to make approximately three litres per minute come out. Then he could sit down on the none-too-clean floor and wait.

On this particular night, Mattias Larsson had plans to take his girlfriend, Hanna Brahe, out to dinner to celebrate the third anniversary of their engagement. At least, if the girlfriend, who seemed to live at the gym and also had a public Instagram account, was to be believed.

He didn't have to wait long on the bathroom floor. After only six and a half minutes, he heard a key turn in the front door lock, followed by the sound of the door opening and a second later closing again and being locked.

Mattias Larsson had come home a full twenty minutes earlier than expected. Perhaps he wanted extra time to prepare for his date. Or maybe he hadn't been able to complete his leg session. It didn't matter. He was ready for him.

At least he had come home alone. There were no voices, only a thud as his gym bag hit the floor and a hummed, off-key rendition of the summer hit 'Somebody that I used to know'.

The first time he'd heard it on the radio, he'd liked it. Remarkable in itself, since he didn't usually like any music written after the eighteenth century. But after hearing it just a few more times, he'd been so sick of it, the guitar intro alone was enough to ruin his mood.

But not this time. This time the humming, which came through louder and louder as Mattias Larsson moved further into the flat, filled him with pure joy.

It sounded like he'd stopped outside the open bathroom door. But he didn't come in. Instead, judging by the sound, he pulled off his gym clothes in the hallway and tossed them onto the bathroom floor. Even his smelly underwear came off.

But apparently not his headphones, because the humming continued as he moved into the kitchen, where the door to the pantry creaked open and the bucket of protein powder from the bottom shelf was picked up and put down on the kitchen counter.

Only then did he stop humming. He was probably reacting to the fact that he was almost out of powder. But he must have concluded that he was misremembering, because soon enough the humming resumed and there were sounds of a bottle being filled with water and shaken. Then he flipped the lid up with a click and drank so loudly even the swallowing could be heard in the bathroom.

After that, it wasn't long before he heard the sound of the bottle hitting the floor, followed seconds later by the sound of the muscular, 190-pound body collapsing.

24

FABIAN WAS BACK in the abyss. In the deep darkness, where it made no difference if he closed or opened his eyes. There was no light anywhere. True, he'd managed to get hold of Tuvesson, who had promised to contact a good lawyer, but that was all. Now, the only thing he could hope for was that Theodor had just been temporarily out of sorts after his first twenty-four hours behind bars and that somehow it would all work out and be behind them before he knew it.

He could only guess at how Sonja was feeling. The silence between them had been unbroken during their return journey across the sound. When they got back, he'd asked if she was okay with him going back to work, and she'd replied that he could do whatever he needed to silence his doubts.

As usual, she understood him better than he understood himself. No matter how fervently he wished it weren't so, work was all that could take his mind off things enough to make the anxiety subside.

But right now, being at work was like dancing through a minefield; every step could be fatal. With the GPS tracker under his car, he risked drawing Molander's suspicion regardless of what he got up to. Suspicion that would hardly be dispelled when he noticed his car had been parked outside his home on Pålsjögatan for almost two hours before he visited Theodor in prison.

Molander had already prodded him with insinuations about how absent he'd been from their investigations, and he wasn't entirely wrong. His own secret investigation was now in such an intense phase he found it to be virtually impossible to sit across from Molander in meetings and pretend that nothing was going on.

But he had to pretend. Pretend that his focus was on the case they were all working on and that everything was right with the team.

That was why he parked his car on Kärngränden, outside the building where the Landgrens lived, took the stairs up and entered the flat, even though it was half past eight at night.

It could have been anyone's home. A completely unremarkable home, characterized primarily by that inescapable chaos that accompanies all families with young children. A home where the children were finally asleep in their beds after toothbrushing, toilet visits and stories. Where parents were cleaning up after dinner so they could then curl up on the sofa with a cup of tea and watch the news.

But the plastic sheets covering the hallway floor all the way to the door where colourful wooden letters spelled out the name *Ester* revealed that this wasn't a home like any other.

According to Tuvesson, the parents were not in a fit state to be interviewed and it was doubtful whether there was any reason to put them through it. The perpetrator had already been identified and now it was all about securing forensic evidence to tie him to the scene.

But that was the easy part. How they were supposed to figure out where he was going to strike next, before it was once again too late, was a lot harder.

When he reached the closed bedroom door, he paused to compose himself for a few seconds before opening it, ready to face Molander and return his gaze unflinchingly.

The problem was that there was no sign of Molander in the slightly untidy room.

'Hi, where's Molander?' he asked the two forensic assistants in white protective suits, who were collecting samples and taking pictures.

'Good question. Definitely not here, though,' one of them said, using tweezers to drop a hair into a small evidence bag.

'Okay. Did he just leave?'

'No, I wouldn't say that. He took off more or less straight after we got here this afternoon. Right, Fredde?' The assistant turned to his colleague, who was taking pictures of the unmade bed where there was a dried-in ring on the sheet.

'Yes, he said something about needing to get back to the lab to sort out something, and that we should get started without him.'

'Okay.' It wasn't like Molander to hand over an entire crime scene investigation to his assistants, but he supposed there was a lot of forensic stuff to get on with. 'So, have you found anything?'

'I guess. The usual.' The assistant placed the evidence bag in a carrying case. 'Some fingerprints and hairs of various descriptions. But I can't tell you if they're relevant until we've had them analysed.'

'And do you have a working theory for how it happened?'

'Not beyond the fact that he must have drowned her, and he could have used practically anything to do that. But my guess is that he did it here, at the edge of the bed. If you look closely, there's a round indentation here.' He squatted down and turned his torch on the rug. 'I think it's from some kind of basin or bowl he filled with water.'

'We found signs of water seeping in under the bed, too,' the assistant with the camera added. 'It made visible tracks through the dust.'

Fabian wasn't listening any more. He'd spotted something else entirely, flashing from among the jumble of markers, loose sheets of paper and fuse bead pegboards. Something that brought to mind the CCTV footage from Ica, where something had flashed just like that in the killer's hand.

He walked over to the table, picked up the object with a handkerchief and studied it. Unlike every dice he'd used as a child, playing Monopoly, Ludo or Yahtzee, this wasn't made of wood or plastic but rather of brushed metal. 'Has this been sitting on this table the whole time?'

'No,' said the assistant with the camera. 'I found it under the bed, but I had to move it to take pictures of the water tracks in the dust.'

Chance. Could it be that simple?

Six sides. Six possible outcomes.

25

HE COULDN'T HAVE asked for more perfect weather. Not a cloud in the dark blue sky. Just uncountable stars reflected in the water. But best of all was the wind. In just a few hours, it had shifted 180 degrees and was now coming out of the south-east at a speed of thirteen miles an hour, resulting in a perfect broad reach up through the sound and on towards Gothenburg.

Frank Käpp hadn't even had to start the engine to leave Humlebæk harbour. He'd just undone the bow mooring lines and pulled the boat out by the anchor rope. Then he'd been able to hoist the mainsail and silently glide out through the inlet.

They were in no hurry, quite the opposite. That was what their around-the-world adventure was all about. Shedding their obligations and letting wind and weather determine the speed of their progress. That's why he'd set an easterly course towards Glumslöv on the Swedish side. Once they passed Ven, he was going to turn north, ease the genoa and set the autopilot on a straight course through the bottleneck between Helsingborg and Helsingør.

This was exactly what he'd longed for and dreamed of during his final years in the office. Being one with the wind and feeling the salt on his face, surrounded by infinity. It was magical. That was the best word for it. Magical.

Unlike during the day, there were almost no other boats out. Other than a few freight ships, he could only see one green side light, close to the water on the port side. He couldn't see a masthead light, however, which meant it must be some kind of motorboat less than twenty-three feet in height.

It was hard to make out at this kind of distance, but it was possible they were on a collision course. He reached for his binoculars and was just about to have a look when Vincent came out of the cabin in his pyjamas.

'Hi, Vincent. Time for bed?'

'Yes, but Dad... Mum said I should ask you if I can sleep with you tonight.'

It was so like Klara to force him to be the bad guy. They'd talked about this a thousand times. 'No, Vincent, I don't think so.' If they gave in to the nagging now, he'd be sleeping between them for the rest of the journey.

'But, Dad, please—'

'Vincent, listen to me. You spent the last two nights in the aft cabin, and it was fine, right?'

'Yes, but we were docked then. Now we're at sea.'

'You might as well get used to it. We're going to be sailing at night a lot over the coming months.'

'Yes, but—'

'Okay, look, you asked, and the answer was no.' Frank peered into the night, looking for the lantern, but he could no longer see it. No green side light and no white stern light.

'Frank, do you have to be so rigid?' Klara popped her head out of the cabin next to Vincent. 'Is it really such a big deal if he sleeps with us?'

'I'm not being rigid.' He raised the binoculars and scanned

the port side but saw nothing even close to the green lantern that had been there just minutes before.

'I think you are. Especially given as how you're the one who insisted we travel tonight, when we could just as easily have left tomorrow after breakfast.'

'The whole point was to do a proper night sail before we leave Sweden. Like we agreed. And yet the two of you have refused every time, and this is our last chance. After Gothenburg, we're off to Oslo.' He did another sweep with the binoculars. But there was no boat to be seen, on either side of them, and that was odd, to say the least. It couldn't have disappeared.

'And what's so terrible about that? What does it matter if we take things slowly?'

'Okay, seriously. What's the problem here?' Frank turned to Vincent. 'I can tell you're exhausted. Just go to bed. I promise, you're going to be asleep in seconds. And then when you wake up, the sun will be shining and we'll be in Bohuslän, on our way into Lilla Bommen, from which we can practically walk to Liseberg.'

'The problem, since you ask, is that you're forcing him to sleep in the aft cabin,' Klara said.

'Okay, Vincent, can you tell me why you don't want to sleep there?'

'It's scary. Last night I had a nightmare about a monster that came in and killed me.'

'A monster?'

Vincent nodded. 'It was super scary.'

Frank turned to Klara. 'If you ask me, that has nothing to do with sleeping in the aft cabin. It's all those computer games you're playing. Look around.' He made a sweeping gesture. 'There's water all around us and soon we'll be out on the open sea. What kind of monster could get you here? I've heard of the Loch Ness Monster, but the Kattegat Monster, that's a first.'

'Frank, I don't think this is the time to be glib.'

'No, I'm sorry, my bad.' He went over to Vincent and hugged him. 'I'm sorry, buddy. Look, it's just that Daddy has put a lot of time and effort into making the aft cabin cosy and nice for you and it actually makes me a bit sad when you don't want to be in it.'

'But I think it's great. I really do. It's just a bit scary.'

'How about this?' Klara suggested. 'Vincent, I'll go with you to the aft cabin and I promise I'll stay with you until you're sound asleep.'

Vincent pondered that and finally shrugged. 'Okay. But you have to promise to stay a really long time.'

'Of course. Come on.' Klara took Vincent by the hand and led him through the cockpit and then the two of them disappeared into the aft cabin.

Frank turned on the radar, both the old one, whose green light swept round and round in a circle, and the new digital one. But the boat, or whatever it was he'd seen, didn't show up on either screen.

It could have been a rubber dinghy. They sometimes escaped the radar's notice. But who would go out in a rubber dinghy in the middle of the night? And with no navigational lights. No, he must have been mistaken. That was the only reasonable explanation. That it had just been some other light reflected in the waves.

Yes, that had to be it.

It had to be.

26

A KILLER WHO for no discernible reason selected victims at random by rolling dice. It sounded absurd; he'd never heard of anything like it. But that could very well have been what he'd been doing every time he stopped and shook his hand back and forth at Ica Maxi in Hyllinge. Maybe the whole thing was dictated by chance.

It was still just a theory, but it would explain a lot. Whether it meant getting one step closer to an arrest, however, was far from a given. Even if it helped explain the past murders, it did nothing to help them predict the future.

Perhaps Molander was mathematically skilled enough to mine the available data and analyse how dice might have been used. He was the last person Fabian wanted anything to do with, but with the help of the previous murders and a pinch of luck, he might be able to narrow down the number of possible alternatives and find a pattern that could be applied to the future.

But despite what Molander's assistants had told Fabian, the police lab was deserted and dark, and there were no signs he might have just missed him. He'd tried to call him three times but had had no answer. Nor was he to be found up in the conference room or in Tuvesson's office. On the whole, the department seemed surprisingly quiet.

At least the lights were on in Lilja's office, though that, too, was empty. But the computer was on and the printer on the floor was spitting out document after document.

He went over and picked up one of the printouts, which was apparently from *Paygoo prepaid MasterCard* and consisted of a long column of purchases made in all kinds of places, from a local Helsingborg swimming pool to *lockpick.se*.

'Well now, look what the cat dragged in.'

Fabian turned to see Klippan and Lilja enter, carrying two pizza boxes from Planet Pizza & Grill.

'Fabian, what are you doing here so late?' Lilja put down a bottle of Coca-Cola and one of sparkling water on her desk. 'Shouldn't you be with your family?'

'Yes,' Fabian nodded. 'And I have been. Did Tuvesson tell you?'

'Molander,' Lilja replied.

Of course it was Molander. God knows how he'd found out.

'It must be horrible,' Klippan said, shaking his head.

'It is.'

'If there's anything we can do, just say the word.'

'Thank you, but I'm sure it'll be all right. Right now, Sonja and Matilda are asleep, so there's not much I can do at home.' Fabian looked around. 'But there seems to be a lot to do here.'

'You can say that again.' Lilja pulled out the bottom box and opened it. 'Did you hear that he lives right next door to my new flat?'

Fabian nodded, grateful that the conversation was moving on. 'Tuvesson told me. Unbelievable.'

'Right? I mean, what are the odds?' Lilja picked up a slice of her pizza marinara, folded it over and started eating, while Klippan helped himself to a slice of kebab pizza and went over to the printer.

'By the way, do either of you know where Molander is?'

'Yes.' Lilja took a sip of water. 'He's at Kärngränden, processing Ester Landgren's room. At least I hope he is, because he promised to tackle Milwokh's lair as soon as he's done there.'

'Then I'm going to have to disappoint you.'

'Why, are you saying he's not there?'

Fabian shook his head. 'I just came from there, and according to his assistants, he left this afternoon and hasn't been back.'

'Seriously, what the fuck...' Lilja sighed. 'I'm getting really sick of this.' She took one more bite, put the rest down and pulled out her phone.

'There's no point. I've already tried several times.'

'He has to pick up some time,' she said, putting the phone to her ear.

'While you wait, I can inform you that it looks like we were right,' said Klippan, who was standing next to the printer, flipping through the printouts.

'He used the Paygoo card to buy things?' Lilja asked.

'He certainly did. He's been splurging. There's everything here, absolutely everything.'

'Hi, this is Irene. Could you call me back, like, right now? And yes, I'm going to keep calling until you pick up or call me back. So just press that little green symbol and put the phone to your ear.' Lilja ended the call and grabbed another slice of pizza.

'And what's that?' Fabian nodded to the stack of documents next to the printer.

'Pretty much everything we could find on Pontus Milwokh,' Lilja replied, trying Molander again.

Klippan held up the stack of papers. 'We have everything from his tenancy agreement to his latest purchases. For example, he's in receipt of full asylum support, which is 6,800 kronor a month. In addition, he gets 3,900 in housing benefits. So his total income is 10,700 a month, which is paid into a Swedbank account, which is in turn linked to a Maestro card. He seems to use that for all his regular purchases, like food, clothes, rent and so on. In other words, nothing out of the ordinary there, apart from one purchase that caught our eye. On Friday 23 September last year, he went to Skånska building supplies north of town.'

'Isn't that just a regular DIY shop?' Fabian said.

'Surprise, it's me again,' Lilja said into her phone. 'And like I said, I'm going to keep at this until you pick up.'

'It is, but listen to this,' Klippan replied. 'I contacted them to see if they could help me figure out what he bought, and they were very helpful. Among other things, there was quite a bit of insulation, plasterboard, timber, paint and filler, as well as a bunch of screws, hinges, fixings and an electric screwdriver, a circular saw and some other tools.'

'What did he need all that for in his tiny flat?'

'Exactly what we asked ourselves. There's nothing to indicate that he owns any other property, but that doesn't necessarily mean he doesn't have access to a small cabin somewhere. The countryside is littered with unused ones. If you ask me, he built some kind of soundproofed box or something like that. Maybe to kidnap someone, what do I know?' Klippan shrugged.

'But that's pure speculation,' Lilja put in, with her phone still pressed to her ear.

'True, but I did some calculations on material requirements, and what he bought would easily be enough for a five-by-five-foot box.'

'Which is pretty cramped, if you ask me. You wouldn't even be able to stand up. But that wasn't what we bumped on, it was the price. Wasn't it?'

'Right.' Klippan turned to Fabian. 'You know what the whole thing cost?'

'No.' Fabian shrugged.

'2,253 kronor.'

'Okay.' He realized they'd expected a bigger reaction. He just didn't know what kind.

'You've never done any DIY, have you! Do you know what the real price would be?'

Fabian shook his head.

'7,253 kronor. More than three times as much. It turns out he used another card to pay part of it. A so-called Paygoo card from MasterCard, which isn't only prepaid but also completely anonymous.'

'So we contacted MasterCard,' Lilja went on. 'And apparently the card is linked to an anonymous PayPal account, and guess which one.'

'Exactly,' Klippan said, before Fabian had a chance to speak. 'We're talking about the same account PetFrame uses. Because that's his little side hustle where he makes the money he uses for the fun things he wants to buy.'

'I don't know about little,' Lilja said. 'Over the course of the spring, he averaged forty thousand a month, tax free, which is a lot more than I take home.'

'But this June, he only made a few thousand. But then, he's been otherwise engaged,' Klippan said. 'Anyway, the Paygoo card has a 5,000-kronor spending limit, which was why he had to use his regular card too. And we're lucky he did, or we wouldn't have known he had it.'

'So what you have there is what he has paid for with his anonymous card.'

'Right you are.' Klippan continued scanning the printouts. 'And from what I can see, most of it's on here. Like the rental car he picked up from Hertz on Gustav Adolfsgatan on 12 June, the day before the laundry room murder in Bjuv. Or 22 April, when he spent 2,495 kronor at lockpick.se.'

'And what did he buy?'

'Given the price, my guess would be a lock pick gun.' Klippan pulled another printout from the printer. 'And this is probably the mask he used at Ica Maxi. He bought that last autumn from realfleshmasks.com for 4,867 kronor.'

'Real Flesh Masks,' Lilja said, looking appalled. 'Is that really the name of the shop?'

Klippan nodded. 'But then, it was very realistic.'

'And what's the most recent purchase?' Fabian asked.

Klippan skimmed the columns. 'On Wednesday last week, he spent 3,487 kronor at trueswords.com.'

'True Swords?' Lilja turned to Klippan. 'So he bought a sword?'

Klippan looked again and shrugged. 'Looks that way.'

'Well, why not?' Lilja shook her head. 'If you can use a washing machine, why not a sword? Especially if you want to sneak around playing at being a ninja. What else do you have?'

'Well, he has gone to the pool almost every day this past week.'

'Could that be our next scene?' Fabian asked.

'It's not impossible. Or maybe he's just doing laps. Yesterday and the day before he also visited Helsingborg Boat Rentals and spent first four thousand, and then three and a half thousand. Probably to avoid exceeding the transaction limit.'

'Okay, I just want to make sure I have this right,' Lilja said, calling Molander yet again. 'So, he has purchased a sword and rented a boat while also going to the pool every day.'

Klippan nodded.

'Anything else? Maybe a clown suit, or why not a nuclear submarine while we're at it?'

Klippan looked up from the printouts. 'No, but speaking of which, we should put the pool under surveillance as soon as they open tomorrow.'

'Of course.' Lilja nodded as a voice suddenly reached them from the hallway.

'Give it a bloody rest, will you?' Molander exclaimed as he entered. 'Don't you have better things to do than harassing me?'

'Yes, many, many things.' Lilja turned to Molander. 'That's the problem. So instead of pretending like you can't hear your phone, you might consider picking up.'

'If I answered my phone every time it rang, I'd never get anything done.'

'And that's why I'm calling. You promised you were going

to process Milwokh's flat as soon as you were done with Ester Landgren, and from what I'm told, you haven't even started yet.'

Molander sighed. 'What do you want me to say? The Landgren flat took longer than I expected, okay?' He shrugged. 'Göran and Fredrik are ambitious and pleasant lads, but no one has ever called them speedy. And you know me.' He looked each of them in the eyes. 'I feel the same way you do – this case is too important for me to leave a crime scene and just hope the two of them do a good job on their own.'

'All right, maybe I misunderstood.'

'Probably.' Molander gave her a curt smile.

'Because from what I was told, that's exactly what you did,' Lilja replied with an even more curt smile.

Fabian realized too late where this was going. This was not how he wanted it to happen. He was still waiting for Stubbs to tell him they had enough proof to arrest Molander. Once she gave the all-clear, he was going to inform Tuvesson so they could come up with a plan for how to make the arrest together.

'What?' Molander turned to Fabian and Klippan and suddenly looked confused. 'Do you know what she's talking about?'

'I suggest we drop this and try to get on with the investigation instead,' Fabian said. 'Because it seems he's rented a—'

'No, I want to know what the fuck's going on,' Lilja broke in. 'What do you mean, you wouldn't leave a crime scene? According to Fabian, you left the Landgrens' flat hours ago.'

It was three against one. Plan or no plan, maybe he should just get it over with.

'And so my question is, where have you been all day?' Lilja went on. 'And what are you so bloody busy doing when you're not answering your phone?'

Molander turned to Fabian. 'I'm sorry, but how is it that you—'

'I went over there.' Fabian felt his body getting ready. 'As soon as Sonja and Matilda were asleep, I went to see if you'd found anything of interest. But you weren't there and according to your assistants you left immediately after you arrived.'

Molander turned to Fabian without speaking.

'And just like Irene, I tried to call you,' he went on. 'Not just once, several times.'

Molander still didn't say anything, just stood there, breathing heavily through his nostrils. For the first time, he seemed shaken. His face had gone pale and his Adam's apple was bobbing up and down as, increasingly desperately, he tried to swallow his anxiety.

Maybe Fabian was mistaken. No, he wasn't. Molander's eyes were wet, filling with tears; if he didn't wipe them soon, his tear ducts were going to overflow.

'Ingvar.' Klippan walked over and put a hand on his colleague's shoulder. 'What's the matter?'

Molander's bottom lip began to tremble as the first tear trickled down his cheek.

'Oh my goodness, Ingvar. Tell us.' Lilja pulled up a chair and helped Molander sit down.

'I don't know,' Molander finally managed to squeeze out, still trying to hold back the tears. 'I don't know where to start.'

'Maybe I can help you,' Fabian said.

'What? She's spoken to you?' Molander looked up at Fabian.

'Who?' Fabian didn't understand.

'Gertrud. She hasn't told me anything. After thirty-four years—'

'Ingvar.' Klippan squatted down in front of Molander. 'Tell us what's happened.'

'She's left me.' Molander burst out sobbing. 'Gertrud has left me.'

'What? Hold on. Are you saying Gertrud wants a divorce?'

Molander nodded and pulled out a handkerchief to blow his nose. 'Yesterday, when I got home from work, the house was empty. I didn't know what was going on. All her things were gone. Clothes, shoes, everything. Her wardrobe was empty. I tried to call her to ask what it was all about, but she didn't pick up. Then I found a letter in my workshop. Can you imagine? After thirty-four years of marriage, she leaves me and the only explanation is a cryptic note.' He shook his head and dried his eyes. 'So if you're wondering why I've been a bit absent today, it's because I needed some time to myself to digest it. I thought I was going to be able to work and just carry on like usual, but—' Molander broke off and shook his head.

Behind him, the door opened to admit Tuvesson, who was in the process of popping a piece of gum into her mouth. 'So this is where you're hiding. I'm glad you're all here, because...' Tuvesson faltered when she noticed Molander. 'Ingvar, what—?'

'Gertrud left him.' Klippan stood up.

'What? Really?'

Molander nodded and looked like he was struggling to keep his emotions under control.

'I'm so sorry.' Tuvesson bent down and gave him a hug. 'I went through the same thing a few years ago, as you know, and if you want, I'd be happy to tell you what it was like for me and how much better I feel now.'

Molander attempted a smile and wiped his eyes with the handkerchief.

'But before I do, I want to ask you to do something,' Tuvesson went on. 'And I'm really sorry to do this, but if you think you're able, I'd like you to put your feelings aside for a while.'

'Astrid,' Lilja said. 'They were married for thirty-four years, and he's just been—'

'I know. I'm not deaf. And Ingvar, I completely understand if you can't handle it, and if so, we'll find another way. But if you—'

'Just tell me what's happened,' Molander cut her off.

Tuvesson stopped chewing and turned to look at each of them.

'What has happened is another murder. Another incomprehensible, meaningless murder.'

27

WHILE TOM CRUISE struggled with making ends meet and trying to convince one of his players, Frank Käpp picked up his wine glass by the stem and swirled it around a few times before holding it up to study the beautiful red colour in the light from the kerosene lamp. It was a newly opened Domaine du Vieux Lazaret, served at the perfect drinking temperature.

He brought the glass to his face, stuck his nose in as far as it would go and breathed in the bouquet. That alone was divine. Even better was tasting the wine, sucking in some air before swallowing. The balance between the four grapes – Grenache noir, Syrah, Mourvèdre and Cinsault – was impeccable.

Klara had, as expected, dozed off thirty minutes into the film and had therefore only had the Rioja that had been open since yesterday and was already so oxidized it would barely do for cooking wine. But at least they'd made up after their fight about where Vincent should sleep.

There was nothing worse than fighting with Klara. He was convinced it was carcinogenic and couldn't understand why it happened so often. It was as though frustration was always simmering somewhere deep inside them, and if they didn't vent it from time to time, they ran the risk of an all-out explosion.

And yet they fundamentally agreed on most things. Fine, so maybe he'd been the one pushing for the idea of sailing around the world. He supposed it was more his dream than Klara and Vincent's. But someone had to take the initiative, or nothing would ever happen. They would be trapped in their offices in Kalmar forever, bitter about never seizing the moment.

It wasn't the first time he'd heard the sound. Even so, he jumped and almost spilled wine on Klara. It sounded like something was pressing against the hull of the boat. Until now, he'd assumed it was a large wave that had set the boat rolling, which could give rise to all kinds of noises.

But this time he didn't notice much of a roll. Besides, the alarm on the radar hadn't warned him about a ship passing close enough to generate waves.

Maybe it was the film. Like the sudden clanging that had alarmed him until he realized it was just one of Jerry Maguire's players banging a locker door in the changing room. That must be it. What else could it be? He took another sip of wine, put his glass down on the table and reached for the TV remote. He had mostly turned on the film for Klara's sake anyway.

The silence that followed was far from silent. He could hear the sound of the wind in the sails and of the water as the bow cut through it. And the faint creaking of the hull when a sudden gust made the boat lurch a little. And yet Frank perceived it as silence. A peaceful, harmonious silence that proved the sound he'd heard must have come from the screen.

He should go up and make sure everything was okay, and he was going to. He shouldn't really be below decks at all until they were out on the open sea. But he wanted to avoid stomping around on deck and risk waking Klara and Vincent, who had finally fallen asleep.

Instead, he took a moment to enjoy how perfectly everything was working. Like the TV and the PlayStation console, the digital receiver and the Apple TV unit, when they had Internet reception. Or the custom-built storage space for wine bottles down in the bilge. The aft cabin, the sound system, the galley. Not to mention the autopilot, which, like a fourth crew member, was currently maintaining a straight course out of Öresund towards Kattegat.

In about a month, it was going to be put to work maintaining a course for days at a time, maybe even weeks, and at that point he would even dare to sleep and trust that everything was working right.

Then he heard that sound again. He couldn't figure out what it could be. It was different from all other sounds, and this time it came through louder, if anything. There was no longer a film to blame, and it definitely wasn't a wave.

In a way, this was exactly why he had pushed for a night sail in Swedish waters, where they were always relatively close to land. But even so, it was with a growing sense of unease that he moved Klara's head from his lap to a pillow and started up the ladder.

Once he reached the cockpit, he raised his binoculars and did a 360-degree sweep. Everything looked normal. Both Helsingborg and Helsingør were where they were supposed to be and every freight ship in sight seemed to be keeping its distance.

Maybe he'd left a fender out after leaving Humlebæk and now it was dragging and somehow getting squeezed against the hull? Motorboat owners chugging around with their fenders flopping about was the rule rather than the exception. But for a sailor, it was a mortal sin.

He turned on his torch, stepped up on deck and leaned across the lifeline on the leeward side so he could inspect the hull. But he couldn't see any dragging fenders. He crossed the boat and repeated the procedure on the windward side.

He found nothing there, either, and it would have been odd if he had, considering that the angle of the boat would have prevented any overlooked fender from touching the water. But he did notice something else.

A black rope was tied around one of the lifeline stanchions and disappeared down into the dark water. He didn't recognize it. Their own ropes were all white, to match the hull. Besides, he would never tie anything around a stanchion; they weren't built for it.

Maybe Vincent had woken up and done something while they were watching the film. That would explain the strange sound, and in a way it would be like him to get it in his head that one of the many stuffed animals he'd insisted on bringing wanted to go for a swim. But where had he found the black rope?

He started to pull on it and instantly realized it couldn't be one of Vincent's teddy bears being keelhauled. In order to make the rope budge at all, he had to use both hands and brace so hard with his legs that he broke a sweat within seconds.

If it wasn't for the fact that they were moving at a rate of six and a half knots, he would have assumed it was an anchor. Now he could only guess what it might be, while part of him dismissed his first thought as impossible and completely improbable.

But apparently, it wasn't.

As though materializing from out of the darkness, the contours of a large rubber boat grew clearer as he pulled the rope. The black colour was so effective at camouflaging it against the mottled surface of the water that, for a second, he doubted his own eyes. He immediately started working on the knot around the lifeline stanchion. It was as though panic had seized his hands before the rest of him, and before he had time to give any thought as to whether or not it was a good idea, he had released the boat into the night.

It had been equipped with an outboard motor, a red petrol can, a heated blanket and two dark, stuffed bags, that much he'd noted. But it was only now he realized there was no passenger on board, and as this dawned on him, the panic exploded through the rest of his body.

His attempts to scream at the top of his lungs came out as faint whimpers that dissolved in the wind. Fuck, he repeated to himself. Fuck, fuck, fuck...

He hurried back across the deck but tripped over the sheet and hit his head on the main halyard winch. He might be bleeding. Or not. All he cared about was getting back on his feet as quickly as he could and going down into the cabin. Nothing else mattered.

Only Vincent.

He grabbed the handle of the aft cabin door and threw it open, and the sight that greeted him was one he knew would haunt him forever. Until the end of his days, it would be tattooed on his cornea, reminding him every time he closed his eyes of the greatest horror he'd ever experienced.

If only he could have climbed down the ladder and swapped places with his son. If only he could have crawled into his child-sized sleeping bag and taken his place. But his role was to stand up there and look down at Vincent in the aft cabin. Down into the claustrophobic space into which he'd forced him. His own son.

Vincent's eyes were petrified. As though they were staring straight into his worst nightmare. Or as though he'd woken up and realized reality was infinitely worse.

A man in dark clothes blocked most of the scene, but the sword in his right hand, which he held pressed against Vincent's throat, was unmistakeable. Harder to understand was what he was doing with his left hand, which was shaking back and forth. But understanding required thought, and right now, thought didn't exist. Only instinct. Pure, unadulterated instinct.

He grabbed hold of something that looked like a sheath across the man's back and pulled him backwards, away from Vincent. In the same fraction of a second, he glimpsed a dice out of the corner of his eye. As though time were standing still, the dice fell out of the man's hand and landed on the sleeping bag.

Frank let out a scream he didn't know was inside him, and maybe the force of it helped him drag the man out of the aft cabin.

As he did, the man turned around and swung his sword straight at him. Frank threw himself to the side, landed hard on the cockpit sole and saw the blade sever the rubber cord connecting the wheel to the autopilot.

The next moment, the blade flashed high above him as the man grabbed the hilt with both hands to drive it down into him. Just then, the boat lurched, as though the waves were suddenly coming from a different direction, which allowed Frank to twist far enough to the side to hear the point of the sword hit the teak sole a few inches behind him.

Without even the semblance of a plan, he army-crawled away as fast as he could, around the table and over to the other side of the steering pulpit, where the wheel was spinning as though it had come to life. The winch handle was in its holder, and he finally had an idea. He reached for the metal handle, lifted it out of its pocket and was just about to stand up when a black boot on his back pushed him back down.

'You might as well give up,' came the man's voice from somewhere above him. 'The dice has spoken, and neither one of us can change that.'

He didn't know what the man was talking about; all he knew was that in a few seconds, it would probably be too late. But he wasn't going to just lie around and wait to feel the sword sink in between his shoulder blades. Without knowing how, he managed to summon enough strength to turn around and hurl the winch handle at the man, who was raising the sword with both hands.

His aim couldn't have been truer. Even so, the man managed to dodge the handle, which continued along its trajectory before disappearing into the sea.

'I told you. There's no point.' The man raised his arms above his head again, unaware that the boat had now turned just enough to make the mainsail gybe and swing over to the other side with full force.

The boom hit the man in the temple and he collapsed across the lifeline with the sword still clutched in his hands.

Frank instantly jumped to his feet and before the man could regain consciousness, he grabbed his legs and heaved them over the line, too. After that, things simply ran their natural course and in the blink of an eye, the man had fallen overboard and disappeared into the black sea.

Frank had no idea how long he stood there, staring out across the glittering water with questions queueing up in his head. Why them? What was the point? Why now, out here, in the dark? What had happened? Had it even happened? Or was he still down in the cabin, sleeping next to Klara?

That was undeniably a tempting notion. To just close his eyes and carry on like nothing had happened. But the shock had chewed its way so deep into his body he was shaking. It didn't matter how improbable or surreal it was. How many questions he had that would never be answered.

It hadn't been a dream.

When he finally dared to breathe again and relax, he stepped back down into the cockpit and went over to Vincent, who was shaking with terror in his sleeping bag. He sat down next to him on the berth and hugged him as hard as he could.

Neither one of them spoke. Maybe there was nothing to say. No words that came close to describing what he felt. That would be apology enough. Instead, he cried for the first time in living memory.

And yet despite the tears, the only thing he could feel was joy.

28

WERE YOU THE *one who assaulted, tortured and raped your wife to death last night?*

Silence. Hesitation.

I don't recall. But I can't say I didn't.

Stubbs continued to flip through the interview Irene Lilja had conducted with Conny Öhman the day after the murder of his wife on 5 April last spring. So far, she hadn't been able to entirely comprehend the case, or, for that matter, figure out what had caused Hugo Elvin to take a particular interest in it, apart from the fact that Molander had been in an unusually good mood the next day.

What was clear was that Öhman had had a truly terrible day at work, which had included being yelled at by his boss in front of all his co-workers. He had then gone to Harry's in Ängelholm for a few drinks and when he got home approximately three hours later, he'd immediately become annoyed at the old bat, as he insisted on calling his wife. According to him, she'd been unsympathetic and rude about his work situation and, simply put, hadn't known her place.

So what did you do? Take to the bottle?

It usually helps.

Helps? In this file I have four police reports made by Kerstin, accusing you of assault, and that's just from the past six months.

The day before, she'd only been able to work for a few hours before Mona-Jill had grown impatient and reminded her she'd promised to help weed the garden, and then they were supposed to listen to *Sommar* on the radio together before riding their bikes around Kranke Lake.

It was only now, well past midnight, when Mona-Jill was at the deepest point of her sleep cycle, that she'd been able to sneak back out to the boat and continue her work.

Yes, I'm an alcoholic, if that's what you're asking. I'm not denying it. But I keep it under control.

You call this under control?

(Conny is confronted with photographs of his battered wife. Silence.)

What I mean is that I decide when the bottle gets opened, not the other way around. No one can say otherwise.

I would actually say these pictures are pretty clear proof you were out of control last night. Wouldn't you agree?

(Silence.)

Yes.

(Silence.)

But I didn't really drink that much. I know that sounds like I'm lying, but it's true.

So you're saying you did this to your wife while you were sober?

No, I'm saying I got drunk much faster than usual. Properly pissed, if that's even what it was. I don't remember. I remember almost nothing. And just so you know, I never black out. It's odd, actually. As if the booze was... Never mind, I don't know.

Öhman's answer was circled with red felt-tip pen, and the last sentences were underlined too. It was so typical of Elvin to highlight a bunch of stuff without the slightest explanation in the margin.

What did you drink?

Explorer. Always Explorer.

Stubbs looked up from the transcripts and scanned the cabin until she found the evidence bag with the Explorer bottle in one of the boat's storage compartments, next to the shoebox with the surveillance owls. So Elvin had gone to the crime scene. Even though he hadn't been working the case, he'd made his way out there and confiscated the bottle.

It was slightly more than half full, and if it was the only bottle Conny Öhman had drunk from after coming home, it could well be true that he was far from intoxicated enough to black out and have complete amnesia. Elvin must have thought the same thing.

And if that were the case, it might mean Molander had been there before the night of the murder to spike the spirits. Probably with Xyrem or some other fast-acting GHB compound that caused a powerful, alcohol-like intoxication but would be out of the victim's system within hours and therefore not show up in a urine sample. The pieces were finally coming together.

Anything else you want to add?

No, other than that I don't see the point of this interview. You've clearly already made up your minds it was me.

Wasn't it?

(Silence.)

Should I take your silence as a confession?

(Silence.)

I guess I should.

Because if you have anything to say to the contrary, this is the time.

(Silence.)

I suppose you could check her phone. She always started filming whenever I got a bit upset.

We already did, and as you say, there's some incriminating things on there. But unfortunately, nothing from last night. I wasn't there, obviously, but I can imagine there were reasons she wouldn't have had the ability to take out her phone and start recording. Or what do you think?

(Shrugs his shoulders.)

Why hadn't they thought of that? Stubbs put the transcript down and pushed her reading glasses up into her hair. Elvin must have had a mobile phone. It should have been in his flat. But there had been no sign of it there, and nowhere else either, as far as she knew.

Had Molander taken it? And if so, why?

So far, she'd left the computer alone. Usually, a computer would be one of the last things she tackled at a crime scene. The most important evidence was almost always physical. What's more, depending on the size of the hard drive, going through one was often so labour-intensive it required several days' work, especially when you had no idea what you were looking for.

But this time, she *did* know when she sat down in front of the computer, booted it up and clicked her way to the DCIM folder. That was where pictures were stored. It didn't matter if you shoved in an external memory card full of photos or connected a phone via the USB port. That was always where they ended up.

And there were pictures in it, a seemingly endless number,

and one day, she would have time to go through them all one by one. But not today. So she sorted the pictures from newest to oldest and scrolled down to Thursday 5 April. But there were no pictures from that date. Nor from Friday 6 April, the day Molander had conducted his crime scene investigation, according to the case file. Nor from the following weekend.

But there was a video.

On Sunday 8 April at 7.17 a.m., Elvin had recorded a video that was four minutes and forty-three seconds long. That was two and a half days after the murder and could have been of practically anything. But it wasn't.

She'd only driven past Munka-Ljungby once or twice. She'd certainly never been to Munka Pizzeria. According to the report, Kerstin and Conny Öhman had rented out part of their house to it, and judging from the footage, which was bobbing up and down as if Elvin was holding the phone while walking, that was where he was going.

He'd probably parked his car some distance away to avoid getting too close to the dark blue Audi whose number plate Elvin was now pointing the phone at. She paused the playback, did a quick search for the registration number and confirmed what she had suspected.

The Audi belonged to Molander.

According to the case file, he'd finished the crime scene investigation on Friday the sixth. And yet there he was, a full day later. Granted, there was nothing irregular about a forensic scientist returning for one last once-over before calling in the cleaners. She'd done it herself countless times. But never in her private car and definitely not without informing the lead investigator, in this case Irene Lilja.

Elvin moved on from Molander's car and walked across the gravel to the back of the house, where he quietly opened the back door and entered. Since he was still holding the phone in his left hand, the video didn't show much beyond a dirty green rug, his orthopaedic Ecco shoes and the bottom of his jeans as he made his way into the house.

But there were plenty of sounds. The creaking floor, the panting breaths and the squeaky door to the living room.

'*Hi there,*' said Molander's voice, and a second later the man himself became visible, standing at the top of a ladder with one hand in the ceiling lampshade. '*What are you doing here?*'

'*Oh, nothing. I just happened to be in the neighbourhood and thought I'd have a look.*'

'*How does anyone just happen to be in Munka-Ljungby at half past seven on a Sunday morning?*' asked Molander, who seemed to slip something into his jacket pocket.

'*Believe it or not, I've actually been out fishing in Skälder Bay. I even caught a codfish that weighed over six pounds. And you? I thought you were done here two days ago?*'

'*You know what it's like. We were in a hurry, and I didn't want to risk overlooking something.*' Molander hurriedly climbed down the ladder and disappeared from the shot.

He was clearly tense, acting as though Elvin had burst in and caught him red-handed. But why was he there, and what had he pulled out of the ceiling light?

'*No, I suppose that makes sense,*' replied Elvin, now pointing the phone at the floor, which seemed to have been scrubbed clean of blood – so the cleaners had already been by to scrub away any remaining evidence, which made

Molander's visit even stranger. '*I guess I didn't realize there were things that needed clearing up.*'

'*Who said anything about clearing things up?*' The phone was turned up and once again showed Molander, but this time from below. '*There's nothing to clear up here.*'

'*So we're sure that Conny bloke, or whatever his name is, did it?*'

The phone was pointed back down at the floor, where two of Molander's aluminium cases were sitting open, revealing technical instruments stored in bespoke compartments.

'*Of course he did it. There's never been any doubt about that, as far as I know. Who else could it be? There are no signs of a third person having been present. Her blood was on his hands, clothes and groin. And according to Lilja he's more or less confessed.*'

'*Calm down. You don't have to sell me on it.*'

'*I'm not trying to. I'm just filling you in on what's going on.*'

'*All right then. So everything's good, in other words.*'

'*Yes, everything's good. There's no need for you to fret.*'

Silence fell and Stubbs heard the sound of the aluminium cases being closed while Elvin continued further into the room and pointed his phone up at the half-empty Explorer bottle on the mantel.

'*So, did you find anything?*'

'*Find? What do you mean, find?*'

'*In the ceiling light. What else were you doing up there?*'

'*Oh, that. Yes, that's a valid question. No, I realized I'd forgotten to check it and as I said, I just wanted to make sure.*'

'*I suppose we have to hope the cleaners missed it, too.*'

'No *need to worry. It was almost as dusty as your house up there.*' Molander let out a forced laugh that faltered when Elvin stayed silent. '*Well, I have to get home. So if you wouldn't mind making your way out so I can lock the door, that would be great.*'

'*Are you in a hurry?*'

'*I guess you could say that. Gertrud will be up in half an hour and she can be foul-tempered if I don't greet her with coffee and croissants. You know what it's like.*'

'*I don't, actually. But you go on, I'll lock up.*'

'*So you're staying. That makes me curious. May I ask why?*'

'*No reason, really. Like I said, I just happened to be in the neighbourhood. Do you have a problem with me hanging around?*'

'*No, why would I? As far as I'm concerned, you can stay as long as you like. Conny Öhman is unlikely to be back anytime soon.*' Molander forced out another laugh. '*All right, well, I guess I'll head out, then.*'

'*Sure, you don't want to be late. And don't forget to send my love to Gertrud.*'

Molander picked up his bags and left the room, and the second the front door closed, Elvin aimed his phone at the mantel again. Not at the bottle of vodka this time, but rather at a number of small black plastic objects lined up in a row.

Stubbs instantly recognized them as surveillance microphones of the exact same model Elvin had used in his owls. So he'd stolen both the idea and the equipment for bugging Molander's living room from Molander himself.

It was also worth noting that as soon as Molander opened his cases, he must have realized that, in his haste, he'd left some of his gadgets at the crime scene. He'd probably felt compelled go back, only to realize Elvin had taken both the microphones and the vodka bottle.

That had probably been all the reason he needed to do away with him.

29

SURFACE TENSION WAS still engaged in a silent yet fierce battle with gravity over the tiny droplet of water trembling at the edge of the tap. But as with every droplet that had gone before it, this one's fate was in no doubt.

Even so, each time gravity finally prevailed, forcing a droplet to let go of the tap and plunge helplessly towards the mirror-like surface of the water in the bath, it was a unique event.

Each time, a crater would erupt in slow motion, sending concentric waves rippling out from the epicentre, just an inch or two above the face with the wide-open eyes and the nose in which a tiny air bubble had become trapped in one of the nostrils.

Yet another victim. Yet another meaningless and completely incomprehensible murder.

That was Tuvesson's only thought when she aimed her torch at the body in the overflowing bath. This time, a naked young man as beautiful as he was muscular. A man who had been planning to take his girlfriend out that very night, to celebrate the anniversary of their engagement. But according to her, he never showed up. Half an hour later, she'd found him dead at his home, in the bath.

What had he done to deserve such a premature ending? What was the point? She shook her head and felt that an ever-bigger part of her was on the verge of giving up and accepting the idea that they may never solve this case.

At least Molander was both focused and full of energy, despite it being midnight and Gertrud having just left him. He was moving around with his characteristic boyish curiosity, shining his torch along the floor, the ceiling and the walls, seeming to know exactly where to start.

'It's too early to say for certain, but I think I've found the cause of the power outage.' Molander turned the beam of his torch towards a temporary power cord running diagonally across the ceiling and down one of the walls before disappearing behind the bath.

Unfortunately, she herself was anything but focused. Her mind didn't know which way to pull her and her thoughts seemed intent on tangling so badly they were soon going to be impossible to unravel.

'The cord is probably split somewhere behind the bath,' Molander went on. 'Because we have the neutral wire at the foot over there and at the head you can see the hot one.'

Tuvesson nodded and noted that a blue and a brown cable had indeed been stripped and taped to the bath an inch or two below the waterline at either end.

'Would you mind holding this?' Molander handed her the torch, grabbed a bath brush that was propped against the wall and slowly dipped the wooden handle down the inside of the bath. Then he pushed the body aside as far as he was able and leaned forwards. 'Just as I thought.' He turned to Tuvesson. 'The ground continues all the way to the bottom.'

'So he was electrocuted?'

'It's one theory, certainly.' Molander put the scrubbing brush down. 'But we should wait and see what Flätan has to say. I don't think I've ever met anyone more allergic to rushing to conclusions than that man.'

'And what's another theory?'

'That he drowned. Obviously.'

Obviously. What else would it be? She had to pull herself together before she made a proper fool of herself.

'What's beyond doubt, however, is that the water level has risen above the cables,' Molander went on. 'And though water may be a poor conductor in and of itself, there's enough dirt and pollutions in it to change that.'

'Enough to be fatal?' Fine, she'd had a drink. She had. But just a small one, certainly not enough for it to affect her work.

'I'd say it depends.' Molander made a weighing gesture with his hands.

'But it's 220 volts, right?' She was probably just tired and needed to sleep. It was well past midnight, after all.

'Yes, but it's not the volts that matter, it's the amperes, and you have to get to at least thirty or forty milliampere for about a minute before the breathing muscles are paralysed and render the victim unconscious.'

'So what you're really saying is that it's too soon to say anything at all.'

Molander nodded. 'Yes, I'm going to have to conduct a thorough investigation of everything from the current of the cables and the conductivity of the water to any other evidence in the rest of the flat before we can be sure of anything. And then there's Flätan, who won't say a peep until he has at the very least had time to open him up and examine his lungs.'

'Fine, but you have to be able to give me some kind of

working theory, though, right? I'll admit the whole things is confusing to me. I mean, if you wanted to kill your victim with an electric shock, wouldn't it be easier to do it without water, taping the cables directly onto his body? Or am I mistaken?'

Molander shook his head. 'I've been asking myself the exact same thing. The only explanation I can see is that this electrical set-up is only part of the explanation.'

'You're saying there's something else? What might that be?'

'Another plan. I don't know.' Molander shrugged. 'That's what my investigation is going to try to find out.'

'Come on. You have a theory. I can tell. You've had one since you stepped through that door. Bloody hell, Ingvar, I know you, don't forget.'

Molander sighed. 'Could I at least have an hour before—'

'You can have all the hours you need. But first I want you to tell me what you think happened here. Think. Not know. If, later on, you come across evidence that points in a different direction, we'll deal with that then.'

'Okay.' Molander took a deep breath and turned to the bath. 'First, Milwokh must have overpowered his victim and subdued him somehow.'

'He might have knocked him out or sedated him.'

'Sure, that may well be what he did, and Flätan's toxicological examination will answer that for us. But either way, that was just to get his clothes off and get him into the bath.'

'Let's hope so. That he at least got to sleep through his final moments.'

'Hope springs eternal, I suppose. But sadly, I'm pretty

sure that's not how it happened.' Molander stuck the brush handle back into the bath and pushed the body aside. 'There are signs that suggest he was awake. Look at this.'

Tuvesson leaned over and saw a steel wire that ran through a hoop at the bottom of the bath and in under the victim's back.

'The other end is probably tied around the victim's wrists, which wouldn't have been necessary if the victim had been kept unconscious.'

'Couldn't it have been precautionary, in case he woke up?'

'Sure. Unless he was meant to wake up.' Molander shrugged. 'Maybe the point was for him to be awake for his own death. If nothing else, the bath makes sense that way.'

'I'm not following.'

'I believe, and I stress the word believe, Milwokh let the victim choose his own death.'

'And why would he do that? I don't see the point.'

'What's the point of shoving someone into a washing machine?' Molander shrugged. 'It would explain the bath, the wire around his wrists and not least, the cables.'

Tuvesson was about to cut in, but was prevented by an exasperated wave.

'Please, let me finish and stop interrupting.'

'I'm sorry, I'm just so—'

'Astrid, I know. We're all groping in the dark here. That's why I want to get to work as quickly as possible. So if you want to hear my theory, you're going to have to listen until I'm done before you smash it to pieces with a thousand objections. Okay?'

Tuvesson nodded.

'As you can see, the ends of the cables are placed fairly

high up, close to the edge of the bath,' Molander continued. 'So high, in fact, that Milwokh had to seal the overflow drain to make sure the water didn't escape.' He pointed to the overflow, from which some kind of grey putty was sticking out. 'So my theory is that he sedated his victim, stripped him and tied him to the bottom of the bath. Then he waited until he woke up. Only then did he turn on the tap and start filling the bath. If I had to guess, I would say he didn't even turn it on fully, just ten or fifteen per cent maybe.'

'And why would he do that?'

'Maybe to give the victim enough time to grasp the gravity of the situation. Who knows? Maybe Milwokh sat right there on that stool and explained what was going to happen.' Molander nodded to a wooden stool by the wall. 'That the water level was going to rise all the way to the cables, and that it was up to him if he wanted to take his own life by drowning or wait for the water to electrocute him, which would be a considerably more painful way to go.'

'Is electrocution really that much more painful?'

'Absolutely. If I had to choose, I'd pick drowning every time. After the initial pain, you don't feel a thing, just float away in a weightless state. Electrocution is far from pleasant. Depending on the strength of the current, you basically fry from the inside. Muscle, tissue, the internal organs. And it can take a while. Ten, fifteen minutes, if you're unlucky.'

'So he either had to drown himself or wait to be fried from the inside?'

Molander nodded. 'But ask me again when I'm done with the investigation and Flätan has done his thing.'

'But shouldn't the fuse have blown the second the circuit

closed?' She finally felt somewhat on the ball. 'I would have gambled on that if it were me in that bath.' Tuvesson flicked the light switch but no light came on. 'The power is clearly out, so the water shouldn't have been live for more than a second or two.'

'That's true.' Molander nodded, looking thoughtful. 'On the other hand, the power didn't just go out in this flat, but rather in the entire building, which would explain...' He left the room and Tuvesson stayed where she was, unsure of what to do.

She'd made some valid comments, she had. Even pointed out some things Molander hadn't thought of. But she wasn't at her best, far from it. She had to fight for every cogent thought, and even so, she mostly felt confused.

But she couldn't blame it on the alcohol. Strange as it may sound, she had in fact taken control of her drinking.

'Found it,' Molander shouted from the hallway.

'What?'

'The fuse box.'

'And? Did you learn anything?'

Like all normal people, she'd managed to find her way back to an equilibrium and now she just had to make sure she didn't fall off the wagon again.

'I obviously need to have a closer look at this in the lab, but it looks like you're right. From what I can see, one of the fuses has been swapped for some sort of home-made device.'

'All right.' Tuvesson left the bathroom and let her torch light her way through the hallway to the living room.

But on Sunday, when she'd made her first attempt, she'd ended up overdoing it. There was no denying it. It was what you might call a significant relapse. But then again, she'd been good for a whole month before that, and if that didn't earn her a relapse, then what did? And maybe it was exactly what she needed to find the equilibrium she was now maintaining.

But there was that one conversation she couldn't stop thinking about.

'I'll go down to the basement and check if it's the same there. That could possibly explain why the power didn't go straight away but only after a fifteen-minute delay.'

She had only a vague memory of it. It had been sometime in the middle of the night and she'd been asleep on her kitchen floor after throwing up in the sink in a desperate attempt to make the world stop spinning. She had no memory at all of her phone ringing; suddenly it was just pressed against her ear and there was a male voice on the other end. Soon after, the call had ended and she'd slipped back into the fog.

The next day, which was to say yesterday, she'd assumed the phone call had been a dream; but going through her call log had confirmed that on Monday, between 12.15 a.m. and 12.18 a.m., Fabian Risk had called her no less than three times. The last time, she had apparently picked up, and a twenty-one-second call had ensued.

What the log couldn't tell her was what they'd talked about. She had no recollection of it. But she had her suspicions and had immediately taken steps.

30

EVEN THOUGH HE'D put on an extra sweater and the sea air was mild, Fabian started to feel cold within an hour. He was tense. That was why. His whole body was on high alert and now, after another thirty minutes, as he raised the binoculars and gazed out across the inky waters of Öresund in the direction of Denmark, the cold had penetrated so deep his hands were shaking.

But there was nothing for it. The two men from the Helsingborg coastguard who crewed the boat had long since started grumbling about wrapping up a mission they felt was nothing but a waste of time and resources.

So no matter how badly he wanted to step down and join them in the warm cabin, he couldn't. To them, it would be a clear signal he'd given up, too, and they would immediately seize the opportunity to turn back towards Helsingborg and their dock behind Parapeten. But so long as he was out here, shakily clutching his binoculars, they had to let him keep at it.

At least he'd managed to speak to Stubbs, who'd told him about a murder case out in Munka-Ljungby last spring that Elvin had been interested in for some reason. She'd tried to explain, but he hadn't fully understood. Either way, tomorrow she was meeting with a certain Conny Öhman, who was serving a lengthy prison sentence for the murder of his wife, and if it turned out she was right about him being innocent, she claimed they had all the proof they needed to arrest Molander.

In a way, he could sympathize with the coastguard's unwillingness to help. He'd forced them out on a virtually impossible mission. Nevertheless, the flat where Milwokh's latest victim was still submerged in his own bath was located only a few hundred yards from Helsingborg's South Harbour and the boat rental suggested it had been his intended escape route.

Where he had escaped to was, however, an open question. He could have gone anywhere. He had not returned to the Råå Marina and Helsingborg Boat Rentals. They'd scoured every square foot of both it and the South Harbour. Then they'd searched the entire coastline from Landskrona in the south to Höganäs in the north and, on Fabian's insistence, they'd even done a few forays further out in the sound.

They were definitely groping in the dark. And yet, he couldn't shake the thought that Milwokh was out here somewhere, bobbing along with his navigational lights turned off, waiting for them to give up.

They knew he'd only rented the boat for two days, which suggested a short trip. Two uniformed officers had been dispatched to keep the boat rental company under surveillance, though they were well aware he didn't necessarily have any intention of returning the boat. But that would suggest he was done for good, and right now, there was nothing to support that. Quite the opposite.

Far likelier was that he'd crossed over to Denmark and pulled the boat up on some deserted beach.

'Hey,' one of the old men called from the cabin. 'How are you getting on? Find anything exciting?'

'No, but if we could pop over to the Danish—'

'Because it's getting to be time to turn back,' the man cut in.

'Yes, so you keep saying, but I'd like to keep going just a bit longer.' Fabian turned the binoculars south in the direction of Ven and focused all of his energy on not shaking visibly.

'I'm sorry, no can do. Both me and Bengan clock out in forty minutes, and we need time to hose her down and refuel and write a report before then.' He shrugged. 'So you see. No can do.'

'Don't you just get paid overtime?'

'Unfortunately, that's not up to us. There have been cutbacks, you know, and word on the street is they're closing our entire unit down and merging it with Malmö. Insane, if you ask me. But that's the way it goes when it's all about the bottom line.' The man turned around and nodded to his colleague at the tiller, who started to turn the boat back towards Helsingborg harbour.

'Hold on a minute.' Fabian lowered his binoculars and stepped into the cabin. 'Look, I hear you. But we're dealing with a killer who in just over a month has murdered at least six people, and there's a small chance he's out here somewhere, just waiting for us to give up.'

'There's also a chance, a fairly big one at that if you ask me, that he's somewhere else entirely,' said the man at the tiller. 'And we've searched the entire coast from Höganäs down to Landskrona. Not just once, but—'

'Not the Danish side,' Fabian broke in. 'We haven't been there.'

'Denmark?' The man at the tiller turned to his colleague for support. 'We can't just go into Danish territorial waters without permission.'

'If that's where you think he is, you'd be better off talking to the Danes directly,' the other added.

'Okay, so who do I call?' Fabian made an effort to keep the frustration out of his voice. 'About the overtime pay and the possibility of crossing the sound.'

'Well, it's not that simple,' one of them said, and he turned to his colleague again. 'Or what do you say, Bengan?'

'I mean, they're two completely separate issues. As far as the Danes go, there are routines, and you need the approval of their Naval Operative Command. Our overtime pay is a budget matter, so that would be Gert-Ove Helin.'

'Then I suggest you start with Denmark's Naval Operative Command.'

The two men sighed and one of them turned to a control panel, picked up a phone receiver with a coiled cord and started dialling.

'Maybe I should do the talking,' Fabian said, and he took the receiver, where ringing could already be heard over the crackling line.

'*You have reached the Danish Naval Operative Command.*'

'Hello, my name is Fabian Risk and I'm a detective with the Swedish police in Helsingborg.'

'*Good evening, how can I help?*'

'I'm on board Swedish coastguard vessel KB 202 just north of Helsingborg. We need permission to cross into Danish territory in pursuit of a suspect.'

'*Fabian Risk from the Helsingborg Police. Is that correct?*'

'Yes, that's correct.'

'*And KB 202. Okay, that's fine. But if anything happens, I would like you to contact us again. Okay?*'

'Absolutely, no problem.' Fabian hung up, pulled out his mobile and turned to the two men. 'And what is this Gert-Ove's number?'

He never got an answer because just then, the shortwave radio on the same control panel crackled to life.

'*Emergency switchboard to KB 202. Over.*'

'KB 202 here. Over,' one of the two men responded.

'*I tried to call, but the line was busy. Over.*'

'Yes, we've been talking to the Danes about permission to cross over to their side. What's this about? Over.'

'*We've had a distress call from a Hallberg-Rassy at Latitude 56.288 degrees and Longitude 12.342 degrees. You wouldn't happen to be in the area, would you? Over.*'

'That sounds like somewhere outside Kullaberg. If that's the case, we're no more than twenty, twenty-five minutes away. Over.'

'*Good. I think maybe you'd better stop by and talk to them and make sure everything's okay. Over.*'

'Sure. What's the problem? Engine failure? Over.'

'*They said something about a black rubber dinghy ramming them and something about a swo... Uh, to be honest, I wouldn't be surprised if they're high, so I would do both blood samples and breathalyser. The whole thing sounded pretty muddled, if you ask me. Over.*'

'All right, we're on our way. Over and out.'

'Hey, hang on.' Fabian hurried over and snatched the microphone out of the man's hand. 'I'm sorry, what did they

say, exactly?' He waited for a reply but heard nothing but
static. 'Over.'

'*Who am I speaking to? Over.*'

'Fabian Risk from the Helsingborg Police. You said they
said something about a rubber dinghy. What else did they
say? Over.'

'*Like I said, it was pretty incoherent and muddled. But
something about a person boarding their boat and attacking
them with a sword. Over.*'

31

'NEW HEAVEN OG Syvende Disneyland – Sexomanisk Mickey Mouse' by Jens Jørgen Thorsen was by no means an appealing painting. It actually looked like something Sleizner could have made himself at the age of four. A riot of bright colours, to all appearances randomly splattered across the canvas, except in one section where one could, with the application of considerable imagination, possibly discern a childish portrait of Mickey Mouse.

Thirty thousand Danish kronor he'd paid for it, convinced it would appreciate immensely. That was why he handled it ever so gingerly as he took it off the wall and placed it on the floor.

He searched the inside of the stretched canvas with both a torch and his fingers, but found neither hidden microphones nor anything else suspicious. He'd already checked the sofa cushions. And the potted plants, the lamps, the bookshelf and the bed. He'd even turned off all the lights and shone the torch at each and every mirror to make sure they hadn't been swapped for transparent ones with hidden cameras rigged behind them.

But nowhere had he found anything to indicate that the flat was bugged, which was a good thing. As a matter of fact, he'd rolled strike after strike recently, not just managing to identify the Chinese fatso but also locating his place of residence and thereby stumbling across the Indian man who'd helped Dunja at the bank. In other words, he was so close he could almost taste the stale smell of her.

He should feel relieved and able to relax on the sofa with a glass of whisky and one of the latest films from The Club. But he was too wound up, and at the moment, his whole body was itching with frustration.

The pictures he'd found weren't much to write home about. Grainy and in some cases completely blurry, taken in a flat, his flat. How the fuck had the miserable cunt managed it? He'd invested in both an alarm system and a top-of-the-range security door when he and Viveca moved into the flat five years ago. Now she'd moved back out and was living with some rich bloody swine out in Gentofte, and in a way he blamed Dunja for that, too.

And yet, she'd managed to get in somehow. He was in some of the pictures, buck naked, having just come out of the shower after a workout. Talk about intrusion and crossing the line, and how had he not noticed?

And it looked so bloody small in the pictures. It was fucking embarrassing. It was always like that after a workout, though he usually pulled on it in the shower to try to make it longer. Of course that was the moment she chose to take pictures. He was going to make her fucking eat it. She was going to goddam fucking suffer.

He walked over to the smoked-glass CD cabinet, picked an album by Sade and pushed the disc into the wall-mounted Bang & Olufsen player. If there was one thing that could make him calm down, it was Sade's sensual vocals.

'Smooth Operator' was his absolute favourite from the album *The Best of Sade*. He didn't care that it was a greatest hits album. People could look down their noses as much as they liked. He didn't give a shit. His entire music collection consisted of greatest hits albums and to be perfectly honest, he'd never understood what was so wrong about cherry picking, about skipping the mediocre dross that was just filler anyway.

He sat down on the edge of the sofa, right in the acoustic sweet spot, and let Sade's sexy groove fill the room while he focused on getting his breathing back to normal.

This was war and they were currently engaged in a game of cat and mouse where they were both trying to be the cat. That much was clear. But she'd crossed a line and now the ball was in his court.

He was going to scout her out and pin her down before announcing himself. And she was going to realize it was already too late. And that's when the fun would begin. Just ending it as soon as he located her would feel as sloppy and undignified as a premature ejaculation. Much as he loathed her, she was still his favourite person to hate.

He wanted to draw it out and relish each successive step. He wanted to lull her into a false sense of security. Then, when he was truly ready, he'd pounce and enjoy seeing the shock in her eyes. Watching as it sank in that she was done for. That it didn't matter how much she screamed for help because there was no Indian man and no Chinese fatso to rescue her.

But that was later. Right now, he needed to find out what she'd done to his flat, and how she'd been able to get in and sneak around even when he was home. He unlocked his phone to go through the pictures he'd found at the Indian man's house one more time, but instead he lingered on one of Dunja walking through the lobby of Danske Bank in Malmö to cash her severance pay.

It was a picture of CCTV footage that had been both out of focus and grainy. But there she was, in her large trainers, ratty sweatpants and camouflage top. Along with the big earrings, the bright red lips and the shaved head, it was very different from what she'd looked like before. Gone were the bland, indecisive clothes, the timid eyes and the last few pounds of baby fat.

The slut had shed her skin and hideous though her new style was, he had to admit she looked tastier than ever. That made him both aroused and even more furious than before.

The phone suddenly vibrated in his hands, and he saw that he'd received a notification from his calendar app about a meeting on Wednesday afternoon. He clicked it and realized it was from that relentless IT bloke, Mikael Rønning. *Security update of your mobile phone as agreed on Wednesday 27 June 2012 1–3 p.m.* He had definitely not agreed to that.

If not for Sade's soothing voice, he would have called that idiot up and yelled at him until he became a bed-wetter again. But as it was, he let it go and instead turned his attention to the pictures Dunja or her little Indian man had taken in his home, and as he did so, he suddenly noticed something he should have seen straight away.

Every picture was taken from more or less the same angle. Which was to say from the panorama windows, or, rather, from outside them. In other words, they hadn't broken into his flat, they'd stood on the balcony and used the zoom. Granted, the balcony was bad enough, but it was still considerably better than having her snooping around his flat.

He chuckled and shook his head. Say what you want, she certainly knew how to keep a man on his toes. He was finally in a better mood. He'd thought he was going to have to crawl around on all fours all night, looking for hidden cameras. Suddenly, the night was young. Maybe he should do a quick workout at home, a few quick sets of push-ups, pull-ups and Turkish get-ups. Just to get the blood pumping before freshening up and heading over to The Club.

He turned Sade up and had already walked over to the exercise corner in front of the mirror wall when another message made his phone buzz. Hoping to be able to dismiss it as unimportant, he glanced at it while unrolling his gym mat and lining up his weights.

Unfortunately, it wasn't something that could just be ignored. That was frustrating, to be sure, but at least it was also something that made him feel happier.

As the head of Copenhagen's homicide unit, he obviously had access to all police databases and reports, as well as countless other documents by default. But since a year or two back, he'd made sure to implement a search function that allowed for the flagging of one or more search terms, and the moment any of them were inputted into a police or wider government database, he was notified by text.

It went without saying that his top two search terms at the moment were *Dunja* and *Hougaard*, closely followed by *Qiang-Wei Hitomu Oisin*. But none of those were in the message. Instead, it was two completely unrelated words that had become increasingly interesting to him since he'd saved the life of the man in question exactly one week ago during a police raid in Snekkersten.

He'd already received them once on Monday. That time, it had been about a visit to Helsingør Prison, which had immediately made him start contacting people and taking the necessary steps. Now, two days later, the same two words appeared again, and he wasn't about to let them pass by unnoticed this time either.

Fabian and *Risk*.

The two words together.

That was all he needed.

32

THE RUMBLING OF the powerful diesel engines rolled out across the dark water as coastguard vessel KB 202 steered up alongside the Hallberg-Rassy, which had lowered both its jib and two-thirds of its mainsail.

Fenders were hung. Ropes were thrown, hauled in and cleated until the two boats became one, though from a distance the yacht, despite its size, looked tiny next to its visitor.

He was sitting about a hundred yards away, feeling impressed by his new biocular device. An Armasight Discovery 5X. It was his first time using it and out here in the dark, in the middle of the sea, it was really showing him what it could do. Gone was the blurry green night-vision image of old. With the Armasight, he could study them in close-up detail. If not for the lack of sound, it would have been like being on board, and he was pleased to conclude that it had been worth every penny.

In a way, he'd been lucky. He could just as easily still have been swimming around, looking for his rubber dinghy. As it was, it had taken him forty-five minutes, and he'd been on the verge of giving up when it suddenly appeared out of nowhere, slowly bobbing towards him. He'd even managed to hang on to the sword, if only because it had got caught in one of the loops on his wetsuit during the few seconds he'd been unconscious.

And yet, lucky was the last thing he felt.

He'd only just finished cleaning up after the debacle with the little girl and had finally been able to relax and look forward to his next task. A task that, no matter how you looked at it, could only be described as a complete disaster.

Was he losing it? Had he just been too busy to notice? His powers, if he'd ever really had any, were they deserting him? It felt a bit like they were.

He was aware, of course, that chance had a will of its own, and maybe on balance he'd actually been lucky. But still, these past few days it was almost as though the dice had been working against him.

At first glance, the Hallberg-Rassy had been the perfect target. The dice had spoken, and for a few minutes he'd been utterly convinced there was a higher purpose to their paths crossing.

Then, everything had gone wrong. Absolutely everything.

Just boarding the boat had been difficult. In order to avoid detection, he'd had to kill the engine a hundred feet away and silently glide the last part of the way. But he'd underestimated his speed and even though he'd rushed to push off, his bow had bumped into their hull.

But no one had seemed to notice the thud. He'd realized why after he stepped over the lifeline and saw the flickering blue light through one of the windows. They'd been watching a film, which was somewhat remarkable considering they were still in the middle of the heavily trafficked Öresund.

But so far, so good, he'd thought as he lowered himself into the cockpit with the dice in his pocket and the sword in its sheath on his back, completely unprepared for that bloody brat to poke his head out of the aft cabin and stare at him, still half-asleep.

They'd stood frozen as the seconds ticked by. The thought of jumping back into the rubber dinghy, cutting the line and hightailing it out of there had occurred to him. But he'd resisted the temptation.

There had been three of them, potential pets not included. That meant each family member had to be assigned two numbers each. As the youngest, the child got one and two, the mum three and four and finally the dad five and six.

The problem was that there had been no time to take out and roll the dice, which was a problem he'd have to solve for future high-stress situations. This time, he'd instead been forced to deal with the boy, who had been pulling air into his lungs to start screaming.

Three quick steps later, he'd been on top of him, forcing him back down into the aft cabin. Then he'd closed the hatch from inside and gone to draw his sword, which turned out to be almost impossible in the cramped space. Especially with a kid kicking and fighting for his life.

In the end, though, he'd managed to get the sword out and the sight of it had subdued the boy, which meant he could use his free hand to take out the dice and roll it. What happened next was something he'd prefer to forget.

He'd suddenly been dragged backwards out of the aft cabin. Granted, he'd recovered quickly and got back on his feet, but the sword had not been on his side. If truth be told, it had turned out to be utterly useless. At least as far as weapons went. He'd kept hitting things with it and missing his target.

Maybe he hadn't practised enough. But in that moment,

he'd felt like a clown, and when the boom knocked him out, the humiliation had been complete. The whole thing had been so embarrassing he'd deserved falling overboard.

But at least the day was still young, so there was plenty of time for him to lick his wounds and recover. If not for the sudden visit by the coastguard, he would have lain down and closed his eyes for half an hour. To compose himself. As it was, he had to keep an eye on how things developed.

The worst-case scenario would be if they gave the family a lift to Helsingborg while a crew member sailed their boat back to shore. Unfortunately, that was also the most likely one. If that happened, he'd have to completely rethink everything. But he'd cross that bridge if he came to it. At the moment, all he could do was hang back in the dark and hope they would be alone again soon.

The crew seemed to consist of three men. And one of them was, strangely enough, wearing civilian clothes. Even stranger, he'd been the first one to step aboard the yacht, and he was the one speaking to the family. He'd been at it for almost forty-five minutes now.

Perhaps he was a police detective. He might even be one of the ones working with that Irene Lilja who had been terrorizing him over the past few days, which was yet another problem.

At first, he'd assumed she was ringing his doorbell whenever she happened to be in the area and that she would give up and leave him alone before long. But when she'd continued to bother him several times a day, sometimes ringing the bell for minutes at a time, it had become obvious she was not the kind of problem that would go away of its own accord. And yesterday, when she broke in and searched his flat, aided by an entire arrest team, he'd barely had time to hide.

It wasn't an unfortunate coincidence. They really were on to him.

Not only had they managed to find out where he lived, they'd sniffed out enough to know his next strike was going to take place out on Öresund. How else could they have got here so quickly?

He had no answer, and ultimately, it didn't matter. He would finish his task regardless. It wouldn't be easy. But then, why should it be? Simple was often synonymous with boring and insipid. Thinking back, it had always been the difficult, almost impossible things that had interested him. Like that time when he was little and had done the impossible by running away from home with both his piggy banks and getting all the way to Tivoli in Copenhagen and having the best day of his life.

Now, instead, he was lying out here in the dark and through his biocular he saw ropes being untied and then the two boats drifted apart.

The wait was over, and he could feel his energy returning. Even the powerful but increasingly distant rumbling from the coastguard ship's engines was like music to his ears.

Even better was that none of the family members seemed to have left the yacht. All three of them were standing in the cockpit with their arms around each other, waving, like in a film with a happy ending when the credits are rolling.

Completely unaware that the film had in fact only just begun.

33

JUST LIKE CLOUDS in a blue sky, the dark waves seemed able to morph into a thousand different shapes in the night, so long as one didn't look too long or too hard. They were all more or less the same, and yet each was also unique, and through his binoculars they merged into an endless series of permutations of shades of black and steely grey.

In a way, he should feel relieved. The family, which, ironically, he had met and talked to just a few nights ago, were still alive and had escaped relatively unscathed apart from the shock of it all. They had the boom that knocked Milwokh unconscious to thank for that. Luck had undoubtedly been on their side, and without it, their trip around the world could have ended very differently.

And yet he felt anything but calm. He wasn't seasick at all, but his insides were churning. Every alarm inside him was going off, flashing and screaming that he was wrong to turn back to shore and leave them alone in their yacht.

He'd offered them everything from accompanying them back to Helsingborg to personally staying with them until they reached the nearest harbour. But the man had turned down every one of his suggestions. In return, he'd sworn to set a new course, for Halmstad, and to make sure they visited a trauma therapist before pushing on towards Gothenburg.

Considering what he'd just been through, he'd seemed

remarkably composed. Same with the wife, who had slept through the whole thing. But they were all in shock, no question about it. Especially the boy, who'd sat wrapped in his mother's arms throughout their conversations, staring out into the dark as though expecting to see Milwokh come flying out of the sea at any moment.

But the risk of that had to be considered minimal. According to the men from the coastguard, most signs indicated that he had drowned and would turn up bloated on a beach in Denmark or Sweden sometime in the next few days. Unless the body was sucked into the propeller of one of the many ships that passed through the sound.

Most would see that as good news. Fabian felt the opposite. Not only because he was opposed to capital punishment, but also because no matter how you looked at it, it was a big failure on their part. They'd done everything they could, but at the end of the day, it was undeniable that they'd simply failed at their jobs, forcing nature to step in and mete out justice.

Even worse was that they'd never get a chance to question him about what was behind the madness. In a way, that was actually the worst part. The way meaninglessness would ultimately triumph when the answer to the question of *why* from the victims' loved ones was that it was all because of a dice.

According to the boy, Milwokh had rolled a dice this time, too. Apparently a five. But what that meant was anyone's guess and now it looked like they were never going to find out. A prospect so dark and depressing he preferred not to dwell on it.

Maybe that was why he saw what he saw. A flight of fancy that manifested as an image on his retina. An illusion built on wishful thinking without any basis in reality. And yet he couldn't ignore what looked like a dark rubber dinghy bobbing on the waves a few hundred yards away.

'Stop,' he bellowed and raced over to the cockpit. 'You have to stop and turn on one of the searchlights!'

'And why is that?' asked the portlier of the two.

'I think I saw the rubber dinghy.'

'Think? Now, look here—'

'Just do as I say!' Fabian cut him off. 'Before we're too far away!'

The portlier man emptied his lungs and turned to his colleague, who, after stroking his moustache for several seconds, finally slowed the engine and turned on one of the searchlights, which shot a beam of light into the night like a canon.

Fabian rushed over to the searchlight and aimed it at the area where he'd just seen the boat. Unfortunately, he could see nothing other than waves surging and rolling over one another in a pattern that was simultaneously systematic and stochastic.

'Are you absolutely sure it was a rubber dinghy you saw?' the portly man asked as he exited the cockpit.

'No, I'm not. But there was something there,' Fabian replied, attempting to sound calm and rational. 'Something dark floating about over there somewhere.' He let the searchlight sweep the area, but there was nothing to see but a billowing darkness.

'If you look at it long enough, you can end up seeing just about anything.'

'That may well be. But I still want us to head over there and search the area, just to be on the safe side.'

'Yes, I'm sure you do.' The portly man let out a chuckle. 'It's like my children. They want Christmas year-round, but that's not something I can give them. This is the exact same thing—'

'For fuck's sake!' Fabian turned to the man, who just stood there with his ridiculous grin, apparently unperturbed by his outburst. 'If it's the overtime you're so damn worried about, I promise you'll get it. Okay? Just do as I say.'

'Okey-dokey. It's a deal. But be prepared to pay it out of your own pocket. Like I said, they've cut our budget to the bone, and I'm pretty sure—'

'It'll be taken care of. The question is, what are you waiting for? We have to get over there now, not six months from now.'

The man gave his colleague a signal that made him go full steam ahead and make a tight turn back to the area in question. About a minute later, they slowed down again and Fabian was able to scan the dark, rippling surface with the searchlight.

But not even with the aid of a vivid imagination could he see anything resembling a rubber dinghy.

'Listen, I have no problem understanding why you're so eager to find that dinghy, or whatever it is. But no matter how badly we want to help, we can't just sit around out here and—'

'Could you ask your colleague to kill the engines?'

'Eh, what?' The portly fellow seemed bewildered.

'I'm sorry, that came out as a question. I was actually ordering you to go back in and tell your colleague to kill the engines. Now.'

The man was about to object, but caught himself and

instead signalled to his colleague to do as Fabian asked. The engines were turned off and the rumbling subsided.

Fabian turned off the searchlight, closed his eyes and took a few deep breaths to slow his racing pulse, which had been pounding in his ears ever since they were hailed by the emergency operator about the attack.

'I'm sorry, would you mind explaining what we're—'

Fabian shushed the man.

His hearing was neither good nor bad. As often as a comment directed at him passed him by, he would pick up on things no one else heard. It could be anything from a faint, high-frequency hum whose source was impossible to locate to some new, strange sound emitted by the car.

This time, though, he was pretty sure what it was as he turned to the other man. 'Can you hear that?'

'Hear what?'

'The outboard motor.'

The man pricked up his ears, then shook his head.

'It's coming from over there.' Fabian pointed west towards Denmark.

The man shook his head again and shrugged. 'That could be anything. It's like my children, when they—'

'Right now, I don't give a toss about your children. The only thing I care about is going over there to see what's making that noise before it's too late.'

Without another word, the man turned and walked back to the cockpit, and moments later they were on their way.

Fabian kept a lookout through his binoculars and at regular intervals told the men to turn off the engines so he could listen for the sound of the outboard motor and adjust their course accordingly.

When he finally saw it again, there could be no doubt. It was a rubber dinghy. Far away, but definitely a rubber dinghy. Too far away for him to see anything other than that there was a dark shape cutting through the waves, leaving a white trail of roiling water in its wake.

'See that?' he called to the others, pointing. 'Over there.'

The men in the cockpit nodded, and he saw the portlier one pick up the VHF microphone and say something while his colleague kept them on a straight course.

They were finally closing in on him. This case was finally going to be brought to an end. This sick, twisted case where nothing had been like anything else. It was still too early for a victory lap. But they were close now. So close he could make out the white foam behind the dinghy even without binoculars.

He pulled out his gun and checked to make sure the magazine was full. He hadn't brought a bulletproof vest. But there should be no need for one. So far, Milwokh hadn't used a gun for any of the murders, and there was nothing to suggest he was armed with one this time either.

His phone vibrated, welcoming him to Denmark. He took the opportunity to type out a text to Tuvesson about being minutes away from an arrest. But when the boat suddenly slowed down and the engines began to idle, he put the phone back in his pocket and hurried over to the cockpit.

'What's going on? What are you doing?'

'We have to turn around, I'm afraid,' the portly one replied.

'What? What do you mean, turn around? We're minutes away from catching up.'

'That's unfortunate, yes, but we have to—'

'The only thing you have to do is what I tell you to do!'

'Sorry. We've had a no and we can't just—'

'What do you mean, a no?' Fabian cut in. 'Who told you no?'

'Denmark's Naval Operative Command.'

'But they gave us a green light just an hour ago. I don't understand.'

'Well, that makes three of us. But the order was unambiguous. They want us to leave Danish territory asap,' said the man with the moustache. 'So we might as well turn around before they get properly surly.' He accelerated and turned the wheel as far as it would go.

'No, no, no! Just calm down and hold on a minute.' Fabian went back out to the deck and saw a big freight ship astern, heading north about fifty yards from them. For the life of him, he couldn't understand why the Danes had suddenly changed their minds. He pulled out his phone and was about to call Tuvesson when it suddenly lit up and vibrated in his hand. He'd received a text in Danish from a withheld number.

Like I told you in Snekkersten. The last thing you want to do is disappoint me.

The two sentences screamed Kim Sleizner. It couldn't be anyone else. A week ago, that same man had saved him from drowning in a jacuzzi in Snekkersten. He'd gone there to arrest Eric Jacobsén, and it would have ended very badly if not for Sleizner.

The Danish detective chief superintendent had wasted no time afterwards making it clear to Fabian that he now owed him, and that repayment in the form of information on the whereabouts of Dunja Hougaard would be greatly appreciated.

The problem was that Fabian had no idea where she was. He'd been trying to reach her himself with no success. He'd explained as much to Sleizner, who apparently didn't believe him and had now found a way to make the Danish Naval Operative Command force him back out into international waters.

The whole thing was absurd and completely unacceptable, but unfortunately tallied with what he'd heard about Sleizner. Calling Tuvesson and asking her to contact Sleizner, or preferably someone above him in the hierarchy, would only be a waste of precious time, and Milwokh would be long gone before they were granted permission to enter again.

He raised his binoculars and watched the Swedish-flagged freight ship MS *Vinterland* pass by them, blocking most of the view with its enormous, dark blue hull. Somewhere on the other side of it was Milwokh, free now to disappear in almost any direction.

He thought about Dunja, who two years earlier had jeopardized her entire career to help him gain access to a perpetrator's car, which the Danish police had impounded, and how it was thanks to her they'd finally had a break in the case.

Whether it was because of that, or simply because frustration had morphed into pure rage, he would later be unable to say. But the moment he felt the cold steel in his hand, he knew he had no other choice.

'Turn the boat around,' he said, sounding significantly calmer than he felt.

The two men's eyes went straight to the gun in his hand.

'Hold on. Are you threatening us?' the portly one said with a glance at his colleague.

Fabian nodded. 'I want you to turn the boat around, and I want you to do it now.'

'You can't do this. It's not our fault. We're not the ones who decided to—'

'I'm fully aware of that. The idiot who did is called Kim Sleizner and he's just trying to mess with me. But that's my headache. All you have to worry about is turning the boat around and getting past that freight ship as quickly as humanly possible. And this—' He held the gun up. 'Think of it as a good argument for when you have to explain this to your boss later.'

The men looked at each other and when the portly one finally nodded, the other reversed their course. A few minutes later, they cut through the backwash from MS *Vinterland* and once again had an unobstructed view to the west.

Fabian spotted the rubber dinghy, which looked like it was heading north-west towards the Danish coast, almost immediately.

'There it is,' he said, pointing with his arm outstretched. 'Now all we have to do is catch up and I'll take care of—' He broke off when the phone on the communication panel began to ring.

'I figured,' said the portly man. 'It's the Danes. What do you want me to tell them?'

'Nothing. Ignore it.'

'But we can't just—'

'We can when I'm holding this.' Fabian waved his gun around, fully aware it was against every regulation and might net him six months behind bars. But it wasn't up to him any more. Milwokh had to be arrested. He'd deal with the consequences later.

'*Naval Operative Command calling KB 202. Over.*'

'Hadn't we better answer, so they know we're okay?'

'*KB 202, do you copy? Over.*'

'No one talks to them until I say so,' Fabian said, his binoculars trained on the rubber boat.

'*We notice that you're back in Danish territorial waters. What is the reason for that? Over.*'

'Look, I get that you're trying to arrest the bloke,' said the man with the moustache. 'But we can't just not answer. Just can't. It goes against every—'

'Fine, I'll do it. You just make sure we stay on this course.' Fabian walked over to the radio and picked up the microphone without lowering his binoculars. 'This is Fabian Risk aboard KB 202. You are correct, we are back in Danish waters. The reason is that we're in pursuit of a suspect attempting to escape in a rubber dinghy. His name is Pontus Milwokh and he is wanted for several murders. We will arrest him with or without your permission. I suggest you take up any problems you might have with that with my superiors. Over and out.'

'*We have received strict orders from our admiral and cannot accept—*'

'You might as well stop talking,' Fabian broke in, keeping his binoculars fixed on a dark shape that looked like a body curled up in the foetal position in the dinghy. 'I know exactly who issued that order. His name is Kim Sleizner and you can tell him I don't give a flying fuck about his pathetic territorial pissing. Besides, I thought out meant out. Over and out.'

He put the microphone down and levelled a stern look at the two men in the cabin, to make sure they didn't get any ideas, before raising his binoculars again.

A vague suspicion had been growing stronger in his mind for a while, but he'd pushed it down, hoping he was wrong. Hoping Pontus Milwokh really did lie curled up, defenceless, in the dinghy. That this would finally end.

But it turned out his gut was right.

The rubber dinghy was drifting aimlessly on the waves, abandoned, a rolled-up black blanket and a water bottle the only signs there had ever been a person on board.

34

IT WAS JUST before half past two in the morning, which meant Fabian had been up for almost twenty-four hours, so no wonder he was feeling tired. But that wasn't the reason he was so distracted he hadn't heard a word of what Klippan and Lilja had been saying.

'He could either duck his head under water and drown himself or he had to wait until the bath filled all the way to the cables and be electrocuted,' Klippan said, topping up his coffee mug.

His mind was somewhere else entirely.

'We'll know which one he opted for as soon as Flätan is done with the autopsy.' Lilja turned to Fabian and waved at him. 'Hello. Are you awake?'

Fabian nodded and tried to look engaged.

'Anyway,' Klippan went on. 'When we heard most signs point to Milwokh having drowned, we felt the best course of action was to get some shut-eye.'

'So we were in the middle of turning out the lights and leaving,' Lilja said.

At first, the thought had been so faint, he'd assumed it was nothing to get hung up on. A gut feeling he dismissed as a result of being stressed and disappointed and, above all, having had nothing to eat all day.

'That's when it hit me,' Lilja continued and turned to the

whiteboard, which was chock-full of the same seven letters in all kinds of combinations. 'It turns out Milwokh has scrambled the letters in his name more than once.'

The thought had come to him the moment the coastguard had radioed them about the attack on the Hallberg-Rassy in the middle of Öresund.

Lilja sighed. 'Am I the only one still awake here, or what?'

'No, I'm listening.' Fabian made a concerted effort to push his own musings aside. 'You're talking about Milwokh, who, if I understood you right, has changed his name again. So that's not really his name, or what?'

'It is. Or at least it has been since he was granted asylum. But...'

'And this is where it gets really interesting,' Klippan added.

But it was hard, virtually impossible. Because something wasn't right about the relative timing of the bathtub murder and the events out on Öresund.

'The thing is, that wasn't the first time Milwokh came to Sweden,' Lilja continued. 'As a matter of fact, he grew up in Skåne and has lived most of his life here.'

'Irene,' Klippan said. 'I think you'd better start from the beginning.'

'All right, sorry. As you know, he rented a car that was parked near the laundry room where Moonif Ganem was murdered, which made us bring him in for questioning. At that point, he was calling himself Pontus Holmwik, and that is what his fake driving licence said, too.' Lilja turned to the whiteboard and pointed to some of the many jumbles on it, with arrows pointing this way and that. 'A week or so later, Klippan realized it's the same exact letters that are on the door of the flat next to the one I just moved into. P. Milwokh. Are you with me so far?'

Fabian nodded.

'It turns out there are more combinations.'

'Five thousand and forty, to be exact,' Klippan interjected. 'And since we're talking about factorial calculations, the proper term is permutations.'

'As you can tell, we've spoken to Molander,' Lilja said. 'The point is that there's a 'permutation' that's slightly more interesting than the others. This one.' She underlined the name *Wikholm*. 'Maybe that rings a bell?'

Fabian had no choice but to shake his head.

'Oh, come on, Wikholm. You don't remember? Soni Wikholm.'

Lilja was right. Something about that name did sound familiar. He'd come across it in some case or other.

'Soni Wikholm was the name of the papergirl who discovered your old classmate Seth Kårheden murdered in his own home. You know, the one who had his moustache cut off.'

Fabian nodded. 'Wasn't she the one filming around Johan Halén's house out in Viken, as well?'

'Exactly, which was why we found her in a shallow grave outside Mörarp just over a month ago.'

'Fine, but what has she got to do with our killer?'

'They're brother and sister.' Lilja spread her hands. 'Soni Wikholm's brother is or was called Pontus Hao Wikholm. They were adopted together from China by Ing-Marie and Börje Wikholm out in Påarp. Isn't that nuts? I was actually at their parents' house just a few months ago, going through boxes of Soni's stuff in their basement. And one of the boxes belonged to her brother, and do you know what it was full of?'

Fabian shook his head.

'Dice.' Lilja paused for effect. 'Dice, dice and more dice. An insane amount of them, along with some well-read library copies of Luke Rhinehart's *The Dice Man*.' She spread her hands and accidentally knocked over Klippan's coffee, flooding the desk. 'Oh no, I'm sorry.'

'Don't worry about it,' Klippan replied, rushing over to try to save as many documents as possible. 'At least it's a big break in the case. I'll fetch a cloth.' He left the room.

'You don't seem very excited.' Lilja turned to Fabian. 'Don't you get it? We've finally figured out his MO. He uses dice. That's how he makes his decisions.'

Fabian nodded. 'Yes, I do get it. I came to the same conclusion myself when I found this in Ester Landgren's room earlier tonight.' He held up a small evidence bag containing the brushed-metal dice. 'And the boy on the yacht told me he used a dice there as well.'

'Okay. Then why didn't you say something?' Lilja snatched the evidence bag out of his hand and studied the dice.

'When was I supposed to do that? We've barely been in the same room until now.'

'Fabian, what's the matter?' Lilja handed the bag back.

'What do you mean?' He shrugged. 'Nothing.'

'Nothing?' Lilja nodded and bit her lip.

'Well, nothing, apart from Theodor being in police custody in Denmark, Matilda talking to ghosts and Sonja seeming to be doing worse than ever. Oh, actually, there's one more thing. I'm bloody tired and I'm going to have to go home and get some sleep soon.'

'Sure, we're all tired and we all want to go home and sleep.' Lilja pulled up a chair and sat down across from him. 'Did you know that this Sunday, we will have been working together for exactly two years, you and me?'

'No – like I said, I've been a bit busy, but, sure, that sounds about right.'

'I didn't know you then. I found you difficult. Maybe it's a Stockholm thing, but I felt like you were keeping us at arm's length.'

Fabian made as if to speak, but was silenced by a raised hand.

'I remember thinking you were an arrogant prick, actually.' She chuckled. 'For a while, I even suspected you of being behind the murders. Certain things seemed to suggest it. But I know you better now. Much better. And though two years may not be that long in the grand scheme of things, it's more than enough for me to be able to tell when something's wrong.'

'Irene, I don't know what you're talking about.' Fabian tried to look at her with honesty and weariness in equal measure. 'I'm sorry if we got off on the wrong foot. But maybe we can get into that more some other time, when things have quietened down a bit. As for right now, nothing's wrong. Other than the things I've already told you about.'

Lilja nodded. 'With all due respect to what you and your family are going through – it's awful in every possible way, and I don't know how I would have kept going in your position. But don't come in here and tell me that's all it is. That those things are what's on your mind, because if you do, I'm going to get proper mad at you.'

He was burning to tell her, but he couldn't. He wouldn't

know until tomorrow how Stubbs's meeting with Conny Öhman had gone.

'For fuck's sake, Fabian. I'm so sick of your bullshit.' Lilja got to her feet with a sigh. 'Sometimes I don't know why we work together at all.'

The door opened and Klippan entered with a coffee urn and a dish cloth. 'I made a fresh pot while I was at it, in case anyone wanted…' He trailed off and looked back and forth between Lilja and Fabian. 'What's going on? Did something happen?'

'No.' Lilja turned to Fabian. 'Fabian's just a bit tired and is going to head home and get some sleep.'

'Right – or, like I said, there's more coffee.' Klippan held up the urn and started wiping down Lilja's desk.

'I don't think Milwokh, or whatever you want to call him, was behind the bathtub murder,' Fabian said.

Lilja turned to Klippan and then back to Fabian. 'What makes you say that?'

'Several things suggest otherwise. None of the other victims had a choice of how to die, for instance. In all other cases, that was the dice's job. Not the victim's.'

'Fine, so it's different from the others. But they're all murders. And besides, they've all been different. You said so yourself, just yesterday. That there were no common denominators and that that was in fact the common denominator.'

'I know. And maybe that's true. Like I said, I'm not sure. But another thing that bothers me is the timing. I don't see how he could have committed both the bathtub murder and the sword attack on board the Hallberg-Rassy.'

'Wasn't it the same thing with Molly Wessman and

Lennart Andersson?' Klippan said. 'Didn't those murders happen on the same day, too?'

'They died on the same day, yes. But Wessman was poisoned a full twenty-four hours before.'

'Fine, but unless I've misunderstood, the bath happened in the evening and the yacht late at night.' Klippan refilled his cup. 'Milwokh might, for example, have picked up the rubber dinghy sometime in the afternoon and brought it over to the South Harbour and walked from there to the flat in Planteringen. Then when he was done, he could get straight back in the boat and head out to sea with his sword.'

'Do you know what time the power went out in the building?' Fabian asked.

'No, but it should be listed on the power company's website.' Klippan went over to the computer and did a search. 'Tryckerigatan, right?'

Lilja nodded.

'Cable fire. That must be it, and if this is to be believed, repairs will be completed "within an hour".'

'Does it say when it happened?'

'The report was received at eighteen minutes past six last night. So sometime after six would be a reasonable guess.'

'I'll leave the proper examination of the rubber dinghy to Molander, but I did find this in one of the storage compartments.' Fabian pulled out a folded plastic document sleeve containing several sheets of paper.

'What are they?' Lilja took it.

'Insurance papers and some general information from the boat rental company. And there are copies of the first two payments from Monday and Tuesday along with the final payment of three thousand eight hundred from yesterday.'

'And when was that payment made?'

'Fourteen minutes past six. Which is more less exactly when the cables caught fire.'

'There goes the theory that he picked up the boat first,' Lilja said.

Klippan nodded. 'Okay, so he must have done the bath first and then gone out to Rå river to get the boat.'

'How long would it take to get from Planteringen to the Råå Marina?'

'I'd say no more than ten minutes by car,' Klippan replied.

'But there's nothing to suggest he rented a car.'

'Fine, say he took a bike and add five minutes. So, fifteen minutes, no more than that.'

'That means he must have left the flat absolutely no later than six,' Fabian said.

'It's tight, but possible,' Klippan said. 'Depending on how long it took the bath to fill up, he could theoretically have left half an hour, forty-five minutes earlier.'

'You're saying he didn't stay to watch the bath fill up and his victim make his choice?' Lilja asked.

'I don't know.' Klippan shrugged. 'I guess if time was short, something had to give.'

'I'm not going to claim I know how his mind works, but shouldn't part of the point of devising and executing such an elaborate death dilemma be to sit and watch how it comes out?'

'Sure, but again, maybe he didn't have time.' Klippan pulled out his phone. 'Maybe something made the whole thing take longer than planned. Maybe the victim got home an hour later than expected. And who knows? Maybe the dice said no, forcing him to leave the flat.'

'Either way, he must have left the tap running if he left the flat before it was over,' Fabian said. 'But if he stayed to watch, he could have turned the water off when it was done. But that would mean he couldn't possibly have made it to the boat rental company in time.'

'Which supports your theory about a second killer.' Lilja sighed and shook her head. 'I just have a hard time imagining that there would be a second lunatic out there capable of something like this. I know you don't agree, but I still say it's too similar to the other cases to indicate a different perpetrator. A lot of the details are different, sure, but we can't ignore the fact that there's a running theme from Evert Jonsson, who was rotting inside a hermetically sealed plastic cylinder, all the way to Mattias Larsson, who was either drowned or electrocuted in his own bath.'

'Could it be a copycat inspired by the other murders?' Klippan asked, with his phone pressed to his ear.

'I guess, but we've made virtually none of the details public. If it's a copycat, it has to be someone with insight into our investigations. Besides, shouldn't there be a limit to how many serial killers we can have in this country? Until two years ago, we hadn't had a single one. Now, they're suddenly springing up like mushrooms.'

The silence that followed begged to be filled with words. But Klippan was staring at his phone again and Fabian was so preoccupied he had a hard time keeping up.

There was only one person with insight into all the investigations who might have done it. Ingvar Molander. He would have no problem planning and staging something like the bathtub murder. Moreover, it fitted with the murder of Inga Dahlberg and a few years later the attempted murder of Ingela Polghed. They had both been similar to other open cases, which had effectively pointed them to other perpetrators.

Could that be why he'd been absent all afternoon and evening? Had the grief at being left by Gertrud been an excuse so he wouldn't have to account for his whereabouts?

'Who are you calling?'

Lilja broke the silence, and the moment he realized what Klippan's answer would be, he also realized it was too late.

'Molander,' came Klippan's answer, like an echo of his own thoughts. 'He was first at the scene, so he should be able to tell us if the tap was on or not.'

'Should we really be bothering him in the middle of the night, considering everything he's going through?' he said in an attempt to redirect Klippan.

'Since when do you care about things like that?' Lilja said.

'I just figured we could call Tuvesson instead, since she was there, too.'

'Hi, Klippan here. I hope I didn't wake you... Oh dear. I understand.' Klippan made a face at the others and made a weighing gesture. 'The thing is that we were discussing the bathtub murder and certain signs point to there being a second perp. A copycat. Hold on, it's better if we can all hear you.' He turned on the speakerphone and put the mobile down on the desk. 'Hello, Ingvar, can you hear us?'

'*Yes, unfortunately,*' Molander replied in a weary voice.

'It's just a quick question, then you can go back to your beauty sleep.'

'*First, I'd like to know exactly what things point to a second perpetrator.*'

'The relative timing of the Öresund attack. He can't have been in two places at once.'

'*What do you mean, at once? One thing happened in the evening and the other several hours later.*'

'Right, but we have a receipt for the final instalment of the boat rental fee – but maybe Fabian should explain. It's his theory.' Klippan nodded to Fabian.

'Hi, Ingvar,' he said, and he cleared his throat to shake off the fatigue. 'So, according to a receipt I found, he picked the boat up at more or less exactly the same time the power went out at Tryckerigatan.'

'*So? What's to say the timestamp on the receipt is correct? Maybe they just forgot to set the internal clock to daylight saving time. Or he could have left the flat long before the water rose high enough to short-circuit the cables.*'

'That's what we were saying, too,' Klippan said. 'So what we wanted to ask you was whether the tap was running when Tuvesson and you arrived, or whether it had been turned off.'

The silence that followed wasn't long, but noticeable.

'*It was running,*' Molander said finally. '*Not fully turned on, but maybe halfway.*'

'Okay, great,' Klippan said. 'That's all cleared up, then. Or what do you reckon, Fabian?'

'Absolutely,' he replied, even though Molander's reply didn't make the slightest bit of difference.

'*I'd actually assumed the point was to give the victim plenty of time to choose,*' Molander said. '*But maybe the real reason was that he wanted to do two things at once?*'

He knew exactly what he had to do now.

35

EARLY DAWN WAS in full bloom when Fabian turned his bike down Tryckerigatan from Västra Fridhemsgatan and saw the white van from the power company pull out of the car park and drive off in the opposite direction.

He wanted nothing more than a few hours of sleep. But that had to wait. Since Klippan had called Molander and spilled the beans, it was time to spring the trap. Not a few days or a week from now. This was it.

As ever, it all came down to the evidence. The case against Molander would have to be more than adequate. If he were to stand a chance of persuading the rest of the team of their colleague's guilt, it would have to be watertight, and then some.

If his suspicions turned out to be correct, this could be the proof he'd been looking for. And time was on his side for once. Unlike previous cases, where he'd had to make do with old case files and pictures, this crime scene was only a few hours old. In other words, there was a good chance there might still be fresh clues to find.

To be safe, he'd left the car at home and taken his bike instead, which had turned out to be surprisingly efficient. He'd made it in fifteen minutes and, as a fringe benefit, the fresh air had blown away some of the cobwebs.

He entered the building and noted that the power

company had been true to their word. Two steps into the lobby was enough to trigger the motion sensor controlling the flickering fluorescent lights overhead.

He found the door marked *M. Larsson* on the second floor. The lock had been changed, as was regular procedure, so he could use his crime scene key to get in.

To avoid attracting unnecessary attention, he left the lights off and made do with a flashlight. He wasn't there to do a thorough search of the whole flat. At least, not right now. The murder had taken place in the bathroom, and that was where he was going.

It was located a few steps down the hall on the left. Flätan, or one of his guys, had already removed the body. But it didn't matter. Whether the victim had drowned or burned to a crisp from the inside was completely beside the point as far as Fabian was concerned.

The only thing that interested him was the tap.

Right now, everything hinged on that tap.

Had the killer left it running or had he stayed until the bath was full before turning it off and leaving? According to Molander, it had still been running when Tuvesson and he arrived. If that turned out to be true, most things pointed to this being Milwokh's handiwork. If not, he had everything he needed to make an arrest.

He leaned closer to the bath and aimed his torch at the three stripped cables taped to the inside. One at the bottom and the other two about an inch from the top at either end.

The fact that they'd been placed higher than the bath's overflow drain, which had consequently had to be sealed with silicone, indicated that the killer had wanted the bath to fill to the brim before the top two cables came into contact with the water. Possibly to make it easier for the victim to drown himself. Or, more likely, to drag the whole thing out so the victim had plenty of time to agonize over his decision.

But those were just more or less likely suppositions. What was beyond doubt was that if the killer had left the tap running, the water must have overflowed and flooded the floor in the hours that followed.

He squatted down and scrutinized the narrow gap between the edge of the bath itself and the decorative panel suspended underneath. But he could neither see nor feel any damp, which was perhaps no wonder since it had been quite a while since Molander claimed to have turned off the tap.

He put the flashlight down on the floor, carefully unhooked the panel and leaned it against the wall. Then he got down on his hands and knees and leaned over until his head hit the floor so he could see all the way to the wall in the light from the torch.

A foot or so from the edge of the bath, there was a floor drain through which the water from the bath was expelled via a pipe. That would explain why the bathroom and large areas of the flat had not flooded – if indeed the bath had overflowed at all – but the drain itself wasn't what interested him.

It was the dust.

There was quite a lot of it. In places, it had gathered into large dust bunnies that drifted across the floor in the draught of his breath.

His suspicions seemed to be bearing out. To be completely sure, he took out his phone, aimed it in under the bath and took a series of pictures that he could then zoom in on and study in detail.

A thick, untouched layer of dust covered almost the entire area under the bath, and there was no sign of water having trickled through it anywhere.

That indicated the killer had stayed and turned the tap off once the cables had short-circuited and everything was over. Which in turn meant the killer couldn't be Pontus Milwokh.

Molander had lied to the three of them and the pictures on his phone proved it. The idea had likely been to make it look like another Milwokh killing, and it would have succeeded if Milwokh himself hadn't struck again at practically the same time.

He found Tuvesson's number, dialled it and listened while it rang. There was no reason to hold off any longer.

Molander was probably at home, asleep. He had keys, so getting into the house and catching him off guard wouldn't be a problem.

'*You've reached Astrid Tuvesson's voicemail. I'm unable to take your call right—*'

Fabian ended the call and redialled. He'd give it three more tries. If she didn't pick up, he'd have no choice but to go over to her house and—

'If I were you, I'd hang up as quickly as I could.'

He recognized the voice, but couldn't place it. He understood, and yet he didn't. Not until he turned around and stared straight into the long cylindrical silencer attached to the gun in Molander's hand.

'*Yes, hello...*' came Tuvesson's incoherent voice from his phone. '*Who is this... Bloody hell, it's the middle of the... Hello?*'

The bike. He'd taken his damn bike. The thought kept echoing through his head, louder and louder, as he watched

Molander wave his gun at the phone in his hand. He was stunned and felt like an oil tanker that had to make a sudden 180-degree turn to avoid running aground. But it was already too late. Long before he'd even had a chance to throw the engines in reverse and start turning, it was too late.

'Is that you, Fabian? Are you calling me again? Hello?'

Should he scream? Was that the right thing to do? Scream and tell her as much as he had time to before Molander emptied his magazine? But how much of it would she be able to catch? Would she even remember that he'd called when she woke up in the morning?

He held up his phone in the dark and pushed the red phone symbol.

'There we go. Good boy. That's wasn't so hard, now, was it?' Molander shot him a smile. 'But then, we already knew you're a good boy. Or you wouldn't be here.' He pulled a stool out of the far corner. 'Have a seat.'

Fabian glanced at the stool and then at Molander with the gun in his hand. Had he been in the flat the whole time? Waiting in the dark for him to turn up. To end things.

In a way, it was the logical conclusion to this story. He was next. And Stubbs. Had he already found and done away with her? Was that why she hadn't picked up when he called earlier?

Regardless, he couldn't just give up. Whatever happened, whatever Molander had planned, it was time for this to end. The problem was that they were standing too far apart for him to knock the gun out of Molander's hand without taking a step forward first. And his own gun was in its holster underneath his jacket. No matter how fast he moved, he'd never make it.

'There's no point. I wouldn't even consider it.' Molander raised the gun and aimed it at Fabian's head. 'Don't take it personally, but I wouldn't hesitate. Granted, this isn't how I planned to do it. But it wouldn't present too much of a problem. So I'll tell you again, for the last time. Please, have a seat.'

'You're never going to get away with this.' Fabian did as he was told and sat down. 'You do know that, right?'

'And your phone, please.' Molander held out his free hand and Fabian gave him his phone.

'Just like I took over after Elvin, someone's going to come after me.'

'And last but not least, that little peashooter of yours. Would you mind opening your jacket with your left hand while you hold your right hand above your head.'

Fabian let Molander undo his chest holster, take his gun and empty it before sticking it down the back of his trousers.

'There, now. Much better! No more unnecessary tension. Right? Now, let's just delete those pictures sitting there taking up precious memory. What's your pin?'

'Ingvar. Wouldn't it be better to just give up? You can't go on like this.'

'Your pin.' Molander took a step forward and pushed the muzzle of his gun against Fabian's left temple. 'If you don't mind.'

'7 3 8 5.'

Molander unlocked the phone and deleted the pictures of the dust under the bath.

'Now what? What are you going to do now?'

'Don't worry. You'll understand in due course. All in due course.'

Molander walked over to the bath, took the showerhead down and slung it over the edge of the bath. Then he turned on the tap, which started splashing onto the floor and in under the bath. 'I honestly hadn't thought about the dust under the bath. And I usually think of everything.' He stepped away to avoid getting splashed and moved in behind Fabian. 'But you did – so much so, you came out here in the middle of the night to check if your theory was correct. It's impressive, I have to give you that. Very impressive.'

'Why?' Fabian said, as Molander started to take off his jacket. 'You're not the first person to have an affair. And I'm sure you're not the first person to be caught by their father-in-law.'

'I'm probably not the first to kill my father-in-law, either,' Molander chuckled as he started unbuckling and removing his holster. 'Far from it. But you want to know the truth, do you?'

'Please,' Fabian nodded, as Molander drew his arms behind his back. 'Explain to me how things went so very wrong.' Moments later, he felt a cable tie tighten around his wrists.

'What makes you so convinced things have gone wrong?' Molander walked around and sank into a squat in front of Fabian. 'Apart from a detail here and there, I'd say most things have gone to plan.'

'You might not be best placed to make that assessment objectively.'

'Tell me.' Molander took a few more cable ties out of his jacket pocket. 'Which colour of Ahlgrens bilar sweets do you prefer? White, green or pink?'

'And what does that have to do with anything?'

'Answer me.' Molander aimed his gun at Fabian's head once more. 'White, green or pink?'

'Neither. They taste exactly the same. The only difference is a bit of food colouring.'

'That's right. But you're forgetting something important. The visual impression actually affects the perception of flavour. At least in this case. I personally prefer the green. The white are okay, but the pink ones. Never.'

'And how does that justify murdering your father-in-law?'

'We were discussing who is wrong and who the more objective.' Molander tied Fabian's legs to the stool. 'You, who can't taste the difference, or me, who would be able to tell them apart blindfolded?' First the right, then the left. 'As far as Einar Stenson is concerned, he had it coming.'

Molander stood up and put the gun back in his holster. 'Did you know he had the temerity to summon me to his summer house and confront me with a bunch of pictures of me and Inga? Talk about doing the wrong thing. Sneaking around, spying on me. As though my life were any of his business. As though he didn't screw around like a bloody rabbit on all those trips he went on.'

Molander shook his head and had to compose himself before he could continue. 'He even tried to blackmail me into divorcing Gertrud. He threatened to tell her everything if I refused. I just lost it and stabbed him with a kitchen knife.'

Fabian was on the verge of saying something, but was silenced by a raised hand.

'I know exactly what you're thinking, and from a certain vantage point, you're right. It was clearly an overreaction. But looking back, I feel no remorse whatsoever. And you know what?' He leaned down until his face was level with Fabian's. 'I'm convinced you would have felt the same in my position. Einar Stenson was an evil bastard. You couldn't tell from looking at him, but behind that warm, friendly smile... Nasty brute, that's all I have to say.' He straightened up, turned his back on Fabian and went over to the bath, where he repositioned the showerhead to make the water flood different parts of the floor. Then he reached for one of the three cables taped to the bath.

Maybe this was his chance. Now, when Molander's back was turned and he was focused on the cables. The thought came to him in the form of a question, but the decision had already been made. He threw himself down and started slamming the stool into the floor as hard as he could, again and again.

Out of the corner of his eye, he saw Molander turn around. Maybe he'd pulled out his gun, too. He couldn't tell, and it didn't matter. He just had to keep banging the stool against the floor. If he could break it, he should be able to kick Molander's legs out from under him and escape into the stairwell.

But the stool refused to break and then Molander was on top of him, holding his legs down until lactic acid rendered them useless.

'Take Gertrud, for example,' Molander went on, nodding for him to sit back up. 'He abused her psychologically from the day she met me. Treated her like air. And that's nothing to how he treated me, even though I did everything a perfect son-in-law should. Everything.'

Fabian tried to sit up, but with his hands tied behind his

back and his legs tied to the stool, it was impossible, and in the end Molander had to help him.

'I went to every goddam Sunday dinner. I sat through them, nodding and pretending to listen to his tedious ramblings. I worked on the house with him and replaced his entire roof. One summer, I dug up the entire bloody foundation by hand because he needed to install drainage but was too stingy to pay a professional. My back has never been the same since.'

Molander turned to a toiletry kit that hung on a hook behind him and took out a small syringe and a tiny glass phial. 'And do you think he ever thanked me? He most certainly bloody didn't.' He pushed the needle into the phial, filled the syringe and squirted a few drops out to remove the air bubbles inside.

'What's in the syringe?'

'The chemical formula is very complex and would require a medium-sized whiteboard to explain. So you'll have to satisfy yourself with knowing that it's a substance I was hoping not to have to use. Unfortunately, however, your behaviour leaves me no choice. Where were we?'

'He was ungrateful,' Fabian supplied, not taking his eyes off the syringe until Molander disappeared behind his back.

'Right. Thank you. So I stood there, watching him thrash around on the floor with the kitchen knife in his stomach, and the bigger the pool of blood grew, the happier I felt.'

Fabian could feel Molander pull his shirt out of his trousers, stick his cold hand into the gap and feel his lower vertebrae.

'Once the old man kicked the bucket, I cleaned up and rearranged the scene. For instance, I polished the floor no less than three times to make sure it was extra slippery. Then

I placed him face down across the open dishwasher door, on top of the cutlery basket. I collected as much of the blood as I could and made sure to keep it moving in the blender to keep it from coagulating until I could pour it over the dishwasher. Stay still now, please.'

There was a pinch when the needle plunged in between his vertebrae, followed almost immediately by a searing pain that quickly intensified. As though it were some kind of acid, corroding everything in its path.

'In a way, it was similar to the way I approach crime scenes as a forensic scientist,' Molander continued, as he pulled another glass phial from the toiletry kit and filled the syringe. 'Just in reverse. It was one of the most fun things I'd ever done. For once, I was in full control and knew exactly what to do.'

The pain subsided, morphing into a dull, thudding numbness.

'It was as though I could see into the future to when Ragnar Söderström from South-west Götaland Police would arrive at the scene.' Molander turned to the toiletry kit again. 'I could almost hear him concluding it was a tragic accident in which Einar Stenson slipped on the newly polished floor and fell onto the cutlery basket, where the kitchen knife happened to be standing point up. It was magnificent.'

When Molander turned around, he was holding a pair of pointed tweezers, and he suddenly stabbed Fabian in the thigh, without warning. 'And you know what it's like. Once you've taken a bite of that apple, it's hard not to take another.' He pulled the tweezers out with a smile and wiped the blood on Fabian's trousers. 'There we are.'

Fabian watched the blood bloom into a dark stain that

kept expanding. But he could feel almost nothing and realized he couldn't move his legs.

'It's a shame you're not pregnant. Then we could have delivered you while we're at it.'

An epidural. Of course that was what he'd given him. He looked up at Molander. 'So you kill your father-in-law, realize you enjoy it and just keep killing people,' he said, feeling his lower body grow increasingly numb. 'What's wrong with you?'

Molander laughed and went over to the bath, where he gently pulled the three cables free, one after the other. 'You have no idea how easy it is to cross over to the other side. There's a line, no doubt about it. But unlike what most people think, it's neither wide nor demarcated by a high wall you have to climb. No, as a matter of fact, it's incredibly fine.'

'Maybe for you, Ingvar. For the rest of us, for healthy people, that line's pretty clear.'

'I happen to be the one who has experienced both sides,' Molander retorted while he studied the three cables and removed another half-inch of insulation with a small knife. 'And I can promise you, I know what I'm talking about. The difference is marginal.' He pulled a roll of thick tape from the bag hanging next to the toiletry kit and once again disappeared behind Fabian's back. 'From my perspective, it's the same bodies and more or less the same scenarios. The same suffering. The only difference is that this is so much more fun.'

'And Inga Dahlberg?' Fabian said, as he heard Molander tear off a strip of tape. 'Did she threaten to expose your little affair, too?' Then he felt a cold wire being pressed against his right wrist and secured there with tape.

'In a way, she did, actually,' Molander replied, taping the other cable to Fabian's left wrist. 'You know how it goes.' He came around to stand in front of Fabian, holding the last cable. 'At first, it's novel and exciting. Then it starts to feel more and more like a chore, and without really knowing how you got there, you find yourself in some kind of polygamous marriage.' He sighed and shook his head. 'I tried to end it amicably. But she refused to let go and became increasingly – well, how to put it – fanatical and crazed, so in the end, I had no choice.'

'But you didn't just leave her. You didn't even just kill her. Apparently, you felt a need to rape and torture her as well.'

'Yes, perhaps I did overdo it, but still, I feel pretty good about it. I pulled off a virtually impossible plan without making a single mistake.'

'You must have made some kind of mistake. If you hadn't, why would Elvin have started investigating you?'

At the mention of Elvin's name, Molander's eyes suddenly darkened. 'The intended scapegoat happened to have an alibi, a ridiculous little alibi that wasn't even half as good as my Berlin one. It was unfortunate, and I suppose it aroused Elvin's suspicions.' Molander shook his head. 'It was the first time something didn't work out as planned.'

'And the second time?'

'Ingela Ploghed. But that was entirely my own fault.' Molander squatted down and pulled up Fabian's left trouser leg a foot or so. 'It was stupid and unnecessary, but what can I say?' He spread his hands in a resigned gesture. 'I'm only human.' He pulled down Fabian's sock and tore off a piece of tape. 'The problem was that I got sloppy, which in turn fanned Elvin's suspicions. I don't know if you remember, but you voiced concern about it not matching the other murders yourself.'

'I do remember,' Fabian said, as Molander taped the last wire to his exposed shin. 'And now what? What are you going to do now? Are you going to kill me, too? Like you killed Elvin?'

'Never start with the dessert, as my mother liked to say.' Molander stood up and shook his head. 'True, I could do it now, no problem. Just a quick flick of that switch over there.' Molander nodded to the light switch on the wall. 'That's all it would take to start ten minutes of hell that would turn you into nothing but a memory in the minds of your loved ones.'

'And you seriously expect everyone to buy it? That I came over here in the middle of the night and committed suicide by hooking myself up to electrical cables? Or that I tied myself up first? And how are you going to explain that I managed to hit a switch all the way over there?'

Molander answered with a smile. 'The dust under the bath. I'll give you that one. But that's the only thing I've overlooked. How was I to know our little Asian friend was going to strike again last night? If it wasn't for that, the dust wouldn't have mattered.' He shrugged. 'But everything else, and I really do mean everything else, has been planned out down to the smallest detail.' He levelled Fabian with an intent stare. 'For the past few days, I've directed your every move. Practically every thought you've had was put in your head by me. Or maybe you thought you came here of your own free will?' He chuckled. 'Nothing could be further from the truth.'

'I came here because of the dust. Your mistake. Nothing else.'

'Are you sure of that? Granted, the events out on Öresund had you questioning the timeline, which in turn led to the question of whether the tap was left on or not. But the only difference that made was that you got here tonight instead of sometime tomorrow like I'd planned. Luckily, Klippan's call tipped me off, so I made it here in time.'

'Why would I have come tomorrow, if not for what happened out on Öresund?'

'Maybe because the fact that the victim was given a choice of how to die had your antennae up?' Molander waited, studying Fabian's reaction for a few seconds. 'Yes. I thought so. Lilja, Klippan and Tuvesson swallowed it, hook, line and sinker. But not you, and you weren't meant to. I know you well enough by now. That thought would have festered and eventually you would have remembered those notes and electrical formulas and calculations you found on my nightstand when you came to my house yesterday.'

Molander knew he'd been there. Even though he'd left his car at home, he knew.

'There we go. The penny finally drops. I even think I wrote something about the impedance of the human body, didn't I? You don't have to look so shocked. If you give it some thought, I'm sure you don't actually believe I would let something like that lie about in plain sight. Come on, you know me.' Molander spread his hands. 'But let's instead ponder the fact that I and the other members of our team will find you here in a few days' time, slumped over the edge of the bath with a wire clutched in either hand.'

'How are you going to explain that to the others?'

'The logical explanation is that you came here, on your own initiative as usual, and were examining the electrical set-up with your prying little hands at the very moment the power was turned back on.'

'And this wound?' Fabian nodded to his thigh where the dark bloodstain now measured four inches across. 'You don't think Flätan's going to notice? Or the missing hair where you pulled off the tape?'

'I'm sorry to have to disappoint you. But you're not going to end up on Flätan's table. I'm going to make sure it's his less meticulous colleague, Arne Gruvesson, who examines you, to the best of his ability, let's hope.'

Molander was probably right. No one would think it was anything but a tragic accident, that he'd obstinately insisted on acting on his own without informing anyone else on the team, as usual. 'So what are you waiting for?' he said. 'Why don't you just go over and flick that switch and get it over with?'

Molander brightened. 'Ah, yes. We're finally making some progress. Let me lay it out for you. As you are well aware, we're in the middle of a complex murder investigation involving a perpetrator who has no qualms about killing an innocent child for his own amusement, and if I'm right about you, you want to see it wrapped up at any cost.'

'Well, then I can inform you the case is pretty much wrapped up already, since most signs point to him having drowned.'

'That's true. At least it looks that way. But we don't know. Not for sure. Isn't that right? And until we do, until we find his body, or at least some part of it, washed up on a beach either here or in Denmark, I want us to keep working together.'

Fabian wasn't sure he'd heard him right. Was he actually seriously suggesting they keep working together after this?

'Fabian, you are without a doubt the sharpest member of our team. My ego might not allow me to show it much, but the truth is that you often both surprise and impress me in our meetings. You draw conclusions and see connections the rest of us miss, and I'm completely convinced we won't be able to finish this without you.'

'You really believe I'm just going to cycle on home and go to bed after this?'

'Of course, what else can you do?' Molander smiled. 'And when you wake up tomorrow, you're going to eat your breakfast, hug your beautiful wife and kiss your daughter's forehead, just like you always do, before getting in your car and driving over to the station.'

'And what makes you think I won't inform the others and have you arrested the first chance I get?'

Molander replied with a smile. 'As much as this investigation needs you, it will never succeed without me.'

'We're going to catch him with or without you.'

'Of course you will. But he won't be convicted. You're only going to be able to hold him for three days. Then Högsell's going to realize there's no binding evidence and demand that you release him immediately.' Molander leaned in closer. 'Every fingerprint and every DNA sample. Every little hair I've found tying him to the different crime scenes. Poof.' He described a small explosion with one hand. 'So it's up to you if he gets to carry on or not.'

'Like I said, a lot points to him having drowned.'

Molander snorted derisively. 'You don't even believe that yourself. That he 'accidentally' fell out of the rubber dinghy after first taping the throttle down while also managing to take all his gear with him. No, what you should be thinking about right now is your own life. And Sonja's, of course. Not to mention little Matilda's.'

'If you lay so much as a finger on either of them, I'm going to—'

'What? Tell me. What are you going to do when you're in a freezer, waiting to be cremated? How are you going to stop me from having my fun with them? Correct me if I'm wrong, but isn't Matilda starting to grow breasts?'

Fabian started to struggle furiously against his bonds.

'And then there's Theodor,' Molander went on. 'What will become of him when he gets out and you're not there? If he ever does get out, that is.'

With his arms tied behind his back and a lower body that no longer belonged to him, Fabian was helpless.

'Or wait, I have an idea.' Molander held up a finger. 'It's a good one, too. Both Sonja and Matilda believe in ghosts, right? So maybe you'll be able to help them from the spirit realm.'

Fabian studied Molander, who was laughing at his own joke. The yellow teeth packed in so tightly they almost didn't fit. The eyes that were both weary and manic. The victory he was already savouring.

How had he ended up here? How had he let things get to the point where the only thing he could do was acquiesce, no matter what Molander demanded?

'And then what?' he said. 'After we arrest him. Then what happens?'

'I've been waiting for you to ask.' Molander paused and nodded, as though he needed to choose his words carefully. 'You hinted at it yourself just now.' He crossed his arms and sighed. 'I can't go on like this forever. I know that, too.'

Fabian was about to speak, but Molander raised his hand pre-emptively.

'I know what you're thinking. That I've lost my mind and have to be considered a raving lunatic. But it's not like that. Not at all, actually. I'm fully aware what I've done is wrong and heinous in every way. That it goes against every sound value and all the things I once believed in.'

'And yet you've carried on.'

'Yes.' Molander nodded. 'Like an alcoholic who wants to quit but can't resist temptation. I didn't realize it at the time, but the moment I stuck that knife into Einar, I opened myself up to something stronger and more addictive than anything else. And the best and probably only way to get clean is, in fact, to come clean and face my punishment, whatever that might be. I'm fully prepared for a life sentence.'

'So why not turn yourself in and let us have the evidence?'

Molander nodded. 'I could, sure. And seen from your perspective, there's obviously no downside. The thing is, though, I don't want to. Like I said before, I've invested too much in this case to jump ship on the final stretch.' He squatted down and leaned in against Fabian's legs. 'I don't know if you've realized, but this is the case of a lifetime. It trumps everything else, and when we tell the media how these cases are connected, all hell's going to break loose. I promise you, books will be written about this. Dissertations. Films. There's no telling how big this will be.'

STEFAN AHNHEM

'Okay, I guess that matters if you're the kind of person who wants to go on morning shows and be famous. But the only thing I—'

'Fabian, what I'm trying to tell you is that we're experiencing something that's never going to happen again. If you think I'm sick for saying that, okay, fine, maybe I am. But just so you know, you're the same.' He jabbed a finger into Fabian's chest and then his own. 'You and me, even though you hate me with a burning hatred right now, we're birds of a feather. When I look at you, I see someone as manic as myself. You have that tunnel vision I recognize from when I'm about to blinker everything but the investigation I'm working on. Imagine if you were the one who had to walk away now, just when everything's coming together…' Molander shook his head. 'You can't, can you? So all I ask is that we finish what we started. No more, no less.'

'So we're supposed to just keep working like nothing's happened?'

'More or less, yes. Though we should be able to focus much better now that we've cleared the air and know where we stand.' He shot Fabian a smile and stood up. 'Why else would I be doing all of this?' He spread his hands. 'If I just wanted to kill you so I could walk away scot-free, all I'd have to do is flick that switch over there. And the reason I don't want to do that isn't that I'd miss you, or feel guilty. Maybe I should, but unfortunately, I don't. No, the only reason is that I'm convinced you're needed to close this case. No offence to Klippan, Lilja and Tuvesson, but without you, we're not going to solve this.'

'And how am I supposed to trust you? How can I be sure

250

you'll uphold your end of the bargain and turn yourself in once this is over?'

'The simple answer is that you can't. On the other hand, what choice do you have?'

PART IV

27–28 June 2012

A FEW HOURS *after the failed grenade attack on the Austro-Hungarian Crown Prince Franz Ferdinand on 28 June 1914, the route his driver was to use to take the Archduke and his wife from the Governor's residence was altered. But in the heat of the moment, the driver accidentally turned down the wrong street.*

At the same time, Gavrilo Princip, one of several Bosnian-Serb nationalists out to get Ferdinand, had decided to have lunch at Moritz Schiller's café when the car carrying the Archduke turned in and got stuck in traffic right in front of him.

Were the two fatal shots that followed the result of pure chance? And if so, should the subsequent events be considered happenstance as well? That is to say, the outbreak of the First World War, which in turn shaped Adolf Hitler and thus would come to affect every aspect of twentieth-century European history.

Was it all just coincidence?

If you believe Charles Darwin, we, too, are the product of chance on the molecular level. We have evolved and developed through random mutations and natural selection.

The question one has to ask oneself is whether everything, all the way back to the origin of the universe, is one big fluke.

36

BEATA SANDSTRÖM WAS standing on the bridge, scanning the sea with the binoculars her husband had given her before this, her first journey as captain of the MS *Vinterland*. In front of her, Anholt island appeared like a few swift pencil strokes against the horizon, and behind her Sweden was dissolving into a light blue haze.

She shouldn't be alone on the bridge; it was against regulations on a freighter this size. But the behaviour of her first mate, Piter Grynhoff, had been so infuriating she'd finally seen no other way but to order him back to his cabin half an hour before the end of his shift.

She checked her watch and realized she had another fifteen minutes before it was time for her second mate to join her. And him, she liked. Jan-Ove Bengtsson was Grynhoff's polar opposite and thankfully refrained from the territorial pissing so many men seemed compelled to engage in just because she was a woman whose orders they had to obey.

Maybe she should call up one of the sailors to keep Bengtsson company so she could get a few hours of rest. But she wouldn't be able to fall asleep anyway. Exhausted as she was after the stress of the past few hours, she was still too wound up.

Maybe it was no wonder. This was, after all, her first journey as captain, and though she'd encountered both conflicts and problems, she'd successfully steered the ship through one of the world's most difficult and heavily trafficked sounds without a major incident.

Granted, they were over two hours behind schedule, which was decidedly more than could be considered passable, and even though they were now doing eighteen knots, they weren't going to be able to make up more than about thirty minutes before it was time to dock in Fredrikshamn.

Two hours. In the grand scheme of things, it was nothing, but in her world it was if not a full-blown disaster, then at least a minor one. Like in the air freight business, the big costs were associated with loading and unloading. The exorbitant port fees, the crane rental and the unloading space for the containers. Not to mention the labour costs. That was where the millions were spent, and in less than twenty minutes from now, they were going to start pouring straight into the harbour as all the hired men sat around idle, waiting for the ship to arrive.

But she would get through this. In fact, she could already feel herself starting to put it behind her and find her way back to equanimity. As though this journey through the sound had given her more experience than all her other journeys put together.

The anxiety had come on the moment they'd sighted the old lighthouse in Falsterbo, and right on cue she felt the first stirrings of both acid reflux and stomach cramps, which had made her question her competence. She, who had finally achieved her dream of being the senior officer on a 500-foot, 10,000-ton freight ship travelling through a heavily trafficked sound. Suddenly, she'd lost all faith in herself and wished she could have been anywhere but there.

When the 121-foot-tall ship passed under the 180-foot span of the Öresund Bridge, sweat had been dripping from her forehead from tension that would not subside until several hours later.

Grynhoff had sensed her anxiety, of course. *I promise. We're not going to hit the bridge*, he'd told her with a smile so condescending she'd felt an urge to keelhaul him. But she'd let the attack pass without comment, knowing the journey through the narrow sound would likely involve situations where she'd need him.

Like passing through the shallowest part of Flintrännan soon thereafter. It was no deeper than 27.5 feet on an average day and considering that the ship when fully loaded had a draught of 22.3 feet, the 5.2-foot margin was on the small side. And with the water level being unusually low, she'd been seriously concerned they were going to run aground and need to be towed.

But everything had gone to plan, and later on, as they passed through the bottleneck between Helsingborg and Helsingør, she'd allowed herself a quick visit to the captain's cabin to wash her armpits, put on fresh deodorant and change her shirt. The sound finally opened out into Kattegat. She would be able to keep the timetable and put her captain's hat back on without apologizing.

But she hadn't even had time to do that when the pitch of the monotonous rumbling of the engines had suddenly changed as their speed was halved. She'd immediately called Grynhoff and demanded an explanation. But none had been forthcoming. Instead, he'd asked her to present herself on the bridge. *Present herself*. Those had been his exact words. As though he were in charge and not her.

By the time she'd made it back up to the bridge, their speed had already decreased by one knot and she had immediately ordered Grynhoff to restore the engine speed. But he had refused, informing her of an all-ships urgency message from the coastguard asking all vessels to slow down.

In hindsight, it had clearly been an attempt to cause a delay. Things had come off too well and it had been up to him to trip her up. But at the time, she'd believed him. Even when he claimed it was something about a suspected murderer being on the loose after attacking a family with a sword in the middle of Öresund, she'd assumed he was telling the truth and ordered the crew to keep a lookout.

But obviously, no one had spotted a lunatic in a rubber dinghy, and when she'd finally called off the search, Grynhoff had objected so vociferously she'd felt compelled to send him below decks. By then, they'd been moving so slowly it had taken them over an hour just to get back up to cruising speed.

Bengtsson would be up in five minutes, and an hour or so after that they would reduce their speed once more and start preparing to dock. She had decided to call in a sailor to assist him. Not so she could sleep, but to give her time to write a detailed report about the events. Hopefully, if put the right way, it would head off some of the criticism.

She went over to the communication panel, picked up the internal phone receiver and was dialling sailor Axel Johnsson's cabin when a shadow seemed to flit by in the reflection from one of the windscreens. She instinctively turned around, and froze.

How had he got in without the slightest sound? How had he got on board? True, Grynhoff had reduced their speed considerably, but at no point had they come close to stopping.

She hadn't believed he existed, much less seen him. And yet she knew exactly who he was. That tight, dark wetsuit. That was all she needed. The swim goggles dangling around his neck. The hood that was pulled up, hiding everything but his face. Those eyes, those hypnotic eyes, boring into hers. She knew.

'*Yes, this is Johnsson,*' a drowsy voice said.

'He's here,' she shouted when she finally got hold of herself again and turned back towards the internal phone. 'Up here, on the bridge! He's—'

That's as far as she got before the shadow in the corner of her eye lunged. The sound of his breathing in her ear and his arm like a vice around her waist. She hadn't even heard him move through the room. The only sound he'd made had been strangely metallic, which was explained when he pressed the cold blade against her throat.

'*Captain Sandström, is that you?*' said Axel Johnsson. '*Hello?*'

'You dialled the wrong number,' the shadow whispered in her ear.

'*Is everything all right?*'

'Everything's fine, everything's under control,' the man continued, and she felt the edge of the blade, about to cut into her skin.

'*Hello? Beata, talk to me. Is everything all right?*'

'Yes,' she finally managed to squeeze out. 'I dialled the wrong number. Sorry. I meant to call Bengtsson, he's supposed to be up in a few minutes.'

'*Are you sure?*'

'Yes, I just wanted to hurry him along, because I'm on my own here at the moment. But everything's under control. You go back to sleep,' she said, and hung up.

'There we are. Good girl. You do know how to behave.'

'How did you get on board?' she hissed. 'Did someone help you?' She had to know. 'Did someone on the ship help you?'

'That's a long story and time is much too short.'

The pain across her throat reminded her the blade was millimetres away from cutting her throat. And yet, for some reason, she wasn't afraid. Maybe because the whole thing felt so implausible. 'Who are you?' she said, noting that her shock was turning into anger. 'And what do you want?'

'Too many questions that will never be answered. Better to listen and obey.'

She nodded and felt the pressure of the blade ease slightly.

'There we are. If we can keep things like this, you're going to get away with nothing but a scar across your throat. Think of it as a small reminder of how luck was on your side this time.'

The sword vanished from her throat and with it, some of the pain. But she could feel the blood, feel it trickling from the cut down her collar and into her bra.

'And if I don't obey?'

'You will. For example, right now, you're going to call that Bengtsson bloke and ask him to stay in bed.'

'There has to be two of us on the bridge. He's never going to agree.'

'I'm sure you'll think of something. And besides, there are two of us on the bridge.'

She picked up the receiver and started to dial while contemplating trying to catch him off guard with a sudden shove. Granted, it had been years since she stopped doing martial arts, but if she could shift her weight onto her right foot, she should be able to do it. He wouldn't be prepared at all and with a powerful backward kick to follow up, he'd be off balance.

'*Yes, this is Bengtsson. I'm on my way up. I just have to—*'

'Jan-Ove, never mind,' she broke in. 'That's why I'm calling. I have the first mate here with me, so you stay in bed.'

'*Grynhoff? I don't understand. Why is he there? Didn't he just—*'

'Piter and I have a few things to discuss, okay?'

'*I suppose that's putting it mildly. Just so you know, you have my full support. He's the one who should apologize, not you.*'

'Thanks, Janne. I'll talk to you in a bit,' she said, and was just about end the call when she heard the metallic sound again. And as though that were the signal her subconscious had been waiting for, she pushed back with all her might. 'Janne, he's here!' she bellowed and followed up with a kick, as planned. 'The guy with the sword is here!' She could hear him falling over. 'Call everyone to the bridge!' High on adrenaline, she turned around and hurled herself at him in one smooth motion.

When she realized the sword was pointed up, it was already too late.

Pain shot through her body like an explosion of welding flames as the steel slid through her and came out the other side.

Somehow, she was more surprised than shocked. Everything was so unexpected. She didn't even understand her own reaction. It was as though she'd left her body. As though none of this was happening for real.

At least she was still alive. The pain made that abundantly clear. The blood may have dyed large sections of her shirt red, but she was breathing.

'Hello, Jan-Ove Bengtsson,' she heard the man say into the phone. 'Now, you listen to me.'

As though she preferred bleeding to death slowly to having it be over quickly.

'Who I am is not important. Quite the opposite.'

And why was she thinking about that now? During her last moments.

'The only thing you are going to do, Jan-Ove, is stay in your little cabin, just like everyone else on this ship.'

She'd never believed in the supernatural, or an afterlife. Once it was over, it was over for real. It didn't matter how much she'd looked forward to the rest of her life. She might only have seconds before everything went dark. She should be thinking of her beloved husband and the children they'd talked so much about but not had the time to actually make.

'The only thing I can say is that if I get the feeling you're trying to sneak up here, your captain won't survive. So for her sake, stay away.' He hung up and turned to Beata, who was lying on the floor in a pool of her own blood, penetrated by the sword just above her left hip. 'Now, that was a tad unnecessary, don't you think?' He squatted down in front of her, grabbed the sword by the hilt and pulled it out.

Then he wiped the blade clean on her trousers, stood

up and slid the sword into its sheath, which was strapped across his back.

She could still see everything he was doing. Follow every movement, though things were becoming increasingly diffuse. She could barely feel the pain any more, and she almost enjoyed lying there, feeling the responsibility drain away.

Then he was back in her field of vision. She hadn't even realized he'd gone. Her shirt. Why was he pulling at it? Rape? Was that what this was about? Maybe after she died. There were people like that. Necrophiliacs, they were called, yes. But still. No... It was too... What was he doing now? The first aid kit. She didn't understand. Why was he taking out the scissors? Couldn't he just leave her alone? Whatever it was he was after, he'd won already.

She saw the scissors catch the light. Saw him cutting. But it didn't hurt. She could barely feel it. Maybe this is what fading away was like. You went numb first. Like a final kindness at the end.

Or was he not cutting her? She was unsure now. No, that was a compress covering her wound. 'Why?' she slurred.

'You're not the one who's supposed to die,' he replied, as he wrapped a bandage around her waist to stop the bleeding.

'Thank you...' It wasn't over. 'Thank you so much...' She was going to survive, and she could already feel her strength returning and the fog clearing.

'There's no need to thank me,' he said, tying off the bandage. 'You're just a pawn in a game. One that's not being sacrificed.'

'But I don't understand. What do you want? Why are you—'

'Your job is not to understand, but to obey.'

'Okay.' She nodded. 'What do you want me to do?'

He smiled, pulled her arm around his shoulders and helped her up. 'I want you to get back to work.'

37

FABIAN HAD TO fight his way out of sleep, and once he opened his eyes he didn't understand where he was, other than that it was outside and he was lying on something hard. Slabs. Square concrete slabs underneath him. A pavement. He sat up, turned towards the nearest house and realized it was his own.

His balance was far from restored, and his legs still felt like they belonged to someone else when he grabbed hold of the porch rail and heaved himself up. It was hard work, and the dull pain in his thigh from being stabbed with the tweezers made itself known as he climbed the six steps to the front door.

How had he ended up on the pavement outside his own house, how long had he been gone and what had Molander done to him? The last thing he could remember was a sudden prick on the side of his neck, then everything had gone dark.

At least he still had his phone, and it claimed it was twenty past six in the morning, almost three hours since he walked into Molander's trap. Three hours that were completely erased from his memory.

His gun was back in its holster, too, its magazine full. Molander had had every opportunity to kill him in that bathroom but had instead opted to let him live. For how long remained to be seen.

The whole affair told him two things. One, that Molander was confident he wouldn't reveal what he knew to anyone else in their team while the Pontus Milwokh investigation was ongoing. Two, that he'd meant it when he said he didn't think they could bring the case home without his help.

Whether he in turn could trust Molander was far from clear. And that he would uphold his end of the bargain and voluntarily turn himself in once Milwokh was under arrest sounded too good to be true.

The door was locked, but his keys were in his pocket, so he unlocked it and entered.

As far as he could recall, Molander hadn't mentioned Stubbs's name once during their conversation, but there could be several reasons for that. Perhaps he didn't want to reveal how much he knew. Perhaps he had a completely different plan for how to deal with her. But the best-case scenario was that he didn't know she was involved at all, and that he didn't know anything about Elvin's boat.

Either way, he was going to have to call Stubbs to tell her what had happened and together they were going to have to analyse this new situation and agree on what steps to take. Should they move Elvin's boat again? Could they keep using their pay-as-you-go phones or did they have to come up with some other way of communicating?

They also needed a plan for how to discover where Molander was hiding the forensic evidence. Without it, Milwokh couldn't be convicted. The question was if he would even be charged, since they'd be unable to point to any connection between him and the murders, other than chance in the form of a dice. Sure, there was circumstantial evidence. But everything hinged on the forensic evidence. Without it, they were nowhere.

The house was asleep and the only sound the soft humming of the ventilation. To avoid waking Sonja and Matilda, he got undressed by the front door. Pulling his shirt off, he discovered a small drop of blood in the middle of the back of it. Seeing that, he also realized he had an itch in a very specific spot between his shoulder blades, and the more he thought about it, the more it itched.

Maybe it was the needle prick from the epidural getting more noticeable now that the anaesthetic was wearing off. But that wasn't where Molander had injected him; it had been a lot further down. At least, to the best of his recollection, to the extent that could be trusted. It might just be a bug bite, of course. He had, after all, slept outside.

He tried to scratch the spot, but couldn't reach it, and after giving up, he sat down on a stool so he wouldn't fall over taking off his shoes and trousers. Then he continued further into the house and up the stairs with the phone in his hand.

He still needed to hold on to the banister, though his balance was returning. The flip side was that the pain from the wound in his thigh was also gradually intensifying, and the thing between his shoulder blades was itching worse and worse. Much as he would prefer not to, he was going to have to wake Sonja to have her take a look at it.

He opened the bedroom door and stepped into the room, kept dark by the blackout blind. 'Sonja,' he whispered the moment he'd closed the door behind him. 'Sonja, it's me. You have to wake up.' He fumbled along the edge of the bed, but it wasn't until he sat down to stroke her that he realized the bed was empty.

Fear washed over him, making his stomach churn. He unlocked his phone with trembling hands, found her number and dialled it, only to notice her phone lighting up among the clothes piled in the armchair.

Was it Molander? Had he kidnapped them to force him to keep his word? Sure, he'd threatened to do all kinds of things to his family if he didn't uphold his end of the bargain. But this took it to a whole new level.

On his way back out onto the landing, he called Molander.

'*Ah, you're awake. I hope you didn't mind waking up in the street. I was going to put you in the back garden. But your neighbour was already sitting out on his terrace, reading the paper, so I'm afraid I had no other choice.*'

'What have you done?' he hissed as he opened the door to Matilda's room. 'What the fuck have you done?'

'*This and that,*' Molander laughed. '*But nothing you should be wasting your energy on right now.*'

The room had completely changed since he'd last been in it.

'*Why don't you make sure you get some more sleep, instead?*'

Gone were the brightly coloured curtains with animals on them, the drawings she'd made. Not to mention the collection of teddy bears on her bed.

'*After all, you have a few hours before our morning meeting.*'

Fabian stared at the neatly made bed, trying to understand what had happened.

'*No offence, but you looked a bit worse for wear when I*

left you, and considering the kind of work we have waiting for us, I can't emphasize enough the importance of being well rested.'

'So you seriously think we can still work together?' Fabian turned back to the landing and hurried over to Theodor's closed door.

'*Of course. Especially now the cards are on the table.'*

Fabian opened the door and stepped into Theodor's room, which was as tidy and untouched as the last time he'd been in it.

'*We can finally focus on what's important, like the crack team we actually are,*' Molander went on.

But Fabian wasn't listening. A mark on the wall some way up the stairs to the studio had caught his eye. He was far from certain, but he thought it was new.

The mark was about three feet from the corner where the stairs turned at a right angle, and when he went closer he realized that not only was the mark in fact a deep dent in the wall, but there was another one further up, too.

At the top of the stairs, he opened the door to Sonja's studio and his eyes immediately fell on her piece *The Hanging Box*. The rectangular wooden box was sitting in the middle of the floor. The artwork, which was meant to be suspended from the ceiling, should have been her big breakthrough, but had instead nearly become her coffin.

Since then, she hadn't wanted anything to do with it and she would have preferred for it to be destroyed once the forensic investigation was complete.

And yet, here it was, and it was the first time he saw the blond wooden box with its lid slightly askew, leaving a gap at the far end.

'Was it you?' he said into his phone as he stepped over the threshold to walk over for a closer look. 'Did you bring the coffin here?'

'*You mean* The Hanging Box. *An incredible piece, if you ask me. And wasn't it lucky she decided to keep it after all?*'

Fabian only had to take a few steps into the room to realize everything was over and nothing mattered any more. There were no words to explain or alter this. Everything had already been said.

Matilda had been right. And Greta. They'd both known someone in their family was going to die and they'd tried to warn him. Wake him up. But he'd dismissed it as nonsense, and now here he was, looking at the consequences.

He ended the call and let his phone fall to the floor as he crossed the room to the open box. He kneeled down and carefully pulled the lid aside so he could see as much as possible of Sonja, who was lying naked on her back with her arms by her sides.

He gently laid a hand over her closed eyes, and even though it was obvious from the moment his skin touched hers, it took him a while to realize she was still warm.

38

Frank Käpp raised his binoculars and let them sweep west along the horizon. Apart from two freight ships, it was uninterrupted. That's how he liked it. Unencumbered with anything irrelevant, an unbroken line where sea met sky all the way around him. It made him feel calm.

But calm was the last thing he felt right now. He was still in shock and couldn't even hold his hands out without them trembling. Images from the night before kept flashing before his eyes, like water torture that slowly but surely breaks its victim down drop by drop. The scene in the aft cabin where Vincent had lain petrified with a sword pressed against his throat would haunt him forever, no matter how surreal and incomprehensible it was.

Klara had taken a sleeping pill and Vincent had been given a half, and now they were both asleep in the forepeak. Nothing could have knocked him out. But then, he was in charge. This entire trip had been his initiative, and he'd sworn on everything sacred that it would go well and that he, no matter what happened, would look after them.

Talk about promising too much.

He sighed, and in yet another attempt to distract himself he once again turned his binoculars towards the horizon and looked at the two freight ships, one of which, the one with the blue hull, looked like it was a lot closer now. But the images of the attacking frogman and his sword soon distracted him once more.

There was no escaping the fact that he was to blame. He'd forced them out on that night sail. Overridden their objections, in fact, and for some reason he couldn't quite figure out, he'd even forced Vincent to sleep in the aft cabin.

In hindsight, that was almost as inexplicable as Vincent's fear of monsters in the middle of the sea. What were the odds of that happening just then? Was it just an unfortunate coincidence or was there something else behind it? A higher power, who wanted to put them in their place. Demonstrate that it didn't matter how far he sailed. That he could never escape his demons.

With a mirthless chuckle, he dismissed that as a positively Bergmanesque fancy, and instead turned his attention to the freighter, which must have changed its course, because it looked both shorter and bigger. The only explanation was that it was heading straight for them.

It was probably destined for Halmstad as well. There was a big commercial port next to the marina. It was a bit odd, though, for such a large ship to change course so abruptly.

He could change his course, too, and skip the detour to Halmstad. Klara and Vincent wouldn't know the difference, and he wouldn't mind pushing on towards Gothenburg like they'd originally planned.

But he was going to keep his promise to the detective and put in at Halmstad to make sure they received any necessary care. They probably needed more than he was ready to admit. It was so like him to want to rush on, away from anything that was hard. As though it would disappear if he just ran fast enough. To some extent, that was exactly what this round-the-world trip was about.

He'd never tried therapy. Klara had wanted them to go together back when things were at their worst, and each time he'd dismissed it, throwing up an argument weaker than the last.

But maybe therapy was exactly what they needed, even notwithstanding the events of last night. To calmly discuss what had been and what they expected from what lay ahead. To clear the air, simply put; to make sure this was the fresh start they so badly needed. If he had to point out a silver lining to this horror, it was that he'd realized how wrong he'd been.

There was still a fair distance between them and the freighter, but there was no longer any doubt they were on a collision course. So Frank turned east and slowed down. It would cost them half an hour, but they were in no hurry.

He could turn the engine off and raise the sails. The wind was perfect for running slowly on a broad reach into Laholm Bay. But if he did, Klara and Vincent would wake up immediately.

Rest and therapy were on the agenda now, and for as long as there was need. When they all felt ready, they'd take their time sailing up to Gothenburg and then spend a whole day at Liseberg.

A lot of people had been through a lot worse, so there was no question they would be all right in the end. It was mostly a matter of giving it time and slowly but surely this would turn into an anecdote no one ever believed when they told it. Maybe one day, they themselves would start doubting it.

But what was with that ship? Just thirty minutes ago, it

had been a dot on the horizon. Now it was once again clearly on a collision course and so close he could read the name on the hull. MS *Vinterland*. He had both changed course and reduced his speed. There was nothing for it but to turn and slow down even further.

'What's going on?' A drowsy Klara poked her head out of the cabin.

'Nothing. Everything's fine. I just have to get out of that ship's way.'

Klara climbed into the cockpit and looked over at the freighter.

'Sleep well?' he went on and Klara nodded.

'When will we get there?' she said in the middle of a yawn and a stretch.

'At least an hour later than planned if that ship keeps pestering us.' He nodded in the direction of the freighter and gave her a hug. 'Good thing we're not in a hurry.'

Klara smiled and shook her head while he held her tighter.

'It's going to be okay. Everything's going to be good again. I promise.'

She nodded and gave him a peck on the lips that quickly deepened into a kiss.

Neither of them noticed that the MS *Vinterland* changed its course again and slowed down by throwing its engines in reverse.

39

FABIAN WAS STANDING in the shower, looking down at his feet, which were almost entirely submerged in water. A sign that it was high time to snake the drain before it overflowed and flooded the bathroom. But it would have to wait until a different lifetime, after all of this was over.

He'd fallen asleep on the studio floor, next to Sonja in her coffin. The piece that had made her question herself and her art. Her whole life. Now she'd done a one-eighty, brought it home and climbed into it. Naked and exposed, into the dark.

When he'd woken up, the box had been empty, apart from a small handwritten note that explained that she was at an important meeting and Matilda had spent the night at Esmaralda's. He'd dragged himself down to the bathroom and stepped into the shower.

He'd stayed under the hot jet for almost an hour. Time, important as it may be, was secondary right now. The drugs Molander had pumped him full of had to leave his system, and with each droplet of water that hit his skin, he felt a fraction cleaner.

After drying off and getting his circulation going, he realized the pain in the wound in his thigh was almost gone. But the itch between his shoulder blades was still there, possibly even worse than before. He could no longer hope it was a regular bug bite. This was different. If it were some kind of insect, it felt more like a parasite burrowing underneath his skin.

He made another attempt at reaching it, but was forever half an inch short. He could scratch it with his toothbrush, but that left him none the wiser, so he took a picture over his shoulder with his phone. It clearly showed there was something between his shoulder blades. He zoomed in and realized it was a few strips of surgical tape covering a small protrusion.

It had to be Molander's handiwork. He opened the bathroom cabinet in search of a more effective poking tool than the toothbrush. The best he could find was Sonja's foot file. With that, he could rub away the tape, however slowly and laboriously, until he could take a new picture.

This one showed a small wound across the little bump, a half-inch-long cut closed with three simple stitches. Molander must have cut him while he was sedated. But why? What kind of surgery had been performed on him? And why was it so bloody itchy?

He should go to a doctor, but Molander's head start was already too big for him to sit around an A&E. Instead, he took the longest tweezers he could find, disinfected them with rubbing alcohol and carefully reached between his shoulder blades. After a few attempts, he managed to push the tip in under the top stitch and rip it out.

He felt blood stream down his back. The pain was considerable and normally he would have been unable to continue. But he was so focused on finding out what

Molander had done to him that he could barely feel the tweezers digging around the wound in search of the next stitch.

Just then, his phone vibrated on the basin in front of him, and he saw it was a text from Molander himself.

Reply and say you overslept, but you're on your way.

Before he could even start processing what that meant, his phone lit up again. This time, it was a call.

'Hello, is that you, Fabian?' Tuvesson said on the other end. 'It's Astrid. Hello?'

'Yes, it's me,' he said.

'Where are you? We're all waiting for you to give us a report on the events out on Öresund last night.'

'I'm sorry, I overslept,' he heard himself say. 'It was a late night last night and I—'

'Fine, sure, I get it,' Tuvesson broke in. 'So long as you get yourself in here asap. We have a lot to get on with and above all, a couple of things to explain.'

'I'm on my way,' he said. 'I'll be there as soon as I can.'

'Good. And by the way, I set Theodor up with a lawyer. Jadwiga Komorovski. According to Högsell, she's an expert on the Danish judicial process, and from what I'm told, she's already in Helsingør.'

'That's great. Thank you. Thank you so much.' Fabian could feel one of many loads being lightened, but he barely had time to end the call before his phone vibrated again.

There now, that went really well, don't you think? But you might want to sterilize that wound so it doesn't get infected. And put a

big plaster over it, in case it starts to bleed. And don't worry. It's
just a little GPS tracker, so I can keep an eye on you.

Had that bastard actually been in his house, installing his
damn cameras? Had he... Fabian did a quick scan of the
bathroom, which at first glance at least looked the same as
ever. Actually, hold on. He was suddenly unsure. Didn't the
potpourri usually sit two shelves lower? And that painting.
Had it always been there?

He had no idea. He'd been so absent lately that Sonja
could have repainted half the house and he wouldn't be sure
what was different.

Molander could simply be assuming he'd found and
started to dig around the wound between his shoulder
blades, of course. If not, he'd somehow installed a hidden
camera in their bathroom. A camera that should be placed
somewhere high up behind him.

He looked up at the saucer-like ceiling light. Like the
one in the bedroom, it had been there when they moved
into the house, and he'd never given it much thought. Now,
he was struck by how beautiful it was with its elegant
glass facets and the brass knob in the middle, holding it
in place.

Maybe it was just dust or dead insects, but something
was blocking the light at the bottom of the glass bowl. He
stepped up on the toilet lid, unscrewed the brass knob and
carefully unhooked the glass.

A layer of dust covered the bottom. But he couldn't see
a hidden camera. Or cables, or a microphone. What he did
find was a folded piece of yellowed paper, which he picked
up and unfolded. A small rusty key fell out of it and landed

somewhere on the floor below. But instead of climbing down to look for it, he read the handwritten message.

Father has gone underground

Working on something profound

In no time some things will be missed

In a room that does not exist

A question: when will it be found?

A poem. Or was it a limerick in the form of a riddle? And who'd written it? Matilda? No, it wasn't her handwriting. On the other hand, she'd changed a lot since the accident, so why not her handwriting, too? It might be her friend Esmaralda. Some kind of game they were playing, perhaps? But the paper was old and yellow and had been buried under a layer of dust.

The first two lines about a father going underground to work could absolutely be referring to him. Over the past month, he'd practically been living in the basement on and off. And sure, he'd been fighting the clock. He still was. But what was that about a room that didn't exist? Was that his improvised basement study or something else entirely?

His thoughts were pulling in a direction he wanted nothing to do with. But he was powerless to stop them, and they made him dizzy; and for the second time that morning, he had to lean on something to keep his balance – this time, the wall. That was when he spotted it. In the potpourri, just as he'd first thought.

The hidden miniature camera and its transmitter.

40

HILLEVI STUBBS WAS already waiting in the interview room when Conny Öhman was shown in by a guard and sat down across from her. He hadn't wanted to speak to her and had sent word that everything he had to say was in the interview transcript. But she happened to know the senior officer at Fosie Prison outside Malmö well enough to have a meeting set up whether Conny Öhman wanted one or not.

'Hi, Conny. My name is Hillevi Stubbs,' she said with a smile, noting that he had both grown a beard and put on weight since his arrest in the spring.

'What do you want?' Conny leaned forward over the table with his chin tucked into his chest and started ruffling his unkempt mop of ginger hair.

'I want you to tell me what you did to your wife, Kerstin Öhman, on the night of the fifth of April this year,' she said, watching dandruff drift down onto the tabletop.

'And why would I?' Conny said, continuing to scratch his scalp. 'I already answered all those questions.'

'But maybe you wouldn't mind doing it again? I would certainly consider giving you a gold star if you cooperate. And if you keep up the good behaviour, you might even be released early.'

'Why would I want to get out? I have everything I need in

here. A gym, a tattooist, porn mags. Even the nosh is better than the old bat's.' Conny let out a chuckle.

'From what I'm told, you're being moved to Tidaholm Prison and that's maximum security, which I promise you is much less fun.'

Conny said nothing, just started pushing the dandruff into a small pile on the table.

'Did you rape your wife that night?' she asked.

'It looks that way.'

'And why did you do that?'

'What do you mean, why?' Conny wet his fingertip with saliva. 'What the hell kind of a question is that?' Then he pressed his finger into the pile of dandruff and stuck it in his mouth.

'Were you angry with her? Or had something happened?'

'Not that I recall. I was drunk and in a foul mood. A fairly potent combo if you ask me.'

'Should I take that to mean it wasn't the first time you raped her?'

Conny burst out laughing and nodded. 'Sure, why not?'

'But this was the first time you raped her to death. Why?'

Conny shrugged and started cleaning his nails. 'I guess she got what she deserved. Or maybe I was in a particularly bad mood.'

'You also supposedly assaulted and tortured her. Was that also common practice for you?'

'I bet you're one of those bloody feminists,' he said, looking at her for the first time. 'The kind that eats pussy the first chance they get.'

'I would appreciate it if you would stick to answering my questions.'

'If you answer mine first.'

'Yes, I'm a lesbian.'

'Well, you've never tasted mine.' He shot her a smile and started to brush the dirt from his fingernails into a small pile.

'Your turn,' she said, her face expressionless.

Conny sighed. 'Sure, I suppose I slapped her about a bit on occasion, if she'd behaved badly. Women are like children, they need to be put in their place from time to time, or they get ideas and start talking back.'

'And what ideas had Kerstin had that night?'

'Who knows. She got all kinds of things into her head.' Conny shrugged and wet his index finger once more. 'Like I said, I was hammered, so my memory's not razor sharp.'

'Are you sure you don't remember? I mean, shouldn't she have been talking back more than usual, given that you actually beat her to death?'

'You'd think, wouldn't you?' Conny pushed his finger into the dirt from his nails and stuck it in his mouth. 'I'm sure she must have.'

'But you don't remember.'

Conny shook his head. 'Nope.'

'No images flickering through your head when you think about it?'

Conny shook his head again.

'Don't you find that a bit odd? There's a big difference between slapping someone about and burning them with a red-hot fire iron.'

Conny lowered his eyes and rubbed at a stain on the table. 'According to the case file, you also shoved the poker into her vagina. She must have been talking back something awful to deserve that, wouldn't you say?'

Conny said nothing, just scratched his fingernail back and forth across the stain.

'And if that wasn't bad enough, you—'

'I don't know,' Conny said, cutting her off.

'You don't know what?'

'I don't know.'

'Know or remember?'

Conny banged his fist on the table. 'I can't answer all these bloody questions! I was drunk, okay? Wasted! So I know, or remember, or whatever the fuck you want to call it, nothing from that goddam night!'

'So what you're saying is, anything could have happened?'

'Yes, and apparently, it did.'

'There might even have been a third person there?'

'What do you mean, a third person?' Conny looked up from the table again. 'What the fuck are you talking about? Who would that be?'

'I don't know.' She shrugged. 'Maybe someone who did all those things to your wife while you were out cold on the sofa.'

Conny studied her. 'What the fuck do you want from me?'

'Just the truth. That's all.'

'I confessed to everything. What more do you bloody want? I've already been sentenced to life.'

'That's true.' She leaned in closer. 'And I'm fully aware you're a terrible person who thoroughly deserves to rot in here, regardless of what happened that night. But as things stand, there's a possibility you're serving someone else's time.'

'I don't know what you're up to. But you don't fool me.'
He stood up. 'You don't fucking fool me. This conversation's
over.'

'This man.' Stubbs placed a picture of Molander on the
table. 'Ring any bells?'

Conny stopped and studied the picture for a long time
before shaking his head.

'Are you really sure? I want you to take a good look.'

Conny ignored her and kept moving towards the door.
But just as he was about to push the intercom to call a
guard, he changed his mind and turned back.

41

FABIAN PUT THE glass jars filled with different kinds of pasta back in the pantry, stepped off the stool and looked around. He'd already checked the cookbooks on the shelf and the ceiling lights. He'd even taken apart and cleaned the kitchen fan without finding anything.

But the hidden camera in the bathroom couldn't be the only one. Something told him they must be everywhere in the house. And yet he hadn't managed to find a single one.

Maybe Molander had only had time to do the bathroom. Maybe he'd figured it was the only place he needed one. Knowing that Fabian was going to stand in front of the mirror and dig around his back. Or maybe he was just looking in the wrong places.

'Hi, sweetheart. You're still here.'

Fabian turned to Sonja, who was coming in from the hallway.

'How are you feeling?' she went on. 'You look terrible. I tried to—'

'I'm fine.' He cut her off and tried to compose himself. 'I overslept and was just on my way out.' There were so many things he should tell her, he didn't know where to start.

'Fabian.' She walked up to him and took his face in her hands. 'I understand if you have a lot of questions and are wondering what I'm up to. And I promise, I will tell you. But first, I want to know what's going on.'

'Not now, Sonja. I can't. I have to—'

'Fabian,' Sonja broke in. 'The only thing we have to do is talk to each other.'

'I know. But it's going to have to wait until I—'

'Until you what? Get back? If you ever do. You were out all night. I know it's just work. That's not the issue. When I saw you this morning with deep gashes in your thigh and back, I obviously knew something had happened and I'm worried. Really worried. I tried to wake you, but I couldn't. It was like you were drugged. And now,' – she took a step back and looked him up and down – 'you look like you're about to collapse.'

'Sonja, I can't do this right now. Not now. It'll have to wait. Okay?'

'Is it Theodor? Did he call, does he want us to—'

'No. All I know is that he has a good lawyer now, who will be with him when they interview him while they wait for the trial to resume.'

'I think about him every second.'

'Me too. But all we can do right now is wait and hope for the best. Anyway, we'll have to talk more later, sweetheart.' He kissed her on the forehead and started to walk towards the front door.

'I've decided to exhibit my work again.'

He stopped and turned to look at her.

Sonja sighed. 'I know. It's not what I've been saying these past few weeks. But Dunkers called yesterday to ask if I wanted to take part in an exhibition. The thing is, it opens on Thursday. Apparently one of the artists pulled out.'

'Thursday this week? Tomorrow?'

Sonja nodded. 'I'm not sure how I'm going to make it. But I have an idea, at least.'

'That's great.' He tried to squeeze out a smile. 'Congratulations.'

'I'm not sure it's all that great. But I believe it's the only way for me to – how do I put it? – process and come to terms with everything that has happened. But who knows?' She shrugged. 'I might die attempting it.'

Fabian walked over and put his arms around her. But though he'd only intended to give her a quick hug of support, she held on to him as though she were in fact supporting him.

He didn't know whether it was the hug or the fact that the last of the drugs had finally left his system. Either way, balance had been restored and for the first time in a long time, he felt firm ground under his feet. Maybe they'd both fallen so far it was finally time to hit rock bottom.

'I actually declined at first,' she said over his shoulder. 'But they didn't need a final answer until today. That's why I brought the box home, to see how I felt about it, and when I woke up this morning, all my doubts were gone. I'm supposed to say hi from Ingvar, by the way.'

'Molander?' He let go of her. 'Was he the one who helped you get the box up the stairs?'

'Yes, why? Someone had to help me and you obviously weren't—'

He cut her off. 'How long was he here for?'

'First, I want you to tell me what you're—'

'Sonja, how long? Are we talking minutes or hours?'

'I don't know what you think happened. But I promise. You have nothing to worry about.'

'Were you with him the whole time? Or did you let him wander about on his own?'

'Fabian, this is Ingvar Molander we're talking about. Your colleague. What do you think—'

'Please, just answer the question.'

Sonja heaved a sigh. 'I don't know exactly how long he was here for. And no, I wasn't with him the whole time. He helped me get the box upstairs and then he needed to use the bathroom. I don't know if he had stomach problems or what. He was in there a long time, and in the end, I had to get going.'

'What, so you left him alone in our house?' Only now did it occur to him, and as it did, the ground disappeared from under him once more.

'Yes. He just had to put the extra keys in the letter box when he was done.'

The basement. He'd obviously been down in the basement and seen all his ideas and clues. Granted, he'd handed most of it over to Stubbs, but...

'Fabian, why aren't you picking up?'

'What?'

'Your phone. Can't you hear it ringing?'

He pulled out the Nokia, declined the call from Stubbs and fired off a text.

Can't talk now.

'Why didn't you pick up? And why are you using your old phone?'

Stubbs texted back:

Ok. When and where can we meet?

'Sweetheart, I don't have time to explain.'

Just finished with Öhman, who has agreed to testify against M,
which means we have enough to make an arrest.

42

'*KIM.*' THE VOICE on the other end sighed and Sleizner could already tell where the conversation was headed. '*I hear you. But I'm sorry, I can't do that.*'

'Why not?' Sleizner got up from his office chair. 'What's the problem?' He always projected more force and gravitas when he was standing up and walking around. 'All you have to do is print the document attached to the email you just received and sign it. I'll take care of the rest.' He went over to the window and looked down at a group of people hurrying across the police station courtyard; the breathing on the other end of the line revealed that his interlocutor was hesitating.

'*Kim, I'm sorry, but I just can't.*'

You're not sorry, you little cunt. It took effort not to let out the sigh that would reveal more about his mood than he wanted known. 'Ingolf Bremer... I must admit you disappoint me.'

'*I'm sorry to hear that, but it can't be helped. After all, I'm in charge of the Naval Operative Command. Not you.*'

Well now, playing the big man, was he? 'Of course, Ingolf. You're in charge. And I've never said otherwise. But it would behove you to slow down and listen to what I have to say.' He paused briefly to show how calm and collected he was. 'Because unless I misremember, you actually owe me a small... Well, what should we call it? Favour?' He was met by silence, a clear sign the battle was almost won. 'I don't care either way, so long as I'm not kept waiting too long.'

'*But Kim, I already helped you out last night. You'd have to say I did, right?*' He was nervous now. It was obvious. He could almost hear the sweat trickling down his forehead. '*When I agreed to deny the Swedish coastguard access to Danish waters, I broke every rule in the book. But I did it anyway. For you.*'

'Yes, you did, and I appreciate it. But I think of that more as a first instalment. A good one, absolutely. But considering what I've done for you, we're still far from even-steven. It's simple arithmetic. Plus and minus.'

'*Kim, I would love to help you, you know that.*' The little bugger was resisting. '*But I went too far last night. And what you're asking now would be unethical and disruptive to the culture of cooperation in Öresund our countries have managed to create over the years.*'

'Ingolf, let me lay it out for you. The least significant aspect of this mess is how you feel about the decision. I have my reasons and that should be more than enough for you. What is significant is that the Swedes completely disregarded the fact that they were denied access. That they just continued into sovereign Danish territory. That's nothing short of a serious violation, and just as if it had been Russia or some other country, we have to lodge an official protest.'

'*Please, Kim, consider my situation. For one thing, we were the ones who acted inappropriately in the first place. Defending our actions now will only make it worse.*'

'Ingolf, this is not only far beyond your remit, it's beyond your capabilities, too. I've already been in touch with Steinbacher at the Foreign Ministry, and he's behind me one hundred per cent. The only thing they're waiting for is an official incident report with your signature on it.' There was a heavy sigh on the other end. It said clearly that Ingolf Bremer was finally on the verge of caving. 'And as far as your situation goes, it seems to me I'm the one who has fully grasped its seriousness. Unless you don't mind a certain video becoming public, of course.'

'*Kim, I'm begging you—*'

'Thirteen years. Too young even to have acne, and unless I'm mistaken, younger than your own youngest daughter. How are you going to explain that to— What's her name again?'

There was a knock on the door and a man popped his head in. 'Oh, sorry, is this a bad time?'

Sleizner sighed and closed his eyes. 'What does it look like?' Ingolf Bremer was down for the count. 'I would recommend that you close that door right this second, crawl back into whatever hole you came from and pretend this never happened.' Sleizner dismissed the man with a wave of his hand and put the phone back to his ear. 'I'm sorry, where were we?'

But instead of leaving, the man stepped through the door and closed it behind him. 'Look, I don't want to be a bother, but we had agreed to meet today. It's already ten past and I have to—'

'Ingolf, two seconds. I just need to deal with something. What meeting? I didn't agree to a meeting.'

'Yes, you did, it's in your calendar. Why else would I be here?' The man moved further into his office. 'You should ask to call back in two hours and hang up. Unless you have another phone you can—'

'Bloody fucking hell.' Sleizner walked up to the man. 'First of all: Who the hell are you? Second of all: What fucking meeting?'

'My name is Mikael Rønning. I've worked in the IT department for the last seven years.'

His name did ring a bell, but too faintly and remotely for Sleizner to remember where he'd heard it.

'I am in charge of, among other things, the security updates on our mobile phones. We've been in touch via email and agreed to install the update this afternoon.'

'Ingolf, I have to go. I'll get back to you about this.' He ended the call. 'So you're the one who has been mail-bombing me over the past week.'

'I'm sorry if that's what it's felt like for you. I'm just trying to do my job.'

'You're not the only one, which is exactly why I'd like you to leave me alone.'

'Believe me. I'd love to,' Rønning replied. 'But this is a fairly important update, not just for you but for the country's national security. It closes a number of significant security gaps, which is why we don't want to delay.'

'Sure, I get that. But...' Sleizner sighed. 'How long did you say it's going to take?'

'Just over an hour, depending on how much memory you have.'

'Fine, then I expect you back here no later than three.' He handed over his phone.

'No problem.' Mikael Rønning nodded. 'I just need the pin.'

'Right, so you said.' Sleizner smiled. 'But that means you can look at all my private pictures and videos.'

'That's correct. Unless you've transferred them to your computer, like I suggested in one of my emails. But if it makes you feel any better, I have better things to do than to go through your holiday snaps. And you're welcome to come with me and watch.'

'That's not happening. The pin is thirty-eight forty—' Sleizner was interrupted by his phone lighting up and dinging. 'Hold on, let me see that.' He took his phone back, unlocked it and read the message from Stig Paulsen, president of TDC.

Found your little Indian man in the archives. Unfortunately, it doesn't look good. Call.

So Paulsen had been able to identify the Indian man, which meant he, too, was connected to TDC somehow. Maybe that's how they knew each other, him and the Chinese fatso. But what problem could be so serious Paulsen wanted him to call? He normally never wanted to do anything over the phone.

'Look, I'm sorry, but it looks like we're going to have to take a rain check after all,' he said to Rønning while he texted Paulsen back.

What's the problem?

'Look, I thought I was being clear about why it's so important to—'

'You made yourself abundantly clear,' Sleizner cut in. 'But

it can't be helped. It's not happening today. Come on, out you go.' He ushered Rønning towards the door, and the moment he shut it behind him, the phone vibrated in his hand.

Like I said: Call.

43

'WELL, WOULD YOU look at this.' Molander spread his arms wide. 'If it isn't the prodigal son, finally gracing us with his presence.'

Fabian nodded on his way into the conference room. 'That's right, in all my glory,' he said, never letting the smile he'd practised in the lift mirror on the way up waver, and adding a wink as the cherry on top.

'You actually look a bit worse for wear, despite probably having had more hours of beauty sleep than the rest of us put together,' Molander went on. 'Rough night?'

Fabian turned to Molander, who was smiling at him with that tauntingly sarcastic expression he so often wore. Before, he'd interpreted it as an innocuous and at heart affable kind of charm. A way to lighten the mood when it risked becoming too heavy. His eyes looked the same, but when Fabian met his gaze now, he sensed a darkness behind it that wanted nothing more than to twist the knife a few extra times just for the sake of it.

'Indeed, as you should know better than anyone,' he said, and he saw Molander's smile slip briefly before he fumblingly slapped it back on, his upper lip trembling slightly.

'What do you mean? I'm not sure I follow?'

'No?' Fabian continued to stare Molander in the eyes and

waited until the silence in the room was palpable. 'From what I'm told, you're the one who helped Sonja transport that piece of art back to our house after threatening to destroy it unless she retrieved it,' he said finally. 'But given her experiences with that particular piece, it shouldn't come as a shock to you, or anyone else in this room for that matter, that seeing it again had a number of emotional repercussions that kept us awake for most of the night. So no, I wouldn't say I've slept much.'

'I'm sorry. I should have known.' Molander nodded. 'I can only blame my own sleep-deprived state.'

Fabian didn't respond. He was going to play along in Molander's charade, but only as far as he had to, and he was going to make sure Molander knew that, or he would eat him alive the first chance he got.

'All right, maybe we should get cracking while it's still light out,' Tuvesson said. 'As you know, we're already running behind schedule and I have to be going soon.' She turned to Fabian. 'So you're going to have to hold off on telling us what happened out on Öresund last night. From what I know, it's still unclear whether Milwokh drowned or managed to swim to shore.'

'That's correct,' Fabian said, nodding. 'I would almost say most things point to—'

'I promise I'll let you know when I'm finished,' Tuvesson cut in. 'Hopefully, if he's alive, he'll want to lie low after the events of last night. But that doesn't mean we have time to be lazy or sleep in. We're behind on practically all of our cases, so let's think of this as our chance to catch up.' She turned around and gestured towards the whiteboard walls with both hands. 'Interviews that should have been conducted a long time ago can't wait any longer. Crime scenes need to be processed and forensic evidence collected.'

Tuvesson was right, of course. They had a mountain of work to get through before the trail went cold. But none of that was even remotely important compared to finding Molander's evidence hoard. Without it, nothing else they did would amount to anything.

'Irene,' Tuvesson continued. 'I want you to talk to Milwokh's adoptive parents.'

Lilja nodded.

'I know you were there just a few months ago. But that time it was about their daughter, and there's an outside chance he'll contact them now that he can't go home. And Klippan. I'm sending you out to talk to the boat rental people.'

'Sure. No problem.'

'Can I ask a question?' Fabian said.

'If you make it quick. Like I said, we're behind.'

'How's the forensic side of things coming along?'

'Right.' Tuvesson turned to Molander.

'I'd have to say swimmingly.' Molander smiled. 'With the exception of the most recent murder, we can tie Milwokh to more or less everything. And I'm not worried about finding something to tie him to the bathtub murder, too.'

'More or less everything?' Fabian said. 'Maybe it's time to be a bit more specific.'

'Look, everything's under control. There's no need to fret.'

'Who said anything about fretting? I just think it's high time for a proper run-through of what you have and what's still missing. That way, we know what to prioritize. So I suggest we continue this meeting down in your lab, assuming that's where you keep the evidence.'

'Great, let's go.' Tuvesson checked her watch. 'I'm heading that way anyhow.'

'Hold on a minute.' Molander held up his hands. 'I apologize if I wasn't clear. As it stands, we have forensic evidence tying him to every crime scene except the flat in Planteringen. That is, in other words, what I should be focusing on. Rather than giving all of you a lecture down in the lab. That's going to have to wait.'

'Okay, how does everyone else feel?' Tuvesson said. 'Do it later?'

'Fine by me.' Klippan shrugged.

'Me too,' Lilja agreed. 'But I would like to know when you're going to get around to his flat. That feels like it should be a priority.'

'And the rubber dinghy, too,' Klippan chimed in.

'As soon as I can. I mean, listen to yourselves,' Molander replied. 'There's a lot to do. So why don't we wrap this up now so we can get to work instead?'

'All right. It's a deal,' Fabian said, without taking his eyes off Molander.

'Good. I think we can trust that Ingvar knows what's in his freezer,' Tuvesson said. She started to gather up her documents as Molander and the others got up to leave. 'Oh, and Fabian. I want you to go talk to Hanna Brahe.'

'Who's she?' he said, his thoughts racing back to Molander's home and the basement with the built-in freezer.

'Mattias Larsson's girlfriend. She was the one who found him in the bath and called us. She wasn't in a state to be interviewed last night. But she's been in touch to say that she's ready now.'

How could he not have thought of that before? That must be where Molander kept the forensic evidence. That was what he'd seen when he was there.

'Okay.' He got up and followed the others towards the door. 'Send me her contact details and I'll get in touch with her today.' He had to get over to Molander's house as soon as possible. Molander could track him with his GPS chip as much as he pleased. It made no difference.

'No, not today. Now, please.'

Fabian nodded and left the room. That he'd agreed to meet Stubbs was unfortunate. But it was going to have to wait. Right now, everything else had to wait.

44

Where are you? Didn't we say Preem on Södra Hunnetorps-vägen?

Fabian turned into Molander's driveway, killed the engine and replied to Stubbs's text. They'd agreed to meet at a petrol station so it would look to Molander like he was filling up the tank. There was also a car wash there and a pizzeria, which should give them at least twenty minutes before it seemed too suspicious.

Can't make it.

But there was no point now parking his car somewhere else and taking the bus or his bike instead. Molander would know exactly where he was anyway. And if he was right about the evidence, they'd be able to arrange for an arrest immediately.

What happened? Can I call?

He hurried around to the back of the house and stuck the white key with the pin code on it into the terrace door lock. Molander had apparently noted his latest visit to the house and must know there was a risk he'd break in again. And yet the key still both fitted and turned smoothly.

No time to explain. Meet in 40 minutes at Skaragatan 12 instead.

Maybe he hadn't had time. Maybe Molander was working against the clock, too. He probably wasn't as well prepared as he wanted to appear. The ambush last night could just as well have been a desperate attempt to put out the fire caused by Milwokh staging an attack at almost exactly the same time Molander was watching Mattias Larsson struggle in the bath.

The notion that he'd planted clues on his nightstand to fuel Fabian's suspicions had to be a frantic post hoc rationalization.

The bugging of Fabian's house, on the other hand, was a different story and likely long planned, as was the threat to destroy the forensic evidence against Milwokh, which was a clear sign he'd been aware for some time that the suspicions against him hadn't died with Hugo Elvin.

He did a quick sweep of the living room, which looked the same as last time he was in it. Granted, that was only twenty-four hours ago, so the real question was if Molander had even been home since.

He continued down the basement steps, well aware of the risk that Molander might be watching every step he took on a screen somewhere. Hopefully, he was too busy to make it over here in time to intervene. When Fabian reached the basement, he pushed his finger through the small hole in the wall, opened the hatch and punched in the code, causing the metal door to slide open.

Of course this was where he kept the evidence against Milwokh. The room with its many shelves and display cases filled with confiscated weapons and all kinds of evidence from older cases was virtually custom-built for it.

He continued over to the built-in freezer at the back of the room and opened it.

It wasn't empty. Far from it. And yet, something wasn't right. It looked the same as before, with a multitude of labelled plastic containers and jars of all shapes and sizes. Or maybe it didn't? Suddenly feeling uncertain, Fabian picked up one of the containers.

Gertrud's liver pâté.

He took off the lid, only to discover the container really was full of something that looked like home-made liver pâté. But there was no discernible smell. He gingerly touched the surface of the pâté. It was frozen. But when he pushed harder, his finger plunged easily all the way to the bottom.

The pâté was, therefore, far from frozen solid. This could only mean that the containers he'd seen before, which had held evidence, had recently been swapped for Gertrud's old leftovers from the fridge. He checked a few more containers; they were all the same. If it wasn't Gertrud's potatoes au gratin, it was Gertrud's lasagne, and nothing was frozen through.

The distant voice sounded like a girl passing by the house while talking on her phone. Or actually, no, it wasn't just some girl. The voice sounded familiar. Too familiar. He turned around to try to locate it and realized it wasn't coming from outside the room but, rather, from inside it – or, more specifically, from one of the many built-in shelves.

'... *are you here?*' he heard when he moved close enough.

'Hello?' he shouted at the shelf. 'This is Fabian Risk. Is there someone in there?'

'Please, answer me if you're here.'

It sounded almost like his own— But no, that couldn't be right.

'Greta, I know you're here. Maybe you don't want to talk without Esmaralda.'

It was her. Unless he'd completely lost his mind, that was Matilda speaking. His own daughter.

'But I'm begging you. Please answer me. I have to know.'

He just couldn't understand how or why.

'Greta. If you're here, please show yourself.'

He started examining the shelf, moving a collection of hand axes and a set of little brown bottles full of various liquids out of the way. But he found nothing to explain the voice.

'It won't take long. I promise.'

Not until he took a closer look at the edges around the shelf, which turned out not to be built-in at all.

'Just give me a sign. Anything. It doesn't matter what.'

In addition to the fact that the right end of the shelf moved a millimetre or two when he jiggled it back and forth, he could also see a thin line between the shelf and the wall on either side.

'I just have one question. Answer it and I promise I'll leave you alone.'

Without knowing how, he must have pushed the shelf the right way, because suddenly there was a click and the shelf swung open like a door in front of him.

'Please, for me. I can't take walking around not knowing any more.'

The windowless space behind the shelves was only a few feet across and furnished with an old desk chair, an overflowing bookcase and a desk on which sat a computer with a speaker on either side of the screen.

'Please, Greta, I'm begging you.'

The screen showed the same audio software that was on Elvin's computer. A programme that had been triggered by Matilda's voice and was now recording what she was saying onto the computer's hard drive.

'You can't just say A and then not bother with B. That's really not okay.'

He studied the sound waves ebbing and flowing on the channel labelled *Basement*.

'So I'm asking you one more time,' Matilda went on. *'After this, I promise I'll never summon you again.'*

The other channels were called *Upstairs landing, Hallway, Living room, Bathroom, Kitchen, Bedroom, Child's room 1* and *Child's room 2,* and finally, *Studio.*

'Who in my family... is going to die?'

Time, his thoughts, the room he was in. Everything was spinning; the ground disappeared from under him yet again and he had to sit down on the chair before his knees buckled.

'Who, Greta? Just tell me who.'

He'd searched virtually the entire house, he'd been everywhere. Yet even so, he'd missed that practically every room was bugged. He tried to scroll back along the time axis to see how far back the recordings went. But that function seemed to be disabled while the programme was recording.

Instead, he noticed a camera symbol in the top right

corner. He couldn't recall seeing that in Elvin's version of the software, and when he clicked it, a new window opened, divided into nine equal parts. Nine moving images that each showed a different room in his house.

45

W*IKHOLM*, SAID A sign on the mailbox outside the house in Påarp where Lilja stopped and parked her Ducati. This was where Pontus Milwokh's parents lived. Or Pontus Hao Wikholm, as he'd been known back then. In a red-brick house with a satellite dish, a carport and a small, meticulously mown lawn, completely devoid of weeds.

Last spring, she'd come here to inform them that their daughter, papergirl Soni Wikholm, had been murdered. That was one of the worst parts of her job. Children should outlive their parents. Period. Now she was there to put them through something even worse by telling them their son was very likely a serial killer.

There was nothing normal about this case. Nothing. The seemingly random coincidences just kept happening, and even though it made complete sense for it to be her delivering the news, she fervently wished Tuvesson had asked one of the others.

It wasn't the news itself she wanted to avoid, it was the parents; before she was even done lowering the Ducati's kickstand and taking her helmet off, she was overcome with the same sense of unease she'd felt the last time she was here. The mood after she told them about their daughter's death had made her want to crawl out of her own skin.

'There you are!' called a woman with powder-white skin and frizzy auburn hair, which looked like it had been brushed for hours in preparation for her visit. 'Hi, welcome,' she went on, waving from the doorway. 'Börje's waiting.'

'Hi, Ing-Marie.' She stepped into the hallway, where everything was a shade of brown.

'So, we meet again.' The woman squeezed past Lilja and reached for the door as if it couldn't be closed fast enough. 'You can leave your shoes here, and then please do come in.' She chuckled nervously and wiped her forehead, which was noticeably shiny.

The living room was brown, too. The floor was covered in beige carpet that had seen better days, and plastic, faux-wood panelling lined the walls. The two windows were hidden behind enormous green plants that effectively shut out most of the natural light. A TV so large Lilja had to wonder how they brought it in was the natural focal point of the room.

The husband was slumped in an armchair and made no move to stand up and shake her hand. Instead, he pushed one of the buttons in the armrest to start the massage function, making the chair whir and vibrate.

'Darling, the police are here.' The woman turned to Lilja. 'Well, then, please sit down and do help yourself.'

Lilja walked around the coffee table, which was set with coffee, cream and marble cake, and sat down at the edge of the plush sofa, unsure whether to cut to the chase or attempt to cushion the blow. 'As I'm sure you've realized, this time I'm here about Hao.'

The woman nodded. 'Yes. We haven't heard from in a long time.'

'No. And I'm afraid I have bad news.' She paused, waiting for a reaction.

Just like her last visit, the man kept his eyes fixed on a spot about a foot or so from his face, and if he hadn't blinked from time to time, she would have seriously suspected he was an incredibly lifelike wax figure. The woman, by contrast, kept swallowing hard, even though she hadn't put anything in her mouth, and her eyes were darting this way and that. To her husband. To the coffee. The marble cake. The eczema under her wedding ring, which was several sizes too small.

'I see,' the woman said at length. 'Has he been murdered, too, then?'

'No,' Lilja replied, taken aback by the question. 'Though we're not sure he's still alive. But what I've come to tell you is—'

'Börje, do you want Mummy to pour you a cup?' the woman broke in, addressing the man, who gave a curt nod. 'We don't want it to get cold, do we?' She let out another nervous laugh, wiped the sweat from her top lip with a napkin and filled a cup with coffee, a dash of cream and four cubes of sugar. 'Here you go, darling.' She pushed the cup over to him with a trembling hand. 'I'm sorry, where were we?'

'Your son,' Lilja said, noting that she clearly wasn't going to be served, which was just as well, since she no longer had any desire to drink coffee and marble cake wasn't her favourite. 'Everything points to him having killed five people in the past month.'

The woman swallowed again.

'You might have read about some of the murders in the papers.'

'We don't really read the paper. Isn't that right, Börje, we don't, do we? They're so full of nonsense and lies, it's enough by half. Isn't that what you like to say?'

The man slurped his coffee as though he wished nothing more than for this moment to end so he could return to his life in front of the TV.

'Okay, well, still, that's how it is. Your son has—'

'We figured this would happen,' the man said suddenly, and he pushed one of the buttons in the armrest, which made his chair fall silent once more.

Just like when she last visited, in the spring, Lilja reacted with surprise. Not at what the man had said, or because he'd spoken at all. No, it was the thin, reedy voice, so incongruous in a man of his considerable bulk.

'Yes, that's true,' the woman agreed, pouring herself a cup of coffee.

'Why is that?' Lilja turned to the woman.

'Oh, I don't know.' The woman raised the cup to drink but put it down again because her hand was trembling too much. 'He was simply too... How do I—'

'He was always a delinquent,' the man cut in.

'Right, delinquent was the word I was looking for.'

'In what way was he a delinquent?' Lilja pictured a tiny dwarf trapped inside the massive body that was positively welling out of the armchair.

'He was always up to no good.' He turned to her. 'It was only a matter of time before it got serious.'

'Yes, that's absolutely true.' The woman nodded eagerly. 'No, we can't say we're particularly surprised. Don't you want some coffee, by the way?'

'No, thank you, I've already had too many cups today,'

Lilja lied, unable to understand how these two had ever been approved to adopt. 'Does this mean you've suspected something for a while? Did you know your son was involved after the first murder, of the little boy in Bjuv?'

'Like my wife said, we don't read the papers.' The man calmly put his cup down. 'Could I have a slice of cake?'

'Of course, darling. Mummy will get it for you.' The woman put a slice of marble cake on a plate and handed it to the man. 'No, we're not big on the news.'

'Well, then I can tell you that your son forced a young boy into a washing machine and started a rinse cycle, which meant he was centrifuged to death twenty minutes later.'

The woman remained silent, but her trembling bottom lip spoke volumes. The man still showed no reaction, just calmly munched away on his cake.

'When did you last hear from him?' Lilja continued. She regretted declining the coffee – not because she wanted any, but it would have been a signal that they weren't done.

'He disappeared the moment he was done with school,' the woman said, serving herself a slice of cake.

'So your son disappeared too, just like your daughter?' She looked back and forth between the man and the woman, waiting for a response that never came.

'I think I'm going to make a fresh pot.' The woman made as if to get up.

'Ing-Marie, I would prefer if you stayed here and answered my questions.'

'I don't know about disappeared,' the man said. 'He'd read some book about a man throwing dice. He tried it himself, and the dice told him to leave us and never come back. And good riddance, if you ask me.'

'But I'm not asking you, I'm asking your wife.' Lilja turned to the woman, whose lower lip was trembling again. 'You haven't heard from him since?'

The woman swallowed and looked around for something safe to rest her eyes on.

'Shouldn't you tell her about when he contacted you and how you were about to transfer him all our savings?' the man said. 'Or have you chosen to forget that? He was in Asia at the time, playing poker.'

'Right.' The woman nodded. 'But—'

'Like I said, we have no idea where he is now. We didn't even know he was back in the country,' the man went on, cutting her off.

'And what you don't know can't hurt you,' the woman added. 'Isn't that right, Börje, isn't that what you always say?'

Lilja wanted to ask the woman how she endured spending more than an hour in the same house as her husband. Whether he hit her. Whether he'd molested their children. And if so, why she hadn't reported it. She wanted to keep digging until she found something sufficiently serious to have him put away for a long time.

'This is my number, in case he decides to contact you.' She pushed her business card across the table to the woman. 'Or if you think of anything else you want to tell me.'

'Oh no, I'm not going to think of anything else.' The woman looked at her husband. 'But I suppose one never knows what thoughts might pop into one's head. Or what do you say, Börje?'

'Unless you want the box in the basement with his things. Feel free to take that.'

'Yes, that's a good idea, Börje.' The woman clapped her hands together. 'Now that we've finally got rid of Soni's things, we can get rid of Hao's, too. Wonderful. What is it they say? Win-win.'

46

WE'RE IN INTERVIEW. The reply came after Fabian's third attempt to reach Theodor's lawyer, Jadwiga Komorovski. *Will call as soon as we're done. We have a lot to talk about.*

Fabian was already deeply worried about how things were going for Theodor, and Komorovski's messages did nothing to allay his concerns. If there had been anything he could do, anything at all, he would have done it in a heartbeat. Without so much as a second thought, he would have dropped everything and run to the rescue. But he could do nothing. Other than wait for her to call back.

He turned into the car park next to the red three-storey buildings on Skaragatan. A little way away, he spotted Stubbs's plump silhouette under a big oak tree. Judging from the way she was pacing back and forth with her arms crossed, she was in a bad mood.

Exactly how many feet away this was from the flat on the second floor of number 12, where Mattias Larsson's girlfriend, Hanna Brahe, lived with her parents, Fabian didn't know. His interview with her was his official reason for being here. That said, he had no idea how accurate the GPS tracker between his shoulder blades was, so ultimately he could only hope Molander wouldn't think his position curious.

He backed into a visitor parking bay and was turning the engine off when his phone began to vibrate.

The number was unknown, but he recognized it from the night before, when he'd been in touch with the coastguard. He declined the call, climbed out of the car and walked over to Stubbs, who had stopped pacing and was glaring at him.

It didn't take a genius to figure out what the coastguard were calling about, and he had no problem understanding why they were upset and probably in the process of reporting him to the police. It would be odd if they weren't. Even though he hadn't taken the safety off his gun at any point, he'd certainly committed a serious crime when he threatened the crew of KB 202.

'Hi,' he called out. 'I'm sorry I'm late, but—'

'Hi,' Stubbs cut him off. 'Do I look like a confession booth to you or something?'

'Eh, what?'

'No, that's right. So do us both a favour and spare us the forgive-me-my-sins bit. Unlike what some people seem to think, we don't have all the time in the world. Here's the deal. I've just been to—'

Even though his phone was on vibrate, it managed to interrupt Stubbs, who threw up her hands in silent protest as he once again declined the call from the coastguard.

'Continue.' Fabian put the phone back in his pocket.

'I can certainly try.' Stubbs gave him a very thin smile. 'I spent the morning at Fosie Prison, speaking to Conny Öhman. And the rest of the day I've been kicking my heels, waiting around for you.'

'And who is Conny Öhman?'

'A wife-beating alcoholic from Munka-Ljungby, who is in prison for killing his wife last spring. At least, that's what he was convicted of. But in reality, Molander was behind the murder.'

'And what's Molander's connection to this Conny bloke, or his wife, for that matter?'

'There probably isn't one.' Stubbs shrugged. 'Other than that he was the perfect fall guy since his wife had already made several reports of aggravated assault to the police. The thing is, I've managed to make Conny see that he's been used, and he has agreed to testify against Molander.'

'Fine, but I still don't understand. If there's no connection, why—'

'Maybe he was experiencing withdrawal, what do I know?' Stubbs shrugged. 'Like with Ingela Ploghed. As far as I'm aware, he'd been on his best behaviour for almost two years, so he probably couldn't curb his urges any longer. Had to vent his pent-up energy and internal frustration. With children, they call it having ants in one's pants. But why don't we leave that to the psychiatrists. The point is, we have enough to bring him in. So I want you to head straight over to the station and get in a room with Tuvesson so you can—'

'I'm sorry,' Fabian broke in, shaking his head. 'I can't.'

'Why? What do you mean you can't? Of course you— That bloody thing of yours is going off again.' Stubbs pointed to his pocket, where the illuminated screen of his phone was visible through the fabric.

The coastguard again. 'It can wait,' Fabian said. 'Now listen to me. The thing is that Molander—'

'No, I'm not going to stand here vying for your attention

with some bloody phone. Either you turn it off completely or you take the call and get it over with.'

Fabian nodded and took a deep breath before answering. 'This is Fabian Risk.

'*And this is Gert-Ove Helin from the Helsingborg coastguard.*'

'Yes, I pretty much figured, and before you launch into it, I just want you to know that I understand if you're upset about what happened last night.' He turned his back on Stubbs in an attempt to block out her angry sighs.

'*Yes, I don't think I've ever heard anything like it in all my years here at—*'

'Gert-Ove,' Fabian cut in. 'I don't want to seem rude. But I happen to be in the middle of an important meeting, so unless you have something else to say, I think you should just go ahead and file that police report and you can count on my full cooperation. Okay?'

'*Yes, yes, I'm sure that will all be fine. Look, I know Bengan and Sylen pretty well after twenty-two years of working with them, and those particular blokes can be proper whingers when they're in that mood. I like to call them the true climacteric threat. Get it? Not climate, climacteric. You know, menopause.*' He could hear Gert-Ove chuckle at his own joke.

Stubbs walked back into Fabian's view and tapped her watch impatiently. Fabian replied by signalling with one hand that the man on the other end wouldn't stop jabbering on.

'The thing is that I contacted our Danish colleagues to get a clearer picture of what happened,' Helin continued. 'And you can say many things about the Danes, but I happen to be on first-name terms with Ingolf Bremer, the head honcho over at the Naval Operative Command, and reading between the lines, the order to deny you access to Danish territorial waters came from higher up the food chain.'

'I am perfectly aware of who issued the order, which was why I acted the way I did. It's not an excuse, but I didn't see any other way at the time.'

'*I hear you. But you have to understand my position.*'

'Look, Fabian, enough.' Stubbs heaved a demonstrative sigh. 'This is ridiculous. You keep doing whatever it is you're doing and I'll go back to doing my stuff.'

'No, hold on.' Fabian grabbed Stubbs's arm.

'*Otherwise, where would we be?*' Gert-Ove continued.

'Exactly, which is why I suggest you do what you feel you have to do.'

'*Yes, until fifteen minutes ago, I couldn't really see a way around reporting you. But when it turned out you were right all along, I decided to stick the whole thing in a drawer. That's what I wanted to tell you.*'

'I'm not sure I follow?' Fabian raised his free hand to pre-empt an outburst from Stubbs, who looked ready to erupt. 'Right about what?'

'*You didn't hear about the ship?*'

'What ship?'

'*Blimey. I just assumed those things were relayed to you guys.*'

'What things?' Fabian could tell his body was about to flood with adrenaline.

'*I don't know if you noticed last night, but a freight ship by the name of MS* Vinterland *was passing through Öresund while you were out on your caper with the boys.*'

'Yes, I remember it well.' He could sense where the conversation was headed and started walking back towards his car. 'It actually passed us close enough that it blocked the rubber dinghy from view for several minutes.'

'Fabian!' Stubbs called after him. 'You've got to be kidding me!'

'I'll explain in the car,' he called back. 'Come on, hurry up. There's no time!'

'It's not really our job to keep an eye on things that far north. But we couldn't understand why it suddenly veered off course a few hours later, turning sharply eastwards. So, we hailed them but had no response.'

Stubbs hadn't moved from under the oak tree when Fabian reached his car and opened the driver-side door. But then she finally relented and hurried over.

'They didn't respond until several hours later. Or, to be more precise, fifteen minutes ago.'

47

THE DRIVE UP to Halmstad should have taken at least an hour, but Fabian pulled up at the Central Station to drop off Stubbs, who was taking the train back to Helsingborg, no more than forty-five minutes after they left the car park on Skaragatan. Even so, a voice inside him was screaming that he could drive as fast as he pleased. It was too late anyway.

In his heart of hearts, he'd never truly believed Milwokh had drowned. But he certainly hadn't expected him to get on board a freight ship and force them to change their course.

Just a few hours ago, this was exactly what he'd been hoping for. For Milwokh still to be alive to answer questions. But now that those answers had to be weighed against the risk of additional murders, he would have infinitely preferred a dead perpetrator and a million unanswered questions.

He'd tried to reach Frank Käpp on the Hallberg-Rassy several times on the way up, but to no avail. Meanwhile, he'd filled Stubbs in on the events of the night before, when Molander had threatened to destroy the forensic evidence against Milwokh if he was arrested before the case was brought to a close.

After going back and forth for a while, they'd agreed to hold off on the arrest until the evidence was safe. Which made finding it their number one priority.

'Okay, I'll be in touch when I've had a closer look at that map I found in Elvin's boat,' Stubbs said as she climbed out of the car. 'If we're lucky, it'll turn out to be Molander's place. If we're even luckier, it's where he's hidden the evidence, and, if we're really shooting the moon, you might even pick up the next time I call.'

She slammed the door shut and hurried off towards her train.

Fabian pulled back out and pushed on towards Slottsbron in central Halmstad. At a red light, he tried Frank Käpp again, but was once again redirected to his voicemail, where his happy voice suggested texting instead of leaving a message.

In the best of worlds, Frank had kept his promise and turned his phone off because they were in the middle of a therapy session. Or he might have forgotten to turn it back on when they were done and going for a walk or maybe even indulging in a glass of wine at one of Halmstad's many restaurants.

He arrived at the marina, which at first glance looked considerably smaller and easier to navigate than the Råå Marina. Granted, it was relatively busy, but it shouldn't take him much more than thirty, forty minutes to search the entire area.

'What's this then?' someone said behind him as he was locking the car. 'You can't park here.'

Fabian turned around and saw an older man with a crutch, dungarees and a captain's hat emblazoned with the Halmstad Marina logo. 'No? It was the only free spot I could find.'

'Is that right.' The man, who was clearly the harbourmaster, tugged on his captain's hat. 'That's the kind of information I file under U for useless knowledge.'

'If there's somewhere I can pay, I'd be more than happy to.' Fabian walked over to the man and pulled out his wallet. He didn't have time for this; he needed to get out on the piers as quickly as possible. 'How much do you want? I won't be longer than an hour, tops.'

'It's free, and as far as I'm concerned, you can park there all day. So long as you're disabled, that it.'

'This is disabled parking?'

'Bingo.' The man brightened. 'Everyone around here knows that, and from what I can see, you don't have so much as a blister on your foot.'

Fabian looked around, but the only sign he could see was a clearly handmade P.

'Yes, I know, the wheelchair symbol has come off,' the man continued. 'It was painted with environmentally friendly bottom paint and that stuff doesn't hold up too well.'

'I see. Well, then I can inform you that it's a crime to post home-made parking signs and tamper with municipal parking bays.' Fabian held out his police ID.

'So you're police?'

He nodded. 'But don't worry, I'm not here to—'

'You know, it's only since I had to start using this,' the man broke in, waving his crutch around. 'It gets crowded here – on a bad day, I have to park all the way over by the crane. And that won't do, not with my hip. The only thing it's good for these days is predicting the weather. Speaking of which, we have a low-pressure area coming in in a few hours.'

Fabian looked up at the sun, which looked unthreatened

in a cloudless sky. 'I'm actually looking for a boat. A Hallberg-Rassy in a guest slip.'

'Hallberg-Rassy?'

Fabian nodded.

'One of the bigger models?'

Fabian nodded again.

'It's in slip 128.'

'So it's here?'

'Came in this morning. A couple with a child.'

'A son of about ten?'

The harbour master brightened and nodded.

He had no trouble locating the boat off one of the four jetties extending out into the harbour. Unlike the first time he'd seen the Hallberg-Rassy at the Råå Marina, it was now berthed with its bow pointing in towards the jetty. Other than that, it looked, as far as he could recall, much the same.

The genoa was wrapped around the forestay, the sheets had been detached and the mainsail was meticulously folded up and covered, exactly how it should be. Everything was in its place, neat and tidy. As if last night's attack had never happened.

Fabian got up on tiptoe to try to see if there was anyone in the cockpit, but the dodger blocked most of it from view.

He grabbed the bow line, pulled the boat closer and tapped his keys against the pulpit. It made almost no sound to his ear, but he knew the metallic clanging would spread through the hull, like when you hit a radiator in a block of flats.

There was no reaction.

He stepped on board and continued sternward along the teak deck to the cockpit. It, too, was neat and tidy. The doors to the saloon and the aft cabin were both locked, and he knocked on them mostly for the sake of having done it.

When he'd been told Milwokh had seized control of the freighter and forced it to turn east, he'd assumed he was going after the Käpp family. But maybe he'd simply wanted to use one of their lifeboats to get back to shore so he could lick his wounds and let the dice choose a new victim in due course.

That was pure speculation, however, and his best option at the moment was to have a seat, wait for the Käpps to turn up and make sure they were safe until Milwokh could be apprehended.

But that turned out to be easier said than done. Just sitting there doing nothing was virtually unbearable. The silence and the slow lapping of the waves against the bow quickly got under Fabian's skin and the calm he'd felt on finding the boat was being replaced by a creeping sense of unease.

Maybe they weren't sipping wine and enjoying the lovely weather. Maybe they'd never got as far as contacting a therapist to set up an appointment.

He stood up and started going through the many compartments in the cockpit. Mostly to have something to do. But when he found a key at the bottom of one of the winch holders, he couldn't stop himself from unlocking the door to the aft cabin, opening it and sticking his head in. Inside, he saw a rolled-up sleeping bag below a shelf filled with books and comics. On the opposite wall was a flat-screen TV and on a shelf next to it, a PlayStation.

But no ten-year-old boy. Or any trace of a sword fight. He left the aft cabin and moved on to the saloon instead, where he was struck by how much roomier it was than he'd expected. The galley looked like it had everything you might need and the ceiling cleared his head by at least a foot.

The saloon was tidy as well. Almost too tidy. Granted, everything needed to be put away on board a boat, but the Käpp family hadn't struck him as neat freaks. Quite the opposite, actually.

The door to the forepeak was closed, and on his way over to it, it suddenly occurred to Fabian that he should probably take out his gun and remove the safety before continuing past the dining table and corner sofa. Once he reached the door, he pressed his ear against it and was greeted by that imploding silence he disliked so heartily. At length, he slowly put his hand on the handle and threw the door open.

The forepeak was empty.

Empty and very tidy.

And suddenly, it hit him like a ton of bricks. The realization that the inner voice that had been screaming itself hoarse had been right all along.

That he was too late.

Pontus Milwokh had got there first using the lifeboat he took from the MS *Vinterland*. He'd carried out the dice's orders and then cleaned the boat until there wasn't so much as a fingerprint left.

But what had he done with the bodies? Thrown them overboard, or had he... Fabian looked down at the carpet underneath his tattered red Converse and after putting the gun back in its holster, he bent down, grabbed hold of an edge and pulled the carpet aside.

The varnished wood sole underneath the carpet was the very picture of craftsmanship at its best. Nothing had been left to chance, and even though it was a shame to cover it with cheap carpet, Fabian could understand why a person would want to protect the wood from wear and tear.

But he was more interested in the three hatches leading down to the bilge, which was bound to be unexpectedly roomy as well.

He had just put his index finger through the flush hatch pull when his phone rang.

'*How are you getting on?*' asked Tuvesson.

'To be honest, I'm not sure.'

'*Have you found them?*'

'Not yet.' He looked down at the closed hatch. 'But I did find their boat.'

'*And?*'

'Too soon to say, but I fear the worst.'

'*Okay. Let's hope you're wrong. The reason I'm calling is that Molander has just completed a triangulation for Frank Käpp's phone, and from what we can see, he's nowhere near—*'

The thud above his head was so loud even Tuvesson heard it.

'*What was that?*'

'Someone has come on board. I'll call you back.' He ended the call and turned towards the companionway as the footsteps above moved sternward.

'What the fuck? Look,' exclaimed a voice, and then a man stepped down into the cockpit and blocked out all the light. A man he'd never seen before. 'Who the fuck are you?' he demanded, staring at Fabian. 'And what the hell are you doing on my boat?'

And with that, everything fell into place.

48

WHEN LILJA MET the Wikholms for the first time that spring, her focus had been on Soni Wikholm, and she had primarily gone through boxes with her name on them. But she'd looked in the one box marked *Hao* as well, and reacted to the large number of dice in it. If only she'd known then what lay ahead.

Now she opened the box again, on the floor of her office at the station, and there it was. The rectangular wooden box filled with dice of every shape and colour. There were regular Yahtzee dice of white plastic. There were wooden dice with gold pips and transparent red casino dice. There were dice with strange symbols and as many as twenty sides.

Dice she hadn't even known existed.

The box also contained a plastic Death Star, a collection of knives and two hardback books and two DVDs with stamped library lending cards from the Påarp Library in plastic pockets on their inside covers.

She'd decided never to read *American Psycho* by Bret Easton Ellis. She'd heard it was far more gruesome than the film, which had been slightly too much for her. The films *Lost Highway* and *Mulholland Drive* were both by David Lynch, and like many others of her generation, she'd gone through a Lynch phase. But she hadn't managed to get through either of those two because she'd found them too weird.

She had, however, read Luke Reinhart's *The Dice Man* and unless she misremembered, she owned both a Swedish and an English version.

At the bottom of the box, she found a photo album with faded pictures of Milwokh and his sister as children, running around the garden, building Lego models and playing Monopoly. But towards the end, the pictures changed, and even though Milwokh didn't look older than eleven or twelve, he seemed to have entered the difficult teenage period, with eyeliner and a perpetual frown on his face.

Between the last two pages of the album was an old envelope from PhotoQuick. She opened it and took out a stack of photographs, all taken during the same visit to Tivoli in Copenhagen.

Pontus Milwokh didn't look older than eight or nine and was in virtually every picture. He'd taken most of them himself in front of various rides. But for some of them he must have asked for help because they were taken from a distance and he was waving at the camera.

There was no sign of his parents or sister in any of the pictures. He could have gone with a distant relative or friend, of course. But after studying the pictures down to the last detail, two, then three times, Lilja had to conclude that it did in fact look like he'd been there by himself.

Given his young age, that was odd. Even knowing his parents, it was strange. But he certainly didn't look upset.

On the contrary, his eyes were so full of joy and happiness it was almost impossible to comprehend that he had turned into such a monster.

49

THE HOT-BULB ENGINE was much too large and so loud a
person could have been excused for thinking they were on
a mid-sized fishing vessel rather than a small, open wooden
skiff. But the harbourmaster needed no persuasion to explain
at very great length why his do-it-yourself contraption was
ingenious.

Within minutes, Fabian had tuned him out, moved to the
bow, far from both the engine and the harbourmaster, and
was using the headset of his phone as makeshift ear buds.
What he wanted was silence. But since not playing anything
through the headphones meant anything but silence, he'd
turned on Brian Eno's ambience album *Thursday Afternoon*,
which helped create a space for his thoughts in the calm
before what lay ahead.

It was only once they reached the open sea that he realized
he'd been feeling that way all week. That everything around
him was just the calm before the storm, before the abyss
opened up in front of him. As though nothing made any real
difference because everything was already preordained.

It was a feeling that went against his nature and everything
he believed, and he would have preferred to pour all his
energy into the complete opposite. Into thinking that of
course it's possible to effect change and make a difference.
That was exactly what he'd been trying to make Theodor

understand. But he hadn't got through, and now he didn't know if he even believed it himself any more.

Once he'd managed to calm down the alarmed family and explain why he'd broken into their yacht, he'd gone to find the harbourmaster to ask him if he knew anyone who would be willing to take him out in their boat immediately. The man had once more warned him of the low pressure that, according to his hip, was about to roll in, but had in the end offered to take him in his own skiff.

With Laholm Bay on their port side, they were moving south towards Hallands Väderö outside the Bjäre peninsula. Visibility could only be described as middling, and there was virtually no wind. Even so, the boat was pitching in waves left over from the previous day's blustery weather, which, although they were evenly spaced and smooth as mirrors, were also long and deep. In other words, it was a day made to cause seasickness, but Fabian was so focused on analysing what he could see through the binoculars as he scanned the vague horizon that he didn't notice. Here and there, he saw the occasional freighter, the size of a matchbox. From time to time, a motorboat whisked past in stark contrast with the yachts that bobbed about, waiting for the evening breeze to pick up, like scattered crumbs on a vast, billowing tablecloth.

The area Molander had identified was based on just two masts. One in Torekov and the other on Hallands Väderö, which, with a maximum elevation of thirty feet, was almost invisible in the thickening haze. It was an impossibly large area, and with the deteriorating visibility, time was an important factor.

The maximum speed of the little skiff was six knots,

which meant they were easily outstripped by any boat running by engine. Yachts with their sails up, on the other hand, were no challenge. But those weren't the ones Fabian was interested in; he was studying the ones lying still, their sails down.

A part of him was hoping they'd be forced to turn back to Halmstad with their errand unfinished. That Tuvesson would call and tell him Molander had just identified a new location further north. That the phone was still moving because Frank Käpp had broken his promise and was pushing on towards Gothenburg as originally planned.

But the sense of unease in the pit of his stomach knew better. It always did.

The dark dot came into sight for just a few seconds before vanishing into the haze once more. It could have been anything. A fishing boat, a light buoy or just a grain of sand on the lens of the binoculars. But it wasn't, and once he spotted it a second time, he felt convinced it was what they were looking for.

He signalled to the harbourmaster to change course and noted that the old man's hip had been correct. Conditions had gradually been worsening since they set out from the marina and a steadily thickening fog had appeared from out of nowhere. Now, just half an hour later, they were unable to see much further than a hundred feet.

'I told you,' called the man from behind the wheel, reducing their speed. 'My hip is never wrong. Never.'

Fabian nodded and gave him a thumbs up. He didn't even have time to start pondering whether there was a scientific explanation for how that worked before a yacht with lowered sails appeared out of the thick fog.

The boat with the characteristic dark-blue Hallberg-Rassy stripe along both sides was adrift on the long, rolling waves, and even if you didn't know what had happened, it was an ominous sight.

Increasingly dense fog banks floated by like big cotton wads in various shades of grey, draining the world of colour and from time to time hiding the yacht from view entirely.

It looked dirty, and both the mainsail and the genoa were dragging in the water. The mainsheet wasn't cleated either, so the boom kept sweeping back and forth with the waves. There was no sign of life on board, and apart from the boom and a stray fender rolling back and forth across the deck, nothing moved.

When they were no more than fifty feet away, Fabian signalled for the harbourmaster to circle the yacht, which was considerably dirtier on the other side. Through the binoculars, he could see that what looked like dirt from a distance was in fact sticky dark-red smears that in places had run down the hull.

Pontus Milwokh had refused to allow circumstance to trump the dice's decision. Against all odds, he had not only survived, but located, caught up with and ruthlessly slaughtered a completely innocent family.

His evil seemed to know no limits. The monumental meaninglessness felt like a few more tons on Fabian's shoulders. He could barely breathe under the pressure, and for the first time he asked himself how much longer he would be able to carry on. How much he was willing to give up to keep going.

Less than five minutes ago, they could have given up and turned back empty-handed. They could have blamed the fog and no one would have questioned it. But it was too late for that now, and there wasn't going to be another phone call from Tuvesson about a new position further north. He was going to have to climb on board and do a quick inspection and then tie a rope to the bow so they could tow the boat back to shore.

The movement in one of the windows was almost imperceptible. But he'd seen it, he was certain. Something had moved inside the cabin. He turned around to see if the harbourmaster had caught it too, but was met by a vacant stare.

'Hello? Is there anyone there?' he called out as loudly as he could, while pulling out his gun. 'If so, come out with your hands above your head!'

Nothing happened. But at least the harbourmaster snapped out of it and moved the skiff in alongside the drifting yacht. The waves made it far from easy, but eventually Fabian was able to step up onto the Hallberg-Rassy and down into the cockpit.

There was blood everywhere. The sticky smears on the white plastic bore witness to a protracted struggle.

'Hello!' he called again, but there was no answer.

The cabin door was swinging open and shut as the boat rolled. Fabian walked over to it and took a deep breath before throwing it open and pointing his gun down into the gloomy saloon, completely unprepared for the scream that greeted him, together with a fist that came flying straight at him.

He fired a shot and then three more in quick succession, before realizing it was just a big seagull with a severed hand in its beak that had been trying to get out and was now dying on the floor among a jumble of body parts that two other seagulls were still feasting on.

It was a bloodbath. A severed foot here, a forearm there. An ear and what looked like part of a torso. One of the seagulls hopped onto the top of Frank Käpp's head, which was sitting on a sofa, and started to peck at the contents of one of the eye sockets.

About a foot from it, Fabian spotted the son's head, mostly hidden under a soiled blanket. Only one ear, part of one cheek and some hair was visible, and even though he would have given a lot not to have to, he walked over and slowly lifted a corner of the blanket.

The eyes that met his changed everything.

'Hi, Vincent,' he said. 'Remember me?'

The boy nodded, and just like that, the feeling of failure and preordained pointlessness Fabian had been carrying around for so long was replaced by something like hope.

Maybe he could make a difference after all.

50

THE FOG AND the dusk. What would he have done without them?

With them on his side, he was able to glide through Helsingborg harbour as though wrapped in a big invisibility cloak. The coastguard ship that had been out looking for him since last night, KB 202, was berthed just fifty yards away on his left, next to Parapeten. But he couldn't even see that far.

For almost three hours, he'd bobbed around in the lifeboat from MS *Vinterland* with the engine turned off so as not to give away his position. At times, he'd been on the brink of discovery. But luck had been with him, and he hadn't had to do anything but sit still, letting them pass him by in the milky fog.

Or maybe luck was the wrong word. Maybe it was a reward for his hard work. After everything he'd been through, he deserved to have things go his way, and for the first time in a long time, he was genuinely proud of himself.

He turned right after passing the first pier and continued towards a small gravel beach where he could pull the boat up and cover it with a tarpaulin.

Pretty much everything had gone wrong, and sure, he'd had moments of doubt. He had no problem admitting it. But he'd turned defeat after defeat to his advantage, and in the end, the complications had been the best part.

It almost felt as though the whole thing had been a big test. A challenge to find out if he was worthy of the dice's grace. There could be no doubt about it now. He hadn't just completed his task. He'd done so with flying colours.

The tide had turned the moment a big freight ship had blocked him from police view. After taping the throttle down, he'd been able to move up alongside the ship, which had been moving unusually slowly, and as though someone was rolling out a red carpet for him, there had been welded steps all the way up the side of it.

About an hour later, he'd left his hiding place and made his way up to the bridge, where the sword had finally been on his side when the female captain had decided to play the hero.

After that, she'd danced to his tune and done his bidding. It hadn't been long before he could see the Hallberg-Rassy without binoculars, and after rewrapping the captain's wound and making sure she wasn't about to bleed out, he'd covered the last bit in one of the freighter's lifeboats.

The sun had been high in the sky and the fog that a few hours later would blanket everything in grey candyfloss had yet to announce itself. There had been no chance of a covert approach, so he'd decided to stand up in the open boat and smile and wave to the man in the yacht instead, like the fond reunion it actually was.

The man had, predictably, sped up and tried to contact the police. But apparently his mobile hadn't been able to make contact with a mast, and before he could get the shortwave radio up and running, the lifeboat had pulled level with the Hallberg-Rassy.

He'd calmly explained to the man that the dice had chosen him, and that neither one of them could change that. To his surprise, the man had listened and let him climb aboard while he made it clear that the best thing he could do in the present situation was to give up without unnecessary resistance, which would only prolong his own suffering and possibly even inflict some on his family as well. The man had nodded without protest, and after that everything had gone his way. There had been no more fumbling with the sword. Instead, the sharp weapon had felt like a natural extension of his arm, and he'd been able to swing it freely.

The whole thing had been like a dance in which the choreography comes naturally. Every swing had landed exactly where it should, and to minimize the man's suffering, he'd started with his head. Seven swings it had taken him, and the thudding sound when the head finally hit the teak floor and the sight of blood spurting out of the man's severed carotid arteries had spurred him to keep hacking away until there wasn't so much as one whole body part left.

The only disruption had been the wife's hysterical screaming once she woke up and realized what was happening. It had been so annoying he'd eventually had to pause halfway through to knock her unconscious. At least the kid had been smart enough to stay calm and let him have at it.

On the way back to Helsingborg, he'd washed his hands and face clean of blood, but his clothes were unsalvageable. Luckily, the harbour was deserted, and he didn't see a living soul until he crossed the tracks via the overpass towards the Helsingborg District Court and turned down Carl Krooksgatan, and even then they were only fleeting shadows in the twilit fog, completely unaware of who they were passing.

Out on the water, he'd pondered where to go now that he'd been identified by the police. It didn't take a PhD to realize they were going to assume he was on the run and doing everything in his power to lie low, which was the only sensible course of action. Maybe that was why the dice had decided he should do the exact opposite.

The workday was over, but the night was still relatively young, so they might still be there, examining his flat. Meanwhile, it was only a matter of time before they found the yacht, if they hadn't already, and then they would likely relocate all resources to dealing with that. But he'd have to see. He'd cross that bridge when he came to it.

After cautiously entering the building, he left the lights off and took the stairs, two or sometimes three steps at a time. With six steps to go, he stopped and waited. At least his door was closed, and he could neither see nor hear anyone lurking outside, watching it, which in the end made him risk climbing the rest of the way.

As he'd noted when he left the flat twenty-four hours earlier, the drilled hole in the door had been covered with several layers of thick tape, and since the locks had been changed as well, he had to use his lock pick gun. *So quick and easy it should be illegal*, the description on the website he'd bought it from had read, and so far, he couldn't accuse them of false advertising. It hadn't let him down once.

Once he'd brought his bags into the hallway, he closed the door behind him and looked around. The bathroom door and the door to the walk-in closet were closed, as usual. Half-open doors had always bothered him. But apart from the damage to his front door, he couldn't see any immediate signs of a police search. There was a hint of a strange smell in the air, but nothing that opening a window wouldn't solve.

He continued into the living room, where he dropped the hockey bag and took off his backpack before going over to the window and peeking out. Nothing in any of the many windows in the façade opposite suggested his flat was under surveillance, which was definitely strange, considering. Maybe the police were simply short-staffed and had their hands full with other things.

The bedroom looked untouched, too. Had they even been there? It almost didn't seem like they had. Maybe they'd just walked around with tweezers, collecting hairs, or maybe they'd been in a hurry and done a poor job.

The wardrobe seemed untouched, too, and opening it confirmed his clothes hadn't been moved.

But it was only after he'd climbed into the wardrobe, closed it from inside, stuck his middle finger into the small hole in the back and pushed the narrow metal plate on the other side to the left, opened the secret door and stepped into his concealed room that he finally dared to relax.

51

THE CAR LOCK clicked behind Fabian as he made his way towards the entrance through the evening fog. He was walking briskly in an attempt to leave the images from the yacht behind. But they stubbornly kept pace with him.

Whatever he looked at became intermingled with the severed body parts in the cabin. Feet, legs, arms, heads. At the moment, they were littering the car park outside Helsingør Prison, and half an hour ago the ferry to Denmark had looked like an abattoir.

He walked through the lobby, showed his ID to the man at the glassed-enclosed reception desk and awaited his permission before proceeding to the security checkpoint, where he handed over his phone, wallet and keys and let them body-scan him.

The severed limbs had been everywhere in the yacht. He'd assumed the foot and the bare woman's leg sticking out from under a sheet in the forepeak had been chopped off somewhere around the hip joint. Then the foot had suddenly twitched. Just a little, almost imperceptibly, but enough to make him pull the cover off the woman, who was slowly waking up.

The uniformed guard swiped his card through the reader and punched in a code, which made the door in front of them buzz open. They continued down an echoing, windowless corridor with cold fluorescent lights and polished laminate flooring.

He couldn't tell if this was a good idea. Theodor had been clear about not wanting visitors. But he couldn't just stand on the sidelines and watch his son dig himself deeper and deeper into a hole.

The boy and his mother had both been in extreme shock and completely unresponsive. Even so, he'd spoken to them continually in an attempt to keep their focus on small details. Like that he was there to help them, that there was another boat they were going to climb into, that they were going to be back on dry land very soon.

To spare them from seeing the worst of it, he'd used a scarf to blindfold the mother and pulled a hat down over the eyes of the boy. Then he'd helped them out into the cockpit and over to the wooden skiff, and they'd waited until the coastguard arrived to tow the Hallberg-Rassy down to Helsingborg, where Molander and his two assistants were standing by to start the crime scene investigation.

He'd accompanied the boy and his mother back to Halmstad, where an ambulance had been waiting to drive them to Helsingborg Hospital.

And then Jadwiga Komorovski had called.

The guard led him down corridor after corridor, but he didn't recognize anything from his last visit with Sonja. It had only been twenty-four hours. But he'd aged at least a year in that time, and if it carried on like this, he was only weeks away from attending his own funeral.

At least he recognized the visiting room, and he could almost hear the echo of Theodor's voice. *I would appreciate it if you left me alone and didn't come back...*

The chairs around the table were unoccupied, as was the armchair and the plastic-covered cot. At least the body parts were gone for now, but the nagging worry remained. Was he doing the right thing, or was his unsolicited evening visit a dire mistake?

A fistfight, Theodor's lawyer had said on the phone. At first, Fabian had assumed another prisoner had attacked his son, but after a while it had become clear it was the other way around. And the fact that they weren't talking about a minor scuffle, but rather an aggravated assault, did nothing to improve matters.

That incarceration was proving tough on Theodor was hardly surprising. But according to Komorovski, he was refusing to cooperate, either with her or with the Danish police. His mental state was also exhibiting clear signs of deteriorating, which was why she'd insisted that Fabian come over and try to set him straight.

Fabian sat down in one of the chairs and stared at the door, waiting for it to open, which took another few minutes. Even so, he woke with a start when Theodor was led in, wearing handcuffs.

'Hi, Theodor.' He almost flew out of his chair to give his son a hug. But Theodor dodged him and sat down, and the embrace turned into an awkward pat on the back instead. 'I'm glad you agreed to see me. So glad.' He was met with silence and realized his own forced smile was about to crack. 'Excuse me,' he called to the guard in an attempt to seize control of the situation. 'I would appreciate it if you could remove my son's handcuffs.'

'I'm afraid I can't,' the guard said, shaking his head uncertainly.

'Oh yes, you most certainly can. I'm not just his father, I'm also an officer of the law, so I think we can both safely assume I'm not in any danger, in case it's my safety you're worried about.'

'Given what has happened, I'm obliged to—'

'You're not obliged to do anything. And as far as my son's concerned, I can inform you he's not a particularly violent person. So whatever happened here, I'm sure there's an explanation, and I intend to find out what it is.'

The guard acquiesced with a sigh, went over to Theodor and unlocked his handcuffs, then left the room.

'There, that's better. Isn't it, Theodor?' He waited for a response, but when none came, he sat down across from his son and tried to catch his eye. 'Hey... How are you doing, really?' But that didn't work either. 'I heard you got in a fight. Is that something you want to tell me about?' Again, he waited but had only silence in return. 'Theodor, I know you and I know you wouldn't just jump a person for no reason.'

Theodor stared at his fingers, which were drumming against the table.

'Your lawyer, Komorovski, claims you're refusing to cooperate. Is that true?' Fabian continued and again had no reply. 'Hey, why won't you speak? We're all just trying to help you.'

Theodor's fingers against the table was the only sound. One by one they hit the tabletop, like an impatient countdown to when their meeting would be over.

Fabian heaved a sigh in an attempt to vent his frustration. 'I don't understand.' But it was already too late. 'Honestly. What do you think you're doing? You don't accidentally get into a fight serious enough to be labelled aggravated assault. And this thing I hear about not working with your lawyer. What's going on?' He stood up and walked around the table. 'And why won't you talk to me? I'm here for you, not me. Theodor, I'm talking to you!' He grabbed his son and shook him. 'Wake the fuck up! Say something! This is about you. You and your life, don't you get that?'

He let go of him and sank into a squat. 'I'm sorry, I just feel so... I'm just trying to help you. Look...' He closed his eyes and tried to calm down. 'I understand if you're angry and disappointed, I really do. With me, with everyone here, with the entire system, but can't we at least try to talk to each other? I promise, you'll feel a lot better.'

Theodor turned to Fabian.

'We belong together, right?' Fabian went on. 'You and me. We're on the same team. Remember that.'

Theodor looked at Fabian for several long, silent seconds. 'That might just be the most cloying thing I've ever heard. Like a line from some eighties' B-movie where the directions are telling us to embrace each other.'

'Well, I'm sorry you choose to take it that way. But cloying as it may sound to you, it's exactly how I feel, and that's why I'm—'

'Please, stop, for your own sake, just stop.' Theodor stood up and took a step back. 'Do us both a favour and leave and we'll forget this ever happened. It's just embarrassing.'

'So?' Fabian shrugged. 'I guess we'll live with the embarrassment.'

'You don't even fucking believe it yourself!' Theodor turned towards the door.

'Theo, wait.' Fabian hurried after him and grabbed him by the arm. 'Whatever you think, I'm here to—'

'You're here for one reason and one reason only. Your own guilty fucking conscience!' Theodor wrenched free of Fabian's grasp and pushed the button for the guard to come and get him. 'There's nothing you can do, and you know that as well as I do.'

Fabian sighed and nodded. 'This wasn't what we thought was going to happen, I'll be the first to admit it.' The door opened and the guard entered. 'But you have a good lawyer. One of the best. The problem is that she can't help you unless you cooperate. Don't you get that? You have to do what she tells you and try to bear it. It won't be long before all of this is over and—'

'Over? What do you mean, over?' Theodor held his arms out to the guard, who started putting the handcuffs back on. 'It's barely even started.'

'Can we, please, hold off on that for a minute.' Fabian pushed in between Theodor and the guard. 'Listen to me. Right now, you're at the bottom of the pit. It doesn't get any worse than this.' He grabbed Theodor's shoulders. 'Being locked up in here with all the criminals just because you want to testify and tell the truth. Because you want to help and do the right thing. It must suck. It does suck.'

'Whatever. I'm leaving.' Theodor tried to sidestep Fabian so the guard could cuff him. But Fabian kept him where he was.

'Please, don't make things worse than they already are. Just try to keep it together until the trial resumes. If you can just do that, I promise you everything's going to be—'

'Where the fuck do you get off promising me anything?' Theodor broke in.

'Because I've been around the block a few times and I know how these—'

'You have no fucking idea! Admit it! You're as lost as the rest of us!'

'I'm not, actually, and neither is your lawyer. She's anything but lost, and according to her you're digging your own grave, the way you're behaving.' His son was right. There was no telling what was going to happen during the trial. 'Theo, I know what I'm talking about. You have to do what she says.' But that didn't change the fact that Theodor had no choice but to tell them truthfully what he knew and hope for a fair judgement.

'Are you seriously standing here promising me everything's going to be all right, so long as I obey her, step into the witness box and tell the truth? Is that what you're doing?'

Fabian was painfully aware of how right Theodor was. He wasn't in a position to promise anything. It was all empty words and wishful thinking at this point. But if there was one thing his son did not need right now, it was prevarication.

So he nodded and did his best to put on a reassuring smile. 'Theodor, there was no warrant out for you. The police weren't looking for additional perpetrators. You came forward of your own free will, and the reason you did was because you wanted to testify and tell the truth. Nothing else. A truth that shows you have nothing to hide.'

Theodor shook his head, fighting back tears now.

'Hey...' Fabian stroked his cheek. 'Do you really think I'd be standing here promising you something if I wasn't sure?'

Theodor shrugged.

'You have to trust me.'

'Do you really mean that?' Theodor was unable to hold back his tears any longer. 'You're not just saying it to make me feel better?'

Fabian shook his head and hugged him. 'Just keep it together for a while longer and before you know it, you'll be back home and we can put this behind us once and for all.'

'Promise?' Theodor hugged him back with a fervour Fabian hadn't felt before.

'Yes, I promise, Theo. I promise.'

Theodor nodded and ended the hug with tears streaming down his cheeks. Then he turned to the guard and held out his hands to be cuffed and led out of the room.

52

LILJA TURNED THE water off and tested the temperature. The bath had an old-fashioned mixer tap, with separate handles for cold and hot water, which at times made it impossible to strike the right balance. Nor did it seem to matter how hard she turned the handles. The tap still dripped, and not at a steady rhythm, either, which made it even more annoying.

But at least she had a bath now, and when she slowly let her feet get used to the heat, she could feel her whole body do the Mexican wave out of sheer joy. She'd missed hot baths.

There had been no bath in the house in Perstorp. Apart from having to live there being generally awful in itself, a bath was probably what she'd missed the most. They'd had a sauna. But she'd never been one for sitting around in the nude, sweating and struggling to breathe.

Hampus, by contrast, had seen it as a big plus when he decided to buy the house and had rambled on and on about how his new healthy lifestyle was going to include nightly runs followed by a good sauna. But there hadn't been any running, and the sauna had mostly been used for storage.

Hampus… She'd barely given him any thought since packing up her things and leaving. Mainly because there had been no time. She'd been on her feet pretty much non-stop the past week.

Burning out had never been her thing. At least, that was how she used to see it. She was someone who dealt with whatever problems came her way instead of curling up in the foetal position. But that was then, before she'd lost herself in this case and before, thanks to Sweden Democrat Sievert Landertz, she'd found herself in the middle of a band of neo-Nazis out to make her life hell.

Now, she didn't know. But she was undeniably fragile, more so than ever, and this was the first time she'd allowed herself to relax and take a break even though there was still a mountain of removal boxes left to unpack. They were going to have to wait, if she wanted to avoid a mental breakdown. A long, hot bath and a few hours of sleep and hopefully she'd be fit for fight again.

She was reaching for the soap when she heard the distant sound of a toilet flushing. It didn't sound the same as last time, when she'd finally realized it was coming from the flat next to hers. This time, she could clearly hear the water rush through the pipes in the ceiling. Even so, she opened the vent and listened, but couldn't hear anything other than the steady whoosh of air.

What were the odds of her moving into this of all flats and becoming neighbours with Pontus Milwokh of all people. And yet they'd managed to let him get away, which in turn meant they now had yet another gruesome murder on their hands.

Molander and his assistants were already processing the Hallberg-Rassy, and if anyone should be close to burning out, it was him. If things carried on like this, they would soon have more crime scenes than they could count. As far as she knew, they'd had to put the examination of the flat in Planteringen on hold to tackle the boat instead.

She didn't know how the processing of Milwokh's flat was coming along. She actually hadn't heard anything about it, which was worrying and suggested they were far from done, and might in fact not even have started. Could that really be the case? Who was in charge of prioritizing? Tuvesson or Molander himself?

If it were up to her, the flat next door would have been first in line. There should be all kinds of interesting things in there, definitely more than what she'd been able to infer from the old dice and photo albums in the box from his parents' basement.

His flat was a mirror copy of her own. That thought had struck her when she first entered, but it had subsequently been lost in the commotion, and it was only now, as she relaxed in the bath, that it resurfaced.

Nothing odd about it, as such. Because of the pipes, bathrooms or kitchens were often placed wall to wall. In this building, the bathrooms were connected to the same mains. The kitchens were at opposite ends. Everything added up, except for the bedroom, which for some reason had seemed considerably smaller in the flat next door.

Milwokh's bed had taken up almost the entire room. She could comfortably fit both an armchair and a big desk by the window in her bedroom. There was probably a logical explanation, though. Maybe she'd just been mistaken. Now that she thought about it, the wallpaper in the bedroom had been dark and the ceiling had been painted black, which was bound to contribute to the claustrophobic feeling.

More than anything, she wanted to let it go, sink into herself and let the sleep she was in such dire need of take over. But she knew herself well enough to realize that no matter how hard she tried, this would bother her until she could find an explanation.

53

HE OPENED THE box as though it were the first time, picked up the two-hundred-year-old, white marble icosahedron and weighed it in his hand. He'd been looking forward to this moment, and more than once during the past few days he'd been convinced it would never come.

It had been a week since the last time he'd held it. That time, its weight had felt like a burden, and he hadn't been sure he was even worthy of holding it in his hand. But his last task had turned him from a blind caterpillar into a resplendent butterfly.

He studied the twenty sides, twenty equilateral triangles whose perfect geometry formed his most valuable dice. It didn't just set the pace, chart the course and determine the agenda for what lay ahead. With its nineteen engraved numbers, plus the ten, which had been replaced with an X, it ruled on whether there would be any more tasks at all.

Rolling a two or higher gave him the number of days until the next deed had to take place, counting from today. A one meant it was over, and not just for now, but for ever and ever.

There had been times when he would have had no problem accepting that outcome. But not this time. He couldn't explain why, but it felt like everything he'd gone through and endured had only been preparation for what was to come. As though each of his tasks had in fact been lessons, tailor-made to help him develop the skills he would need.

The dice was getting warmer in his hand, and his entire body itched to perform the first throw. To make sure there was no dirt that could affect the outcome on the green felt board, he dragged his hand across it before shaking the dice until he was convinced there was nothing to impede chance.

Then he let the dice fall and watched it bounce on the felt before coming to a stop.

A twelve.

He was relieved but also slightly disappointed. It wasn't over yet. Another task was going to be set, but it would be almost two weeks before he could complete it. The question was whether he'd be able to wait that long. Maybe there was a point to it, though. Maybe the preparations were going to be so extensive he'd need the time.

He moved on to the next step to find out who his victim was going to be this time. For that, he needed his collection of six-sided, anodized aluminium precision dice. He picked up one of them to determine if he was supposed to use one or two dice and shook it in his hand before releasing it onto the felt.

A three.

In other words, one dice. He picked it back up, shook it and rolled.

A one.

He turned to the map of Skåne pinned to the wall in front of him. The map was cut into a square that was further divided into 144 smaller, numbered squares. Twelve columns numbered west to east and twelve rows from north to south.

For the first time, he was going to execute his mission in the first column, which extended south from Mölle on the beautiful Kullaberg peninsula, in many ways a perfect setting for a murder.

He picked up the dice again, shook it and did another pre-roll.

A four.

That meant the row was going to be determined by two dice. He picked up another one, shook both and released them onto the felt.

Two sixes.

He didn't even need to check the map to know the southernmost square in column number one was Copenhagen. The idea of getting to do something in Denmark had been there since the day he drew the grid on the map, but that it would be the bottom-left square had been beyond his wildest dreams.

An online search revealed that there were approximately 2,300 street names in Copenhagen, and to find out which letter the street name should start with, he once again did a one-dice pre-roll.

A five.

This time he could use up to six dice, so he took out five, shook them in his cupped hands and rolled.

A three, a four, a five, a one, a six.

Together that made nineteen, which corresponded to the letter S.

The column of street names starting with S was much too long to fit on the computer screen, so he repeated the procedure to determine the subsequent letters T O L. That narrowed it down to Stoltenbergsgade, and a few more rolls gave him street number 9.

The street was fairly centrally located, and judging from Google Maps, the building in question had six floors including the attic, which looked like it had been converted into flats. A few rolls later, the dice had settled on the flat to the far right on the third floor, and he was able to do a search on Krak.dk to find out who it was that had only twelve days to live.

At first, he didn't understand what it said. How that could be someone's name. When he realized a few seconds later that it wasn't the name of a person at all, but rather of a Danish government agency, something sparked to life inside him.

The National Police of Denmark.

No wonder he'd need time to prepare. Just determining who exactly the intended victim was would require going there and letting the dice decide at the scene.

He'd only had three people to choose between on the boat. At Ica Maxi, there had been so many potential victims, he'd made the colours of their clothes correspond to numbers on the dice. That had worked out okay. But there, he'd been able to walk around unnoticed.

Repeating the same procedure in an office building full of police officers was something else entirely.

To find out how that was supposed to work, he picked up one of the dice again and shook it. First, he needed to know which category he was doing next. An uneven number meant getting out the list of murder weapons, from rifle to slingshot. An even number meant the list of different ways to die.

A four.

He took out the list of twelve possible causes of death and did a pre-roll.

A four.

So he had to use two dice.

A five and a four.

According to the list, the chosen victim, whoever that might be, was supposed to die in a fire twelve days from today. Something that at first glance might seem relatively straightforward. The difficulty lay in isolating the fire so no one else got hurt. But it was nothing that couldn't be solved with some preparation. After all, he had twelve days.

He already had several ideas of how to proceed and felt eager to get started. But before he did, he needed the final confirmation from the icosahedron. So he picked up the marble dice, which had gone cold, and warmed it in his hands. Then he shook it thoroughly before making his throw.

This time, it rolled around for a long time before looking like it was going to settle on twelve, but then, for some unknown reason, it tipped over and landed on X. The chance – or, if one preferred, the risk – of that happening was one in twenty. And yet this was the fourth time he'd rolled an X.

Every number on the dice except X meant the task was set in stone and that he could get started on the preparations. Now, instead, he was going to have to get out the notebook in which he'd written down 120 different additional tasks and then roll the icosahedron again.

Twenty.

The outcome meant he was supposed to use no fewer than

twenty six-sided dice to determine which of the additional tasks would be required. It was the absolute maximum number. He took out another box of anodized aluminium precision dice and counted out twenty.

They barely fitted in his cupped hands, and more than once he dropped one while trying to shake them and had to start over again. But after a while, he felt convinced they were sufficiently randomized and released them onto the felt.

He looked at the dice – no, he stared, utterly speechless. What lay before him on the green felt was inconceivably improbable. It looked like someone had deliberately adjusted each dice.

All twenty dice had come up six.

Twenty sixes, which added up to 120.

He'd never heard of anything like it, much less experienced it himself. But there they were, each one with its six pips pointing up, as though it were the most natural thing in the world. But it was anything but.

Individually, each dice was just as likely to roll a three as a one or a six, of course. But put together it was something else entirely. The probability of all of them coming up six in one throw was negligible. Winning the jackpot at a casino was considerably more likely than rolling twenty sixes. And yet, that was what he'd done.

He still couldn't quite believe it, but there they were, twenty sixes that together made 120, which ordered him to do the last of the additional tasks. A task he'd never thought he'd get to perform. A task more complex and challenging than all the ones he'd already done put together. A dream scenario that was too good to be true, and to make sure he wasn't about to wake up and realize it was all a dream, he pinched his arm so hard he drew blood.

Persuaded that he was, indeed, fully awake, he went over to the shelves and took down the notebook with a big X on the cover. Then he sat back down and turned to task 120, and a shudder went through him the moment he laid eyes on the header, written in all caps.

FORGET EVERYTHING

Time, place, victim, weapon and method.

Forget everything. This is a task like no other.

54

THE PRINTER FINALLY whirred to life. Stubbs, who was already in a foul mood, could only hope it wouldn't take as long to print a page as it had taken to start up. One thing she really didn't enjoy was waiting. Sluggish printers that refused to connect to her computer were another.

A third one, since she was on a roll now, was musicals. She'd never been able to understand why actors should suddenly break into mediocre song and attempt to dance. And the songs were hardly ever good enough. No, if she wanted to see a film, she went to the cinema or watched TV. If she felt like listening to music, she put on a record. Mixing the two was like mixing ketchup and trivets.

Rocket wasn't a favourite of hers either. She honestly couldn't fathom how something as bad and foul-tasting as rocket could still be in vogue. It had come out of nowhere, and suddenly every little café with pretensions had to put rocket in everything. In their burgers, on their sandwiches and, of course, in all their salads. For a while, she'd felt like she couldn't even order a cup of coffee without it being garnished with that unappetizing weed.

But working late was unquestionably number one on the list of things she never wanted to have to endure, and yet here she was, doing just that for the second night in a row. That had soured her mood more than anything, and as she waited for the printer, she mused that Mona-Jill was in fact directly to blame for introducing all of those evils into her life that night.

Her plan had been to scan the map she'd found in Elvin's boat using the multifunction printer, immediately after dinner. But when she'd discovered the meatballs on her plate were full of finely chopped rocket, she'd asked Mona-Jill how she could possibly have forgotten that the diabolical little leaves were definitely not her thing.

During the discussion that followed, it turned out Mona-Jill hadn't forgotten. On the contrary, she'd deliberately chopped up the spiky abominations and mixed them into the mince in an attempt to trick her into realizing how tasty rocket actually was. At that point, the fight had been unavoidable, and she'd said a number of things she'd wanted to take back and for which she'd apologized as soon as the dust had settled.

But the mood had still been tense when they cleared the table after dinner and when Mona-Jill had suggested they watch *Mamma Mia!* – because it was a feel-good film that made people happy – she'd felt too guilty to say no. After all, Mona-Jill had opened up her home to her, not the other way around.

Two hideous hours later, she'd finally been able to lay a blanket over Mona-Jill, who had fallen asleep on the sofa, and sit down in front of her computer to try to get the bloody printer started. She preferred not to think about how much time she'd lost. But at least the map had been scanned and was filling the screen in front of her.

That it was a plot of land had been clear from the first. The question was where it was located. There were no names or property details to guide her. The only hint was a handful of numbers on the various buildings and Elvin's virtually indecipherable notes. But she wasn't going to give up until she'd zoomed in and scrutinized every millimetre as though it were a melanoma.

Whether the plot was in any way connected to Molander was anyone's guess. But why else would Elvin have been interested in it? A search of the Property Register had only returned one hit – for his house in Ramlösa – and repeating the search with Gertrud's name hadn't returned any hits at all, so whoever was listed as the owner, it wasn't Molander.

It was a very unusual plot of land, that much she could tell. A number of blue patches indicated some kind of water reservoirs. Or maybe ponds, which was peculiar in itself, and judging from the rectangular shapes, they seemed man-made, to boot. As though they were part of a water treatment plant, or maybe some kind of fishery…

She had an idea and to check that she'd remembered correctly, she took out the set of keys Fabian had given her. It contained seven keys, and on one of the two marked with white tape, there was a hand-drawn fish. Maybe it was a coincidence, or maybe she was on to something.

A blue line meandered along the bottom of the map. It was probably some kind of river or stream, and according to the map it formed the southern boundary of the property. A red four-lane road ran along the top of the map, cut through in the upper right corner by a grey and white line that looked like railroad tracks.

The plot was, in other words, bordered by a stream, train tracks and a motorway. There must be a thousand plots of land of that description, and she could spend the rest of her professional life searching for the right one without any guarantee she'd ever find it.

Her only chance was to make some educated guesses. Like, for example, that it was in Skåne. Molander was a dyed-in-the-wool Scanian and had even, as a young man, talked about Skåne seceding from Sweden.

There were quite a lot of streams and rivers in Skåne, Kävlinge and Helge rivers being the major ones. But if it was in the vicinity of Helsingborg, it had to be Rå river. It was eighteen and a half miles long and emptied into the Råå Marina.

She went to Google Maps, zoomed in on Rå river and started following it as it wound its way east through Skåne.

She had always felt that Stockholm, with its archipelago of thousands of islands, was by far the most beautiful part of Sweden, and she probably still did. But north-west Skåne was a close…

She sat up with a start, her eyes fixed on a number of green patches on Google's satellite image. It would have been easy to dismiss them as vegetation and keep scrolling east. But the rectangular green formations had caught her eye, and when she zoomed in, she could clearly see that they were, indeed, ponds. Algae green, overgrown ponds near enough identical to the ones marked in blue on Elvin's map.

What's more, they were located on a plot of land that, according to Google Maps, was wedged in between a four-lane motorway by the name of Rausvägen, Rå river and the tracks of the local commuter train.

55

LILJA PUSHED HER feet into her well-worn Birkenstocks, slipped on a pair of leather gloves, opened her front door and walked over to Pontus Milwokh's flat, determined to get to the bottom of why her bedroom was so much larger than his.

She put the key the locksmith had given her into the lock, turned it and entered, and after finding the light switch, she closed the front door and continued into the living room. Molander and his men were supposed to have been here and done their thing two days ago. But the black backpack and the hockey bag in the middle of the floor revealed they weren't done yet.

It was probably the assistants who had left some of their equipment. It certainly wasn't Molander, since he always carried those aluminium cases with cut-out compartments no one under any circumstances could so much as look at. He would never leave them lying around, not even for one night.

She continued through the room to the closed bedroom door, opened it and turned on the overhead light. Everything looked exactly like before. Maybe they hadn't even started the examination of the bedroom, which would explain why Molander hadn't reacted to the discrepancy in its size.

She'd measured her own bedroom to be eighteen feet across from the window to the wall facing the hallway and bathroom. In this room, the outer wall was at most three feet from the foot of the bed, which meant the difference was no less than eight feet.

She walked over to the wall shared with her own bedroom and continued around the bed to the small nightstand in the corner. There, she turned on her phone flashlight and studied the corner and inner wall by the head of the bed.

Molander had taught her that if a wall had been added as an afterthought, any telltale signs were most likely to be found along the edges and in the corners. It could be anything from an unintended gap letting light through to inconsistent moulding.

But that wasn't the case here. As far as she could tell, it was the same dirty-white skirting board all the way around. The same was true of the classic dark-blue wallpaper, which overlapped in the corner. In other words, there was nothing to suggest the wall was not original.

The last trick Molander had taught her was to listen. She tapped the wall in a few different spots. Granted, it didn't sound the same as the wall facing her bedroom. But that was probably mostly because it wasn't load-bearing. Regardless, it sounded solid and not remotely jerry-built.

She dismissed her phone's low-battery warning and turned the flashlight onto the nightstand. But that didn't seem to be hiding any secrets, either, so she moved on to the wardrobe wedged between the bed and the other wall.

She'd started to examine it the last time she'd been here but had been interrupted by Klippan. Now, she opened it again and noted that everything looked the same as before.

The sparse hangers with a jacket, a pair of trousers and two shirts. No more, no less. It was exceptionally ascetic and probably an indication that Milwokh kept his clothes elsewhere.

She pushed the hangers aside, leaned in and started to look around in the light from her phone. Again, it was the edges that normally gave things away. Unfortunately, her phone gave up and turned off, and since she herself blocked most of the output from the ceiling light, it was too dark to make anything out. She took off one of her leather gloves and ran her fingers along the side of the back of the wardrobe.

There was a gap there, all the way up one of the sides. But that could be innocuous. The backs of the Ikea wardrobes she and Hampus had put together in Perstorp had been like that. The flimsy panels that were supposed to be secured with tiny nails all the way round had kept coming loose again and again.

She tried pushing on the back, but it didn't budge. Not even when she put her back into it did it give so much as a millimetre. No, it definitely felt a lot more solid than their Ikea crap. Hampus's Ikea crap.

In the middle of the back panel, at approximately waist height, she discovered a round hole about an inch or so across. She wondered why it was there and couldn't recall if the wardrobes in Perstorp had had the same kind of hole. Maybe it was to aid assembly or intended for power cords for lights.

To make sure she didn't overlook anything, she stepped into the wardrobe, bent down and put her eye to the hole. But the only thing she could see was an impenetrable darkness, which was exactly what one would expect to see behind a wardrobe. Even so, she couldn't shake the feeling that something wasn't right.

But a feeling wasn't enough. She needed something concrete. Something to back up the feeling. And until she found that something, she was stuck. In the end, she saw no alternative to giving up, stepping back out of the wardrobe and leaving the bedroom. Thinking she might have moved too fast, she decided to start over and went back to the hallway, where she stopped and looked around.

Apart from the front door, there were two doors, both closed. One led to the bathroom, which was an exact mirror copy of her own with a bath, basin and toilet. She knocked on the wall that was shared with the bedroom. It sounded more solid that the one in the bedroom.

Stepping back out into the hallway, she opened the other door, which in her flat led to a small storage room she'd crammed full of removal boxes. Milwokh, on the other hand, had divided the space into two separate areas.

One half housed a collection of tools that would make the most inveterate power-tool geek cry for joy. Saws, drills and electric screwdrivers were jostling for space with toolboxes, bottles of glue and screws of every conceivable size. There was even a powerful nail gun in there, as well as pieces of timber of various lengths and some other sundries. As they had surmised after seeing his purchase history at Bauhaus, Milwokh had clearly built something. But what, and more importantly, where?

The other half of the space served as a walk-in closet, apart from the vacuum cleaner and mop in one corner. Behind a curtain were neatly folded trousers and sweaters on shelves, a long row of shirts, sorted by colour, and drawers full of socks and underwear.

From what she could tell, the space was the same size as her own, which only fuelled her suspicions. She managed to start her phone back up and squeezed the last drop out of the battery by illuminating the back wall, which was adjacent to the bedroom. But she couldn't see anything out of the ordinary here either, so when her phone finally gave up, she tried knocking on it in a few places, only to realize she was no longer able to tell if it was any different from the other walls.

But it absolutely couldn't be the same wall as the one in the bedroom; they were too dissimilar. So she went back to the living room, took out her measuring tape and measured the distance to the outer wall. Ten feet. That looked consistent with the location of the inner wall in the bedroom and left eight feet between it and the hallway and walk-in closet unaccounted for.

Eight feet that had been erased from the bedroom. She'd sensed it from the moment she stepped into the tiny room. But it was only now it dawned on her that she'd been right all along.

There was another room in the flat. That much was beyond doubt now. A room that had been so carefully concealed that neither she herself, nor Molander and his team had managed to find anything that even resembled a way in.

She returned to the walk-in closet to examine it more closely. But hard as she tried, she couldn't find anything to suggest there was a way through the back. She was probably just too tired. She should go home and sleep on it and make sure to get Molander over as early as possible tomorrow.

She decided to do just that, so she stepped out of the closet and was continuing into the bedroom to turn out the lights when the pieces suddenly fell into place and made her freeze mid-step.

The walk-in closet wasn't the problem, it was the wardrobe.

Its mere presence was odd. In a bedroom so cramped it was hard to move about without bumping into things. And the fact that it contained only a handful of items of clothing made it even more suspicious. The wardrobe was not meant for clothes storage. It served a completely different purpose.

The back panel was the key. It had to be. At first, she'd figured the solid feeling she'd had when she pushed it had meant everything was in order. But in fact, the opposite was true.

She opened the wardrobe door again, climbed in, located the hole and inserted her index finger. To her surprise, it didn't find a wall but only empty air. The wardrobe looked like it was flush against the wall. She inserted her middle finger instead to extend her reach.

She felt around the hole on the other side of the back panel, first down each side and then underneath, without discovering anything of interest. It was only when she reached up as far as her finger would go that she discovered something made of metal, something she was able to push to the left after a few failed attempts.

There was a faint click and then the back of the wardrobe slid open. With her hands held out in front of her, she walked straight into the dense darkness, and with the sound of her own breathing echoing in her ears, she fumbled along the walls for some kind of light switch.

When she found it, the tiny space was suddenly bathed in such bright light she had to close her eyes.

56

IT HADN'T TURNED out too badly, the voice in Fabian's mind told him as he climbed the stepladder in the middle of the living room and started examining the brass chandelier and its eight arms. If anything, it had gone rather well. As well as he could have hoped, if not better.

That Theodor had talked to him and even hugged him back had to be considered positive. True, he'd cried and not been himself. But that was hardly surprising given where he was and what he'd been through. Hopefully it would be over soon.

Maybe he'd gone too far when he promised everything would turn out all right. But what was he supposed to do? If anything, the outcome was less certain than ever. Especially after the assault. Why would they believe him over the others once he stepped into the witness box?

Was that why he had a headache? His head normally never hurt. As a matter of fact, his whole body felt achy and uncomfortable, as though it didn't belong to him. Maybe it was the price he paid for not going for a run or hitting the gym for weeks.

But he hadn't had the peace of mind to pull on his shorts and head out into Pålsjö Forest. And right now, he had to locate and remove the cameras Molander had installed around his house. At least that was easier now he'd seen the camera angles.

The bathroom, bedroom and hallway were already done. As was the basement, the upstairs landing and the kitchen, where the camera had turned out to be hidden in the wall clock, of all places. In the children's rooms they'd been inserted into cacti Molander must have rigged and brought with him. Sonja was currently in the studio, busy preparing for her performance piece tomorrow and not to be disturbed under any circumstances, so he was leaving that camera up for now.

The only other camera left was the one in the living room.

He'd examined the picture frames, the display cabinet, the curtains and the potted plants in the window with a magnifying glass, to no avail. He'd even gone over the brass chandelier in the ceiling twice. But there was a camera somewhere; he'd seen it on the screen in Molander's basement. An eye placed somewhere high up and angled down towards the middle of the room.

Maybe he should just give up and not bother. Almost everything had been said between Molander and him anyway. They'd searched each other's houses and Molander had most likely gone through his office in the basement, so there was really nothing left to hide.

More than anything, he needed to relax, if only for a few hours. Forget his worries and the guilt over Theodor. Forget Molander and Milwokh. And himself.

He stepped off the ladder, went over to the record collection that covered one of the walls and let his eyes rove across the CD spines for something to take his mind off things.

Other than Brian Eno's *Thursday Afternoon*, he hadn't listened to anything for ages, and he suddenly realized how much he'd missed it.

In front of him were countless albums he never had time to play. So many songs just waiting for their chance to fill the room. Together, they formed an almost impenetrable wall of choices so overwhelming he was unable to make a decision.

Maybe that was why he closed his eyes and let his fingers roam across the spines and the hard, angular plastic. Whatever the reason, it felt good and he continued to let his hand wander along the rows of albums, some of which were broken and jaggedly sharp. When he suddenly came across something sticking out between two albums, he opened his eyes and saw the tiny camera squeezed in between the xxs' debut album and their second, *Coexist*, in the electronic indie section.

Relieved, he pulled the camera out and disconnected the battery cable. Then he pulled out the debut album, and after studying the stark white X against the black background for a while, he pushed the disc into the player and turned up the volume.

57

THE VERY LAST additional task was almost too good to be true. It was over a year since he'd written it down, but he remembered it like it was yesterday. It was the longest of the texts, and he'd never imagined it would become reality. But rolling twenty sixes had made the impossible possible.

There could no longer be any doubt the dice had forgiven him and considered him worthy of a new challenge. But that it would be another X task and number 120, to boot, was so astoundingly amazing he'd had to go out for a big dinner at Charles Dickens to let it sink in.

There had been enough people there for him to enjoy his steak and pints unnoticed. He'd even been able to read the evening paper, noting that the police were playing their cards close to their chest. There was no picture of him and his name wasn't mentioned, and nowhere could he see anything about the events on Öresund and the murder on board the yacht. There was quite a lot of information about some bathtub murder, however, and at least they'd finally found the body in Klippan.

Eventually, he went home, stuffed and slightly tipsy. But that was okay. Maybe it would even help him get the good night's sleep he needed so badly before starting on the preparations.

He stepped into the hallway, closed the front door behind

him and realized immediately that something was wrong. When he got back from Öresund a few hours ago, the doors in the hallway had been closed. Now they were open.... Either the place was haunted or someone was having him on. Or...

He popped his head into the bathroom. It looked untouched. It was highly unlikely the police technicians would come back this late. Unless the flat was under surveillance and his return had been noticed.

The door to the walk-in closet was hard to close and sometimes opened of its own accord. But that didn't explain the bathroom door. Maybe he'd left it ajar himself, after all.

He went into the bathroom, turned on the tap to fill the bath and started to pull off his clothes. He had been looking forward to this. A steaming hot bath in which he could get some well-needed rest with the floating pillow under his neck. Then, without opening his eyes, he would make a mental list of everything that had to be done before he could leave.

He would, for example, have to construct some kind of device to help him roll a dice while running. He didn't have any ideas so far, but one would come to him. They always did. He also had to go through and make sure all his weapons were in good working order. Once he started, there would be no room for mistakes.

That, in turn, meant he was going to have to repack his backpack from scratch. He had to make it several pounds lighter. Anything that wasn't strictly necessary would have to go. Like the extra provisions he'd brought in the boat. His meal at Charles Dickens had been enough for several days; he'd have to get by on a bottle of energy drink.

Being able to access as much of his equipment as possible without stopping was going to be crucial, too. Because that was the name of the game. To keep moving and finding the flow. A groove where he could pick off one person after another until the dice told him to stop.

He pulled off his underwear, peed and tested the water in the bath. The temperature was perfect and the bath was almost full. He went back out into the hallway and continued into the living room to get a glass from the kitchen.

But he never made it that far.

Instead, he stopped in the middle of the room with his eyes fixed on the glow spilling out across the floor from the overhead light in the bedroom.

58

'*SHE NEEDS TO DIE,*' intoned a male voice over the computer's speakers. '*She doesn't deserve to live anyway. The only thing she deserves is you.*'

Lilja had found the audio file while going through the computer sitting on the small desk in the secret room, which could be no larger than about seventy square feet. It had been labelled *Assar's voices.*

'*You can do what you want to her. Whatever you want. So long as it ends with her dying.*'

So that was how Pontus Milwokh had persuaded the mentally ill Assar Skanås to kidnap Ester Landgren from the playground in Slottshagen and molest her.

'*We know you want to.*'

By playing him recorded voices that Skanås, in his confused state, must eventually have assumed were in his head. *I was just doing what the voices said, he'd told them in one interview. They told me what to do.*

'*You've been waiting for this. Longing to finally let go of your inhibitions. You deserve it. You more than anybody.*'

To avoid doing the deed himself, Milwokh had dragged a paedophile into his sick game, enticing him with an opportunity to molest and rape.

'*You know she's supposed to die. It's only right.*'

But what was the point of bringing in someone else

instead of just doing it himself? It must have been incredibly complicated and labour-intensive. Not to mention the increased risk of things going wrong, which is exactly what had happened when she'd finally found Skanås and stopped him from completing the rape.

'*You know what to do.*'

Maybe the idea had been to throw them off track. Set them running in the wrong direction. It had undeniably worked.

'*And you like children. No one likes children as much as you.*'

Or had the dice decided that, too?

She looked down at the green felt next to the keyboard. The dice sitting on it were the same kind as the one Risk had found. Like that one, these were made of gleaming brushed metal and looked made for fateful decisions.

For some reason, they were all sixes. Twenty of them, in all. Lilja could still remember the time when she was nine years old and rolled five sixes on her first try in Yahtzee. She'd never come close to anything like it again. Rolling twenty was unbelievable.

Was that really what he'd done? As with so many other aspects of this investigation, both chance and probability seemed warped. But the question she should be asking herself was what the twenty sixes meant, if anything.

She closed her eyes. Her brief burst of energy was fading now. She'd hoped to discover something that could move the investigation forward and possibly even put them a step ahead. But everything she'd found pointed back in time, to things that had already happened. Things they already knew. Sure, there were answers here to several of their outstanding questions, but not to the most important one of all.

Where and when was Milwokh going to strike next?

She looked up at the map of Skåne pinned to the wall in front of her. She'd already studied it once. But seeing the little notes and crosses corresponding to almost every murder Milwokh had committed over the past few months had made her burst into tears. This time, she was going to try to be more analytical.

She started with the cross in column 6, row 3. It marked the town of Klippan. A note next to it read *25 May 2012, Evert Jonsson, cause of death: asphyxiation*, which tallied with the autopsy report they'd had from Flätan.

The cross in column 5, row 4 was similar. *13 June 2012, Moonif Ganem, weapon: machine of some kind*. She was trying not to let her emotions get the better of her, but it was difficult. Despite the cold, factual tone of the notes, it still hurt to think of that morning when she'd received the call-out about the missing boy in Bjuv on her way in to work.

She continued going through the crosses and their associated notes detailing the date of each murder, the name of each victim and which murder weapon or cause of death had been used.

In some of the squares she also noticed smaller crosses accompanied by two-digit numbers. But she had no idea what they stood for. The absence of the bathtub murder of Mattias Larsson was conspicuous as well. There was no cross in the square just south of Helsingborg and no note referencing it.

Maybe Fabian was right about Milwokh not being behind that one after all.

Another thing that caught her attention was the square in the bottom left-hand corner, which was almost entirely taken up by Copenhagen. In it was a big cross, a small cross and the number 120. That was all. No date and no note about the weapon used or the cause of death. She hadn't heard anything about a Danish murder as spectacular as the ones on the Swedish side of the sound.

And then there was the cross in the middle of Öresund, just north of Ven Island, with the accompanying note *27 June 2012, Frank Käpp, weapon: sword.*

That was today's date. Trails didn't get any hotter than that. The murder had, for obvious reasons, taken place considerably further north than intended, but both the name and the weapon were right. That he'd known what weapon he was going to use was pretty much a given. But that the name was correct as well was actually a bit odd. Did that mean Milwokh had known who his victim was before he went out or had he somehow, after the fact... No, it probably just meant they still knew far too little about how he operated.

She rubbed her temples to get the blood flowing. Anything to help her think.

In front of her, the screensaver took over and she stared vacantly, wearily at the mesmerizing shapes. As though she were about to nod off. But she wasn't. Somewhere deep inside her, something had stirred.

She turned around in the chair and looked at the bed, which seemed to have been hastily made. There was still an indentation in the middle of the pillow from Milwokh's head and the duvet was bulging and creased like when Hampus had made the bed. Except in one spot, where it looked as though there were something underneath it.

Lilja got up, pulled the duvet aside and found herself looking at a yellow notebook with an X on the cover. Even though she couldn't possibly be sure, she knew instantly this was what she'd been looking for all along. She picked up the notebook, carefully pulled off the rubber band and began to flip through the pages.

On every page was a handwritten note, some filling as much as half a page. Most, however, were only a few sentences long and a handful consisted of just a few words.

You have to be blindfolded, was, for instance, what the note on the page numbered 73 said. On page 11, she read: *Also take the victim's closest colleague, neighbour or friend. The dice decides whom and how much time must pass between the two tasks, as counted in hours.*

Tasks. So that's how he saw it. Tasks that had to be completed at any cost. She turned the page.

Frighten the victim before it's time.

Break into the victim's home at night. Sedate the victim with hexane gas. Then let the dice choose one or several of the following alternatives:

1. Rearrange the kitchen cabinets.

2. Take a trophy from the victim's body.

3. Turn on the victim's stereo, put the music of your choice on repeat and turn the volume up.

4. Tattoo something on the victim's forehead.

5. Leave all the victim's windows wide open.

6. Take a picture of the victim using the victim's phone, hack into it and set the picture as the new background picture.

That was exactly what had happened to Molly Wessman. Milwokh had both cut her fringe and broken into her phone before poisoning her a day or so later. So this was some kind of addition to the main task.

Lilja had an idea and went back over to the map to find the cross in column 3, row 5, where the note said *16 June 2012, Molly Wessman, cause of death: poisoning.* But this time, she was more interested in the smaller cross and its associated number.

X 97

Back to the open notebook and sure enough, the number at the bottom of the page was 97.

Maybe the note wasn't another cross but an X.

She located the square containing Hyllinge and the note *16 June 2012, Lennart Andersson, weapon: item from murder scene.* That, too, had an X followed by a number.

X 28

She turned to page 28 of the yellow notebook.

The task has to be executed in front of witnesses.

That explained why he'd stabbed his victim in the middle of Ica Maxi instead of in some more secluded spot. It also explained why he'd been wearing a mask. There hadn't been a racist or xenophobic angle. He'd wanted to hide his face, plain and simple.

Why he'd killed both Molly Wessman and Lennart

Andersson on 16 June was explained by the brief additional task on page 13.

Start a new task and let it run in parallel with the original one.

Even the bizarre involvement of Assar Skanås in the kidnapping of Ester Landgren was explained by reading page 47.

This is not your task.

Choose someone else, according to your own preference, and let that person complete the task in your stead.

Whether guided by instinct or chance, she couldn't say. But for some reason, her eyes were drawn to the dice on the desk. The twenty dice that somehow had all come up six and together totalled 120.

120... She turned to the map and took a closer look at the tiny notation in the square that contained Copenhagen.

X 120

Then she checked how many pages there were in the yellow notebook and quickly realized there were considerably more than 120. But page 120 was the last one with an additional task. The last and by far the longest:

FORGET EVERYTHING

Time, place, victim, weapon and method.

Forget everything. This is a task like no other.

Time:

A new time will not be given. Complete all necessary

preparations, but don't dawdle. Act as quickly and efficiently as you can. If possible, within the next few days.

Place:

Take the location of the discarded task as your starting point and choose the largest public space you can find in the vicinity. A place where as many people as possible can be found in a limited area.

Preparations:

Roll the dice to determine victim, weapon, appearance and position according to the criteria. Only then will you enter the designated area and execute the first sub-task. Each time a sub-task is completed, the dice is immediately rolled again. The outcome will determine which of the six criteria below will change for the next sub-task, which will commence without delay.

One:

The task has been completed. Wrap up and retreat.

Two:

Change your location. Roll again.

Keep moving

Utilize a mode of transportation or something that is in motion

Get to the highest point you can find

Get to the lowest point you can find

Find a secluded spot

Push into the crowd

Three:

Change your weapon. Roll again.

Knife

Crossbow

Rope

Rifle

Your own body

Poison

Four:

Change the colour of the victim. Roll again.

Red

Orange

Yellow

Green

Blue

Purple

Five:

Change your appearance. Roll again.

Wig

Glasses

Jacket

Trousers

Headwear

Shoes

Six:

No changes. Keep going.

Lilja put the book down. This was one of the sickest, most horrifying things she'd ever read. It was all just a game to him; he was playing. Like a videogame with VR glasses, with the crucial difference that this was real.

These were real lives being taken. Real people, innocent and completely unaware they'd been reduced to being just bodies, prey to be selected, hunted and slaughtered for no other purpose than to give the player a kick.

She was far from certain. And yet she felt no doubt when she looked back and forth between the dice, the open notebook and the map with a cross marking Copenhagen in the bottom left-hand corner.

Everything added up.

She'd seen it in the pictures in his photo album and been struck by it even then. The almost ecstatic joy in his eyes. The thrill and feeling that anything could happen. That was what he was trying to recapture. The feeling he'd had once as a child. That kick. Of course that was what this was about. So there was a motive, after all.

But the only thing that mattered was that now she knew, because she did. She knew both where and how he was going to strike.

Suddenly, she registered a movement out of the corner of her eye and whipped around. But the back of the wardrobe had already slid shut and the metal plate was pushed back into its bracket with a click.

'Hello! Who's there?' she bellowed as she went over to the wardrobe, where she grabbed the metal plate in an attempt to open the door again. 'Hello, I'm still in here! Let me—'

The bang sounded like a gun firing at close range, and before she could even flinch, she saw a nail erupt through the back of her left hand. The pain didn't register until the blood had already run all the way down her arm to her elbow.

She only just had time to yank her hand free before another nail burst through the wood with a bang. A second later, there was a third bang and Lilja was forced to retreat and watch nail after nail penetrate the wood all around the back of the wardrobe.

59

'CAN YOU EXPLAIN *something to me?*'

He could hear music. He couldn't understand why. Loud, too. The kind of volume that usually meant Theodor. He reluctantly opened his eyes and realized he was in his own living room. Right, he'd put the music on himself. The xx, which was now running on repeat. He must have fallen asleep.

'*Fabian? Can you hear me?*'

It was Stubbs's voice. He knew that much, but he couldn't figure out where it was coming from.

'Hello?' he said eventually, and realized he was still lying on the sofa. 'Hillevi, is that you?'

'*No, it's Barbra Streisand. Would you mind explaining to me the point of keeping an extra phone if you never pick up?*'

He sat up on the sofa and looked at the Nokia in his hand. 'I'm sorry, I must have dozed off. What time is it?'

'*What are you talking about, dozed off? It's ten to nine in the morning. I've been up all night, staring at Elvin's map until my eyes bled.*'

Fabian stood up and walked over to the kitchen island, where he'd left his iPhone. It was true. It was ten to nine. He must have slept all night.

'*Hello? Are you still there?*'

'You've been studying the map. And? Did you find something?'

There was a loud sigh on the other end. '*Why else would I be calling? To tell you that Mona-Jill is grumpy as an old rag just because I don't happen to like—*'

'Hillevi,' he broke in. 'What did you find?'

'*I'm sorry, I'm just exhausted from pulling an all-nighter.*' Just as Stubbs heaved another sigh, Fabian spotted a handwritten note on the coffee machine. '*Anyway, that's my thing you're doing now. I'm the impatient one who gets frustrated. Not you.*'

Hi Fabian,

I know that you're busy and in the middle of a big case. But I would never ask you if it wasn't important, and this time it's more important than ever. For me and for you. For us. For that reason, I want you to come and see my performance at Dunkers at seven tonight.

Sonja

'*It turns out I was right about the map. I think I know where Molander's little hideout is. Though it's anyone's guess if that's where he's stashed the forensic evidence, obviously,*' Stubbs went on while he read the note. '*Does Rausvägen 28 ring any bells?*'

Their marriage depended on this.

'*Hello? Houston calling!*'

'I'm listening,' he said, dashing upstairs. 'I know where Rausvägen is. But that's all I know. What is it? A house?'

'*From the satellite pictures it looks like several small houses or barracks. I honestly can't make out what kind of place it is.*'

'Is Molander listed as the owner?' Fabian said, hurtling up the second flight of stairs to the studio.

'*No, it's a company called Warhammer.*'

'And who owns the company?'

'*My God, what's with the third degree?*' Stubbs griped, but he could hear her typing in a search on her computer. '*You're right. Here he is, in the form of Gertrud Lisbeth Stenson. That must be her maiden name. You're not as dumb as you look, I guess. When can you be there? I would suggest as soon as possible.*'

'I can't. I can't go out there.' He pressed his ear against the closed studio door. He just wanted to hold Sonja and assure her he would do everything in his power to be there to support her. 'Molander will know what's going on immediately and we have no idea what the consequences might be.' When he didn't hear anything, he opened the door and peeked into the studio. 'You should head out there by yourself, and I'll do what I can to keep him busy.' Only to discover that both Sonja and the wooden box were gone.

60

Bang! The sound of one tin of ravioli hitting another rang in Lilja's ears, even though she'd used the stuffing from the pillow to make earplugs.

Bang! At first, she'd missed her target several times, hitting either the hand holding the screwdriver she'd found in a drawer or nothing at all. Bang! But she wasn't missing now. She was like a machine running on autopilot.

She closed her eyes – it made no difference anyway – and raised the tin behind her like a javelin before thrusting it with all her might against the other tin, which she had emptied and placed over the handle of the screwdriver. Bang!

Several hours had passed since the world went dark. Time was racing by as if it couldn't get to the point where Milwokh would start his diabolical game soon enough. Bang!

And then there was the darkness. The claustrophobically suffocating darkness that kept pressing in closer. It was even darker than a winter night with a sleep mask and blackout curtains, and she honestly didn't know how much longer she was going to be able to hold on to her sanity.

That frightened her more than anything. The prospect of eventually collapsing in a sobbing heap on the floor, unable to do anything but curl up in the foetal position and shake uncontrollably. If it came to that, it would all be over. With her down for the count, Milwokh would be free to act, and long before the others would figure out what he was planning, it would be too late. Bang!

She still hadn't got over the murder of Ester Landgren, the innocent little girl who at six had already survived more than anyone should have to go through in a lifetime. She hadn't discussed it with anyone else in the team and, in a way, it was only now she realized it fully herself. But the anger she felt at Ester Landgren's fate made her willing to go to any lengths to stop him.

Pontus Milwokh. It had to be him. And yet she couldn't quite believe it. That he had returned to his flat was one of the most unexpected developments in this case where everything was unexpected. For a perpetrator to return to the scene of a crime was a relatively common occurrence, but going back to his own home, his hideout, after it had been discovered by police, was completely bizarre.

She'd screamed at him to stop, but the thick nails had kept punching through the back of the wardrobe in a never-ending stream, and once the nail gun fell silent, the electric screwdriver had taken over, then a circular saw had revved up, cutting through one plank of wood after another.

Two hours it had taken him to turn his hideout into a prison cell with no way in or out. Then silence had fallen and a minute later he'd turned off the main circuit breaker and everything had gone black. The computer, the harsh overhead light. Everything. Bang!

Once it had sunk in that she couldn't get out, panic had made her scream at the top of her lungs, and, hoping that a neighbour might hear her, she hadn't stopped until her vocal cords gave up.

It was only then that she'd managed to get a grip on herself and once her breathing had returned to normal, she'd been able to formulate a plan of action. Bang!

This was the third tin of ravioli she'd gone through. She'd broken the other two hitting the handle of the screwdriver directly, and each time, tomato sauce had exploded all over her. At least she didn't have to look at herself in the dark. Bang!

The first thing she'd done was rip a strip of fabric from the sheet on the bed and wrap it around her left hand to stop the bleeding from the nail. It was only at that point, after she'd finally managed to calm down, that the pain had begun to make itself known in earnest. A sharp, burning pain that radiated through her hand and up her forearm.

Then she'd fumbled around in the dark and concluded that both the wardrobe and the wall facing the bedroom were perforated with so many nails and screws it would take her weeks, if not a month, to open up a hole big enough to squeeze out. A smaller hole to try to reach an outlet would be pointless since the power was off in the entire flat. That was why she'd turned instead to the wall Milwokh's secret room shared with her own flat.

Just above the skirting board, she'd found an electrical socket and with the help of the screwdriver, she'd loosened the screws and pulled the entire thing out of the wall. That had created an inch-deep recess in the wall, and by sticking her hand in, she'd been able to determine that the core of the wall consisted of bricks. She'd focused her attention on the mortar between them, and with the screwdriver it had proved relatively easy to hack deeper and deeper into the wall.

At least at first. But what should have taken no more than

an hour had turned into an interminable struggle. When her right hand started to bleed from rubbing against the edges of the tin, she'd wrapped that in fabric, too.

But she was at the end of her tether. Despite her tireless banging and all the mortar she'd been able to remove, the brick inside the wall was refusing to budge. She was sure there was an explanation for that, but she was too tired to think. Too tired to carry on forever and strike at the screwdriver with every ounce of strength she could muster for the five hundred thousandth time.

The tin burst in her hand. Even though she'd put one of the broken tins over the screwdriver, she was once again spattered with ravioli, and this time something snapped inside her. Something that made her throw down the tin and furiously attack the wall with nothing but the screwdriver.

The wrappings around her hands came undone and her wounds opened as they rubbed against the ridged surface of the handle, which was becoming slick with blood. The pain was almost unbearable, but still nothing compared to the frustration of all those wasted hours. All her pain and her increasingly desperate struggle. Neither would stop Milwokh.

It sounded like a tooth cracking. A barely perceptible little click, that was all. But to Lilja, the sound was something new. Something that could change everything.

She put the screwdriver down and wiped her hands on her trousers. Then she stuck her hand into the hole and let her fingertips explore the edges of the immovable brick. Unfortunately, it felt much the same as before. True, quite a lot of the mortar around it was gone, but she didn't find the explanation for the sound she'd heard until she ran her fingers over the surface of the brick.

The crack was probably thinner than a hair, but even so, using her fingernail, she could clearly feel it zigzag down through the brick. She tried to grab the edges of the brick, but it was as stuck as it had been before she began.

She grabbed the screwdriver again, placed the tip of it in the middle of the brick and with her free hand reached for yet another tin of ravioli from the stash under the bed and struck the handle again. This time it was a small tap rather than a great big swing. It was all that was needed to split the brick in two, and the screwdriver suddenly sank into it as though it had turned into butter.

She stuck her hand into the hole and could feel that the brick had split open far enough for her to be able to push her fingertips into the break. And one half of the brick was finally loose and could be pulled out without much difficulty. The other half, however, was still stuck and after another thirty minutes of fruitless work, she gave up. Apparently, the weight of the entire building rested on it.

She found the cord to the extension lead under the desk and pushed the plug into the hole she'd made. Then she tried to stick her right hand in after it, but no matter how hard she shoved, there wasn't room.

She slumped onto the floor and considered just closing her eyes and letting exhaustion take over. No one could say she hadn't tried. She'd probably be asleep in seconds, and maybe she'd dream of something wonderful while the rest of the team figured out where she was.

She might have, in her previous life. A life full of naive wishful thinking in which she had shared a bed with

Hampus, unaware of who he was, and would never have considered setting fire to a neo-Nazi clubhouse. A life in which she'd long since given up and was instead focusing all her energy on licking her wounds, waiting and hoping that somehow, things would change for the better.

But that life didn't exist any more. That Irene didn't exist. She realized that now. The process had begun weeks ago and her old self had slowly faded away, growing ever more diffuse and vague. It had been a painful process, and she'd felt more confused than ever before. But now she could see who she had become. Here, on the grubby floor in the pitch dark, she could finally see it, clear as day.

She let her hands examine one another. A minute or two later, she'd settled on the left. It was already injured from the nail, and she depended on it less than her right. And so she got to her feet, found the bed and pulled it out from the wall.

Once the bed was in position against the far wall, she lay down on her stomach, placed both feet against the edge of the bed to brace and pushed her left hand into the hole as far as it would go. She was strong, she knew that. But strong wasn't enough. Not by a mile. She needed to go beyond that, into uncharted territory, to the kind of primal strength it took to lift up a car if her daughter were trapped under it.

She didn't have a daughter. But she did have Ester Landgren, and the thought of her made Lilja push so hard with her legs her hand moved a millimetre deeper. She didn't know if she could push any harder, but she had no choice, so she kept going until she heard something break inside her hand.

A devastating, indescribable pain shot out from her hand

to the rest of her body as the knuckles of her fingers were crushed against each other. It felt like her broken hand was on fire. Even so, it wasn't the pain she would remember, but the crunching sound of cartilage and bone.

She took a short break and tried to gauge how her hand was doing. If she really tried, she could still wiggle her middle and forefinger as well as her thumb, but she had no contact whatsoever with her ring and little fingers, and maybe from this day forward they would simply dangle there like two dead relics, reminding her of this moment.

She was now able to fold her hand over, knuckles and all, like a deboned chicken, and strangely, doing so didn't increase her pain. It was probably maxed out. Or maybe the endorphins had finally begun to sand down the sharpest edges, because her hand was beginning to feel more and more like an amorphous lump, which finally broke through the hole.

She was through. She was really through.

She focused on breathing for a few seconds and then explored the small space between the brick wall and her own bedroom wall. She judged it to be about an inch. There was a wooden board almost immediately to her left, and the extension lead plug was waiting right next to her hand. Straight ahead, she could feel old insulation that could easily be pushed aside.

She'd been hoping the inside of her own wall would consist of old reed-reinforced plaster. Instead, it was some kind of modern plasterboard, probably installed at some point during the nineties. Luckily, the screwdriver had perforated it enough for her to pick off pieces with her thumb and forefinger.

Once the hole was big enough for the daylight from her own bedroom to start trickling in, she momentarily forgot about the pain and let out a shriek of joy that came out as a dry hiss.

It wasn't too difficult to wiggle the plug through the hole into her bedroom, and her hand after it, and once she'd pushed her whole forearm through, she was able to not only bend it but also to locate the outlet and insert the plug, which turned both the desk lamp and the computer back on.

61

STUBBS TURNED INTO a free parking bay outside Ica Maxi in Raus, set the parking disc and placed it on the dashboard before climbing out of the Jeep, picking up her backpack and hurrying off across the car park. She had three hours before some overzealous parking attendant would give her an exorbitant fine.

Driving all the way up to the property would have been easier, but she didn't dare to risk it. Molander was bound to have installed cameras to watch both pedestrians and cars passing by the property.

For that reason, she also pulled down the ski mask Mona-Jill had lent her as soon as she'd crossed the big thoroughfare called Rausvägen onto the much smaller road running parallel with it, which was inexplicably also called Rausvägen.

She turned left and jogged down the road, which after about twenty yards narrowed considerably, making her feel like a trespasser, even though she was still in a public space. A sweaty trespasser.

Mona-Jill had purchased the ski mask for a trip up to Lappland to go cross-country skiing in temperatures of eighteen below. A sweltering twenty-six was something else entirely.

On her left, bushes and trees formed a green wall of leaves

that blocked out the sights and sounds of the bigger road. On her right was a tall barbed-wire fence and on the other side of that, a paved area. She couldn't see any cameras, though that did nothing to ease her mind.

She wasn't just dripping with sweat, she was panting like a dying centenarian, too. She could already hear Mona-Jill lecturing her with one of her I-told-you-so speeches about how she should start working out, get fit and above all lose weight.

She stopped to catch her breath at a double gate topped with barbed wire and displaying a sign that warned against trespassing. The message was underscored by a thick chain and a sturdy padlock.

Whether this was Rausvägen 28 or some other number altogether was impossible to say. But she could glimpse two of the ponds she'd seen in the satellite pictures up ahead, and something that looked like a derelict little fishing boat pulled up on shore.

She took out the old extra phone Fabian had insisted on and fired off a short text to say she was about to enter the property. They hadn't been in touch in the past hour, and if he was holding up his end of the bargain, he was busy distracting Molander. That was probably why he wasn't replying straight away. He couldn't exactly pull out his old Nokia and wave it about in front of his colleague, he'd have to find a moment to step away.

While she waited, she pulled out Elvin's keys, selected the one marked with white tape and a drawing of a fish and tested it in the padlock. According to Fabian, it was the last key left to identify. Fishing ponds, an old fishing boat and a picture of a fish. Why not?

Sadly, it didn't fit. She couldn't even get it to go in all the way. She tried the rest of the keys. Mostly so no one would ask her later why she hadn't. But to no avail. None of them came close to fitting.

After another minute of twiddling her thumbs, she was unable to stop herself from taking off her backpack, pulling out the pliers she'd brought and cutting a hole in the fence. She couldn't just stand around wasting time, waiting for a text from Fabian that might never come. If she set off an alarm, well, so be it.

Six minutes later, she was inside and she raced on with sweat pouring down her face inside the ski mask. She knew the layout from Google Maps and the map from Elvin's boat: the three ponds on the left and the slightly larger one on the right. The many hours of staring herself blind at the screen the night before were finally paying off.

The problem was that she had no idea where she was going. Time was too short and the property too large for her to wander about aimlessly. The forensic evidence could be hidden pretty much anywhere, if this was even where Molander kept it.

Wherever it was, though, the evidence was likely still being kept frozen to ensure the samples remained intact and didn't degrade. That suggested there was a freezer or some such in one of the buildings. She'd counted six cabin-like buildings on the map. In addition, she could now see a number of sheds, a large skip and an abandoned fishing boat next to a pile of fishing equipment.

That alone would take all day to go through.

Without any real plan, she walked on towards the end of the road and did a sweep out towards the three ponds on her left, looking for something, anything, to guide her search. But apart from a large outdoor scale, a bath and a pile of junk, she saw nothing to make her pulse quicken.

Instead, she lowered her eyes and began to study the gravel. There were a number of tyre tracks, but none that continued past the end of the road into the foot-long grass. And she couldn't make out any footprints.

She continued down towards one of the sheds and climbed a ladder propped against the roof. From up there, she had a better view and was able to make out something in the tall grass. It was too early to say whether it was tracks. It could just be that the soil was less rich in that spot.

Either way, it did look like the grass was flattened and slightly yellow. Kind of like a faint fairy ring, except that this was a relatively straight line that disappeared off between two of the ponds.

She climbed down the ladder and followed the track through the grass, past the ponds towards a red wooden house, where she found her explanation in the form of a wheelbarrow, parked upright. Of course that was what had rolled through the tall grass, and judging from some sections of the track, it had been heavy.

She walked over to the green door and studied the white enamel sign, which read *Warhammer*. A few older screw holes and a frame of green paint around it that looked slightly less faded than the rest of the door suggested the sign had been replaced at some point in the past few years. The same seemed to be true of the locks and the door handle.

She pulled out Elvin's keys while she pondered what *Warhammer* might signify, but didn't get very far because the key with the fish on it slid smoothly into the lock.

The house didn't smell bad, exactly. A bit stuffy, perhaps, and dusty, but there was also a hint of coffee. The grimy curtains of the room's only window were closed, but the thin fabric and the gap between them let in enough light for her to look around.

Normally, people like Fabian and his colleagues were first on the scene. She was called in at a later stage, and she'd never had any trouble thinking of it as if it were any other job. She'd never been bothered by the blood or the maimed victims sprawled out in front of her. She'd always been able to compartmentalize and approach her task pragmatically.

But this time was different. This time, she was first on the scene, and even though the room was neither soaked in blood nor littered with body parts, she had to fight back a growing sense of unease. Maybe it was because of all the things she couldn't see, all the things that were hidden but that her subconscious had already taken note of and her brain was now putting together.

She forced herself to move further into the room and suddenly heard a distant but increasingly loud high-frequency screeching from somewhere outside. She pulled open the curtains and peered out of the window but could see nothing to explain the sound.

Instead, her eyes fell on the desk next to the window, on which were scattered a handful of paintbrushes and surgery pliers of various sizes, a hacksaw, a chisel, a number of syringes and several pairs of scissors. There were also bottles of various sizes, a couple of small jars of paint and ten or so painted plastic war figurines.

Was that why Molander had named his company Warhammer? She vaguely recalled both Molander and

Elvin having been obsessed with a game called Warhammer during their years at the police academy. Was that still a hobby of his, or was it just cover?

The high-frequency screeching was now so loud it hurt her ears. Moments later, it was explained by the sudden roar of a train passing by just a few feet from the window, on the other side of the bushes. Everything on the desk shook and shifted and one of the tiny jars of paint slipped over the edge and fell to the floor.

Moments later, silence returned as if it had never been broken, and she squatted down, pulled out her torch and looked under the table. Apart from several more jars of paint, there were a number of war figurines, in various stages of completion, a scalpel with what looked like dried blood on it and a few sheets of paper held together with a paper clip.

Vaginal hysterectomy – a manual.

She didn't need to read on to know what the bed in the far corner had been used for, or what the two posts with some kind of leg supports on them were doing there. She didn't even need to take a closer look at the patch of dried-in blood on the mattress to know that this was where Ingela Ploghed had been robbed of her uterus two years earlier.

So this was where Molander had taken her so he could drug her and perform the surgery before dumping her in Ramlösa Park to bleed out. That explained why she'd reacted so strongly to the screeching rails and the roar of the trains, as mentioned in one of the reports in the case file.

Stubbs turned to the door next to the bed, pushed it open with her foot and peeked into a small kitchen with a worn wooden floor, a grimy old rag rug, brown cabinet doors and peeling ceiling paint. In the far corner she spotted a blowtorch, and on a table next to the window stood a coffee cup, a chipped bowl full of sugar cubes and an opened packet of biscuits. On the kitchen counter sat an old coffee maker, a thermos and a packet of Zoegas coffee.

She entered, picked up the thermos and shook it. It was half full, and after unscrewing the lid and noting that the coffee was cold but still smelled relatively fresh, she concluded that Molander had been here at some point during the past few days. But why? She looked over at the blowtorch in the corner but it didn't offer any new ideas.

A sudden noise made her jump. A sound so familiar she wouldn't normally have even noticed it. But this wasn't normally, so when the compressor hummed to life behind her, she turned to the old refrigerator and berated herself for being so distracted she'd overlooked it.

She opened the fridge door and saw a number of ready-made soups with expiry dates in July and several bottles of water. What she couldn't see was any forensic evidence. Not until she opened the freezer compartment. There, in neat little containers, tagged and labelled, was what she was looking for.

Relieved, she pulled out the Nokia to contact Fabian, but in her excitement, she dropped it on the rag rug she was standing on. Once again, it was the sound that caught her attention, because it was all wrong. She picked up her phone, pulled the rug aside and discovered a trapdoor in the floor.

She grabbed hold of the flush hatch pull and heaved it open. The trapdoor led straight down into the crawlspace beneath the house, to another trapdoor a foot further down.

That one was round and made of iron and looked like it led straight down into the ground.

She grabbed the handle of the second trapdoor. It was so heavy she had to plant her feet on either side and use both hands to lift it.

The stench hit her with such force she didn't have time to duck out of the way – of it, or of the swarm of flies that shot out of the hole and got caught in her hair and lost in her nostrils. But the reek and the flies were nothing compared to what lay slumped in the dark below the sturdy grate welded to the rim of the hole.

She couldn't quite make it out. And yet she already knew – that this was the heavy load Molander had pushed through the tall grass in his wheelbarrow. That this was what he'd needed the blowtorch for. That they'd all been deceived, that she hadn't finally seized the opportunity to leave him after all their years together.

Which was why she wasn't the least bit surprised when she could finally bring herself to turn on her flashlight and point the beam down into the dark root cellar that had been converted into a prison. Down at Gertrud, who was lying motionless on the hard dirt floor with her eyes closed.

62

THE LIGHT AT the intersection of Tågagatan and Drottninggatan turned red, as though it were completely out of sync with the rest of the intersections. But Fabian, who was already ten minutes late, accelerated, forcing the other drivers to slam on their brakes as he burned through the intersection and turned down Bogseraregatan in Helsingborg's North Harbour.

The moment he'd ended the call with Stubbs, he'd contacted Tuvesson to tell her he wasn't going to be able to make the morning meeting. She'd wanted to know why and had, to his surprise, not accepted his explanation about needing to be with his family.

Even when he'd insisted, she hadn't let him take so much as a half day off. What's more, she'd reprimanded him for being so absent lately, pointing out that he'd overslept as recently as the day before and was now asking to stay home even though the investigation was in a critical phase. That Lilja hadn't showed up either and wasn't answering her phone had done nothing to improve Tuvesson's mood.

The conversation had gone on for quite a while, and he'd come close to telling her. But with all the questions and explanations, there hadn't been time. It would take hours, maybe days, to persuade her to consent to an arrest. In the end, he'd seen no other option than to lie to her face and promise to come to work just so he could get off the phone.

By then, he'd already been late, and if he knew Stubbs, she wasn't the type to hang around, so she'd likely already entered the property. He could only pray Molander was too busy with the Hallberg-Rassy to have time for anything else.

Fabian parked his car and hurried out towards the piers and jetties of the North Harbour Marina on foot, past the restaurant where every table was occupied by holidaymakers in sleeveless shirts and pastel shorts.

He spotted the Hallberg-Rassy about fifty yards further on, moored alongside a pier. Granted, only the mast was visible, but he instantly recognized the double set of spreaders and the radar and anemometer at the top. The rest of the boat was hidden behind crime scene barriers that blocked off parts of the pier.

Fabian pulled out his police ID, pushed through the inevitable gaggle of rubberneckers standing around with their phones at the ready, stepped over the police tape and walked up to a uniformed officer, who led him in behind the privacy barriers.

Close up, any similarity between the Hallberg-Rassy and the rest of the boats in the marina was gone. The once white hull was still smeared with dried blood. The mainsail had been taken down, but only hastily tied around the boom. The same was true of the blood-spattered genoa that lay loosely rolled up on the foredeck.

It was a gloomy sight, and by rights the boat should be destroyed as soon as they were done with it. But that would never happen. It was too valuable and, at the right price, any number of buyers were bound to be willing to ignore its past.

One of Molander's two assistants was in the cockpit, dressed in full protective gear, picking up things from the floor with tweezers. The other, also wearing full protective gear, was taking pictures of the body parts lined up in a row on a folding table shaded by an umbrella before packing them into coolers.

Molander was busy, too, but not with the yacht. Instead, he was standing next to the van with the top half of his protective suit tied around his waist and his eyes glued to his phone.

'Ingvar,' Fabian called out.

Molander looked up from his phone and turned to him.

'It's only me,' he continued, and he caught himself waving to his colleague, which he normally almost never did. He had to act natural. At least he wasn't walking too fast.

'Don't sell yourself short.' Molander managed a smile. 'To what do I owe the pleasure? I thought you were tied up in the morning meeting with the others.'

'We had to push that back. Apparently Tuvesson can't get hold of Lilja.' Fabian stopped in front of Molander and focused all his attention on returning his smile. 'So I thought I'd stop by and make sure you're not standing around playing Murder Snails during work hours.'

Molander laughed and pocketed his phone. 'I wish.'

'I thought you loved this stuff.' Fabian gestured towards the Hallberg-Rassy. 'Shouldn't this be right up your alley? And speaking of which, how are you getting on?'

'Is that why you're here? To ask how we're getting on?'

'Among other things.' Fabian looked over at the assistant

in the cockpit, who was disappearing into the aft cabin. He was playing for time. It didn't matter how, but he had to keep Molander busy for as long as possible. 'I would obviously be interested to know if you've secured any forensic evidence against Milwokh.'

'No need to fret. I'm sure we will both secure and take care of the evidence.'

'I couldn't be further from fretting.'

Molander chuckled. 'That's what you say. But it's not what I see.'

Did he already know Stubbs had gone in?

'But I'd say it's as expected,' Molander went on.

'Pardon?'

'You were asking how we're getting on.'

'So you haven't found anything that stands out, something that could point us in the right direction?'

Molander shook his head. 'But who knows what might turn up. We're far from done.'

'How long do you think you'll be?'

'How long is a piece of string? Speaking of which, maybe we should get back to doing our respective jobs. That is, after all, how we can be most useful.'

'Right now, this is my job. I'd appreciate it if you could show me what you have so far.'

'A person can appreciate many things in this world. I, for example, would appreciate an answer to the question of what that could possibly achieve, other than wasting precious time.'

'It might be that I see something you don't.'

'I hardly think so. But if you have nothing better to do, who am I to stand in your way?' Molander turned to the assistant on the pier. 'Fredrik! Could you give Fabian a quick run-through of what we've found?'

'Absolutely! I just have to get these sent off to Flätan!'

'No rush. Fabian seems to have all the time in the world. See you.' Molander gave Fabian a curt nod before turning towards the van and reaching for the handle of the driver's door.

'Hold on, where are you off to?'

'To Kjell & Company on Bruksgatan,' Molander said without turning around. 'I'm sorry it's not somewhere more exciting.' He opened the door. 'The camera's memory card is full, you see, and—'

'Maybe Fredrik could do that instead?'

Molander let go of the door handle and turned around. 'And since when are you in charge of how my staff and I do our work?'

'Unless I'm misremembering, you were the one who went on and on about the importance of you and me working together if we were to have a shot at arresting Milwokh and having him convicted. Is it really so surprising that I would prefer to be shown your findings by you rather than your assistant?'

Molander said nothing, just stood there, as though he could see right through Fabian and knew exactly what it was really all about. 'Of course,' he said finally, and nodded. 'You're right. Let's get it over with right now.'

Fabian was just about to reply with a smile when his phone went off in his pocket.

'Don't you need to take that?' Molander nodded towards his trousers.

Luckily, it was his iPhone, which was why he decided to

pull it out, and when he saw it was Stubbs, he put the phone to his ear as quickly as he could to block the screen from view. 'Yes, this is Fabian.'

'*If you're wondering why I'm not calling the other number, I can only say it's because doing so is completely pointless, since you never pick up.*'

'I'm sorry, who am I talking to?' He could feel Molander's eyes burning a hole in the side of his head and his only option was to turn to meet them and try to look genuinely confused.

'*Is this a bad time?*' Stubbs said. '*Is it because you—*'

'Oh, it's you. Hi,' Fabian broke in. 'Would you mind if I called you back later, in, say, an hour?'

'*Is it Molander? Are you with him right now?*'

'You might say that, yes. So, like I said, I would prefer if we could talk about this later, when I'm done here.'

'*No, this can't wait,*' Stubbs replied. '*So you listen to me and don't you dare hang up. You hear me? Don't. Hang. Up.*'

'Fine, but make it quick.' Fabian shrugged apologetically at Molander, who was now staring at him as though he had no difficulty seeing through his charade.

'*I've found the forensic evidence. Do you hear me, Fabian? I've found—*'

'I'm sorry, I don't know if I'm—'

'*The evidence against Milwokh! It's all right here in front of me in an old freezer compartment.*'

'Right, so you're saying—'

'*Exactly. So just arrest him. There's no reason to wait.*'

'I see.' Fabian nodded and smiled at Molander.

'*And I found Gertrud, too.*'

'Right, well, what do you know. And? Was everything all right with that?'

'*I'm afraid not. The bastard has trapped her in a root cellar, and the problem is that I can't get down to where she is.*'

'What? I don't understand—'

'*Fabian, the only thing you need to understand right now is that you have to arrest him. Not in a few hours or a little while, right now.*'

There was a click in Fabian's ear as she hung up.

'Yes, okay, agreed,' he said, still holding his phone to his ear. 'I understand, sounds good. Bye.' He put his phone back in his pocket without taking his eyes off Molander.

So Gertrud hadn't left him. She'd been thrown into a root cellar the moment she became a liability. The handwritten letter had just been one more smokescreen so no one would go looking for her.

He almost couldn't believe it. Not even of Molander. That a person could just sacrifice his own wife like it was nothing.

Neither of them spoke. But it was clear. The looks and the silence carved the situation in stone, hardening it into a memory that would haunt them both forever.

Molander knew. He had figured it out. Maybe not exactly who had broken into his property and found the forensic evidence. But he'd worked out that Fabian wasn't working alone and now he was busy considering his options. You could almost see it in his face, in his eyes, which although they were still fixed on Fabian were nevertheless turned inward, busy searching for a solution. A way out.

Fabian had nothing to ponder. The moment he had both longed for and dreaded was finally here, and it was up to him to make the first move. He was the one who was going to end the impasse by arresting Molander, his own colleague. He was going to handcuff him in front of his own assistants, in the middle of their crime scene investigation.

But it couldn't be helped. In time, they, too, would understand. They and everyone else. They would see that no matter how strange it seemed to them, Fabian had right on his side.

If only it were that easy. In reality, it felt more like throwing himself off a cliff blindfolded, with no way of knowing how far he would fall or where he would land.

His handcuffs lay ready and waiting in his right jacket pocket. All he had to do was pull them out and ask Molander to hold out his hands. Maybe it would be exactly that undramatic, over in a few seconds. Now that he thought about it, Molander shouldn't have any interest in causing a scene. He probably wouldn't even require handcuffs, just an explanation and a hand on his shoulder.

'Ingvar,' he said finally, breaking the silence.

The rest all happened in the wrong order.

The first thing that hit him was how wrong his assumptions had been. The pain came several seconds later, radiating out from his solar plexus. Only then, as he stood doubled over with his hands pressed against his midriff, did he realize Molander had punched him as hard as he could and was now climbing in behind the wheel of the van.

Pain crackled inside him as he hurried towards the cab and he could almost see himself jumping off the edge of the cliff and hurtling through the air.

Without knowing how it happened, he caught hold of Molander's leg and clung to it as though it were his last lifeline, trying to pull his colleague out of the cab despite kicks raining down on his hands and face. At the same time, the van door was slamming into his head, again and again, as though it had come to life and was taking Molander's side.

He should have given up and let go. Remembered all the things he had to live for. All the things that really meant something. But he couldn't. Despite the kicks that left deeper and deeper gashes in his forehead, despite the blood getting in his eyes and making it hard to see, he couldn't let go.

Maybe because the pain wasn't getting worse but rather, more distant. As though his body was tuning out all unnecessary distractions, the white noise, and encapsulating itself in the realization that if he let go of Molander's leg, he would keep falling and lose everything.

He could hear the distant screaming of the two assistants. Whether it was because he was trying to make himself heard over their shouting or if it was just some kind of primal force, he would never know. But suddenly, he could hear nothing but his own roar, and moments later, Molander lay flat on his back on the asphalt in front of him.

He'd managed to pull him out of the van, and for a brief moment, he managed to register that his colleague was flipping onto his stomach in an attempt to get back on his feet, while his assistants tugged and pulled at Fabian from behind. But they were all too late. He had already lunged.

When he landed, he was on top of Molander. The struggle was over, and he pressed his colleague's face into the asphalt with one hand while reaching for his handcuffs with the other.

'Hey! Fabian?' The assistant's voice started as a vague

murmur of disjointed words but quickly became clearer, as though his hearing was being reconnected. 'Have you lost your mind?' Soon after, he felt two hands start to tug at him again.

'Let go of me!' he bellowed, trying to fend them off and cuff Molander's hands behind his back at the same time.

'Bloody hell. What the fuck are you doing?' said the other assistant, and the two hands became four and together they managed to pull him off Molander and drag him away across the asphalt. They didn't let go of him until he drew his gun.

'Listen to me,' he said as he got to his feet, wiped the blood out of his eyes with his jacket sleeve and glanced over at Molander to make sure he was still on the ground. 'Odd as it may sound, Ingvar Molander, your boss and my colleague, is suspected of committing a number of murders. I'm respectfully asking you to back away so I can arrest him. Okay?'

The assistants looked from the gun in his hand to Molander and back again.

'What are you talking about, murders?' one of them said finally. 'Are you saying Ingvar—'

'Yes, I'm afraid so. But this isn't the time for questions. I can't say any more about it right now anyway,' Fabian replied. The blood kept getting in his eyes. 'So I'll ask you again. Back off and let me do my job.'

The two assistants didn't seem to know what to do.

'Back off!' he roared, and he aimed his gun at them, which made them raise their hands above their heads and back away while he wiped the blood out of his eyes with his sleeve again. 'There. Good. Now I want you to—'

'Drop the gun!' interrupted a voice that didn't belong to either of the assistants or to Molander. 'I said, drop it!'

He recognized it, but couldn't place it until he turned around and saw Tuvesson approaching with her own gun held firmly in both hands.

'Astrid, calm down,' he said, raising his free hand. 'Let me explain.'

'I want you to drop your weapon! And I want you to do it now!' Tuvesson stopped about ten feet from Fabian with her gun pointed straight at him.

'For fuck's sake, would you let me explain—'

'Just do what I say or I'll shoot!'

Fabian put the gun on the ground and shook his head. 'This is a mistake, Astrid. Just so you know. Your biggest ever.'

'Oh yeah? I'm the one making a mistake?' Tuvesson nodded. 'Interesting. So you're not the one who's been pursuing his own agenda over the past few weeks, completely neglecting our biggest case ever? It's not a mistake when you point your gun at the coastguard one day and your own colleagues the next?'

'Astrid, I can explain,' Fabian said, while Molander started to get up. 'If you would just let me…'

'I don't know how many times I've told you we work as a team,' Tuvesson cut him off. 'That we're honest with each other and share our thoughts and ideas. And yet you continue to lie to my face again and again. You say you need to look after your family but in reality, you're somewhere else. Or like now, when you promised to come straight to the meeting and instead you drove over here. Yes, you don't have to look so surprised. I've been watching you recently, via a GPS tracker on your car, and it's been interesting, to say the least.'

'Are you done?' Fabian said, mentally going over the last few days in an attempt to understand what it meant that the tracker had been Tuvesson's and not Molander's.

'I don't know. I'm asking you. Am I? Because honestly, I have no earthly idea what this is all about.'

'It's about Molander. Simple as that,' Fabian replied. 'He's not who you think he is. The truth is, he killed both Hugo Elvin and his—'

'Elvin?' Tuvesson broke in. 'Killed? What are you talking about? That was suicide.'

'No.' Fabian shook his head. 'It was just made to look like it, and I'm afraid Elvin's not Molander's only victim.'

'Hold on a minute. Are you seriously standing here accusing Ingvar, a member of our team, of having—'

'Astrid, if you think I've been distracted and you've suspected me of having my own agenda, you're absolutely right. Ever since Elvin's funeral, I've been working on my own investigation, of Molander. An investigation Elvin himself started a few years ago.'

Tuvesson shook her head as though she were unable to take in what he was saying.

'I swear,' Fabian went on. 'I wanted to tell you. But I couldn't. Not until I had enough proof, and I didn't, not until just now. Astrid, he's killed at least five, probably six people. I was about to arrest him when you arrived. Call Hillevi Stubbs if you don't believe me. She's been helping me and can confirm every word I've just said.'

Tuvesson's face was ashen and she was holding her gun as though it were the only thing keeping her from falling over. 'Is this true, Ingvar?' she said, turning to Molander. 'Is what he's saying true? Ingvar, answer me? Is it?'

'Both yes and no. It's true Elvin started his own secret investigation. But it wasn't about me, it was about Fabian, because he suspected Fabian was the one who drugged Ingela Ploghed, his old classmate, and cut out her uterus, which later caused her to commit suicide. He brought it up with me several times, but unfortunately, I didn't take him seriously until he died.' Molander swallowed. 'Don't ask me how, but somehow Fabian must have found the case file.' He shook his head and looked as though he was about to burst into tears at any moment. 'It's just awful. Elvin was one of my best friends.'

'Astrid, come on,' Fabian said. 'Surely you don't believe—'

'You stay where you are!' Tuvesson shouted at Fabian.

'For fuck's sake! He's just making stuff up! Can't you tell—'

'I said shut up! Not another word!'

'Making stuff up?' Molander threw his hands up. 'Why would I make stuff up when I can prove he killed both Elvin and Ploghed?'

Tuvesson looked from Molander to Fabian and back again, still clutching her gun.

'Think about it,' Molander continued. 'Fabian's been here for two years. That's as long as any of us have known him. Two years, which coincides with when all these problems began. Right? I don't know how much you know about his history in Stockholm, but two of his closest colleagues there died under mysterious circumstances. Just a few months later, he moved down here. And then there's his son, who's in custody in Denmark on suspicion of being a member of the Smiley Gang?'

'But Ingvar, I don't understand? Why didn't you say something?' Tuvesson asked. 'If you knew about all these things, why didn't you say something?'

Molander turned to Fabian, swallowed, and then looked back at Tuvesson. 'Gertrud,' he said finally, his bottom lip trembling. 'I said she left me, but that's not true. It's Fabian... He's taken her.' He took off his glasses and wiped his eyes. 'So what was I supposed to do? You of all people should know how much I love her.'

Tuvesson thought about that for several seconds before finally nodding. 'So that's why you called in the middle of the night, both last night and on Sunday?'

'What? What do you mean, called?' Molander said before realizing Tuvesson had turned to Fabian, who was nodding.

'Astrid, how long have we worked together, you and me?' Molander went on. 'It must be fourteen, fifteen years. Right?'

'Sixteen this August,' Tuvesson replied, turning back to him.

'We've been colleagues and friends for almost sixteen years.'

'Yes, we have.' Tuvesson nodded and fixed him with a level stare. 'And yet I've never been able to fully trust you.'

'What? Why wouldn't you be able to trust me?' Molander spread his arms.

'That's a good question. But I haven't, now that I think about it. Not ever.'

'Astrid, when haven't you been able to trust—'

'Get back down on the ground, face down, arms and legs out.'

'Are you serious? Are you going to—'

'Ingvar, I'm begging you,' Tuvesson cut him off, looking like she was fighting to hold it together. 'Don't make this harder than it already is.'

Molander thought about it for a moment before finally gritting his teeth and lying back down. Tuvesson nodded for Fabian to go over and handcuff his arms behind his back.

After everything Fabian had been through, it went surprisingly smoothly and when he was done, he and Tuvesson pulled Molander to his feet and started to walk him towards the car park in silence.

No one spoke. Not even Molander's assistants. It was as though every word they might need had suddenly gone missing, replaced by silence. A vacuum-like silence that spread to everything around them. To the tourists who suddenly stopped chattering and the cars that stopped passing by on the street. To the dogs that were no longer barking and even the gravel underneath their feet, which no longer made a sound. It was as though the world was holding its breath.

The sound that suddenly broke the stillness made them all stop and turn to each other.

Three different sounds from three different pockets at once.

Fabian and Tuvesson pulled out their phones.

The message was from Lilja and had been sent to the whole team, including Molander. It looked like it contained quite a lot of information. But Fabian only needed to see the words *Milwokh* and *Tivoli* in the subject line to know Tuvesson was going to have to take Molander back to the station by herself.

63

GERTRUD MOLANDER HAD waited forever. Through a hell of grief and pain, she'd waited for it to come. Longed for it. But it was only after she'd given up all hope of surviving. Of anyone coming to rescue her before it was too late. It was only then it had finally appeared.

The light. The light above her. So high above her.

It looked just like she'd imagined it would, and it made everything feel feather-light and wonderful. Gone were her hunger and thirst. Gone were all the things that hurt and all the thoughts of how stupid and naive she'd been. Of how she should have known. Of how, under all the protective layers, maybe she had guessed. None of it mattered any more.

The uneasy conscience, the tightness in her chest and the constant stomach ache had faded away and all she could feel now was an intoxicating harmony that made her so light she was on the verge of soaring up off the dirt floor.

That a drop of water fell from somewhere high above meant nothing to her. Nor that it landed on her top lip and trickled into her mouth. It was too late. Her body had finally given up and was on its way to somewhere else. That the drop was soon followed by another and then another made no difference.

It had been different before. When she'd lain there dreaming the same dream over and over again in an attempt

STEFAN AHNHEM

to think of something that hurt less. The one in which it began to rain. In which the sky suddenly opened, releasing torrents of water that flooded the land and found its way through all the minute cracks in the ground, all the way down to her parched throat.

But no rain had come. So that drop must have been just another dream, conjured by some part of her that was still refusing to give up.

And yet she felt another one. She did. She felt it land on her nose and trace its way uselessly down her cheek. But it couldn't be true. It just couldn't.

Actually yes, something was happening, she realized now. It was as though everything was moving in the wrong direction. Backwards and away from the light somehow. She'd only just noticed. She hadn't even realized she'd been moving forwards. Or had she imagined the whole thing? Like when you think the train you're on is moving when in reality it's standing still and it's the train next to yours that's leaving the station.

No, there could be no doubt now that she was being pulled back to where she'd come from, even though she'd lain in the same spot all along. She didn't know if it was a good thing. But she'd always preferred to travel forwards rather than backwards.

No, she didn't want to go backwards. Not back to the cold hardness. To the pain and hunger. To the humiliation and horror. The fear. She didn't want it.

She could remember what it had felt like. The pain must have subsided gradually; there was no other explanation for why she hadn't noticed the shift that eventually made her let go and let herself be lifted up towards that blinding, warm, lovely light. And now she was descending again. Down towards all the things that hurt so badly.

The next drop of water hit her lower lip but trickled the wrong way down her chin and throat, where it veered off towards her ear.

Before the next one landed, she opened her mouth a little bit wider, and once the droplet hit the sandpaper that had once been her tongue, she was not only convinced it was water, but also that she was still alive, whether or not she wanted to be.

64

HE HADN'T BEEN to Copenhagen since he was a little boy. But it looked the same. The colourful old timber-frame houses, the cobbled streets and all the different kinds of bikes going every which way. Nothing seemed to have changed during the interceding years. Every pavement stone looked like it had always been where it was. Even the smells matched the ones in his memories.

But he'd never seen the city like this. From below, it came off as significantly calmer than usual. The stress was confined to street level. That was where time flew by and people dashed around like headless chickens. Down here, the pace was turned down, like in a parallel reality where everything moved in slow motion.

His breathing deepened and slowed. As though he were entering a meditative state in which body and mind existed in perfect balance, even though he was on his way into the heart of a teeming metropolis.

But then, this was the first time he'd arrived by sea and been able to glide silently past The Little Mermaid and the hordes of tourists crowding the promenade, exclaiming at how small the sculpture was. Past the new opera house and Nyhavn and along the canals under the bridges.

His harmonious state was unmarred by distractions and maybe that was exactly what he needed to prepare him for what lay ahead. A last moment of calm before every part of him would need to perform at its absolute best.

He passed a sightseeing boat full of Asians, who waved to him like it was the first time they'd ever encountered a person of their own skin colour. He waved back but turned his face away when they started to take pictures. About fifty feet further on, the canal made a ninety-degree turn to the left into the darkness underneath yet another bridge, where the sound bounced between the surface of the water and the damp bricks above his head.

When he re-emerged into the light, a number of boat slips appeared on his right and he was able to squeeze in between the other little boats and moor at the low wooden jetty.

None of the pedestrians or cyclists passing just feet from him reacted. Not even the parking attendant taking down the registration number of a Nissan Primera noticed him when he berthed the lifeboat from MS *Vinterland* in the middle of the city centre.

On his way down towards Copenhagen, he'd made sure to hug the Danish coast, in case a situation developed. But not once had he seen anyone who appeared to be looking for him.

His one real setback had been that policewoman, Irene Lilja, who for some reason had gone back into his flat and managed to find his secret room. That could only be described as a significant blow, and much as it hurt, he had to accept that he would never be able to return there.

Only time would tell what the damage might be. Unfortunately, this time, the dice had said no to taking her life. But at least he'd had enough timber left over to trap her so comprehensively it would take her a long time to break out, even if she had help from the outside, and by then, he would long since have completed his task.

He checked his equipment one last time. He was wearing beige cargo shorts, trainers and a thin grey hooded jacket that came down to well below his hips. He'd also put on a baseball cap and sunglasses. Granted, the get-up was far too warm for a summer's day like this one; he was going to sweat profusely. But it couldn't be helped.

He'd replaced his backpack with no less than six belt bags, worn around his torso, each filled to bursting and relatively easy to reach. To his own surprise, he still had almost full range of motion, despite all the gear, and with the jacket covering everything, he just looked a few sizes broader than he was.

The rifle had been the biggest challenge. It was a Finnish hunting rifle, a Tikka T3x TAC AI with sniper scope he'd purchased over a year ago and hidden in his neighbour's attic storage space. It weighed just eleven pounds, which had to be considered incredibly light for a full-scale rifle.

But when he'd pushed it into the padded, custom-made inner pocket of his jacket, it had felt considerably heavier and more cumbersome than he'd thought it would. A few adjustments to the sword sheath had allowed him to carry it on his back instead.

The crossbow weighed around eleven pounds as well, but folded up and wrapped in a piece of cloth, it fitted relatively easily into the satchel along with the bolts, a change of clothes and a bottle of water.

Even the problem of having to roll the dice on the run had been solved. By cutting the bottom off a water bottle, taping the sharp edges and making two little holes just large enough to insert a cable tie, he'd been able to construct a perfect device on board the lifeboat from things he had with him.

When he was sure everything else was in order, he tied the device upside down around his left wrist with an aluminium dice inside and tried shaking his arm to make sure the dice couldn't fall out. Then he got out of the boat, climbed the wooden steps up to the street and flashed the parking attendant a warm smile before strolling down Frederiksholm Kanal and turning left onto Stormgade.

To avoid becoming too dehydrated before things even got started, he was careful to keep to the shade under the portico. Moments later, he crossed Vester Voldgade and then H.C. Andersens Boulevard and now he was so close he could hear the shrieks of excitement from the rides at Tivoli.

65

FAREED CHERUKURI. NOT only was the name impossible to remember, the little Indian was the worst kind of hacker, too, according to Stig Paulsen at TDC. During his years at TDC, Fareed had worked his way around every last firewall, infiltrating all the way to the inner core of the company's code, which made it possible for him not only to eavesdrop on every mobile phone call relayed through TDC's network, but to perform triangulations, read text messages and who knows what else.

Over the past month, they'd had a whole team working around the clock to fix all the security breaches and clean up after him as quickly as possible. But it had turned out to be more complicated than they'd thought, which was why they were still unable to give an end date when the network would be one hundred per cent secure again.

But that was Paulsen's headache, not his. He used Telenor. Besides, they'd agreed not to report it to the police but rather to deal with it internally. Partly to protect TDC's good name, but mostly so he could resolve the situation in whatever way he pleased. Which he was now looking forward to doing more than ever.

Suddenly, he didn't just have little Dunja to take care of. He also had a tiny Indian man and an obese Chink with an elephant fetish, and he could already sense that the whole affair was going to be a treat like none he'd ever experienced before. A treat that, if all went to plan, was waiting just around the corner.

Now that he knew the Indian man's real address and was sitting in his car outside Amagerbrogade 150, keeping an eye on the entrance between Synoptik and Punkt1 through his rear-view mirror, his last outstanding question was hopefully going to be answered imminently. His working theory was that all three had swapped flats with each other, which meant Dunja should be hiding in this hideously ugly building in the middle of Amager. That fact alone did wonders for his mood.

Because Amager was one of the most depressing areas of Copenhagen. No wonder the island was nicknamed Rubbish Island. Once upon a time, it had been Copenhagen's landfill, and it still smelled worse than anywhere else. As though soap hadn't made it here. Everyone wore second-hand clothes that reeked of mould and nowhere would you see more hammered, stinking Greenlanders than on Amager.

Islands Brygge, where he himself lived, did have a geographical link to Amager. But that was all. Culturally, not to mention economically, the two neighbourhoods were like night and day, and he was convinced the battle to introduce the postcode 2301 *Islands Brygge* would soon end in victory, thus severing the last connection to Rubbish Island.

But enough about that. Right now, he was dealing with that little whore, and he was almost certain his fingers would soon be wrapped around her throat.

And yet he felt anything but calm. Deep down inside, he was furious. Even after a double dose of Omeprazole, he could feel the searing burn every time his oesophageal sphincter opened, releasing stomach acid into his throat.

He should really just let what happened go and stop caring. Focus on more important things. But, true to form, he'd let aggravation get a firm grip on him and as usual there was no way to shake it.

Fabian Rask. Or was it Risk? Whatever. That prick had seriously crossed a line on Wednesday night. Going into Danish territory after being denied access – that was, quite simply, a declaration of war.

Fine, so the question of whether or not they had been right to deny the Swedish coastguard access to Danish waters was maybe open to discussion, as Ingolf Bremer of the Naval Operative Command had pointed out during their conversation. But this wasn't about right and wrong. Let the politically correct Swedes wring their hands about those kinds of namby-pamby considerations.

No, this was about one thing and one thing only. About giving that Risk bloke, who was chummy with Dunja to boot, a proper slap on the wrist to show him who was boss. If he'd just accepted it, taken his punishment and slunk back to Sweden with his tail between his legs, the whole thing would have been over and done with and balance restored.

But no. Instead the prick had been overcome with hubris and violated Denmark's sovereignty. He'd given him the finger, clear as day. *I don't give a flying fuck about his territorial pissing*, he'd said on the recording of his conversation with the Naval Operative Command. No one talked to him that way and walked away unpunished. Least of all a fucking Swede.

He'd tried to run the matter all the way up the flagpole

to Morten Steinbacher for an official statement on the ministerial level, which would in turn lead to the Swedish ambassador being summoned for a meeting. That would stir things up, and their relationship with their Swedish neighbours would deteriorate even further. And that was exactly the kind of environment in which he thrived. When the world was engulfed in chaos and everyone else felt like shit.

But he needed Ingolf to be on board, and since he was insisting on being obstinate, he'd switched tactics. He was going to sit on his hands and pretend he hadn't even noticed the declaration of war. As though it had passed by unnoticed without so much as a raised eyebrow.

Then, one day, when everything seemed blessed state fucking peaceful, he'd pounce. Then Mr Rusk would find out what it was like to have him as an enemy. It would hurt, really goddam fucking hurt. Granted, he'd already laid the groundwork, but exactly how and when he would strike in earnest was still an open question. Maybe tomorrow. Maybe a year from now. The only thing he knew for sure was that when the opportunity presented itself, he would be ready to unleash an Armageddon that would obliterate that son of a bitch and everyone around him.

In the end, it was his phone that broke the silence, and when he saw that it was the useful idiot Jan Hesk at Homicide, he answered, mostly to distract himself. 'Yes, what do you have for me?'

'*Hi, Kim, it's only me, Jan.*'

'I know, and I wouldn't mind if you cut to the chase.'

'*Right, well, the reason I'm calling is that I just spoke with Astrid Tuvesson from the Helsingborg Police and—*'

'What, wait, hold on,' he broke in, glancing up at the mirror aimed at the entrance. 'You've been in touch with the Swedes?'

'*Yes, but I wasn't the one who*—'

'Ap-ap-ap, let's calm down and rewind the tape. Haven't I been perfectly clear about all contact with the other side of the sound being conducted by me and no one else?'

'*You have, but, like I said, she called me. I didn't call them, and since you weren't here*—'

'You should have referred her to me.'

'*And I did. But she insisted and in the end, I had no choice.*'

'Jan, I have to say I'm disappointed. You of all people should understand what—'

'*Kim, if you want to keep bickering about this, that's fine,*' Hesk broke in. '*But if I were you, I'd listen to what she had to say instead.*'

Hesk had never talked back or interrupted him like this before. 'You would, would you?' he said, and let the silence between them grow. 'I see.' Hesk had never liked him, that much was certain. Ever since that Christmas party a few years ago when he'd stormed into his office trying to play the hero after seeing Sleizner on top of Dunja on the sofa, he'd held a grudge. 'But then, you're not me, you're you. At least, I hope that's the case.' Hesk had never mentioned it again, but he'd concealed his growing dislike behind a thick layer of sycophantic smarm. Until now. 'And if I were you, I'd seriously consider plastic surgery, then I would think carefully about what I said and above all, to whom.'

'*Look, I didn't mean to sound rude. If that's how it came*

off I apologize, and for what it's worth, I would never call you unless it was important.'

There. Back in your hole. 'All right, let's hear it.'

'From what I gather, for the past few weeks they've been hunting a perpetrator of Asian descent suspected of committing a number of murders on randomly selected victims. And they now believe he has crossed the sound to strike here, at Tivoli.'

'They believe?'

'Yes, they found his notes, and though they don't explicitly mention Tivoli, they're saying it's highly likely that's where it's going to happen. The problem is that they don't know exactly when. It could be tonight, tomorrow or the day after. He might even be there now. So what they're suggesting is working together to formulate a plan of action to—'

'Our cooperation with the Swedes will be kept to an absolute minimum.'

'Yes, I know that's the official line, but—'

'Absolute minimum! Am I making myself clear?'

'Right, I hear you, but what does that mean in real terms? We can't just ignore this. From what I'm told, a detective called Fabian Risk is already on his way over, and if it turns out they're right about—'

'Risk?' Of course that prick was involved. Fucking fantastic. 'Just so you know, that man has already violated our sovereign borders once. So if he's planning to run around Tivoli, waving his gun around, our top priority is to have him arrested. Okay?'

'Okay, but surely we still have to—'

'No buts! If you want to retain whatever slim chance you still have of getting promoted, you'll make sure that bastard's arrested! As far as the other thing goes, it's all guesswork, no more, no less. You know what it's like. He might be on his way to Tivoli or he might not. He might come tomorrow, he might come never. We don't know,' he said, just as he saw the door between the two shops open. 'That being said, of course we will take the threat seriously.'

Out stepped none other than the Indian man and the obese gook, scanning the street like two freaks in cheap sunglasses. It was almost enough to make him believe they suspected they were under surveillance.

'*Okay, so what do you suggest we do?*'

But he wasn't worried, not in the slightest. They could look around all they wanted. They would never spot him.

'*Kim, are you still there?*'

Granted, he'd hoped to see Dunja herself, but this was almost better. That half of Asia had just been in there and were now parting ways suggested they'd had some form of meeting at her house.

'I'm going to have to call you back,' he said, and climbed out of the car.

And that should in turn mean she was still in the flat.

66

ACT AS QUICKLY *and efficiently as you can. If possible within the next few days*, the instructions had said, according to Lilja's email. That could mean pretty much anytime. Even so, Fabian sprinted up the stairs from the parking garage underneath the Confederation of Danish Industry's building, next to Tivoli.

He came out on H. C. Andersens Boulevard and raced around the corner to Vesterbrogade, where crowds of tourists slowed him down.

During the drive to Denmark, he'd been in more or less constant contact with Tuvesson, once she'd dispatched Klippan and a team of uniformed officers to assist Stubbs and made sure Molander was safely locked up until he could present his evidence.

She'd read him the message from Lilja in which Milwokh's impending attack was outlined with the help of a number of rules for how the dice was to be rolled, which in turn determined who was supposed to be murdered next and how. The whole thing had exuded a cynicism and coldness they'd never come close to before.

People were staring at him. True, he was forcefully pushing through the crowd. But that wasn't it. Their looks were fearful, and he had no problem understanding why. His face, cut and bruised after his fight with Molander, must look terrifying, and even though he'd washed off the dried blood in a bathroom on the ferry to Helsingør and put plasters over the deepest gashes, it clearly wasn't enough.

Together with Tuvesson, he'd come up with a plan that, in simple terms, consisted of her contacting the Danish police to inform them and initiate cooperation, while he rushed to the amusement park and began to search it as best he could.

The queue outside the main entrance with its grand arch was absolutely grotesque. Every family in the capital must have had the same thought when they woke up that morning. It was a welter of screaming children with dropped ice-cream cones, frustrated parents, shrieking hen dos and bellowing bands of young men. Not to mention the groups of tourists from all over the globe. In a word, it was bedlam.

But the worst thing about it was that Tivoli's own security guards didn't seem to have the situation under control. It was as though they'd been caught off guard by the onslaught. True, they were conducting the occasional security check, but very sporadically and mostly for show.

Was that why he saw Milwokh's face everywhere? Because he did.

Like in the group of Asian tourists of various ages taking pictures with their selfie sticks and iPads ahead of him. Of course they all looked different. But not to him. Every last one of them could have been Milwokh, and he saw no alternative to pushing through the queue and searching them one by one.

'Police. I'm from the police,' he repeated over and over

again, holding out his police ID while he patted them down and searched their backpacks and belt bags.

'Hey! You!' one of the guards shouted at him as he approached. 'What do you think you're doing?'

'My name is Fabian Risk, and I'm from the Swedish Police Authority.'

'You're a Swede?'

Fabian nodded. 'My superior, Astrid Tuvesson, is supposed to have contacted the Danish police to inform—'

The guard cut him off and grabbed him by the arm. 'I don't understand you, but it doesn't matter. Either way, I'm not going to let you run around making people uncomfortable. You're coming with me.'

'No, wait.' Fabian resisted. 'A killer's on his way here. Maybe today or—' He broke off as he spotted an Asian man passing under the arch.

The man was wearing a baseball cap, a grey jacket and beige cargo shorts, and even though he couldn't see his face, he wrenched his arm free and broke into a run. It was Milwokh. All the alarms in his head were going off like mad.

The guard shouted after Fabian as he pushed through the sea of people. A child got in his way and fell over on the asphalt, crying. The mother shouted at him and the dad grabbed hold of his jacket, or maybe it was someone else. But it didn't matter. The only thing that mattered was getting to Milwokh before it was too late.

He eventually managed to push all the way up to the tills where he could climb over the barriers and finally start running after the man, who was now walking briskly past the elephant-headed mirrors towards the Pantomime Theatre.

'Police!' he shouted at the top of his lungs. 'Stop!' But the man kept walking without looking back. 'Stop or I'll shoot!' He pulled his gun out of its holster and disengaged the safety.

He could vaguely hear panicked screaming all around him and out of the corner of his eye he saw people running in every direction. Only now did the man look back over his shoulder, straight at him. Then he broke into a run, just like everyone else.

'I said stop!' Fabian shouted again and fired a shot into the air, which finally made the man stop and put his hands up.

'Get on the ground, face down! Arms and legs out,' he shouted, but the next moment he felt a number of hands grab him and push him down on the asphalt.

'No! It's not me, it's him!' he bellowed as the guards wrenched the gun out of his hand.

'Face down,' one of the guards shouted at him, and put a knee on his head.

'I'm sorry, I don't speak Danish,' he heard Milwokh say as he walked over towards them. 'Was it me he was after?'

Or maybe it wasn't Milwokh? Had he been mistaken?

'We don't know yet,' one of the guards replied.

'Search him,' Fabian said, trying to wriggle his head out from under the knee. 'Listen to me! You have to search him!'

The three guards exchanged looks and then one of them finally walked up to the man who at least looked a lot like Milwokh and began to pat him down. But all he found was a wad of Danish notes in one of the many pockets of his shorts. No knife, no gun, no rope. No weapons of any kind.

'It's okay, you can go,' the guard said and the man nodded, turned his back on them and continued into the amusement park.

67

ELECTRICAL ROOM – NO UNAUTHORIZED ACCESS read the only sign on the door. No name and no letter box with stickers saying no to circulars. Nothing that suggested anyone lived there. But it took more to fool him. This was where the little Indian man had been registered as recently as a few months ago, before he'd gone to ground with Dunja.

The lock pick's performance was impeccable this time, too, and the moment Sleizner stepped into the hallway and quietly closed the door behind him, he was sure he was in the right place.

True, the hallway looked much the same as other hallways, a rectangular passageway with doors on both sides. But other than a basket full of threadbare slippers and a coatrack with a see-through raincoat, it was empty. There was virtually no furniture and the bare walls were as empty as you might expect in the flat of a shady hacker who cared about nothing but the light from his screen.

The door on the left stood ajar and led into a windowless bathroom. He turned on the naked bulb above the bathroom mirror, looked around and immediately spotted the top prize on the edge of the bath in the form of a pink Venus razor and a bottle of intimate soap of the exact same brand he'd seen in Dunja's bathroom during one of his visits.

This was where she lived. Just as he'd thought, Dunja, the

Indian man and the Chinese elephant freak had swapped flats.

He dragged his finger along the inside of the bath and noted that it was still wet. He was close. No question about it. With a bit of luck, he might even surprise her in the bedroom before she was dressed.

He picked up the razor, sniffed it and counted about ten pubic hairs stuck between the blades, plus quite a bit of shaving cream. So the little slut was freshly shaved.

He extracted the dark pubic hairs from the razor with a pair of tweezers and dropped them into a small sealable plastic bag. You never knew when they might come in handy. Then he stepped back into the hallway, popped his head into a messy kitchen whose grimy windows looked out on a smaller side street and turned to the closed door opposite.

There were no signs on it, nothing specific to indicate it was a bedroom door. And yet he was completely convinced it was. He just knew, and why wouldn't he? Until now, his gut had been right at every juncture. Everything was how he'd thought it would be.

He went right up to the door, administered a few puffs of mouth spray and waited until every muscle in his body was tense and poised, then he opened the door as quietly and quickly as he could and entered.

As expected, it was a bedroom, with an unmade bed and a nightstand topped with a stack of books. Clothes were piled on a chair in one corner. Blouses, a red bra and a pair of knickers that unfortunately smelled clean, so he didn't bother pocketing them.

A clothes rack with a small number of hangers stood along one wall and each item of clothing on it looked like it had been purchased at some moth-eaten second-hand dump. There were tattered dark jeans, a few sets of gym clothes and tops with different patterns, each more hysterical than the next, which was apparently part of her new feminist look, along with a shaved head, bright red lipstick and big earrings.

He pulled out his phone and took a picture of each piece of clothing as well as the trainers and the heavy boots on the floor. Then he walked over to the nightstand to take a closer look at the books, which all seemed to be about bugging and surveillance. That was concerning, but worse was the receipt lying next to them, which revealed that they had all been purchased at Bog & Idé in Holbæk, of all places. That could be a coincidence, obviously, but something told him he should be seriously worried.

A sudden gust from the window, which was open a crack, interrupted his reverie. Somewhere a door had opened, creating a cross-breeze that subsided as abruptly as it had arisen. He hurried back into the hallway, only to discover that it was as deserted as before. Had the little bitch really managed to sneak out behind his back? Or had a window been opened? There was, after all, one last closed door at the far end of the hallway.

He walked up to it, pressed his ear against it and thought he could hear someone walking around whistling on the other side. So this was when it was going to happen. The moment he'd been looking forward to for months was finally here.

The door seemed to open of its own accord the moment he put his hand on the handle, with the effect that his entrance ended up not being the surprise he'd envisaged. He literally staggered into the room and almost fell over before managing to right himself.

The room was considerably larger than all the others put together, and apart from a single removal box in the middle of the floor, it was virtually empty. Or, more accurately, emptied. But that wasn't what made the ground disappear from under his feet. Nor was it that there was no sign of Dunja. It was the realization of what the room had once been.

The walls were lined with desks, emptied of computers, screens and everything else. What was left were cut cables, stray extension leads and a handful of soldering irons, and on one of the desks, a small transistor radio playing the whistled melody he recognized from a Tarantino film.

This had been a proper command centre. He could see it. The computers, screens and strange boxes with blinking, multicoloured diodes. The wire harnesses, exposed circuit boards and control panels. All to get under his skin and hit him where it hurt the most.

Goddam fucking hell... The words echoed through his mind. Goddam bloody fucking shit hell... He had to sit down on the floor in the middle of the room to keep from falling over and try to slow his heart rate by breathing like he'd learned at yoga.

When he stood back up, he realized he was in a different building than the one he'd originally entered, and that there was a door at the other end of the room. He walked over to it, opened it and discovered it was in fact another front door leading straight into a stairwell that would take him down to the side street. This, too, said Electrical room – No unauthorized access. Was this how she had escaped while he was in the bedroom? He could certainly feel the same cross-breeze as he had done then.

He closed the door and looked around the abandoned room. They must have known he was coming. There was no other explanation. Somehow, they'd bloody well figured out he was going to show up today, right now.

He'd thought he was a step ahead. That he was in control, with a firm grasp on the tiller. When in reality, the opposite was true. Pathetic, was what it was. So goddam fucking pathetic.

The only silver lining was the removal box on the floor. Granted, it could be them taunting him again. After all, this was Dunja Hougaard, a goddam fucking bitch cunt. He prudently studied the box from every angle before finally bending down and opening it.

The sight of the piles of circuit boards, cables and disassembled mobile phones was enough to let him know they'd been so rushed they simply hadn't managed to take the box with them. Whatever it was, it wasn't something they'd want him to have.

He picked up one of the phones, which was connected to a circuit board via a number of electrodes and thin wires. That meant nothing to him, but there was bound to be someone back at headquarters who could explain it to him. Deeper down was a small, resealable plastic bag containing ten or so SIM cards. At least he knew what they were for.

It was the eight digits, written in felt-tip on the bag, that finally made the penny drop and for the second time in just a few minutes, he had to sit down in order not to fall down.

They could have been any eight digits. But they weren't. Together, they formed a number. His phone number.

68

THE QUEUE WAS insane. They'd been inching their way forward at a snail's pace for forty minutes now. He could almost see the slime trail behind them, and yet it would be at least another fifteen before they were in. A virtually hour-long, near-death-experience wait for one minute and fifty-eight seconds of bumper cars. That really wasn't on.

Yeah, that really was how long the ride lasted. He'd timed it, or his name wasn't Ib. Not just once but all thirteen go-arounds that had taken place while they were waiting, and no matter how you counted, the average time was exactly one minute and fifty-eight seconds.

That they had the temerity to flog all-day passes for several hundred kronor each on a day like this was nothing short of daylight robbery.

If he was completely honest, he'd never really seen the draw of amusement parks. Waterparks were the worst. He'd rather strip naked, smear honey all over himself and be eaten alive by termites than spend one day at Lalandia. And Legoland, Bakken and Tivoli weren't much better. They were all about one thing – to herd people into long queues and steal all their hard-earned money.

Twice in a lifetime was enough. Two dutiful visits, no more. Once when your parents made you and once when your kids did. And yet this was his fifth trip to Tivoli, at least, and as always, he was the one who had to fork out a minor fortune for the privilege of queuing all day, surrounded by a horde of screaming brats.

But the children, as Mette liked to say. *Ib, we do it for the children*. The children… her constant go-to. As though they weren't helicoptered enough. As though they didn't already get everything they pointed to. He wondered if they could even spell the word *no*.

They were never whinier than at Tivoli. It didn't matter how much ice cream and candyfloss you bought them. When you finally said no to some grotesquely oversized lollipop that would inevitably be left unfinished to get gross and gather dust at home, all hell broke loose. Scenes were made and you had to hear that you were the stingiest human on the planet.

At least it was finally their turn now. Not that he was looking forward to forcing his legs into the miniscule bumper car and getting hit by a bunch of maniacs from every direction. No, he would happily forgo that. The only silver lining was that at least the queueing would be over for a few minutes.

He hated this with a burning passion. But he did it anyway and kept his thoughts to himself. No one could say he didn't. He even put on the safety harness after the little coloured boy pointed out that he hadn't. Perhaps his smile was less than completely genuine, but there he was, enduring, for the sake of his family and the children, accelerating as hard as he could in a car that insisted on driving diagonally backwards.

At least he had his baseball cap on. Mette had badgered him about leaving it at home, of course. But he'd refused, and the row had been unavoidable. She'd rehashed her litany of tired arguments. About how the Danish People's Party's logo bothered people and that you really didn't have to force your own political views down other people's throats.

What she didn't understand was that the hat with the DPP logo on the blue background was his bulwark on a day like this. He'd made so many compromises since he woke up that morning that without it, there would be nothing left of Ib.

Besides, he couldn't see what the problem was with making his political affiliation known. If anyone wanted to come up to him and have a discussion about something, why not? Like the importance of keeping Denmark pure.

He didn't mind explaining to people what was really going on in the world. How the Muslims' wet dream was to come in and take their jobs and pensions while also forcing their sick values on everyone. These were facts. Not to mention all the Swedes who on days like this flooded in across the sound and made trouble. Without them, the queues would have been half as long.

No, kick out the riff-raff so real Danes could have some peace and quiet. What was so hard about that?

There was a loud thud and the entire car shook as he was rear-ended moments after he'd finally managed to make his car stop reversing. And if that wasn't bad enough, he felt a sudden pinprick in his neck and then an intense pain spread down his shoulders and back.

Was it whiplash? Was this what it felt like? It would be just his luck to get injured in a goddam bumper car. He turned around as much as he could and saw a happy Chinese bloke go by, smiling at him.

Of course it was a Chink. Go figure.

69

THIS WAS MADNESS. Utter madness.

While waiting for the two Tivoli guards to make contact with their supervisor, Fabian kept his eyes down. He could almost see time slipping through his fingers, spilling onto the table and over the edge. Every second he'd been ahead before, he was now falling behind. All while thousands of blissfully ignorant visitors were milling about just outside in the mistaken belief that this was just another beautiful vacation day full of sunshine and spinning carousels.

Three times he'd got up and explained to the Danes that this was no time for red tape, that they had to call in more staff and, above all, proper police support. He'd even had Tuvesson explain the gravity of the situation to them. But each time, they'd simply told him to calm down and carried on making internal calls.

'Well?' he said when they finally turned to him. 'Did you get hold of him?'

'I'm afraid not,' said the one whose Swedish was at least functional. 'His daughter is graduating today, so his phone is probably turned off.'

'Okay. But then someone else must be in charge, right? Or what? You can't just disregard security every time someone's daughter's graduating, right?'

'All right, settle down,' said the other guard, raising a warning hand.

'No, I'm not going to settle down, and you shouldn't either with a killer about to attack this place any minute.'

'Do you know how old Tivoli is?' The guard spread his hands. 'One hundred and sixty-nine years. So we know what we're doing.'

'Know what you're doing? Then how come we're sitting in here instead of being out there trying to apprehend him?'

'Because you're the one who came storming in here, firing a gun and attacking one of our visitors.'

'I thought it was him, and I still do.'

'Yes, you've made that clear. But the only one armed in that situation was you.'

Fabian was about to argue but stopped himself. He still believed it was Milwokh he'd seen, but he couldn't be sure.

'Fine, it's possible it wasn't him, and since we didn't bring him in for questioning, we can only pray you're right and I'm wrong. But that doesn't change the fact that we have to be ready when he does get here, because he will. He is coming here. Do you understand me?'

'Yes, we understand, but—'

'Then why aren't you doing anything? Why are you just sitting here? Don't you get that he's going to pick them off one by one as the dice directs him? Children, old people, women, men. No one will be safe. It's only after he rolls a—' He gave up with a sigh.

There was no point. They'd stopped listening and much as he hated to admit it, he could see why. Everything he said sounded insane and the more he'd tried to argue with them and make them understand the gravity of the situation, the more obvious it had become that everything was based on loose assumptions. He couldn't swear he would have believed them if their roles had been reversed.

'And this must be Fabian Risk, unless I'm mistaken,' said a voice behind him.

He turned around and saw a man with a determined smile on his face enter the room.

'Thank you. I'll take it from here.'

The guards nodded and left the office while the man took a seat across from Fabian.

'My name is Jan Hesk and I work for the Copenhagen Police.'

'Finally, someone from the police,' Fabian said. 'I don't know how much you know about the situation. The thing is that we have a suspected killer who may be about to attack—'

'Stop, stop,' Hesk broke in, raising one hand. 'One step at a time. Is it true that you broke into the park armed with a gun and proceeded to fire it?'

'Yes, that's correct, but it was a warning shot, into the air. What's important right now is that—'

'I have to ask you to give me your weapon.'

'I'm sorry, the guards already confiscated it, and though I would love to have it back as soon as possible, what's important right now is that we get plain-clothes officers out there and start evacuating the visitors before—'

'Is it also true that you were the one who violated Danish territorial waters yesterday, despite being denied access?'

Fabian nodded with a heavy sigh and was about to explain, but couldn't get a word in.

'Great. Then I would ask you to sign here and here.' Hesk

pushed a document across the table and pointed to the dotted line at the bottom.

Admission of illegal violation of Danish territorial waters and illegal possession of a firearm.

Fabian didn't have to read past the first word to realize the Danish police had no interest in Milwokh.

70

Pontus Milwokh was in the Star Flyer, a swing ride, spinning round and round, 250 feet above the ground. From up here, he could see not only Tivoli and every one of his potential victims, but all of Copenhagen spread out before him.

When he'd come here as a young boy, this ride hadn't existed, so it was his first time trying it, and he had to admit he felt like the thin chains his seat was suspended from might snap at any second.

As they began to descend again, he shook his left arm and watched the dice tumble around like it was dancing, led by chance, inside the modified water bottle. So far, he had no complaints. The dice had provided a virtually perfect warm-up sequence of sub-tasks and he was starting to feel ready to up the ante.

He'd done five already. Five victims that at the moment had no idea that's what they were. If it kept on like this, he'd run out of ricin. But he felt sure the dice had that under control.

Four – Change colour

At least it wasn't a one. Granted, he wouldn't have had to go home empty-handed if it had been, and sure, he'd had fun. More than fun, it had been a blast. But he was far from done and couldn't wait to sink his teeth into his next sub-task.

He shook his arm again and let the dice jump around under the plastic dome while he climbed out of the swing and walked down the steps. This was exactly what he'd been chasing. The feeling that anything was possible. That adventures, each one bigger and more thrilling than the next, lay ahead. It was intoxicating and helped him put the difficulties he'd encountered getting in behind him.

It had been his own idea to enter the park without his gear. He'd thrown his equipment in over the fence behind The Demon, Tivoli's largest roller coaster, and that had turned out to be ingenious. That the dice had ordered him to use the main entrance to Tivoli, rather than one of the smaller side ones, was, perhaps, not ideal.

Maybe it had just wanted to add some spice to proceedings because suddenly, someone claiming to work for the Swedish police had started chasing him and had even fired his gun. He wasn't sure, but he thought he might have recognized him from his night on Öresund.

He'd never been able to figure out how they'd come so close to catching him that time. He was even more stumped today. It was impressive. Really impressive, and he had only his lucky star to thank for not having had his gear with him. He would have been arrested if he had and then he wouldn't have got to experience any of the fun that awaited him now.

One – Red

New colour, new victims. There were so many to choose from he'd decided to pick the first one he laid eyes on, to avoid turning it into an active choice.

As soon as the guards had let him leave, he'd casually strolled over to the exit from The Demon, and in the quiet between two trains he'd hurried up the short flight of steps and jumped over the railing to a hidden patch of grass where his gear had been waiting for him next to two large bins.

In that secluded spot, he'd been able to take his time strapping on the back holster and all the belt bags without anyone noticing. When he was ready, he'd simply unlocked the gate in the red wooden fence from the inside and started the game, and since then, everything had gone like clockwork.

The boy looked to be about ten and was wearing red shorts. That was all he needed. It was almost like stalking himself on that day almost thirty years ago when he'd made his way here all by himself and had the best day of his life. Nothing, despite all his attempts and experiences, had ever compared to it.

Not until today.

There was no sign of parents. Maybe he was lost. But he didn't seem upset, so more likely he'd been allowed to walk around by himself for an hour or two so the adults could catch a break in the sunshine.

He followed the boy into the Grand Prix, a circular room underneath the Ferris wheel where you could place bets on postmen racing round and round on their bikes. As a boy he'd loved the cycling puppets, but just like the boy in the red shorts, he'd been afraid to gamble away any of his money, and so he'd continued out the other side and walked up towards Fairy-Tale Lane.

In reality, it was called Smøgen, but to him it had always felt like stepping into a fairy-tale world. Wedged in behind the old roller coaster, it was easy to miss, but it was where all the fun stands could be found and all the best lollipops were sold. But above all, it was where you could feel like no one else knew where you were.

The boy stopped at a stand where you could shoot all kinds of animals with a laser rifle. He could remember standing in that same spot as though it were yesterday, waiting for his turn as one inebriated group after another pushed ahead of him.

He could almost feel the frustration from back then, when he'd finally screamed that it was his turn to play and yanked one of the men's ponytails so hard he fell over. The man's mates, who all wore leather jackets with the same patch across the back, had applauded and put him on a stool so he could finally shoot the animals.

It was happening again. As though time had glitched and was running on a loop, the little boy was waiting his turn when a group of drunk idiots pushed ahead of him. He wanted to go up to them and stab them, one by one. But sadly, it wasn't their turn. So instead, he walked over and tapped the biggest one's shoulder.

The man turned around and tried to focus his bleary eyes on him.

'What do you think you're doing, fucking Chink?'

'The rules are there to be followed,' he replied calmly. 'And one of them is that everyone has to wait their turn.'

The man cleared his throat. He could hear the phlegm travelling up from his lungs to his mouth. But somewhere in his boozy haze, he must have sensed how serious the situation was, because he spat the mucus out on the pavement and stepped aside so the boy could get to the rifle.

Once his time was up and the rifle went out, he held out a twenty-kronor note so the boy could go again. But the boy shook his head, and before he could react, he'd been swallowed by the crowd.

Milwokh hurried after him and bumped into several people on his way through the milling throng. This was not part of the game. This simply couldn't happen. He'd had several opportunities to finish the task. Instead, he'd allowed himself to get sucked into a swirl of saccharine nostalgia and been completely blinded.

He could maybe choose someone else. He saw potential victims wearing red all around him. The rules said nothing about that or how to handle the situation that had suddenly arisen. But in his heart of hearts, he knew that wasn't the intention. The first one he saw was the one. No one else.

Then he finally spotted the red shorts again, just as they disappeared into the Fun House with its moving staircases, suspension bridges and revolving tunnels. The best thing about the Fun House was that you could stay as long as you wanted. On this occasion, however, his main concerns were the poor air quality, the loud screaming of the hordes of children and the boy.

It felt significantly smaller than the last time he was here, but it was still large enough that it could potentially take him hours to find his target.

'Why are you following me?'

The voice behind him was more high-pitched than he'd expected, and as he turned it dawned on him that the boy might be even younger than he'd thought. Just as suddenly, fumbling around for the least implausible lie became irrelevant.

'You remind me of myself at your age. I think that's why.'

The boy thought about it and eventually nodded. 'But

maybe you could stop now, because I don't like it. Not at all, actually.'

'Absolutely,' he said, nodding. 'On one condition. That you let me give you a hug.'

The boy instinctively took a step back.

'You might not be able to understand this, but I'm just here to close the circle, and when I saw you, it was like seeing myself.'

'Do you promise to leave me alone if I let you?' the boy said, swallowing hard.

He nodded and smiled. 'I promise.'

'Cross your heart?'

'Cross my heart.'

'Okay.' The boy took a step forward and hugged him and a fraction of a second after the needle penetrated the cotton of his T-shirt and then the skin above his hip, he flinched.

It was over in seconds, and yet it felt like an eternity as he held the boy close for as long as it took to empty the entire syringe before allowing him to run off.

71

FABIAN MOVED AS quickly as he could without knocking
people over. Sometimes he ran, sometimes he had to
skirt around large groups of people, but he kept moving
and turning his head constantly to try to take in as much
information as possible.

He had to avoid getting bogged down in irrelevant details
and only focus on things that stuck out. Whatever that
might be. Most of the things he reacted to were completely
normal at an amusement park.

People were screaming all around him. Usually out of sheer
thrill, but on occasion out of fear or even panic. Children
were crying and adults shouting. People's movements were
different, too. They were either standing still in groups or
ambling around aimlessly without any discernible purpose.
Others were running like they were being chased. All of
it had to be considered normal. Not even the occasional
fistfight was eyebrow-raising.

His decision not to sign the admission of possession
of an illegal firearm but rather to stand up and leave the
guardhouse hadn't strictly speaking been a decision at all.
He'd simply had no other option, and what the Danish
Police Authority, under the sway of Kim Sleizner, chose to
do about it wasn't something he had time to care about
right now. Jan Hesk had seemed to secretly agree with

him, since he'd let him go without so much as a word of protest.

Since then, he'd managed to do two complete laps around the park. This was the third time he'd turned away from the lawn in front of the main stage and continued in between the Promenaden and Frikadellen restaurants.

So far, he hadn't noticed anything out of the ordinary. The man he'd been about to arrest was nowhere to be seen. At the time, he'd been convinced it was Milwokh. Now, his doubts were growing with every step. What if that hadn't been him, what if this wasn't where the attack was taking place?

Both he and Tuvesson had taken Lilja's conclusions on faith. And yet all they'd seen was a description of the task itself and Tivoli hadn't actually been mentioned once. *Take the location of the discarded task as your starting point, it had said.* A public space in the vicinity with as many people as possible in a limited area. With Copenhagen marked on the map with a cross, it was reasonable to assume it had to be Tivoli. Particularly since Lilja had also found pictures of Milwokh as a child at the amusement park. But there was no escaping the fact that he might just as likely be planning to attack the Zoo. Or why not the central station, just a stone's throw from Tivoli?

He'd been in frequent contact with Tuvesson to inform her of what was happening. When he ran into problems with their Danish counterparts, she'd been firmly on his side, promising to do everything in her power to get in touch with Sleizner and making sure an official protest was lodged by someone higher up.

They'd also agreed he should continue to search the park

until closing. Then they'd have the night to go over the clues Lilja had found and hopefully share enough about the case with the Danes to persuade them to help patrol Tivoli, the Zoo and some of the other venues that could conceivably be in Milwokh's sights.

A sudden burst of screaming from the old roller coaster made him turn around, but a row of clothes on display blocked his view. It wasn't unusual for there to be screaming on a roller coaster, of course, but the screams themselves caught his attention. These were not shrieks of joy brought on by the thrill of the ride. These were pure, unadulterated terror.

He hurried back towards the roller coaster through the crowd and climbed the stairs to the platform where the train would normally stop to let the passengers off. But this time, it continued straight ahead and rammed straight into the parked train in front, where people were just climbing into their seats.

The platform instantly turned into an inferno of screaming and crying people. Chaos erupted, some people were limping, others were rubbing their necks or bleeding. But no one seemed seriously injured, except for a man who lay motionless between two of the carts halfway down the train that had come in too fast.

A guard behind him was shouting something about everyone needing to get off the platform, but Fabian ignored him and instead pushed his way over to the motionless man, who was dressed in a red and green Tivoli uniform. It was his job to manually apply the brakes in the old trains, and for some reason he'd lost consciousness, which must have been why the train had been out of control.

Fabian checked the man's pulse while listening to voices saying the train had stopped in a dark tunnel and stood still for over a minute before continuing at maximum speed. But he couldn't find a pulse, nor did he seem to be breathing. Another voice behind him said the man driving the train had been slumped over after the tunnel and in the next drop he had fallen out of his seat. The man was definitely dead. But why? There was no blood. Could he have had a stroke or a heart attack?

It was only after he lifted up the man's chin and saw the dark blue strangulation marks from a rope that the penny dropped.

Milwokh was here.

He must have rolled a three for rope.

Fabian stood up and scanned the milling mass of shocked passengers and the Tivoli staff trying to impose some sort of order. Chances were, he was right here. Pretending to be part of the crowd being ushered away from the scene of the accident. But he couldn't see him. Not on the platform and not down among the curious onlookers who were beginning to gather.

With his eyes fixed on a man in his fifties who was strolling by, seemingly indifferent to the accident and the attendant commotion, he pulled out his phone and called Tuvesson.

'Hi, Fabian, how are you getting on?' Tuvesson said on the other end, just as the man suddenly collapsed mid-step. It looked like a stumble after one too many Carlsbergs. The problem was that he didn't get back up.

'Astrid, he's here, and he's already hard at work,' Fabian said. He ended the call and started making his way towards the man, who was now the centre of everyone's attention.

'I think he's dead,' said a woman who was checking the man's pulse.

Fabian nodded and, just to make sure, he lifted up the man's chin to check his throat. But there were no marks to be seen this time.

Then he spotted a small hole in the dark red shirt by the man's left pectoral. He took a closer look and realized the shirt was soaking wet, then he turned his hand over and stared at his palm, which was covered in blood.

The woman pushed up the man's shirt and studied the ragged exit wound in the area of his heart, from which blood was still pumping out. 'Oh my God, he's been shot,' she exclaimed.

'Yes, so everyone please stand back,' Fabian said as he rolled the man over onto his stomach and found the much smaller entry wound just above his right shoulder. 'The best thing you can do right now is leave the park as quickly as possible.'

So the shot had come diagonally from above.

Fabian turned around and looked up at the old roller coaster, and at the very top, on the side of the fake mountain peak, he spotted the dark outline of a crouching man.

72

JAN HESK HAD felt like a deer. A terror-stricken deer standing petrified on a road in the middle of the night, staring into the headlights of an oncoming lorry.

Putting the so-called admission in front of Swedish detective inspector Fabian Risk and asking him to sign it had been a new low point in his police career. But he'd done it. Even though the shame of it would haunt him for the rest of his life, he'd followed Sleizner's explicit order.

But when the Swede had shaken his head, stood up and made clear he was about to walk out since there was a suspected terrorist out there to arrest, he'd been unable to do anything other than stand there in the middle of the road, staring into the headlights.

And now he was sitting at his desk in the open-plan office with his phone to his ear, overcome with anxiety. He, who was usually always hungry, hadn't been able to get so much as a bite down since breakfast. Even a few sips of water had necessitated a dash to the bathroom, where he'd thrown them back up along with a lot of bile.

His body was on strike. But then, he was in deep shit and about to drown. And yet he would have done the same thing again if given the chance.

He gave up on his fifth attempt to get hold of Sleizner to inform him about what had happened and cracked his neck to try and dispel his headache. Making up a story in which the Tivoli guards hadn't managed to apprehend the Swede or in which he'd pulled his weapon to get away from them would only make matters worse once the truth came out.

No one could sniff out a lie like Sleizner, and then he could forget about promotions and having his own office, more money and, above all, being in charge of the interesting cases. They were going to have to put off redoing the kitchen, too, and he would have to have that conversation with Lone about closing her plastic-free baby shop and finding a real job instead.

She would obviously fly off the handle and launch right into her well-practised diatribe about how she'd stayed home with the children so his career wouldn't suffer, and it was her turn now, even if she had to divorce him to get it.

And that was just the Sleizner aspect of the problem. The real meltdown would happen if the information the Swedes had given them turned out to be correct. Then it wasn't just a lost promotion he needed to worry about, he was going to have to find a new job.

The best he could hope for now was that all of it would amount to nothing. That it would turn out to have been conjecture, like Sleizner had said. At the end of the day, most alarms were in fact false. Ninety-six per cent of the time, the fire department was called out needlessly, for instance.

The same was true of terror attacks. How many false rumours to each one with substance? At the same time, every last one of their recent big terror attacks had been preceded by warnings of some kind, that was undeniable. Warnings that had been played down, overlooked and for various reasons consigned to the spam folder.

The question was whether this was going to be yet another in a series of attacks where it was revealed afterwards that they'd been aware of the threat but hadn't taken it seriously. If that happened, his head would be the one to roll. Especially when it came out that he'd put all his energy into trying to arrest the one police officer who had actually tried to stop the attack.

But the whole thing was just a bunch of flimsy suppositions. He didn't really know anything. Not until he spotted his colleague Morten Heinesen's stressed yet restrained gait as he made his way through the open-plan office towards his desk.

It was no longer flimsy supposition.

The Swedes had been right.

It was really happening.

Whatever it was, it was happening right now.

73

PONTUS MILWOKH SHOOK his arm as he gazed out across the area below the roller coaster. Paramedics had arrived and were just now concluding that the man in the red shirt was beyond their aid. The shot had been perfect, even though he'd been in motion, and the fact that no one else had been hurt definitely merited a gold star.

He'd never understood the people who stood around watching. They were everywhere. As soon as disaster struck, they popped up out of nowhere with their dull eyes and camera phones. It was as though they took pleasure from the fact that it hadn't happened to them. That they weren't the ones being covered and carried away on gurneys.

At least the Danish police seemed to have finally caught on. Sirens were wailing in the streets outside Tivoli now, and he could even see special operations teams arriving. But he wasn't worried. He left things up to the dice. Like now, for example, when he stopped shaking his arm and checked the outcome.

Three – Change weapons

It was the third time since he started. If it had been up to him, he would have had a few more goes with the rifle. It was undoubtedly the best weapon from up here at the top of the roller coaster.

But the dice had spoken and he could only hope it would

choose the crossbow or the rifle again. What he would do
if it was the knife, rope or poison, he had no idea. Or even
worse, if he rolled a five, which meant he could only use his
own body.

Another train full of Tivoli visitors was unlikely to go by
anytime soon and he wasn't allowed to change his position
at will. In the worst-case scenario, he would have to wait in
place until the police came to arrest him and at best get one
of them before it was all over.

Was this the dice's way of telling him it was time to wrap
up? That it was tired of him? He hadn't made so much
as one mistake since starting this task. On the contrary,
he'd delivered more than could reasonably be expected,
considering the pressures of the situation.

Only the boy had bothered him. It was the first time he'd
felt an instinctive resistance to obeying the commands of the
dice. But he'd checked himself and done as he was told, and
strangely, afterwards, he'd felt stronger than ever.

Maybe that was the point. It almost felt like it might be.
As though the boy had been significant. As though the dice
had decided it was time for the circle to be complete so he
could move on. Was there a better way of escaping your
childhood than destroying yourself as a child?

He shook his left arm again until he was sure the dice was
ready to make a decision.

Two – Crossbow

It was the second-best option, though a crossbow was far
from easy to operate. Especially at a distance. Granted, he
had imported a Revengeance from Barnett in the US through
Amazon. It was relatively easy to arm, despite reaching bolt
speeds of almost 250 miles an hour. But at this distance,

wind was a factor. And if the target was moving, there was a considerable risk the bolt could miss, which was out of the question under any circumstances.

He unfolded the two cam limbs, cocked the thick string and placed the bolt in the flight groove. Then he let the weapon rest against the edge of the grey plastic that was meant to look like a mountainside and put his feet against the track for support.

He judged the distance down to the open space between the Ferris wheel and the swing ride to be about three hundred feet and set the scope accordingly. The moment he put his eye to it, he felt like he was down there in the crowd.

Like an invisible spectre, he hovered there right in front of them. He could even see the fear in some people's eyes when they realized someone had been shot nearby.

What he didn't see was panic. No crowds stampeding in every direction, trampling each other to save themselves, like during a terror attack. Just a general worry about what had happened, which suited him perfectly. The calmer they were, the better.

The man who finally caught his attention was, however, not on the ground, but rather sitting alone in one of the gondolas of the Ferris wheel with a red pocket square in his breast pocket. He looked like he was well into his sixties and, unlike the other visitors, was formally attired.

He adjusted the scope and watched the man through the cross hairs as he went round and round until the Ferris wheel suddenly stopped and his gondola swung back and forth at the highest point while waiting for the lowest gondola to empty out and fill with new passengers.

Meanwhile, the cross hairs wandered up to the red

pocket square and then his index finger squeezed the trigger, releasing the latch holding the string, which, aided by the two limbs, sent the bolt flying.

It was over in less than a second, and it took him a while to realize the bolt had missed. Judging from the man's surprised face, it had passed by about a foot to his left.

The Ferris wheel began to turn again, which gave him plenty of time to cock the string, place another bolt in the flight groove and get into position. The man seemed to have regained his composure and was enjoying the view when the Ferris wheel stopped once more, setting the gondola swaying.

This time, he adjusted his aim about a foot to the man's right before releasing the bolt, which shot through the air almost soundlessly, pierced the left side of the man's chest and, judging from the heavy bleeding that immediately soaked his shirt, went straight to his heart.

74

THE SOUND WAS coming through inverted. All the high frequencies in the clamour around Fabian had been turned down so low it had morphed into a constant deep rumble, like distant thunder. The only thing he could hear was his own hammering pulse as he pushed his way back up onto the roller coaster platform.

Even though it had been fifteen minutes since the trains crashed into each other, the platform was still a pandemonium of guards, injured people and rubberneckers. 'Police,' he said, holding up his police ID for one of the guards blocking his path to see.

'Get out of here!' the guard bellowed. 'Come on, get!'

'I'm police! I have to get up there!' He pushed past the guard. 'Hello? Can you get me up there?'

'You're not going anywhere,' the guard roared, grabbing him from behind. 'Fucking wanker, get out of here, and I mean now!'

Fabian spun around and smacked the guard's arms aside. Twice now he'd come stumblingly close to an arrest. He was not going to miss his third chance. But the guard didn't back down.

He did, however, turn to look when screaming suddenly broke out over at the Ferris wheel, which let Fabian wrest free of his grasp and climb into the empty train. Hoping for the best, he released the handbrake and the train began to move forward into the tunnel.

Behind him, the guards were screaming, both at him and each other, but the further into the tunnel he got, the more distant they sounded, and once the chain between the tracks hooked onto the carts and started to pull the train up the lift hill, he could barely hear them at all.

Two visitors had already fallen prey to Milwokh. Two completely innocent people. At least two. He was going to catch him this time. At any cost.

The train came to a halt in the middle of the incline; someone had probably pushed the emergency stop. He saw no other option than to get out of the car and climb the last bit. But it was steep and considerably harder than it looked. He was positively dripping sweat and the injuries from his fight with Molander were making themselves known again. His entire body was screaming that it had had enough and needed a rest.

Once he reached the top, he literally staggered across the fake lawn with the grazing cows on it towards Milwokh, who was standing with his back to him, shaking his left arm.

'Pontus Milwokh,' he shouted. 'This is the police, and I'm ordering you to put your hands up and turn around!'

Milwokh slowly raised his hands above his head. But instead of turning around, he disappeared over the edge.

No... no, no, Fabian repeated again and again as he hurried over to the edge, where he spotted Milwokh, who had landed on an adjoining roof about ten feet further down and was now crawling away, vanishing around a corner moments later.

The fall was too high, but that realization came too late; like Milwokh, Fabian had thrown himself over the edge without any idea of how to land safely.

As he hit the roof, his phone fell out of his jacket pocket and bounced over the edge. Worse still was that despite his best attempt to bend his knees on impact, he could both feel and hear something snap in his hip.

But it didn't matter. Right now, only Milwokh mattered, which was why he clambered down from the roof to a smaller terrace from which he could hop a fence and get down to the ground via a column.

He looked around as he half lay down on the ground and, defying the pain, pulled his leg as hard as he could in the hopes of popping his hip joint back into place. But Milwokh was nowhere to be seen.

'Which way did he go?' he shouted at some people standing around staring at him as he pushed himself back onto his feet. 'Answer me! Where did he go?'

'I think he ran that way,' a woman behind him called out just as he spotted something whizzing by a few feet away, so quickly it was almost invisible.

Fabian didn't understand what it was until it had already burrowed into the stomach of the woman, who had been walking towards him, but who now collapsed instead.

He limped over to her. She was lying on her back in a growing pool of her own blood with the bolt sticking out of her stomach.

'What happened?' she said.

'You've been shot in the stomach with a crossbow bolt,' he said as calmly as possible. Then he took off his jacket and tied it as hard as he could around the woman's waist and the wound as curious people began to congregate around them. 'But it's going to be okay,' he continued. 'Everything's going to be okay. You just have to stay awake.' He looked up at the crowd. 'Could someone call an ambulance. Please! Anyone! An ambulance!'

'I'm a Swedish doctor and I'm already in contact with them,' said a man in shorts, sandals and a HIF baseball cap, who emerged from the gaggle with a phone to his ear and immediately knelt down and began checking the woman's eyes as he talked to the paramedics. 'Yes, she's conscious. But I would guess there's severe internal bleeding.'

'Could someone call my husband?' the woman asked in a voice that sounded distinctly weaker than before. 'Someone has to call my husband.'

'Where's your phone?' Fabian asked.

'In my handbag.'

'The ambulance will be here very soon,' said the doctor, who was already examining the bloody area around the bolt.

'My husband, he's waiting for me. He won't like it if no one calls him.'

'Don't worry, everything will be fine.'

Fabian opened the red handbag the woman was still holding and took out her phone. That was when it hit him. The colours. Milwokh was choosing his victims by colour. The man he'd strangled on the roller coaster, the one who had been shot right after and now this woman.

They'd all been wearing red.

In the form of a red-and-green Tivoli uniform, a shirt or, in this case, a handbag.

'My husband,' the woman said. 'You have to call my husband.'

'Could you help her call her husband?' Fabian handed the phone to a young woman and turned to the people standing behind him. 'If you're wearing anything red, remove that piece of clothing immediately,' he shouted as he kicked off his red trainers, only to discover that the toes of his socks were also red.

People gave him and each other uncomprehending looks.

'Listen to me!' he went on, pulling off his socks. 'I'm a police officer. You have to take off anything red! And you have to do it now!' Then he stood up, yanked the red baseball cap off the doctor's head, started pushing through the crowd and limped away in the direction the bolt had come from.

Most signs pointed to the dice having ordered Milwokh to change position from *as high up as possible* to *keep moving* or possibly *push into the crowd*.

Both alternatives should mean that he was still nearby. But he couldn't see him anywhere, and in an attempt to get a better overview, he climbed onto a bench, leaning on his uninjured leg. But there was still no sign of him. Maybe he'd been ordered to change positions again. Maybe he'd rolled a one and was on his way out right now.

At least some people had heeded his advice and removed their red clothing, though most were busy filming with their phones as though they were on a beach, completely unaware that a tsunami was on its way.

Once again, Fabian noticed the almost imperceptible movement through the air, invisible to most. This time, he realized instantly that it was another crossbow bolt, and instead of following it to its victim, he looked in the opposite direction and saw a man standing with his back to him about a hundred feet further down the path. A man with shoulder-length black hair, who was already shaking his left arm again.

75

THREE DEAD AND one seriously injured.

So far, Jan Hesk thought grimly to himself as he received the information from one of the Tivoli guards with a curt nod, after which he went on alone towards the big lawn in front of the main stage. How many victims there would be before this was over was anyone's guess.

Once the first shock had worn off and the dust had settled, there would be a lot of questions. That much was certain. People would ask how something like this had been allowed to happen. Why the public still wasn't safe after all the things that had already occurred, and if there had been any warning signs.

Every stone would be turned, and investigative journalists would dig ever deeper into the shit. Conspiracy theories would surface about how the police had known but tried to cover it up, and in part, they would be right.

But only in part. No one would fully take into account the fact that everyone involved was human. People with flaws and shortcomings. Regular people with rents and car loans to pay. Who were trying to do their best despite having a boss with his own, radically different agenda.

None of that would be considered extenuating once it became clear the Swedes had done everything in their power. That they'd contacted and informed the Danish police the second they'd discovered signs pointing to Tivoli. That they'd reached out to him again and again to try to work together.

And now here he was, stuck so deep in the shit he risked falling over if he so much as twitched. The slightest error at this point, and he would have to go into exile.

But dark as things may look, there was still a chance he could turn this into something positive, and if he failed, he had only himself to blame.

No one knew where Sleizner was. For the past forty minutes, he'd been refusing to answer his phone. Normally, that would have aggravated Hesk's ulcer, but this time he was fine with it, because it gave him a chance to step up, take charge and show what he could do.

In fact, most of the anxiety he'd been feeling just an hour ago had evaporated. It was a relief no longer to have to wonder but rather to know that all hell had broken loose and that it was up to him now.

The mood at the amusement park was definitely different to usual. No widespread panic yet, luckily, but it was simmering beneath the surface and risked bubbling over any second.

Panic was something they wanted to avoid at all costs. Once panic broke out, there was no way back, and the death toll could quickly rise into double digits when twenty-five thousand visitors started trampling each other to get out.

For that reason, they'd left most of the rides running, except for the old roller coaster and the Ferris wheel. The important thing was to perform an orderly evacuation while making sure the killer wasn't able to slip through their checkpoints. It was a difficult balancing act, but to his mind, it was their only option under the current circumstances.

At least no one was running around spraying the crowd with automatic gunfire. If that had been the case, they would have had hundreds of dead people just in the first fifteen minutes. The downside was that now they had a more protracted scenario on their hands and a perpetrator killing clandestinely was much harder to locate.

That's where Fabian Risk came in. In fact, it was all about him now. The Swede who had stormed in with his gun drawn, without inhibition and with a demeanour that said nothing was going to stand in his way.

He'd sensed it the moment he stepped into the room where Risk was being held. The darkness and the firm determination that showed he was ready to go all the way, no matter what the consequences.

In a way, he envied Risk. He'd always tended to think more about the consequences than the goal itself. He was no hero, and he never would be. The truth was that he was mediocre. But he was smart, and this time he had no problem letting someone else play the hero.

76

MILWOKH PUSHED ON and made sure to keep moving like the dice had ordered him to. He walked around calmly to avoid drawing unwanted attention to himself and tried to look like he was one of all the oblivious visitors, enjoying the sunshine, unable to think of a better place to spend an afternoon.

Most people apparently had no idea what had happened, though he saw some who seemed to be fighting a gnawing sensation that something was awry. A few had realized and were hurrying towards the exits where the queues were growing longer, dragging their loudly protesting children with them, and here and there he saw discarded baseball caps, backpacks and shirts, all at least partially red.

He hadn't counted on that, and he could do nothing about it. A change of colour would have been helpful, but the dice had instead opted to change his weapon again, to the knife, which in a way was preferable since he was running low on crossbow bolts.

He'd worried about the crossbow, but looking back, he had to admit it had been the most fun weapon to use. It even beat the sword. There was something elaborate about the whole thing that really hit the spot. Physics at its best. Not to mention the bolts. He couldn't think of anything sexier than the way they silently sailed through the air and penetrated their target without permission or apology.

He stopped by the fountains outside the concert hall and looked around. Maybe it was just in this particular spot, or maybe more people than he'd thought had removed their red clothing. Either way, the fact was he hadn't seen any red whatsoever in the last four minutes. There should obviously be an unlimited supply, but for some reason it was as though his eyes could no longer perceive the colour red.

He continued past the outdoor seating area of Nimb Brasserie, where a girl of about twelve was sitting with her parents holding a large ball of light-red candyfloss. The urge was instantaneous, but the question was if candyfloss even counted. Or the red lighter on the table between the parents.

'No, I think we should leave now,' the mother was saying. 'This place doesn't feel right.'

His thoughts were a clear sign of his growing desperation. He knew full well only clothes and accessories counted, nothing else. Besides, the candyfloss was more pink than light-red. And, off-topic, he couldn't understand how a responsible parent could puff away like that in front of their child.

'You're being hysterical,' the father replied. 'Look around, everything's nice and calm.'

He considered staying around until they got up, to see who would pick up the lighter. Once one of them did, it would definitely count as an accessory and the girl would be burdened with one less irresponsible parent.

A few steps later, he finally spotted something red in the form of a scarf around an older woman's neck, about fifty feet away. She was sitting on the edge of the wishing well in the park outside Nimb with the same serene facial expression as the bronze statue behind her. She didn't look like she was waiting for anyone, more like she'd found the perfect spot in the shade.

For some reason, she'd already noticed him, and she was looking at him without the slightest hint of fear in her eyes, as though she had no problem with him approaching her. It was almost as though she knew what he was going to do, even though he was smiling back and keeping the knife hidden in the sleeve of his hoodie.

But, then, everyone reacted differently to danger. Some started to scream and tried to run. Others broke down and begged on their bare knees to be spared. This lady apparently faced death with a smile.

'Yes? And what can I do for you?' she said, standing up.

'Nothing,' he replied, and took another step towards her. 'Just relax.' Without taking his eyes off hers, he let the steel sink into her midriff and in that moment, it dawned on him that he had completely misunderstood her.

The shock in her eyes surprised him, and he had to put one hand over her mouth to keep the scream from escaping while he continued to dig around her insides with the knife. But eventually she calmed down, and he could finally let her fall to the ground and hurry away from the agitated voices.

77

KEEP WALKING. THERE was nothing else. Keep moving forward, even though every step seemed to rub another layer off his hip joint, intensifying the pain. If it hadn't been for the pain, he would have been able to move considerably faster. As it was, he was hobbling along barefoot, trying to put as much of his weight as possible on his right leg so he could make any progress at all.

But it wasn't fast enough. He'd lost sight of Milwokh a few minutes ago, which could mean he'd rolled a one and left the park.

He rounded the corner of Nimb Brasserie and instantly realized there was another victim when he spotted the crowd by the wishing well. The pain in his hip was now so debilitating it took him several minutes to push his way to the older woman, who had already received care to stop the bleeding.

'Has anyone called an ambulance?' he said, noting the red scarf around her neck.

'Yes, they're busy, but they'll be here as soon as they can,' someone replied. 'From what I hear, she's not the only victim.'

'What, there are more?' someone else piped up.

'I heard someone got hit by an arrow.'

'Can you hear me?' Fabian said, bending down over the

woman, who nodded, almost imperceptibly. 'Where did he go? Did you see in which direction he ran?'

Her mouth opened, but he couldn't make out any words. Just ragged breathing. He defied the pain, knelt down and put his ear about an inch from her mouth.

'The stairs...' she said on a trembling exhalation. 'Up the stairs...'

Fabian struggled back onto his feet, spotted the stairs, which looked like they led up to the indoor section of Nimb Brasserie, and started limping towards them.

'Take these,' someone said behind him.

Fabian turned around and saw an older man on crutches. 'Thank you,' he said, taking them. The crutches allowed him to move much faster. The pain was far from gone, but certainly more bearable. When he entered the restaurant, he was greeted by a waiter.

'We're closed.'

'What, closed?'

'Yes.' The waiter nodded. 'All of Tivoli is closed on account of the terror attack.'

'And the Asian man with long dark hair who just came in? Where did he go?'

'Towards the hotel,' the waiter said, pointing.

Fabian continued through the dining area on his crutches and found himself in an unmanned hotel lobby facing the street and the central station on the other side of it.

A person could just walk out. No staff. No guards. Nothing, just straight out into freedom.

But if he knew Milwokh, he would only have done that if he'd rolled a one. It was a one in six chance, which meant the chance of him being somewhere nearby was considerably greater.

A flight of stairs led up to the first floor, and since Fabian couldn't see a lift, he started slowly working his way up it. At the top of the stairs, he found a deserted hallway with numbered hotel rooms on the Tivoli side that led him to a large, palatial ballroom with three enormous crystal chandeliers suspended from a high, vaulted ceiling. A bar ran along the wall on his right and here and there were groups of brown leather sofas and large potted plants.

But there were no guests or staff to be seen. Having pushed and shoved his way through crowds for so long, he now felt like the last man standing. The hotel had been evacuated, which certainly made it the perfect location if Milwokh had rolled a two and followed up with a five.

Find a secluded spot, he muttered under his breath as he continued towards the three sets of tall double doors on his left. Two were open, so he hobbled up to the third set and paused to compose himself before entering.

The rectangular room was furnished with a big black conference table decorated with candelabra and flowers. Silver-framed photographs alternated with sconces along the walls on either side, and above the table was a large domed skylight.

At the far end, by the triple window, stood Milwokh, still wearing his shoulder-length wig, gazing out at Tivoli, where quite a lot of people were still moving about.

'Secluded place. Knife. Red,' Fabian said, and hobbled into the room on his crutches. 'Maybe not the easiest combination.'

Milwokh turned around with the bloody knife in his

hand and looked from Fabian's battered face to his dirty linen shirt, tattered jeans and bare feet.

'Sorry. No red.' Fabian spread his crutches. 'But then again. Maybe you're counting the blood stains?' He smiled. Despite the gravity of the situation, there was something so absurd about the whole thing a smile might be as good a way forward as any.

But Milwokh's face remained expressionless as he continued to look him up and down as though to make sure he hadn't missed anything, which had to be taken as a sign that blood was not well received by the dice.

'Pull your jeans down,' he said finally, and took half a step forward.

Fabian had no idea what colour underwear he had on. It could easily be red.

'Take them off,' Milwokh said again, and held the knife out in front of him as though he was getting ready.

'And if I don't? Then what will you do? Surely you can't kill me unless the dice gives you the okay?'

'I can just ask.' Milwokh started to shake his left arm, making the dice inside the plastic dome jump around. 'One, two or three, that's all I need.'

'Why not the other way around? Or odds and evens?'

'Because what's decided is decided and it's not up to me or you.' Milwokh stopped shaking and held out his arm so Fabian could see the outcome too.

A two.

'The dice has spoken. The ball's in your court. Either your jeans come off, or one minute from now you'll be bleeding to death. It's up to you.'

The idea of taking two steps forward under the pretence

of checking that it really was a two, grabbing his arm and pulling him down onto the floor never got beyond the realm of vague fantasy. Images from the Ica Maxi CCTV footage in which Milwokh had hurled himself over the meat counter and stabbed Lennart Andersson were still flashing before Fabian's eyes.

He wouldn't stand a chance.

One last time, he tried to recall what he'd put on that morning. But he had no idea and saw no other way than to unbuckle his belt with trembling hands and undo the buttons of his fly. Then he pulled down his jeans and lowered his eyes for the verdict.

It was a pair of cheap H&M pants Sonja had been on the verge of binning on several occasions. But each time he'd put up a fight, arguing that as long as there were no holes, they should be kept in rotation. Now, the yellow and green stripes were saving his life.

'Pull your shirt up,' Milwokh continued and Fabian did as he was told.

The elastic was white with green text spelling out the name *Dobber* all the way around. The tag with the laundry instructions may have been red or white. But he'd long since cut it off.

Fabian exhaled and looked up, only to see that Milwokh had suddenly pulled his arm back as though about to attack. 'Come on, are you colour-blind or something? There's no red. You can't just—'

But the knife had already left Milwokh's hand and all Fabian could do was watch as it spun past him, about a foot away. When he turned around, unsure if it had missed, it had already plunged through the red tie and was deeply embedded in the chest of a waiter standing in the doorway.

With blood pumping out of his mouth and gushing down onto his white shirt, the waiter collapsed on the floor and started flapping his arms and legs about in a desperate attempt to get back up, like a beetle on its back.

A moment later, Milwokh was standing over him, pulling out the knife and stabbing again and then again until the flailing limbs slowed and finally grew still.

Then he wiped the knife clean on the waiter's clothes and pulled the body far enough into the room to allow the door to close.

The whole thing was over so quickly Fabian only just had time to pull up and button his jeans.

Meanwhile, Milwokh shook his left arm again, noted the outcome and shook it again. 'I would like you to leave me be now.' On his way back towards the windows, he sheathed the knife and in one smooth movement pulled the rifle out of the holster strapped across his back.

'That's not happening. You know as well as I do I'm here to arrest you.'

'You're free to go. Consider it a gift before the dice asks me to change to green victims.'

'Another option would be for you to take control of your life and end this, even though you haven't rolled a one.'

'Take control?' Milwokh let out a chuckle.

'Yes. It's just a regular dice. A stupid fucking Yahtzee dice.'

'Leave.' Milwokh walked up to Fabian with eyes that had suddenly gone flat. 'For your own sake, just leave.'

'You're a slave, don't you get that? An insignificant little slave with a lot of sick compulsions—'

Pain flashed through him as though something had exploded in his face when the butt of the rifle hit him with full force. But just as quickly, it faded again, into the black of unconsciousness.

78

KIM SLEIZNER LOCKED his car and hurried through the garage under Copenhagen's police headquarters, away from the sound of sirens. Away from the traffic jams that had made the drive in from Amager take forty minutes. Away from the chaos and confusion. But it was impossible.

Even in the lift, where a vacuum-like calm normally reigned, all he could hear was a cacophony of wailing police cars and ambulances. He hadn't even known they had so many cars. And he was the one who never missed an opportunity to beat his drum about the police not having enough resources.

He didn't know exactly what was happening because he hadn't dared to turn his phone on. What little information he'd had he'd gleaned from the radio, where they were talking about a terror attack at Tivoli with a number of dead and injured.

That was terrible, of course. But what was worse was that the Swedes had turned out to be right, again. If it got out that they'd warned the Danish police but had been ignored and dismissed, it wouldn't look good. He'd already been in trouble once because of Dunja. If it happened again, he'd be hard-pressed to avoid repercussions.

And for this to happen on the day he discovered his phone had been hacked was just beyond the fucking pale. How many of his calls had the little cunt listened in on? How many texts had she and her two pet freaks read? Had they been going through his emails and triangulating his position the moment he entered The Club? Or had she been able to access the microphone and listen to any conversation that took place while the phone was around? Or the camera. What if she'd had access to that?

It was a perfect shitstorm, concocted by Satan himself. As though the entire world had decided to stick it to him, of all people.

The light in the tunnel was Hesk. He was the one the Swedes had actually spoken to. He was the one who had been slippery and evasive. He was the one who had been more interested in tripping up Risk than taking the terror threat seriously and prioritizing the safety of the public. He was the one who seemed to have forgotten why he'd decided to join the police once upon a time.

'There you are,' said the annoying voice of Morten Heinesen before the lift doors had even opened fully. 'We've been calling and calling, but—'

'I know,' Sleizner broke in as he stepped out of the lift. 'I had to keep my phone turned off. Someone's hacked it.'

'Hacked?' Heinesen hurried after Sleizner. 'I'm sorry, are you saying it might be connected to what's happening at Tivoli?'

'It's possible,' Sleizner lied, and he continued down the corridor, which opened into a small open-plan office that was currently in a state of considerable commotion, with phones ringing and people talking over each other. 'That's why I'm going to need yours.' Sleizner held out his hand.

'I'm sorry, my phone?'

'Bingo. Come on.' He waved his hand impatiently until Heinesen finally handed over his mobile. 'And the pin?'

'3 2 8 7,' Heinesen replied. 'But for how long? I'm going to need—'

'Just an hour or so. Don't worry about it,' Sleizner said, cutting him off. 'Fill me in on what's going on instead.'

'Um, well, the problem is that no one really knows.' Heinesen followed Sleizner down yet another corridor. 'Quite a few things point to some kind of terror attack, but the thing is that it's different from anything we've seen before.'

'In what way?'

'The attacker doesn't seem to have done any of the usual things, like storming in with an automatic rifle and opening fire on the crowds to try to kill as many people as possible in as short a time as possible, which we're obviously grateful for. Instead, he's been using a range of methods. Some of the victims have been stabbed and others shot with a crossbow. We've even been told one of the victims was strangled.'

'And what kind of numbers are we talking?'

'Nine dead and five injured.'

At least it was single digits. 'Let's hope it stays that way.'

'Hope springs eternal,' Heinesen replied, trying to keep up with Sleizner as he strode down the hallway. 'But according to the latest information, it's not looking good for two of the injured. And four people have reported someone pricking them.'

'Pricking them?' Sleizner stopped and turned to Heinesen. 'What do you mean, pricking them?'

Heinesen shrugged.

'Well, whatever, people get paranoid. Just you wait. Soon they'll be calling in to report blisters on their feet, thinking the attacker caused them. But fine. The question is what we do to minimize the number of victims and catch this bloke. How's the evacuation coming?'

'It's slow. The total number of visitors is over twenty thousand and they all have to be searched and checked, and then there's the possibility of widespread panic. But we've already started—'

'Started?' Sleizner interrupted. 'Started what? Mayhem? Because that's what I'm seeing when I look around.' He waved his hand about as he continued walking. 'People running around like headless chickens with no direction whatsoever.'

'Well, actually, I think most people know what they're doing,' Heinesen said. 'It's obviously a high-pressure situation, but—'

'Please don't interrupt me again,' Sleizner said, stopping outside the closed door to the IT department. 'A better use of your time would be to make sure we close off H. C. Andersen, Vesterbrogade, Bernstorffsgade and—'

'Tietgensgade,' Heinesen cut in, drawing a stern glance from Sleizner. 'I'm sorry, but we're already closing the streets around Tivoli so we can move the visitors into an outer zone more quickly and check them there before releasing them.'

'Okay? And who gave that order?'

'Hesk.'

'Did he now?' That prick hadn't been able to resist stepping in. 'Good, then. At least something's being done. And the special operations teams?'

'Two have already gone in and four more are on their way, two of which will be—'

Sleizner raised a hand to silence Heinesen and opened the door to the IT department without knocking. He couldn't bear to listen to whatever else Hesk had ordered. He'd only been gone for a few hours and the ingratiating little amoeba had already succumbed to megalomania.

Mikael Rønning was on the phone at a desk at the far end of the room. 'Hey, I'm going to have to call you back.' He ended the call and looked up at Sleizner.

'Private calls during work hours,' Sleizner said, entering the room. 'Not good.' He started cleaning his nails. 'Not good at all. Especially considering that we're in the middle of a terror attack. What do think of that, Morten?' He turned to Heinesen, who didn't seem to know what to say.

'It wasn't private.' Rønning stood up. 'I was actually talking to—'

'Calm down,' Sleizner cut him off with a chuckle. 'Ever heard of a little thing called a joke? You know, ha-ha.' He looked from Rønning to Heinesen and back but neither so much as cracked a smile. 'Fine, forget it. The main reason I'm here is to apologize for being so surly about giving you my phone.' He added a smile. 'Better late than never, so I'm here now and I would like you to install that security update as quickly as humanly possible.'

'As you might recall, I had set aside the whole afternoon yesterday, and given what's happening at Tivoli, I have other things to see to.'

'Then I suggest you reconsider your priorities. This doesn't have to be difficult.'

'I'll see what I can do. Put it on the table over there with the pin code on a Post-it note.'

'You have two hours. Then I'll be back and I expect it to be ready.'

'Then count on being disappointed. I won't be able to even start until tonight, so there's no point stopping by until after breakfast tomorrow morning.'

Sleizner put his phone down with a snort of derision and started walking back towards the door.

'Don't forget the pin,' Rønning said and picked up his phone again.

Sleizner gritted his teeth, went back, jotted down his pin code on a Post-it note and stomped out with Heinesen hard on his heels.

'But, Kim,' Heinesen said. 'I don't think I can be without my phone until—'

'One more thing, before I forget.' Sleizner stopped and turned to Heinesen. 'That Swede. Rusk, or whatever the fuck his—'

'You mean Fabian Risk?'

'Right. Has he reared his ugly little head yet?'

'I think you'd better talk to Hesk about that. He's at the scene and—'

'But I'm talking to you now.' Sleizner smiled. 'Hesk has other things to think about. So I'm asking you to keep an eye out for Rusk. Unless I'm much mistaken, he's going to do everything he can to be the one who apprehends the killer so he can hog the spotlight. But we will not let that happen, under any circumstances, are we clear? In Denmark, we do things by the book. That's all I wanted to say.' He patted Heinesen on the shoulder. 'We'll be doing the arresting today.'

'And what does that mean?' Heinesen swallowed. 'I mean, if it turns out he is there, and—'

'I think you know exactly what that means.'

79

HE HEARD A SHOT. It was distant but loud enough for Fabian to wake up and open his swollen eyes. He instantly recognized the sound of something hard clattering against plastic as the dice bouncing around the plastic dome Milwokh wore strapped around his left wrist.

But he couldn't see anything. Only blurred patches of light. Pain was throbbing in practically every part of his body but nowhere more than his face and hip. It was as though his body had finally accepted all its injuries and instead of screaming in panic it had changed gear and was trying to heal.

He was lying on his side, that much he'd puzzled out, with his hands tied behind his back. Diagonally above him was a considerably lighter, round patch, which suggested he was still in the rectangular room with the domed skylight. Further away, he could also just about make out Milwokh, silhouetted against the triple window, aiming his rifle, then another shot rang out.

'Why?' he said, rubbing his eyes against his shoulder in an attempt to get some of the dried blood out of them. 'Why are you still doing this?' Pain seared his face, an indication of just how badly bruised and injured it must be, but at least he could see a bit better.

'I'm not the one you should be asking.' Milwokh, now

wearing a black baseball cap over his wig, turned to him and started to shake his left arm.

'The dice, I know. A one, and it's all over. But what if it's not a one?'

'Then I'll keep going. What else would I do?'

'Cease and desist. Haven't you done enough damage?'

'Apparently not.' Milwokh walked over to Fabian, sank into a squat and held his arm out so he, too, could see the dice bouncing around under the plastic dome. 'But let's see what it says. Maybe it's had enough.' He shrugged. 'Maybe it's hungrier than ever.' He stopped shaking and held his arm completely still.

Four – Change colour

'What do you know? A four.' Milwokh started to shake his arm again. 'Let's see if your luck holds.'

He was wearing blue jeans, he knew that much. And his underwear was yellow and green. Three colours represented by numbers three, four and five. It was fifty-fifty. 'I don't get it,' he said. 'What makes you want to be a slave to chance?'

Milwokh put the muzzle of his rifle against Fabian's forehead without letting the dice stop. 'Ever given any thought to your own relationship with chance? Of the two of us, I'd say you're more profoundly in its hands than me. Or what do you reckon?'

'At least I have free will. That's more than you can say.'

'Free will? Milwokh sneered. 'Your so-called free will is an illusion. Like most people, you're just an algorithm that has got stuck on repeat, like a scratch in an old LP. I bet you'd rather be at home with your family than here, beaten all to hell with a rifle pointed at your head. But your algorithm has programmed you to want to arrest me at any cost. So no matter how much your so-called free will would prefer to stay home on the sofa and read about the Tivoli attack in the papers, this, a dice throw from death, is where you find yourself.'

'It's true I'm the one who's tied up at gunpoint. But of the two of us, I'm not the victim, you are. Don't you get that? You're the sick one. You're the one who has no say. Who can't make the smallest decision without asking chance for permission. Like a little kid who has to beg for sweets.'

Instead of responding, Milwokh stopped shaking his arm and held it out so Fabian could see.

Two – Orange

'You should hit a casino. With your luck, you could be rich.' Milwokh stood up, went over to the window and immediately started to scan the area outside through the scope on his rifle. A minute later, a shot rang out, accompanied by scattered shouts and screaming.

'You and me and everyone else, we're all victims of chance whether we want to be or not,' Milwokh went on, starting to shake his left arm again. 'It's everywhere, all the time. We might be run over by a bus. A plane could crash into this building before I finish this sentence. If you're really unlucky, you get a bullet through the chest just for wearing an orange baseball cap.'

'The former are tragic accidents. The latter is murder.' Fabian managed to push himself up into sitting position despite his hands being tied behind his back. 'You can blame chance and your damn dice all you want, but what you're doing is murder, plain and simple.'

Milwokh came over and squatted down next to Fabian again while the dice danced under the plastic dome. 'Just a few minutes ago you claimed I was a slave to chance. That I'm unable to make my own decisions and that I'm just a puppet whose strings are tied to the dice. The truth is, you're the one who's a slave to chance. You and everyone else. You're all slaves. You just don't know it. You think you're in control. That you're in charge of your own lives. That you genuinely want to get up early every morning, sit around in traffic and once you get to some bland open-plan office with terrible ventilation you actually want to write reports you know no one's ever going to read. Your pre-programmed algorithms dictate, and you move in circles like cute little goldfish.'

Milwokh shook his left arm more and more violently and the dice was bouncing so hard against the plastic it sounded like it was about to crack. 'But then one day, it turns out your boss at, let's say, the bank has been more interested in his mistress's new fake boobs than your reports about suspected money laundering, which leads to a scandal and tanking stock prices. There's a run on the bank and you're one of the many thousands fired. Unfortunately, you've just hit that age when you're either too qualified or too old. A few years later, your wife has had enough and the only thing you can afford after the divorce is final and the mortgage repaid is a small one-bed flat in some drab three-storey building on the outskirts of town and there you sit, wondering what the hell happened. You were in charge of your life. You knew exactly what you wanted.'

He kept shaking his arm as though he was never going to stop. 'And then there's me. I have chance under control. Unlike the rest of you, I've managed to tame it and boil it down to six sides. Six possible alternatives, all defined by me.'

Fabian had to agree. In a way, everything he was saying was true. 'You're right,' he said, nodding. 'So let's follow your line of thought and take control of what happens next. You and me, together. Let's do it. Let's list the options and then the dice will decide.'

Milwokh said nothing, but his eyes gave him away. He was going through the permutations and calculating the outcomes.

'I can tell you're tempted,' Fabian continued. 'But hey, maybe you're too scared. Maybe you don't have the guts.'

'What's that supposed to mean?'

'Maybe you're afraid of what the dice would tell you. Of the outcome. I'm surprised by that, actually. Isn't it kind of undignified? Right? After everything that's happened, after everything you've done, you don't even have the guts to let the dice settle something that straightforward.'

'You don't think I know what you're doing?' Milwokh shook his arm harder than ever, savagely, as though Fabian's attacks were getting to him. 'Don't you think I get it? But you're not in charge of this. You don't make the decisions.'

'No, and neither do you. The dice does. So isn't the least we could do is ask it what it thinks?' Fabian forced out a smile. 'Wasn't that what you said a while ago? That you can just ask. And what was it again? One, two or three, that's all you need.'

Milwokh didn't react, but suddenly stopped shaking his arm.

A *three*.

'Would you look at that, it said yes. The dice is on board,' Fabian went on. 'Roll a one and you win.' He hadn't given the suggestion even a moment's thought and it only sank in a few seconds after he said it that he had put a number on his own life, just like that. Like a price tag on his forehead saying how much he was worth. He had no idea why he'd picked one. But it didn't matter. It was too late to back out.

'And two to six?' Milwokh asked. 'What do they represent?'

'You give yourself up, let me arrest you and accept your punishment.'

Milwokh let out a sharp laugh and shook his head. 'I'm not the one who's tied up. I'm not the one who's desperate and fighting for my life against the odds. I can just get up and walk away.'

'Not until the dice gives you permission and orders you to change your position. Until it does, you're going to stay and see what it has to say about where you and I go from here.'

'A six, and I give up and let you arrest me.' Milwokh looked Fabian in the eyes. 'A one, two, three, four or five and you're done.'

'Your suggestion against mine,' Fabian said. 'I guess there's just one way to settle it: we let the dice choose. One, two or three, my suggestion wins.'

Milwokh didn't have to think long before he started to shake his arm again. The sound of the dice hitting the plastic had been loud all along, but only now was it starting to bother him. As though each tap against the dome was a step closer to the end. Once the sound stopped, he was almost too afraid to look.

A *five*.

'Sorry.' Milwokh shot him a brief smile. 'But did you really think it was going to side with you?'

Fabian didn't know what to say. Every muscle in his body was on the verge of giving up, and he sagged as though his body was preparing for what was coming. He had tried everything. Absolutely everything. And yet, this was how it was going to end. With a dice throw he would lose unless it came up six.

It was five times more likely his brains would end up on the wall with the killer still on the loose. A killer who was going to continue his game of dice somewhere else, pursued by other police officers who were going to search in vain for the motive that could help them understand.

He could hear Milwokh start to shake his arm again, but he couldn't bear to watch the bouncing dice, so he kept his eyes closed. If his hands hadn't been tied behind his back, he would have covered his ears so he didn't have to listen to the sharp clacking sound that was boring into him.

Deep down inside, he'd always known he might be killed in the line of duty. He hadn't spent any sleepless nights wondering exactly how it would happen. But he certainly hadn't pictured himself tied up and battered, waiting for a dice throw.

In a way, though, it was typical. Everything he'd fought for, everything he'd been through, just for it to end like this. And what had he really been fighting for? In hindsight, on his deathbed, he honestly had no idea. Maybe Milwokh was right. Maybe he was just an algorithm stuck on repeat until one day it was over. Until the battery ran out.

A new murder case, that was all it took for him to drop everything he cared about and start chasing the white piece of cloth like a slobbering racing dog. His family, his friends, if he even had any, and everything that really meant something to him, none of it had ever been able to compete with the prospect of solving another crime.

So maybe it had better end now. If that ghost Matilda claimed to be in contact with turned out to be right, he was glad it was him and not someone else in his family. If you boiled down everything they'd been through, all the pain they'd endured and all the difficulties they'd fought their way through, there was no escaping the fact that he was the problem and the root of all that evil.

If not for him, things would have been different. He'd let everyone down. If Sonja, Theodor and Matilda had had a husband and father who was there for them, not just in thought but physically, everything would have been so much better.

The problem was that he wasn't ready to go. Not yet. Somehow, he was convinced he had more left to give before he was done. He hadn't even said goodbye. To Matilda. To Theodor, who was counting on him to be there for him once the trial resumed. To Sonja, who was expecting him to show up at her performance tonight. She'd told him she needed him by her side, and his death would just be another in a long line of betrayals.

If he could just have one more chance, he'd do anything, absolutely anything. Maybe he should change careers. Quit policing and do something else entirely. Though what was the point of thinking about that. What was the point of thinking at all, now that—

He suddenly realized everything had gone quiet. That the beating of the dice against the plastic dome had stopped. He didn't know how long since, just that there was an outcome. A ruling.

'Don't you want to see what it is?' Milwokh said in an unreadable voice.

'Just do what you have to do and get it over with,' he said, and opened his eyes.

80

KIM SLEIZNER HURRIED around the corner from Stoltenbergsgade to Bernstorffsgade with the phone pressed against his ear. He was walking as briskly as he was able without overheating. Turning up sweaty, oozing desperation, would not do. He was in charge and people who were in charge didn't turn up with pit stains the size of dinner plates, looking frantic.

No, this was his organization, his town, his country. He called the shots. He gave the orders and laid down the law. Not some sycophantic fucking amoeba who didn't know which hand to hold his cock in.

But why was that daft fucking cow not picking up? Why was she keeping him waiting after spending half the day trying to reach him? The strange thing was that the phone kept ringing. There was no voicemail or intercept message. Nothing but this goddam fucking ringing, on and on and on.

At least the police station was less than half a mile from Tivoli, so he reached the police cordon on Tietgensgade in minutes. It was a mess of cars, cyclists and pedestrians who didn't know where to go. Not to mention all the fucking journalists and rubberneckers getting in his way.

'Hey, you!' someone shouted behind him just as he'd managed to push to the front of the crowd and reach the police tape. 'Stop right there. This street is closed to unauthorized personnel.'

Sleizner turned to face the uniformed officer standing behind him. 'Well, then, aren't we lucky I am authorized, or, more exactly, the head of Copenhagen's Homicide Unit.' He smiled through his fury.

The uniformed officer swallowed. 'I see. Do you have some form of ID to confirm that?'

'ID? Who the fuck do you think you are?' He gesticulated angrily with his free hand. 'I'm Kim fucking Sleizner, and you're a goddam nobody who's about to piss himself.'

'*Yes, this is Astrid Tuvesson at the Helsingborg CID,*' a voice suddenly said in his ear.

'You know what I think of people who sound like they don't know who's calling even though they can see it on their screen?' Sleizner said as he shoved his ID in the uniformed officer's face and ducked under the tape.

'*You'll have to excuse me, all I can see is a Danish number,*' Tuvesson replied. '*But now that I hear your voice, there can be no doubt. Hi, Kim.*'

Fuck, right, he wasn't using his own phone. 'You've been trying to reach me.'

'*Yes, that's correct. We've unsuccessfully been trying to get in touch with you guys all day so we can work together. But given recent events, it seems a bit late to come crawling now.*'

'What the fuck are you talking about? Working together? Crawling?' he said, holding out his ID to yet another uniformed officer to avoid another scene as he walked through one of Tivoli's entrances. 'Is storming in, waving a gun around and opening fire in public what you call working together?'

'*What was he supposed to do? It was a desperate situation.*'

Sleizner lowered the phone, covered the microphone and turned to the uniformed officer. 'Take me to whoever's in charge as quickly as possible.'

The officer nodded and led the way.

'I'm sorry, where were we?'

'*I was saying that this is about saving lives. Not marking territory!*'

'Settle down, Miss Tuvesson. I'm not the one who has a lunatic running around Tivoli. You are. Or actually, you have two armed lunatics running around. You've lost every semblance of control. Luckily, the organization I'm in charge of is better run and working hard to evacuate the public and arrest the perpetrator as we speak. That's all I wanted to tell you. That in Denmark, we're on top of things because we follow the rules.'

'*And what does that mean in relation to Fabian Risk?*'

'Don't ask me. That's completely up to him.'

81

A SIX.

His first thought had been that his eyes were deceiving him. But it was a six. The dice had decided that he would be allowed to keep breathing, and Milwokh had already put his rifle down without protest and started to unbuckle all the belt bags strapped around his torso.

He still didn't dare to believe it. It was as though he needed more time to overcome his conviction that everything was really over and his life had reached its end. He'd been wrong. The odds had been wrong. Because he was walking, or rather hobbling, out of the hotel and down the front steps, leaning heavily on one crutch. He was carrying the other one over his shoulder as a hanger for all Milwokh's bags and weapons.

Pontus Milwokh was walking next to him with his hands tied behind his back. Just as they'd agreed, he'd consented to being arrested the moment the dice under the plastic dome had landed with its six pips facing up.

It was over. It was really over.

All the work he and the team had put in over the past month. All the hours. All the theories and assumptions. All the dead ends and mistaken suspects. All the times they'd thought they'd hit upon a solution when they'd in fact been on the wrong track. Together, all those things had contributed to Milwokh finally being under arrest.

But truth be told, chance had played the biggest and most important role. They had chance to thank. If not for chance, they would never have—

'Put your hands up and get down on the ground!' someone shouted through a megaphone.

Fabian turned around and saw men wearing bulletproof vests and helmets and armed with automatic rifles advancing on them from opposite directions. 'It's already over,' he called back. 'He's given himself up, you can just come and get him.'

'I said put your hands up and get down!' shouted Jan Hesk, who was standing off to the side with the megaphone in his hand.

'He can't! His hands are tied,' Fabian shouted back and he turned to Milwokh, whose eyes were darting back and forth between the two special operations teams. 'Pontus. You should do as they say and lie down.'

'Face on the ground!'

'Calm down! He's doing it! Just do as they say so no one else gets hurt.'

'Okay,' Milwokh said finally, getting down on his knees and then his stomach.

'Good,' Fabian said. A split second later, he heard a bang somewhere behind him.

It sounded like a handgun firing, thin and hollow, like a medium-sized firecracker. But it couldn't be a handgun since the special operations officers were carrying automatic rifles and Hesk was only holding a megaphone. Fabian didn't understand and was feeling increasingly confused, and in the end, it was as though the uncertainty morphed into a physical condition that made it increasingly difficult to keep upright.

Then he noticed the blood blooming across the leg of his jeans and realized he'd been shot, that it really had been a gunshot he'd heard. As he fell, he managed to twist around and catch a glimpse of Kim Sleizner walking towards him with a gun in his hand before his head hit the ground and everything went dark.

82

SHE'D BEEN HOPING Fabian would be one of the first to enter the venue when the doors opened. That he would hang back in a corner and let her do what she needed to do, while also being ready to step in if anything went wrong or anyone took things too far.

She'd prayed that this time he'd listened and taken her seriously when she'd expressly told him she needed him by her side. That this time was more important than all the other ones.

But he hadn't been one of the first. He wasn't standing in a corner, waiting for it to start. He wasn't even there.

She was sure there was an explanation. There always was. But right now, tonight, the explanation didn't matter. Whatever it was, regardless of how reasonable and plausible it was, she'd needed her husband by her side.

Being in the foetal position on the floor made her even more vulnerable and she had no choice but to let the visitors make their way in and spread out in the space. There was no manual. No instructions for what was expected of them. Nothing, other than herself.

The audience was bigger than she'd dared to hope. Much bigger. Exactly how many was hard to judge, but certainly a hundred, maybe more. She wanted to get up and run away. Bolt. She didn't know where to, but as far away as possible.

That was exactly why it was so important that she remain on the floor. That she endured and pushed through this agony. If she failed, she would never come out the other side. She would forever be stuck in the feeling she'd been carrying around with her for the past few months. A feeling that she was waiting for something to end, unaware that it already had.

She'd felt it over the past week or so, and she could feel it now, stronger than ever. This wasn't for the audience. This wasn't her way back to art.

They may be in an art gallery and the programme may have called this a performance piece, part of an exhibition, but it wasn't. This was something she had to do for herself, for her own survival, as an attempt to find her way back to a place where she felt like she still had things to live for. That she hadn't reached the full stop. The audience were there as extras, spectators who contributed their gaze, like witnesses.

Without them, it was meaningless. Without them, what was about to happen would never have taken place.

Then the doors closed. The distant din from outside subsided and the soundscape in the room became more intimate. After another minute or so, the anticipation was palpable. The air trembled with it. Or was it just her?

The room was dead quiet now, but she made herself wait a little longer still. This wasn't something she could just force to get it out of the way. Stay in the pain, she repeated inwardly like a mantra. Stay and endure.

Then she slowly got up, first into sitting position and then, just as slowly, onto her knees. Finally, she stood, her back straight, her arms by her sides. The silence was now so profound it felt like every last molecule in the air was holding its breath.

She held a man's gaze until he looked away. It didn't take long. Not long enough. She picked a woman instead. She did better, but in the end she, too, gave in and averted her eyes.

She needed to pick the next one more carefully, so she walked around studying the spectators for several minutes. Their different styles, body shapes and personalities. One person smelled strongly, another was in a wheelchair and a third gave her a weird smile.

The man she eventually settled on was her age, maybe slightly younger, fit and with clean features. She instantly sensed that he was the bold type who wouldn't just crawl into his shell. And so she let the minutes pass while they looked at each other, and when she had assured herself he would be able to take it, she began to unbutton her blouse, one button at a time.

She had been sure her hands would shake, but they didn't. The man held her gaze until her blouse was completely unbuttoned then looked away, allowing her to retreat into the middle of the room and let the blouse fall to the floor.

She looked down at her breasts and the red lace bra Fabian had bought as part of a set for Christmas a number of years ago. She'd found it sexist and demeaning and had given him a stern talking-to and refused to wear it.

The set had stayed in a drawer until she'd started her affair. And now. She'd wanted to burn it, turn it into ashes as though it had never existed. But instead, she'd put it on and it was dazzling everyone with its redness.

Next, she picked the wife of one of the slightly older men,

who was virtually devouring her with his eyes, walked over and turned her back to her. Once again, she let the minutes pass; she'd lost count of them by the time the woman was able to summon enough courage to unhook her bra, allowing her to walk back into the middle of the room and let that, too, fall.

This was what she looked like. She normally didn't even want Fabian to see her. And yet here she was, standing in front of a hundred strangers, feeling her nipples harden. Whether it was because of the mood in the room or the cool air from the vents in the ceiling was impossible to say. She hadn't seen it coming, but it made her feel stronger.

Then she unbuttoned her wide-legged trousers and let them fall. Only her knickers were left.

In the end, she removed those, too, and stood there, naked, exposed.

She had only a vague sense of what her audience were thinking. Before, that would have been what mattered. The opinions behind all those gazes. Now, it was like they cancelled each other out.

All but one.

She'd seen him and yet she hadn't. The man in the wheelchair. As cowardly as everyone else, she'd quickly moved on to the next person, sidestepping what looked like overwhelming pain. All those cuts and bruises. Only now was she brave enough to see it. Now that she herself was naked and just like him had nothing left to lose.

She didn't know what had happened to him. What he'd been through, other than that it must have been horrifyingly violent. The only thing she knew for sure was that he'd listened. Despite everything he must have been dealing with, he'd heard every word.

Because there he was, the one who belonged to her, and just like that, she felt calm.

She turned to the wooden box sitting on the floor a few feet behind her and slowly walked over to it. When she reached it, she turned to her audience and waited another minute before stepping into it, lying down with her arms along her sides and closing her eyes.

She woke up when the lid that had been propped against the box was placed over her. Then she could hear some of them pick up the screwdrivers scattered on the floor, grab a screw and start fastening the lid to the box. From time to time, someone dropped a screwdriver, which suggested they were taking turns.

When the lid was in place, silence descended on the room once more. As though it had just dawned on them that they had all participated in burying her. Then she drifted off again. At least it felt like she did. She couldn't be sure. Time seemed to move in circles.

In the end, someone must have made a decision and persuaded at least one other person. Maybe more. But she could clearly hear the four steel wires dangling from the ceiling being hooked onto the hoops at the four corners of the box.

Then she was raised higher and higher, further and further from the grave she had been on her way down into just a few weeks ago.

83

ASTRID TUVESSON ENDED the call, put her phone in her handbag and looked out from the balcony. Apart from the banging and the angry buzzing of saws in the bedroom, it was a pretty nice evening. The kind of evening when summer really shines, with a perfect, balmy breeze.

And yet the pavements and the outdoor seating area of the restaurant down the street were virtually deserted. Only the occasional car drove past below. Instead, everyone was sitting in their living rooms, glued to their TVs in some kind of collective shock.

Not because of the European Football Championship semi-final between Germany and Italy, but because of the news. She could see as much through several of the windows across the street. The news from Tivoli in Copenhagen.

A few hours ago, this had been just another day of glorious summer weather in the middle of the holiday season. A few hours ago, people had been blissfully unaware of the darkness simmering just beneath the surface. Now they were all going to remember, for the rest of their lives, where they were and what they'd been doing when the news reached them.

So far, only the Danes had held a press conference, with Kim Sleizner taking the lead, basking in the glory of the arrest. That would all change tomorrow, when she held her own press conference and told the world about all the things the Danes had decided to sweep under the rug. About how difficult the Danes were to work with. About all the other cases they had thought were solved but which now turned out to be connected. And about Molander...

She still hadn't been able to digest that. She hadn't even had time to think about it, and at the moment she had no idea how she was going to approach it when she was standing on the podium tomorrow.

She sat down on the balcony chair with a heavy sigh. The handbag in her lap was still open, and there, next to the phone, on top of the silvery bag of gum, it lay, waiting for her say-so.

She had been good, she really had. The past twenty-four hours had been like nothing she'd ever experienced in all her years on the force. But they had pulled through. She had pulled through.

Now they were just waiting for the noise from the bedroom to die down. Then they were officially done, and they would all be able to look themselves in the mirror and feel proud. Fabian, Klippan, Irene and her. Proud that despite their failings, they'd managed to do the right thing in the end. If she didn't deserve a tipple now, when would she ever? Just a sip, a small one.

Before she'd even made a conscious decision, one hand was already pulling the flask out of the handbag while the other unscrewed the cap. Then the spirits burned on her tongue and left a hot, pulsating trail all the way down her throat. As if on cue, warmth spread through the rest of her body and she instantly felt her shoulders relax. She took another sip and then another before she could get hold of herself, put the flask away and shove a couple of pieces of gum in her mouth.

'So this is where you're hiding.'

Tuvesson whipped around to discover Klippan standing in the doorway. 'Oh my God, you gave me a fright.' She closed her handbag and stood up. 'I just talked to Högsell. Apparently, the Danes are insisting on taking over the case and holding the trial there. But the last word hasn't been said yet.'

'I'm sure it'll be all right,' Klippan said, and he closed the balcony door behind him to muffle the racket from the bedroom. 'Astrid. Are you okay?'

'No.' Tuvesson sighed and shook her head. 'How could I be after a day like today?' She wiped the moisture from her eyes. 'A day with so many innocent victims and Molander, who... So no, I'm far from okay, since you ask, and yes, I've had a drink, but just to clear my head a little. How about you?'

'I don't know.' Klippan shrugged. 'What I do know is that you're not the only one who needs to get their head together.'

Without a word, Tuvesson opened her handbag, pulled out the flask and handed it to Klippan, who unscrewed the cap and took a few deep gulps.

'When you called to tell me,' he continued after a long pause, 'I couldn't comprehend it. I heard what you were saying. Every word of it, but I didn't understand. The words just sort of ran through me like they didn't mean anything.' He took another sip and handed the flask back to Tuvesson. 'It wasn't until I saw Gertrud lying there at the bottom of the root cellar. Until then, I didn't fully get it.' He shook his head, fighting back tears. 'Eighteen years we've worked together, him and me. Eighteen long years, sharing everything. At least I thought so. I don't know what it was like for you, but for my part, I considered him not just a colleague but a friend as well. Maybe not my best friend. But still, a friend that I—' He trailed off and shook his head, lost for words.

As Tuvesson walked over and put her arms around him, the balcony door behind them was opened by a uniformed officer.

'We're almost through.'

Tuvesson nodded and she and Klippan followed him into the black-painted kitchen, through the equally black living room and into the bedroom, where the bed had been turned on its side and two more uniformed officers were working on making a hole in the wall big enough for a person to get through.

Tuvesson stepped through the hole with Klippan right behind her and spotted Lilja lying on a narrow cot. 'Hi, Irene. How are you doing?' she said. She sat down on the edge of the bed and looked around, trying to imagine what Lilja had been through.

At the computer and all the dice. At the cloth wrapped around Lilja's hands, which was stained dark red, at the tinned food and all the ravioli on the floor. At the extension lead that disappeared through a hole in the wall.

'Tell me you got him,' Lilja said finally. 'Tell me I was right. Tell me everything worked out, that you caught him before he killed more people.'

'You were right,' Tuvesson said, and swallowed. 'You were completely right. Wasn't she, Klippan? Tell her.'

'Absolutely,' Klippan said, nodding his agreement.

'And yes, we did catch him in the end, Irene. Fabian caught him,' Tuvesson said. 'He's sorry he couldn't be here, and he asked me to tell you that if it weren't for you and what you did, many more people would have lost their lives.'

Lilja said nothing, as though she needed time to digest the significance of what Tuvesson had just said.

'But there's one more thing we have to tell you,' Tuvesson went on, and she turned to Klippan for help.

84

It was, without a doubt, one of the finest albums ever made. Kate Bush's *Hounds of Love*. On his list of personal favourites, it was up there with *Abbey Road*, *Computer World*, *Nevermind*, *Hunky Dory* and a few more.

'Running Up That Hill' was not only one of the best songs in the world, it was an epic masterpiece clocking in at just under five minutes, and every time he heard her sing *Tell me, we both matter, don't we?* in a voice as fragile as a butterfly's wing, he welled up. He couldn't explain why; for some reason the line just got to him.

But that wasn't the song he picked now; he went straight to the second-to-last song on the album, 'Hello Earth'. It was Sonja's favourite, and when he turned up the volume, her reaction was instantaneous in the form of a smile from the kitchen where she was putting together a simple dinner.

'How about a glass of wine?' she said, holding up a bottle of red.

He nodded and she immediately set to opening it and getting glasses out. She couldn't have been more right about her performance at Dunkers earlier that evening. Once the audience had left the venue and the staff had let the box back down and opened it, a new Sonja had climbed out and walked over to him.

Gone was the insecurity and the introverted darkness.

The coldness. Instead, there was a strength in her now that reminded him of their first few years together. Before the children, when it was just the two of them. When life was an open door and nothing was impossible.

She filled both glasses and he wheeled himself over to the kitchen island, took one and raised it in a toast. She picked up the other, clinked it against his and kissed him. Gently, so as not to inflict any more pain on his battered face.

It still hurt. But he didn't care. The intimacy was back and that was all that mattered. The intimacy and tenderness that said so clearly that if there had ever been any doubt about it being the two of them, it was now banished forever.

At the same time, the anaesthesia from his surgery at Copenhagen's main hospital was wearing off, and he could feel the pain from the gunshot wound in his thigh returning. But it was nothing compared to what his body had endured earlier in the day, and since no vital organs had been damaged, the doctor had reluctantly agreed not to keep him in overnight for observation and had instead arranged for him to be transported to the Dunkers Culture Centre in Helsingborg.

Now they were finally home, and Fabian didn't want to be anywhere else, and even though they both had so many things to tell each other and so many questions, the past hour had been virtually silent. They had all the time in the world, and right now, all the questions, answers and explanations felt like unnecessary ballast they'd do best to jettison.

'Dad...'

Fabian turned and saw Matilda looking at him from the hallway. 'Hi, Matilda,' he said and smiled, even though it hurt.

For the first time in weeks, he recognized her, his own daughter. It really was Matilda, standing there staring at him, his Matilda. True, her eyes were wide with shock and concern, but they were her eyes. Hers and no one else's.

'Dad, what happened?' She hurried over to him. 'What did they do to you? You look... awful.'

'Matilda, I promise I will tell you. I promise I'll tell you all about it. But not right now. Right now, I just want to have a nice dinner and enjoy us being together. Okay?'

Matilda nodded, bent down and hugged him as gently as she could. He hugged her back and Sonja joined in as well. Only Theodor was missing.

EPILOGUE

28 June–1 July 2012

LATER THAT NIGHT, the official casualty count of what would become known as the worst terror attack in Danish history stood at eleven dead and five injured. The debate about the lack of cooperation between the Swedish and Danish police authorities that followed was fierce and protracted.

Of the six people who were poisoned with ricin, only the young boy survived. He had his parents to thank for it. Particularly his mother, who insisted on taking him to the A&E in Malmö the second she realized something wasn't right. The other five died of severe stomach pains over the course of the next few days.

Kim Sleizner used the press conference held in the wake of the attack to explain that his colleague Jan Hesk and the entire Danish police had, under his leadership, demonstrated an ability to act decisively, coupled with an efficiency few countries could rival. According to him, there could be no doubt the Swedish serial killer would still have been on the loose if not for them.

Fabian Risk was not mentioned once during the almost two-hour-long live press conference. Not a word was said about the role he played during the attack. He did figure in the description of the arrest itself as *another Swede accompanying Milwokh*, who was shot in the leg when he refused to obey the Danish police's orders to get on the ground. Later, however, Jan Hesk would clarify that the Swede had turned out to be an officer of the law and was doing well under the circumstances.

In which country Milwokh will be facing trial is still unclear. The forensic evidence against him is, however, so overwhelming there can be no doubt he's looking at a lifetime sentence.

The extensive work of collecting forensic evidence against Ingvar Molander is well under way. It will be supplemented with interviews with a large number of witnesses, such as Conny Öhman and Fabian himself.

Most signs point to a lifetime sentence for him as well, though it is still not known whether key witness Gertrud Molander will be able to testify. Having been declared dead at the scene, she is now being treated in the intensive care unit at Helsingborg Hospital, where doctors are cautiously optimistic that she will make a full recovery.

The same is unfortunately not true of Irene Lilja's left hand. After countless complex surgeries, mobility could only be achieved in her thumb and fore and middle fingers. The surgical fusing of her pinkie and ring fingers will forever serve as a reminder of what she endured.

Within days of Sonja's performance at Dunkers, word had spread in art circles far beyond Sweden's borders. Art shows, galleries and museums lined up to host a repeat performance.

But even though she'd finally managed to create something meaningful, not just to herself but to everyone who had attended, *The Hanging Box* was a closed chapter for Sonja. She had emerged from it a new person, more whole and stronger than ever, and she was never climbing back in.

Over the next few days, Fabian, Sonja and Matilda travelled to Helsingør as often as they could to meet with Jadwiga Komorovski and support Theodor while they waited for the trial to resume after the weekend. But that Monday, they received the unexpected news that the trial had been postponed again. This time for reasons unknown.

MIKAEL RØNNING SIPPED his mineral water, in which the ice cubes had long since dissolved and the pips from the lemon slices were bobbing about like tiny olive pits gnawed clean. It was his second glass, and even though he was sweating in the evening sun, he made sure not to drink so much he'd have to go to the bathroom and risk missing her.

Café Diamanten was, apart from its convenient distance from the police station, an odd choice for a meeting. Especially the kind of meeting they were going to have. With an outdoor seating area overlooking the canal along Gammel Strand, it was anything but secluded. Even worse, the place was so crowded you couldn't help overhearing the conversations at the tables around you.

If she ever deigned to show up. It had been over an hour since their agreed meeting time, and so far there was no sign of her. And he'd studied every single guest that had come and gone.

But then again, she had never been one of his more punctual friends. For her, being half an hour late was the rule rather than the exception, and back when they'd hung out regularly, he'd often told her the film, concert or whatever they were going to started half an hour before it actually did, which had worked great until she figured it out.

But it had been months since he'd last seen her, and they weren't going to the cinema. This was a very different kind of rendezvous, one he'd been very hesitant to agree to. The only reason he had was that it was her, and now she wasn't even here.

Had something happened, or was it just that her casual approach to timekeeping had got even worse? Regardless, he didn't feel good about this. Especially since he didn't even have a number he could reach her on.

He made eye contact with the waiter and signalled that he wanted to pay. Given how crowded the café was, it would probably be a while before the bill was on the table.

It was odd to think that the world just kept on turning, even though it had only been hours since that Pontus Milwokh guy had attacked Tivoli. Sure, people expressed their sympathy by adding the Danish flag to their Facebook profile pictures, and it was bound to dominate the news around the world for days to come. But right here, everything was the same as it always was, even though he could still hear the occasional police siren and the streets just a few blocks away had been cordoned off.

The waiter came by with his bill but disappeared before he could get his wallet out and find the right card. When he looked up again, a woman had sat down across from him. He'd seen her sitting two tables down, together with two foreign-looking men, and decided to make it plain to her he wasn't interested.

'Hi, Michael,' she said, putting her hand out on the table. 'It's great to see you again.'

Until he heard her voice, he didn't realize it was Dunja Hougaard, the person he'd been waiting for all this time. She looked completely different with her short, silvery bleached hair, big earrings and bright red lips. But that wasn't why he hadn't recognized her.

'You too,' he said, and took her hand. 'You have no idea how much I've missed you.'

Nor was it her svelte body, denim shorts or heavy boots. 'I've missed you, too.'

It was because of her eyes. They were what had changed.

'And I'd love to hold your hand,' she went on. 'But it's going to have to be some other day. We don't have much time.'

'I'm not the one who's been wasting it.' He took out Sleizner's phone and the Post-it note with the pin code and placed it in her hand. She furtively passed it to one of the men who had been sitting at her table and was now sidling past them.

'I had to make sure you weren't followed.'

He nodded and looked over at the table where the two men were already busy deconstructing the phone and hooking it up to a laptop.

'Thanks,' she said after one of them nodded an okay and signalled with his fingers that they would be done in three minutes.

'It was nothing,' he lied. 'When can I see you again? You're my favourite straight person, you know.'

'And you're my favourite gay.' She smiled and chuckled, apparently unable to answer his question.

But he already had the answers he'd been looking for.

That she didn't know.

That this might be the last time he ever saw her.

That she no longer had anything to lose.

Author's thanks

THIS WAS SUPPOSED to be an easy book to write. If such books exist. All I had to do was follow up on and wrap up what I'd started in *Motive X*, I figured. But as the book was read by more and more people around the world and expectations mounted, for a while I felt there was no way I could live up to them. Despite the praise lavished on the first four books about Risk and their success, insecurity is always lurking around the corner.

That's when you need a good team around you. A team that believes in you, builds you up and gives you strength. A team that slaps you about until you wake up and realize you have the best job in the world. A team that makes you push through and find the fun again.

Mi, you're one of them. Thank you for being there for me and putting up with my brooding when I'm mulling over a plot problem. Thank you for reading, commenting and sulking when I don't do exactly what you want. Thank you for possessing the ability to remember every single chapter I've written so you can point out when I'm being repetitive. I don't think anyone knows Risk's universe as well as you do.

Except maybe my editor, Andreas. We've made five books together, and I feel like you are as deep into Risk's world as I am. A big thank you for that.

Tor at Salomonsson Agency is another rock. Together with Julia and Marie, you steer this ship with a firm hand, despite my whims and insistence on going my own way, which is not always the straightest. Big thanks for bearing with me.

I tip my hat to Adam and everyone else at Sveavägen. You have done and are doing a wonderful job getting the books published. Since day one, I've felt well cared for and now, five years in, Sveavägen is like a home away from home when I'm in Stockholm. Thank you, thank you, thank you.

Reidar Jönsson, it's been forever since we worked on various film scripts together. For that reason, I'm incredibly grateful that you, with your substantial experience as a sailor, agreed to read, fact-check and answer all my questions. A big thank you for that.

Nils, considering how many book covers you design every year, it's nothing short of a miracle that you manage to outdo yourself every time with mine. A big thank you for never letting the smallest detail escape your loupe.

Filipa and Kasper, thank you for your support, questions and care.

Noomi and Sander, you are still too young to read my books, though you've figured out that Daddy writes about scary things. But thank you for existing and thank you for bursting into my office and hugging me every day when you get home from school.

Finally, I want to give all my publishers around the world a big thank you. Some of you I've met in my travels, others I will hopefully meet before long. In case I forget to say it then, I'm saying it now. You are amazing! A big thank you for all the work you put into getting my books to readers in countries I never dared to dream I'd reach.

About the author

STEFAN AHNHEM grew up in Helsingborg, Sweden, and now lives in Denmark. He began his career as a screenwriter, and among his credits is the adaptation of Henning Mankell's Wallander series for TV. His first novel, *Victim Without a Face*, won Crimetime's Novel of the Year, and became a top-ten bestseller in Germany, Sweden and Ireland. *Eighteen Below* was a top-three bestseller in Germany, Sweden and Norway. Stefan Ahnhem has been named Swedish Crime Writer of the Year, and has been published in thirty countries. The Fabian Risk novels have sold more than 1.8 million copies worldwide.

About the translator

AGNES BROOMÉ is a translator of Swedish literature. She holds a PhD in Translation Studies, and has translated a number of works including *The Expedition* by Bea Uusma, which won the August Prize.